China Red

CHINA RED

A Caleb Frost Novel

Ralph Sanborn

iUniverse, Inc.
Bloomington

CHINA RED
A CALEB FROST NOVEL

This is a work of fiction. All of the characters, names, incidents, organizations, and dialogue in this novel are either the products of the author's imagination or are used fictitiously.

iUniverse books may be ordered through booksellers or by contacting:

iUniverse
1663 Liberty Drive
Bloomington, IN 47403
www.iuniverse.com
1-800-Authors (1-800-288-4677)

ISBN: 978-1-4759-8293-0 (sc)
ISBN: 978-1-4759-8294-7 (hc)
ISBN: 978-1-4759-8295-4 (e)

Library of Congress Control Number: 2013905101

Printed in the United States of America.

iUniverse rev. date: 3/28/2013

This book is dedicated to my mother,
Francenia Alibone Budd Towle.
*She inspired me through her own
elegant poetry and prose. She would
have read this book ... because I wrote it.
No greater love hath a mother.*

'Cause you told me that I would find a hole
Within the fragile substance of my soul
And I have filled this void with things unreal
And all the while my character it steals.
—From "Roll Away Your Stone" by Mumford & Sons

1

The grip of the SIG Sauer P226 pistol in his coat pocket reassured Caleb Frost. He stepped off the Métro car as the doors swooshed open. Heavier and taller at six foot four and 205 pounds than the average Parisian, he made his way easily through the crowd waiting to board. Warm, body-odor-laced air from the packed Métro car collided with the cold, damp-clothing smell of the impatient, homeward-bound crowd. Out of habit, Caleb slipped his hand more deeply into his pocket, feeling for the security of the SIG Sauer's textured grip.

Women glanced at him, appreciative of his youthful appearance, his longish blond hair, and his open-faced honesty. Without question, women found him attractive. At thirty-two, he still looked as if he were in his twenties. His look of innocence served him well in the world in which he had to survive. The images resident deep within his pale-gray eyes told another story. They had witnessed and recorded scenes and events most people would not be able to assimilate and then continue with their normal lives. His resilience to the onslaught of life's ugly realities left him a tortured force within a deceptively benign exterior.

Caleb Frost was a professional—a professional assassin. He was on the payroll of the US government, and he was an expert in black and very wet operations.

Pausing, he scanned the crowd exiting the cars and spilling onto the platform behind him. He didn't expect to see anyone following him, but evasion lessons, drilled into him during long days of training, had become second nature. This was his sixth change of Métro lines over the past two hours.

When he was a child, his father had made a game out of shadowing. If he could follow his father to the local ice-cream store without being seen, the prize was chocolate with sprinkles in a sugar cone. Sometimes, the roles were reversed. And sometimes, his mother played the game. By the time he was twelve, his techniques for both evasion and shadowing were equal to his parents' skills. Or so they said. And, as he came to learn a couple of years later, they were professionals.

He emerged from the depths of the Métro onto Boulevard Saint Germain in the Sixth Arrondissement. A freezing January rain pounded Caleb's leather coat. He strode past a café and inhaled the harsh odor of Gauloise and Gitanes cigarette smoke. It melded with the more subtle smell of espresso and perhaps the fragrance of a grilled *croque-monsieur* sandwich dripping cheese. The windows of the café and the small shops along the street were etched by condensation, blurring his view of the people inside. Hand-cleared peepholes wiped by comfortably seated patrons allowed them to look outside. The blurry apertures permitted him to see threads of steam floating from wet shoulders and heads. Customers fondled their small cups of espresso. He envied the lucky souls who had escaped the biting wind and angled spears of rain stabbing the city; they gathered the café's cloaking warmth around them. In Paris, the cold climbed inside bodies, chilling them to the core; it slicked the skin with moisture, dampening clothes and souls.

A maze of small streets and passages leading toward the Seine branched off Rue Bonaparte. He followed them until he arrived on Boulevard Dauphine, at the end of which he could see the Pont Neuf gracefully spanning the river. Each ornate light along the bridge was haloed by the fog rising from the gray water.

He stepped into the Hotel d'Aubusson's elegant lobby and took a seat that allowed him to see through the front window into the street, while keeping an eye on the revolving door at the hotel's entrance.

His SIG Sauer was a pleasant weight on his thigh. Upon his arrival in Paris, he had picked up the weapon in a back-alley porn shop run by an American operative of one of the alphabet-soup agencies. The P226 had a double-stack magazine holding fifteen nine-millimeter Parabellum rounds—sixteen slugs, if there was one in the chamber, as there was tonight. Among handguns, it was Caleb's favorite. He found that his accuracy with this gun was exceptional, even at distances of as much as fifty yards. While the P226 would win no beauty contests with its dull, dark-gray, flat finish, there were few guns as functional or reliable in its class. Caleb was going to do some work with it that night.

Turning his coat collar up against the rain, he left the hotel's comfort, assured that no one was following him. Only one man knew where he was going to be tonight—at least that was how the script was written. But one never knew.

He took a left down Rue St. Andre d'Arts, a dark and narrow street. These buildings had been overlooked during the facade-cleaning program, which had turned the edifices along the major boulevards and rues of Paris a glistening white. Above his head, on a metal bracket attached over a door, was a bravely flickering, red neon sign that simply announced, "Hotel." A number of *à louer* signs hung in filthy windows. Signs announcing studios and galleries for rent were frequently so faded and aged that it was unlikely that whatever had been available at the time of posting the ad was still for rent. At the end of the street was a plaza with the mandatory café. Inside, students huddled around small tables or stood at the zinc bar engaged in intense "save-the-world" and "condemn-the-American-involvement-in-the-Middle-East" conversations. He suspected that the abused country was now Afghanistan or, perhaps, Yemen. Caleb had spent a year as a student in Paris, and although the times and issues changed, he found that the Franco-American love-hate relationship continued unabated.

He stepped into the shadowed doorway of an elegant apartment building and waited five minutes. He was on time for his rendezvous with the informant. His father had always insisted that if something was worth doing, then preparation and anticipation of eventualities—if it can go wrong, it may well go wrong—were critical to the success of the venture. "Visualize the conclusion," he would say, "and keep that objective in mind." Being early was an advantage as well.

Across the Seine, at the tip of the Île de la Cité, an oppressive ceiling of dark-gray clouds, their underbellies illuminated by the city lights, rolled above the towers of La Cathédrale de Notre-Dame. The blunt towers of the cathedral stood as pillars, shouldering the heavy skies above them. In the distance, he could see the Préfecture de Police and L'Hotel Dieu, the center of administration and security for the city of Paris. A large plaza separated the government office buildings and La Cathédrale Notre-Dame de Paris. The substantial expanse between these buildings belied the close proximity of the mutual interests of the Church and the State.

Caleb walked down Rue Cloitre Notre Dame to the Pont Saint Louis, a bridge connecting the larger Île de la Cité to the smaller, but incredibly more affluent Île St. Louis. Many of the buildings housed families whose heritage spanned a couple of centuries on the small island in the middle of the Seine. The old money, the *corps diplomatique*, whose political service or family connections had earned them postings to Paris, or the seriously nouveau riche businessmen found that the Île St. Louis address enhanced their positions. Five-story buildings crowded along the streets nestled up to thin sidewalks. Tall, narrow rows of windows observed the streets and river traffic below with a haughty indifference. Many apartments had their gray, horizontal metal-slat shutters closed for the night. Yellow light glowed through them, warm and inviting, as Caleb passed by in the chilling rain.

At the end of the bridge, Caleb paused to prepare for his descent to the quays below. He leaned on the bridge railing and peered down, searching for anything out of place. The quays' broad, cobblestone expanses circling the islands and along the Seine's banks had served for centuries as the loading docks for river barges delivering goods to the city and taking away Parisian artisans' products. Long, sloping stone stairways clung to towering sandstone walls leading from the surface streets to quays at river level.

Caleb sensed his heart rate increasing. Relaxing his hold on the SIG, he drew in a deep, fog-laden breath in preparation for his meeting at the river's edge.

2

For two weeks, Caleb Frost had worked with a *mélange* of former Interpol associates, French law enforcement contacts, and sleazy informers who were intimate with the Muslim underworld in Paris. He had spent days developing intelligence on the daily habits of an Iraqi national, Amahd al-Tikriti. As a representative of Saddam Hussein's regime to the country of France, al-Tikriti had been officially attached to the Iraqi embassy as the deputy ambassador for academic cooperation. With Operation Iraqi Freedom in 2003, the French had cancelled the diplomatic credentials of all Iraqis in the French capital; the papers the French had so readily provided in 2001 when Saddam sent al-Tikriti to Paris became worthless. The French government advised him to leave the country as rapidly as possible.

With the fall of his benefactor and the death of the dictator's sons, there was little to lure al-Tikriti back to the desert. The prospect of incarceration by the American infidels held little appeal, as did the thought of answering to the Shiites, whose anathema toward a major Arab Socialist Ba'ath Party thug would be substantial and unpleasant. Moving rapidly, al-Tikriti procured false papers. Over the course of the years he had spent in Paris, there had been many opportunities to submit false expenses and to skim major amounts from the accounts he managed. Now, those Euros were snug in a number of accounts in several small, very private banks in France and some large banks in Switzerland. Financially set for years to come, al-Tikriti had melted into La Goutte d'Or section of Paris.

Most people who knew al-Tikriti's history and predilections

preferred to keep any child of theirs well away from him, as his preference for young children, boys or girls, was widely rumored in Baghdad. Two of his best friends were Saddam's sons, Uday and Qusay Hussein. Matching sadistic enterprises one for one, the three tore through Baghdad killing and maiming at will. One night, al-Tikriti's personal bodyguards snatched a six-year-old boy for whom al-Tikriti had developed a sexual desire. The child was kidnapped right out of his mother's arms, and she was severely beaten as she attempted to rescue her child. Al-Tikriti proceeded to have his way with the screaming child, penetrating him repeatedly and viciously beating the little boy, ultimately causing the boy to bleed to death. His naked body was found lying on top of a garbage heap the following morning.

The murdered boy's father was a highly placed Ba'athist Party member and powerful in the Chaldean Christian community. Saddam had made the Christian a minister of minor importance in his government as a token non-Muslim. There was no doubt whatsoever as to the identity of the beast who had killed the little boy. However, no public recognition of the murder appeared in the Iraqi media. That would have had exceptionally unpleasant consequences for the publishers, editors, and journalists, all of whom worked at Saddam's pleasure.

Despite the risks associated with taking on a favorite of Saddam and the bosom buddy of the dictator's sons, the boy's father requested an audience with Saddam Hussein. He demanded al-Tikriti's arrest and beheading. Saddam Hussein was at his most compassionate and shared his grief for the family and the little boy. He sent al-Tikriti to Paris.

Uday and Qusay visited him in Paris frequently, and, if necessary, their methods of disposal of used-up bodies were more carefully planned. If the police had their suspicions, they did not act on them; no charges were ever brought. Aside from al-Tikriti's infrequent ceremonial duties for international academic cooperation, he spent his days happily enforcing Saddam's wishes in the Iraqi community and feasting on those children in the community who caught his fancy.

La Goutte d'Or, the Drop of Gold, was a section of Paris known for harboring immigrant populations, including Algerians, Iranians, Iraqis, Yemeni, and Saudis mixed in squalor with Africans from the Côte d'Ivoire, Senegal, and other former French colonies. The mixture made for an evil brew of discontent and hatred for their hosts and for any Muslim, Christian, or, most frequently, Jew, they saw as hindering them from attaining their rightful rewards in life.

The mindless fervor among the Muslims in La Goutte d'Or, justified by gross distortions of the messages of Islam's holiest of books to suit their own purposes, continued to stun Caleb even though he had, at times in the past, lived undercover in Muslim communities in Isfahan, Iran, and Mosul, Iraq. He wondered how the moderate Muslims could permit the continued funding of the dregs of their cultures. But millions of dollars from all over the world flowed through insurgent cover organizations' coffers. Caleb knew the ins and outs of the fractured nature of Islam and the social structure in which alliances were strongest at the family and tribal level. The local sheiks were the first bricks in the foundation of the power structure. They were the base of the social pyramid. At the top were the clergy and the politicians sitting on a precariously balanced, fluid, and volatile construction of personal interests and power struggles. They were also responsible for crafting inflammatory misinterpretations of a beautiful religion to achieve their own goals. Some of the historic tribal feuds existed over several centuries and were still blood hot.

Despite knowing full well the extent of criminal activities rampant in La Goutte d'Or, the police and the government were either unable or unwilling to take control, so crime, conspiracy, and drug trafficking flourished.

Thoughts of his recent search for al-Tikriti filled Caleb's mind as he started down the long stone stairway to Quai d'Orléans. The stone steps were worn from years of traffic. One of his sources, a one-eyed Afghan, had contacted Caleb with word that a former Iraqi embassy guard had information about al-Tikriti's whereabouts. It would cost one thousand Euros in cash in advance of the rendezvous. The ex-guard would meet Caleb on Quai de Bourbon, arriving by boat at 9:00 p.m. sharp. Be there on time or the informer would leave immediately, the go-between had said. Money changed hands.

The rain released the musty odor of decades of rotted vegetable matter, dead meat, blood, mud, and all manner of collected filth from within the cracks between cobblestones. Lining the top of the walls, standing along the sidewalks and roadways above the quays like a ragged, black fringe, were kiosks and stalls. Their backs to the Seine, they awaited the next day's brisk business.

Caleb walked slowly down the quay, staying close to the wall and within its shadow, to Quai de Bourbon on the north side of the island. He could see the Seine through the threads of rain splashing on thousands of cobblestones stretching into the distance. The blurred lights of the city and the river traffic reflected off the surface of the river. The putt-putt of an outboard motor grew louder. Caleb quickly crossed the width of the key to its edge, peering intently into the darkness, searching for the boat.

He felt a tug to his coat sleeve and a burning sensation on his left forearm. Almost as an afterthought, he heard the soft report of a shot. He dived for the ground. What the hell was he doing meeting out in the open like a rank amateur? How could he really have believed that an ex-Saddam guy would sell out for a lousy one thousand Euros—ten thousand maybe, but for chump change, what was he thinking? Set up like a dummy. He could hear the putt-putt of the rendezvous boat receding.

A second shot, splashing off a cobblestone inches from his left eye, sent a fragment of the bullet's jacket spinning like a circular saw. The copper chip zipped through Caleb's left eyebrow and buried itself in his coat's shoulder pad. He stifled his impulse to shout out in pain and rage. The rest of the bullet ended up in the back of a kiosk across the Seine above Quai de l'Hotel de Ville. Tourists enjoying a late supper aboard a passing *Bateau Mouche* tourist sightseeing boat had no idea how close they had come to having a bullet enter their boat's Plexiglas canopy. Nor would the couples scurrying to find sanctuary from the rain across the light-dappled black strip of river know that evil was present in the soft thud heard from behind a kiosk.

Caleb wrestled the P226 out of his coat pocket and rolled over to face the direction from which he sensed the shots had come. He lay prone, giving as small a target as possible, arms outstretched, hands tight around the SIG Sauer's grip, safety off, searching the darkness. He blinked furiously to clear the rain and blood out of his eyes as he searched the recesses in the quay wall for the gunman. He did his best to melt into the cobblestones. The thought of getting up and running like hell appealed to him for a millisecond.

Blood oozed like warm chocolate from the gash above his eye. It collected on his cheek under his eye. His forearm burned. The corner of his mouth filled with blood. It overflowed onto the cobbles mixing with the collected sludge of centuries in the cracks beneath his face. At street level, atop the high wall, the apartment buildings' shuttered windows gazed down as if pondering his plight—or maybe they observed it with amusement.

A third shot rang out, also clicking off a cobblestone and tugging once again at his sleeve's cuff. He was being bracketed as he lay, sprawled motionless on the ground. Eventually, that guy would get lucky and pop one into his head. This time, he had seen the flash from deep within the right side of the recessed alcove at the foot of the wall. With a slight adjustment in elevation, he squeezed two rapid shots into the blackness. There was no sound. No bullets striking stone or the metal door at the back of the alcove that housed the entrance to what he presumed was a maintenance storeroom. A wayward thought crossed his mind about the puddles forming beneath his body, soaking his shirt and pants. Were they sweat, rain, or blood? A muzzle flash streaked out of the doorway into the sky. The angle and direction of the brief lightning bolt from the weapon told Caleb that the bullet would be flying aimlessly over the slate rooftops of Paris.

A figure in a long, dark overcoat, an outstretched arm holding a pistol, staggered into the dim light afforded by the street lamps along the avenue high above the quay. The man's shadow extended outward toward Caleb, who stayed still on the cobbles aiming his weapon at his chest. The figure took a step, instinctually trying to maintain his balance, as if confused as to where to go. A drooping mustache slashed across a long face. It glistened in the rain. The man's lips were pulled back into an involuntary grimace as if expressing incredulity and defiance.

Dark blood poured from a ragged spot in the white forehead, lengthening the appearance of the man's mustache as the thick liquid ran to the corners of his mouth. Gouts of blood spurted rhythmically from the man's neck where one of Caleb's shots had drilled into flesh, hitting the artery. Another flash from the end of the dying man's outstretched arm and a slug showered sparks as it gouged the cobblestones some feet from Caleb's head. Slowly, like a tree clinging to its deep roots as it toppled from the woodsman's ax, the body fell forward. The overcoat billowed like a black cloud around the figure on the quay—a suitable black shroud.

From a window in an apartment building high above the quay, a woman's voice shrieked, "*Que se passe-t-il donc la bas? Dégagez bande de voyous!*" Caleb suppressed an urge to shout at the lady that he had just assassinated a pedophile. That was what was going on.

Caleb rose, fishing his handkerchief from his back pocket, and pressed it against his eyebrow. He ran to the body and turned it over with his foot. Black, sightless eyes stared fiercely into the cloud-laden sky. Rain spattered on al-Tikriti's face, giving it the appearance of momentary life, but he was dead. The world would not miss this piece of shit, Caleb thought as he slid his weapon into his coat pocket and mounted the stone stairs.

Climbing the stone steps to street level, Caleb quickly calculated his moves. The job was done. He needed medical attention for his eyebrow and his arm. Neither injury was life threatening, but both were open wounds and leaking blood into his clothes and down his face. They were hindrances, distractions, and could well draw unwanted inquiries. As soon as he was safely away from the scene, he'd call Vesuvius for a safe doctor. Vesuvius maintained a worldwide, ultra-private list of resources. Safe houses, doctors, documents, transportation, weaponry, communications support, and even military and police assistance were all available from the bottomless pit of international affiliations Vesuvius could access. Caleb had never tried to understand the Vesuvius network's provenance. Its origins were never discussed. All he knew was that it was a resource that had never failed to assist him in his missions.

His mother had once advised him to gain in-depth knowledge of whom and for what purpose he was working—and then to give absolute loyalty to that employer and ideology. Since the beginning of his career, he had never had occasion to doubt the singular importance of his assignments. They were all designated by the same organization and the same man, his controller. Shortly after the conversation about loyalty with his mother, she and his father had been brutally slaughtered in an ambush. Caleb often wondered what she would say now about trust and loyalty.

Caleb had yet to identify his parents' murderers. The perpetrators of the horrendous killing were one consideration. The individual who ordered the operation was something else. That person was his ultimate target.

The stairs led him up to Rue Deux Ponts, a residential street lined with empty-eyed doorways. He crossed the street, searching for shadows, and strode toward the Métro Jussieu a couple of blocks away.

A ball of white hair cannoned around the street corner Caleb was approaching. The tiny bichon frisé's arrival was followed immediately by a woman attached to the dog by a leash. She had stylish, short dark hair and wore a Hermes scarf wrapped around her neck for warmth against the misty cold and the rain, which had now become a persistent drizzle. A gusting wind fluttered her raincoat around her legs as she kept pace with the dog's brisk trot. She wore stovepipe jeans beneath her belted raincoat. The clicking of her bright-red, four-inch heels echoed in the silent streets. As his startle reflexes, ignited by the abrupt appearance of the dog, settled, he appraised the woman.

He decided that she was very attractive. Maybe under less stressful circumstances, he speculated … well, it wouldn't happen tonight. He figured that the blood-soaked handkerchief covering his eyebrow probably did little to improve his appearance.

He said, "Bonsoir, mademoiselle." Stepping over the leash, he hurried down the sidewalk.

Her reflexive response, a murmured "Bonsoir, monsieur," whispered after him in the damp air.

Approaching the corner and the entrance to the Métro, he sensed that she had turned to watch him. He could almost feel her eyes scanning him. He paused and glanced back. She was staring at him, memorizing the moment, the details. It was time to get out of Paris. Too bad.

3

Wrath's blunt fingers, nails defined by half-moons of compacted grease, slowly rotated a maroon beer stein on the battered tabletop he used as a desk. A barely legible gold college crest made its statement as the stein revolved. His hands were large, his knuckles scarred. Next to his right hand, a Glock 22 forty-caliber pistol rested on top of a deluxe edition of Robert's *Rules of Order*. Both the stein and the weapon were fully loaded—the mug with Samuel Adams Winter Lager and the Glock with one in the chamber and a fifteen-round mag in the grip. A gold Cross pen and a yellow, lined legal pad adorned with scribbled meeting agenda completed the table's setting. The margins around the agenda were covered with jottings and doodles. A psychiatrist would have had a field day, albeit a scary one, with Wrath's subconscious as revealed by his sketches.

Leaning back in his easy chair, Wrath listened to the discussion of the club members. From beneath his long black mane of hair, which hung down to touch his broad shoulders in a jumble of curls, his intense, blue, almond-shaped eyes roamed lazily across the faces of the men seated haphazardly around the Visigoths' MC mother chapter's clubhouse living room. As he turned his face to track the conversation, his long, aquiline nose stood out like the bowsprit of a sailing ship—a pirate ship.

Wrath intuitively recognized souls like his own. Some of them he knew from the same gutters he had survived in the streets of Oakland. His father spent most of his time failed and jailed. His mother was a drug-addicted prostitute. When he put his "business plan" in motion, he knew how to harness the intense, close-to-tears fury and frustration of these men's lives. It was an easy sale. He gave them a way to give the finger to the establishment assholes, while making a living off middle-class weaknesses. The business plan called for an outlaw motorcycle gang. Muscle. Courage. Hunger. Security. And loyalty to the only forgiving and supportive family these men had ever known.

As the chapter meeting's agenda wound its way through the afternoon, Wrath took an inventory of the twenty-four men in front of him and their value to his business. An outlaw motorcycle club prided itself on being counter-establishment in as many ways as the group could adopt. To Wrath's amusement, as he recruited his membership, there was a sameness among all of his candidates. The group was a subculture, dressed, speaking, and reacting identically. They were unkempt, by mainstream standards, jeans-and-vest clad, T-shirted, mechanically skilled, and angry men. Yet, beneath the similarities, each man, like his white-collar brethren, was different and had unique skills acquired and honed in the streets, in jail, and, for that matter, in mainstream corporate business—all important contributions toward achieving the objectives of the business plan Wrath had created three years earlier for a course project at the Harvard Business School.

Several members of the Visigoths Motorcycle Club were convicted murderers. There was no one criminal act that someone in the club had not been intimately engaged in at some time in the recent past. The only crime the men were not allowed to indulge in was heavy drugs. Grass and alcohol were the lifeblood, but the hard shit was out. No mixing pleasure with business.

As in most outlaw motorcycle clubs, all of the members were required to have day jobs. One held a job at Cisco Systems as a network programmer, a skill of considerable value to this particular organization. Another was a biochemist employed by Genentech, nicknamed "Designer," who could analyze and manufacture almost any drug. For a variety of reasons, loyalty to Wrath and doing his bidding was the number-one job for each of the Visigoth members.

Overstuffed, dilapidated sofas and easy chairs filled the room, furnishings collected from the street curbs of Oakland and Alameda. Several of the members' ol' ladies, skillful with needle and thread, kept the worst of the rips sewn shut.

Floral-patterned wallpaper from fifty years ago covered the walls of the living room. Water stains added random shapes to the wall covering. Throughout all the rooms in the house, shredded pieces of wallpaper panel sagged like long drooping flags stuck to the walls. They revealed peeks of underlying layers of past wallpapers and, in some instances, simply yellowing plaster walls. The air was redolent with a powerful mixture of sweat, smoke, and stale beer. The house had no heat, so mold, gathering during years of dampness, clung in fermenting layers behind the walls. The mold contributed its own distinct stench.

All of the members were competent in the use of firearms and some form of hand-to-hand fighting. Many had weapons of choice, such as knives, chains, guns, or iron bars. The preferences for weapons seemed to define the characters and styles of his men. A fellow known as "Strike Force" had been abused by his family and his fellow soldiers in the military. Since he had spent so much time in the embrace of his tormentors, he had developed a fondness for shivs, stilettos—thin, deadly needles suited for close work. Simon Warfull, a bodybuilder, welded a metal sheath on the side of his bike to carry his chromed, twenty-pound sledgehammer. The club also owned an assortment of rifles, shotguns, and machine pistols for the traditionalists.

"Creek?" Wrath said, addressing the behemoth sitting to his right. "New business, please. The subject is chapter house security, I believe?" he said checking his agenda.

Creek stood and shambled to a blackboard nailed to the wall. His worn biker boots compressed the brown shag carpet. With a glance at Wrath, who was drinking from the maroon stein, Creek turned to the members. Small animal bones tied into his shaggy head of hair and full beard clicked merrily as his long, greasy hair swept across his bulky shoulders. His florid face was acne-pocked and featured small, piggy eyes, bright and menacing, sitting atop pillows of red-veined cheeks.

At six-foot-five and three hundred and twenty-five pounds, Creek made an immediate bad impression when he entered a room. His arms, bare and forced through a soiled gray T-shirt, were thigh sized with biceps stretching the shirt's short sleeves as he moved his arms. The knuckles on his huge hands bore the prison-tattooed letters F, U, C, K on the right and Y, O, U with an exclamation point on the pinkie finger on the left. His denim pants were so filthy they appeared shiny, black, and rigid with grease and dirt and food-messed hand-wipings. The only creases on the jeans were behind the knees and across his ample lap.

His leather vest was emblazoned with several colorful scatological biker patches. The 1% and Harley-Davidson patches prominent among them. The 1% symbol was one of several genius marketing concepts produced over the years by the motorcycle gang culture. The Hells Angels in particular had shown a superior marketing instinct. An executive of the American Motorcycle Association decried the anti-establishment behavior and violence of outlaw motorcycle clubs by saying that 99% of all motorcycle riders were law-abiding citizens. The benefit of co-opting the remaining 1% was an acknowledgment heralding Hells Angels membership as being unique and therefore special. Every outlaw MC adopted it.

The back of Creek's worn leather vest had two black rockers with a grinning death's head smiling from between them. The top rocker read, "Visigoths," stitched in silver thread. Beneath the skull was the embroidered chapter location, Alameda. A fourth patch sewn close to the Visigoths rocker had an "MC" on it. Motorcycle Club! But not your average American Motorcycle Association member's club.

The grinning skull was a piece of genre art. Wrath had sketched the basic design himself and then had the girl he was sleeping with in Boston finish it on the computers at her art school in Cambridge. Many outlaw clubs' colors featured a variation of the skull. The jaws were always set in a rictus grin. The black, hollow eye sockets glared from deep within the bone head with a malevolence promising imminent violence. A Visigoth helmet sat on top of the skull, jauntily tilted forward on the forehead.

Creek earned his name and validated his position as sergeant at arms for the Visigoths based on an incident up at the Russian River, north of San Francisco. The Visigoths' weekend run had ended at an off-the-road picnic and camping spot. A hapless member of the Riatas MC, another outfit down south in Salinas, followed them off the road thinking that he would be met with comradely acceptance and a beer or two.

As the riders roared into the recreation area, the hikers and campers picnicking or setting up their tents for a weekend's outing suddenly decided that the weather was going to get unseasonably stormy and they should leave, rapidly. Children's questions about why they were being uprooted were met by glares and shushing sounds. Soon the Visigoths had the tables, fireplace grills, and volleyball court to themselves. And the Riata guest was accorded a couple of beers and some hot dogs as the women got the fireplaces blazing.

Wrath knew that the Riatas had a methamphetamine lab in the area and that the stash of meth and money was probably quite large considering their distribution network across Northern California, Oregon, Idaho, and Nevada. If someone OD'd on meth up north in Portland, the odds were good that the Riatas' product was involved. Maybe the product had been stepped on a couple of times and possibly contaminated by middlemen, but basically, it came from the Riatas' lab.

Wrath called Creek aside. "You suppose you could get this guy to tell us where the Riatas' methamphetamine stash is? Any persuasion you could devise to encourage him to tell us?"

"Sure," Creek said looking around the area. Wrath could see the anticipation in the man's face as he considered the persuasion possibilities. His fingers cracked like Chinese New Year firecrackers as he intertwined and kneaded them. The waterway running through the picnic area intrigued him.

"Ask him first," Wrath advised. "No sense in ruining his day if he's willing to share."

"Unhuh," Creek had said as he lumbered off to initiate the business discussion.

The recalcitrant Riata refused to share the location of the stash despite the generally pleasant nature of the initial questioning. Moving the persuasion up a notch, Creek cuffed the guy's hands behind him and wrapped duct tape a couple of turns around his head and mouth. By then, the man was resisting violently.

"Now, you're sure you don't want to cooperate and save your ass from getting wet?"

The tape smothered his answer.

Creek tied long ropes around each of the thrashing biker's ankles. He tied the ends of the ropes to sturdy trees on opposite sides of the narrow, fast-running stream.

Grabbing the man's face in his huge hand, Creek told him, "Listen close, motherfucker. You goin' swimmin', ya hear me, man? When you want to save your fuckin' ass and tell us what we want to know, lift your head outta the water and nod … a lot. Then I'll pull you out. You got that?"

Wrath could feel his excitement grow as he watched. His feral being cried for this violence. It bordered on being a sexual urgency. He watched with fascination as Creek, with a roar, grabbed the collar of the man's denim vest and the seat of his pants, raised him over his head, and launched the flailing Riata into the water, head downstream. The thrill ran through his body like an electric shock.

The man was never able to keep himself afloat long enough to get air or to signal. He drowned in front of the entire Visigoths chapter and their ol' ladies. When he floated, motionless, facedown in the stream's burbling water, everyone applauded Creek's efforts. The fierce and feared street name, "Creek," was bestowed.

The Visigoths listened up as Creek began to draw an outline of the Craymore Street property. Wrath had bought the sixty-year-old, three-story clapboard, 2620 Craymore Street house when he founded the Visigoths. The house sat on a lot reminiscent of the days when a house came with a half acre or more. A long driveway ran up the middle of the front lawn ending in a circular parking area. A walkway of cracked and tilted slabs led from the front gate to the sagging stoop and the front door.

The clapboard house's exterior paint was a cracked and peeling gray. Outside, the lawn was mainly dirt surrounding an occasional clump of hardy grass. Large bushes edged the front yard. Between the bushes and the barbed-wire-festooned redwood fence surrounding the property, a well-beaten pathway allowed guards to move around the property unseen from the street entrance. A ninety-foot-deep backyard ended against an easement running the width of the property. Dense bushes grew around the perimeter of the backyard. Well-concealed gates, intended for escape, or surprising intruders, were built into the outer fence.

Wrath had bought the house from the heirs of an old man who had lived there for forty years and died so alone that it took two months before he was discovered dead, facedown in a plate of Spaghetti-O's. A bottle of cheap red wine sat on the old man's table. There was a concrete-like block of Italian bread and a bowl of wilted and rotted something. The wine, like the deceased, had breathed its last.

People visiting the Visigoths' mother chapter house frequently commented on the faint unpleasant odor wafting about the house every now and then.

The main floor of the house featured a large living room where the chapter meetings were held. A ramshackle bar was set up in what used to be the dining room across the entry hallway from the living room. Sawhorse tables made up the bar furniture. Whatever furniture had existed in days gone by had been broken or otherwise destroyed. Wrath chose to keep the bar's floor space clear for the games the boys might choose to play. "Sit on the fuckin' floor," was his response when anyone had the gall to complain about the lack of seats or couches. The kitchen at the back of the building was a free-for-all, both in terms of use and appearance. It was usually the mamas who would clean up when even they couldn't stomach the rancid mess. A regularly scheduled meal might be served for a chapter event, but never otherwise.

A large room across the front of the second floor served as a dormitory with room for ten bunks. Eight smaller rooms—four across the back of the house and two on either side of the second floor's central hallway and staircase—had been built out. All of the rooms had views of the perimeter and, therefore, decent lines for defensive fire.

To all appearances, the purpose of the third floor was to provide recreational opportunities for the members. Access to the floor was by the back stairway, which climbed up from the cellar to the third floor against the back wall of the house. A pool table and some couches filled the center space of the attic. The Visigoth armory was located on the third floor. Racks holding weapons and containers filled with ammunition, flares, and hand grenades stood behind the expertly concealed panels. Other containers held chains, nunchakus, knives, and other tools for creating mayhem. There was one highly polished and sharpened cutlass hanging on a bracket attached to the inside of the sloping roof.

When Wrath had purchased the chapter house, he had also purchased a second house. The property backed up to the same easement as the Craymore house but faced one of Alameda's better streets. The house on 2727 Clifton Way was a very well-kept Victorian. Realtors frequently pointed it out to promote sales in the area. The owner of the Victorian, they reported, had done a considerable amount of renovation and modernization. The real estate salespeople rubbed their fingertips together implying "big money" lived there—a very respectable lawyer or a financier of some stripe. The realtors never had tours on Craymore Street and were unaware of the construction work completed on 2620 Craymore at about the same time as the work on 2727 Clifton Way.

"According to the chapter by-laws and the rules national has approved for everybody," Creek continued as the room settled down, "we got to keep six brothers on security detail seven by twenty-four." His guttural delivery filled the room as his words rumbled out of his long beard. The clicking from his beard continued for a split second after he shut his mouth.

"All of us got fuckin' jobs, Creek. You're asking for twenty-five percent of the motherfuckin' membership on each shift," John Tabor said. He accentuated his comment by pulling a Bud tab and gulping beer. "You gonna assign som'a the ol' ladies? Give 'em goddamn weapons? I don't trust my bitch with a fuckin' butter knife."

"I smelled like you, John, you turd-eating asshole, I'd wanna be put outta my shit-eating misery anyhow," a member dubbed "Coyote" said, ducking the half-full beer can John Tabor threw at him.

Stained yellow teeth filled the slit in Creek's beard as he grinned. "John, don't forget; I know your ol' lady, and I'd take her on my fuckin' patrol over you, pretty boy, any goddamn day."

"Or ... night!" half a dozen men shouted in unison, and the crowd roared with laughter. John Tabor was blushing, and his eyes cast a baleful sweep around the room. His regret that he had spoken up at all was obvious. Tabor was more style than vile.

The butt of the Glock tapped once, and the room fell silent. Heads turned to the table at the front of the room. Wrath stood. He was six foot six and about two hundred and thirty-five pounds of whippy muscle. He leaned forward, fingers splayed on the scarred surface of the desk. His eyes met the eyes of each man. When he spoke, it was in a soft voice demanding that everyone listen closely.

"Guys, the Visigoths' business is doing well. From everything I can gather, we are in better fuckin' shape the past coupla years than the goddamned Angels an' Diablos. We haven't lost one fuckin' ounce of product, and, more importantly, not one of our guys has been off'd or busted doin' our business. Thanks to your skills, our bikes are in perfect condition. Course, the financial support we get from national helps a bunch. We got as much supplies and ordnance as we'll need for a year 'cording to our quartermaster, right, Obit?"

A sallow young man nodded and waved a grease-stained hand with his thumb raised skyward. "Yo," was the extent of his commentary.

"So we're in good shape, guys. You are all doin' a good job. Thanks. Any questions?"

"Yeah, Wrath, I got one fer ya," said a young member sitting in the back of the room. His voice held a timorous quaver as he asked, "If we in such good shape, how come Creek's busting our balls and tightening security?"

Wrath moved from behind the desk and sat on the corner of the table gently swinging the heavy black boot on his left foot. He gazed at his loosely clasped hands in his lap. With a slight grin on his full lips, he looked up from underneath his eyebrows. He reached back, grasped his stein, and took a slow sip. "Creek tells me that his left nut is itching. If his nuts itch, gentlemen, it's time to pay attention and watch our backs. Scratch for us, Creek!" he commanded turning to the bearded giant. Creek dug his left hand inside his jeans and scratched his crotch gritting his teeth as if in ecstasy. The men laughed and hooted appreciatively. "So, I suggest you bastards hear him well. Our sergeant at arms does not take his assignment lightly, and you shouldn't take his advice lightly either." Absolute silence met the comment.

"Creek, bring 'em up-to-date. Finish it up," he said waving his hand in a forward rolling motion. "We got another meeting."

"Yeah, okay, Wrath. Listen up, you assholes. I don't want no sass talk on the schedule, or you'll discuss it with me out back. Any takers?" With a scowl filled with meaning and threat, he scanned his audience. Nobody moved a muscle or met his gaze either. He returned to his drawing of the property and the outline of the house. He labeled the streets, identified the houses in the neighborhood, and drew patrol routes, lines of fire, and inside positions to be manned in case of a fight.

Pointing a chalk-powdered finger at a slouched figure on a couch at the back of the room, Creek said, "Guys, Kirk's ol' lady works at the Alameda pig sty. She's got access to the fuckin' reports comin' inta the chief. The Feds in Washington, the local bozos in San Francisco, and some Sacramento weenies was asking about us. Not only us, but other Visigoth chapters as well. The Albuquerque chapter got rousted at their clubhouse last Tuesday night. Fuckin' twelve bikes were put out of commission. Fuckin' bastards ran a Hummer over them. Can you believe those motherfuckers?"

Creek held up his hand to quiet the mutters. "National authorized a buy to get everybody back on a bike. Six were damaged beyond repair, including a '36 EL Knucklehead in cherry condition. If I knew who the bastard cop was who made that decision, I'd find 'im and skin him alive." His brow dark with fury, Creek snorted with an effort to control himself. The noise abated, and he lifted his head. "Mebbe I will someday." He shook his head, and the animal bones clacked their anger. "Anyway, you know Wrath's policy. We replaced 'em at no cost to the members, ya know. 'Cept for the '36 Knucklehead. That's gone, goddamn it."

"Fuckin' cops," a bald biker said, his long side hair swirling as he shook his head in disgust. His chaps were worn and greasy, as was the "Live Fast and Die Later" T-shirt covering his bowling-ball paunch. Wrath smiled appreciatively as Knobby tightened his fists into fur-covered hammers. "Why not go tear that whole motherfuckin' town a new asshole, Wrath? You can't go fuckin' up guys' bikes that way. Let's kill a few of those fuckin' sonsabitches. Mess somebody up for that."

"'Cause, you do that, Knobby, an' we won't be able to ride down Route 40 without bein' hassled by the cops. And that's bad for our business, you know?" Wrath said. "There's times to chill, man, and now's one of 'em. We made good on the members' hogs. Ain't nobody got dinged too bad; a couple arms broken and a mouthful of teeth lost is all. All covered. Let it slide. We'll remember those bastards and get ours back someday soon."

Wrath paused and looked at the yellow pad. "The agenda says after we get our security assignments, you guys have to plan the ride to Redding. The Diablos are having a ride too, so I called over and suggested we all meet at the Sundowner Ranch off Ninety-Nine on Saturday for some barbecue and contests."

"Yeah, baby," came from the back of the room. "Wet T-shirt contests. Tits, tits, and more tits, man." Some of the older members looked bored. That was a young man's fun. Many of the mother chapter members were married and had kids.

There were no women in the meeting or membership. Aside from their usefulness in the kitchen, the bedroom, and at their jobs bringing in money and information of value to Wrath, women's concerns were ignored. Women were basically chattel and were treated as such most of the time. The tougher married women and girlfriends, the ol' ladies, pushed the line as far as they dared to keep their men at home.

Some of the older women, known as mamas, hung around to feel the glow of speed, violence, and power. They were frequently less attractive women by virtue of age, abuse, or incident. They may have been cast off by a member and couldn't let it all go. So they stayed on the fringe. They made themselves available to anyone who wanted any service, including sex, whenever, wherever, and however they liked it. It was a pay-as-you-go arrangement for these women.

Outings like the run to Redding meant the women would be expected to go along. Dressed in leathers and denims with low-cut jeans and tight T-shirts, they would add an air of excitement for the members, as well as the citizens who watched the spectacle roar pass. Colorful scarves would wave from beneath the women's helmets. Every Visigoth wore a skull cap helmet at a minimum. Some sported the spiked Prussian helmet, though none of them had it chromed—an unforgiveable affectation among Visigoths. The club wore helmets because Wrath reasoned that it was not smart to break a law unless the return on the investment in the crime was worth jail time.

For purposes of safety and ownership of the road, bikers rode in a protective, staggered formation, which was traditional among motorcycle clubs—outlaws or not. Cast a big shadow and get respect. Coyote, the Goths' road captain, was in charge of the ride, setting the details in advance and managing the formation on the road. Wrath, as the president, and Coyote rode at the front. The other officers were behind them, then the members, and finally the probies who were applying for membership.

Wrath kicked at Coyote's outstretched feet.

"Get everybody there, Coyote. I want everyone on the ride. Tell the probates. Let 'em come along for the day. See how they ride. How they handle 'emselves. They can do the fuckin' cooking with ol' ladies. Make sure the van follows with whatever you think we might need. Tell Molly to drive. Can't imagine a problem with the Diablos though, can you, Creek?"

The large man shook his head, rattling the bones.

Molly O'Shaughnessy's follow van would be loaded with food, drink, spare parts, some gasoline, and an assortment of weapons concealed under the floorboards—just in case. A few ol' ladies served as drivers for the Visigoths. The van never exceeded the speed limit and never needed new lights or better tires or more gas at a critical moment. Molly O'Shaughnessy was a fifty-year-old welder on the Alameda docks. She was one of the few women who owned her own bike and could maintain it as well as any of the members. She played house with Rattler Bosworth. Bosworth was noted for carrying a fully fanged and juiced rattlesnake with him on his bike as a pet. Bosworth had named the snake Sidney. Wrath wasn't sure about Rattler's mental stability. In a knock-down, drag-out fight between Molly and Rattler, many of the guys would have backed Molly to clean Rattler's clock, barring his use of Sidney. Still and all, Molly was not a member, could not attend meetings, and was really only allowed on the property when she was repairing her own bike or cooking for social events. She was the best follow vehicle driver, however, and her disarming motherly looks had dissuaded many a cop from issuing a citation.

Wrath held up a hand and told Creek to post his security assignments on the second-floor bathroom door and leave it to Coyote to set up the run to Redding. He asked for a motion and a second to adjourn the meeting. Eager members called out motions and seconds. Wrath banged the Harvard stein on the table and declared the meeting adjourned. Shouting above the conversations and laughter filling the room, he called the Visigoths' executive committee members to join him downstairs in the conference room. Glock stuffed in his waistband, stein swinging from curled fingers, and boots thumping as he left the room, he led the way toward the kitchen and the back stairs.

4

The 747's rumbling engines lulled Caleb Frost's thoughts away from the itching on his brow. He had made a coded call to Vesuvius requesting a doctor. The clandestine Vesuvius service directed him to a residential neighborhood in Neuilly-sur-Seine across the Périphérique from the famous Porte Maillot entrance to Paris. Exiting the Métro at Avenue de Madrid, he walked to a point midway across the Pont de Neuilly and dropped his SIG Sauer into the Seine. He would later drop his gloves in a trash barrel at the airport.

After the doctor, who had artfully repaired his eyebrow and forearm wounds without questions, had finished stitching, patching, bandaging, tch-ing, and hiding the tiny stitches under the smallest bandage he could provide, Caleb thanked him profusely and went to find a dark corner from which to call his people in Burlingame. He reported the success of the mission and reassured them regarding his health. Then he took the Métro to L'Arc de Triomphe and caught the shuttle bus out to the suburbs of Paris to the sprawling Aéroport Charles de Gaulle.

His return trip tickets, in the name of John Davidson, from Aéroport Charles de Gaulle to New York's JFK with a continuation to Chicago on American Airlines, were in order, as were his passport and his continuation ticket on a United flight to Chicago's O'Hare. The flight to New York proved uneventful.

Caleb preferred to fly business class. First-class people received more attention, while business-class people were assumed to be just that, businessmen and women who were lucky to get a perk from their companies. He asked the flight attendant for a blanket. The Parisian doctor had supplied him with powerful painkillers for the trip. Sleep came quickly.

Caleb passed through JFK's customs without a hitch. Entry into the United States was the least friendly entrance into any country in the world, but had they been searched by TSA, his carry-on bag and briefcase would have been found to be totally innocuous. He made a point of carrying no electronics, except for the businessman's requisite iPhone.

The interterminal bus took him to the United Airlines terminal. Using John Davidson's ticket to Chicago and ID, he passed through TSA security.

At a newsstand, Caleb collected a copy of *The New Yorker* magazine and a couple newspapers, a *Wall Street Journal* and a *New York Post*. He added a Mounds candy bar and laid a one-hundred-dollar bill on the counter as payment for his purchases. The counterman took the materials and asked if he would like a bag. He said yes, and the counterman gave him his change for the one-hundred-dollar bill without comment and placed the purchases in a bag he brought up from behind the counter. He passed it to Caleb.

Seating himself on an unoccupied hallway bench across from the shops, he looked at the contents of the bag. Included with the magazine and the newspapers were a boarding pass from a United Airlines flight from San Francisco to New York six days earlier, the return business-class ticket, and a boarding pass for that day's flight. The bag also contained a variety of business cards bound by a rubber band. Three credit cards, a driver's license, a Social Security card, and some company papers, all in the name of Harry Wilcox, were also included.

According to the papers and a name badge strung with a skinny white elastic cord, Harry had attended a consumer electronics convention at New York's Javits Center collecting business cards in the traditional card exchange with exhibitors and attendees. A packet of colorful trade brochures touting new products and inviting his attention were bundled by a large paper clip. An expense account form had correctly dated receipts attached to it. The collection of paper remnants from food stands, taxis, bars, and his hotel charges proved that Harry Wilcox had been there.

Caleb distributed the assorted bits and pieces into his jacket pockets and John Davidson's nondescript, worn briefcase.

In a men's room stall, he dropped his Davidson passport and driver's license, the contents of Davidson's briefcase, including letters of credit and business documents confirming his credentials as an investment banker, pictures of his wife and daughter, and his return ticket to Chicago into the toilet. The special plastics and papers dissolved in the chlorinated water soundlessly and without smoke or odor. He flushed. John Davidson's life went down the drain. Literally.

Harry Wilcox, salesman for Brinkman & Sons Electronics, boarded a nonstop flight to San Francisco.

5

The plane banked westward into the evening skies, the engines producing a rhythmic throb beneath Caleb Frost's head. He reviewed the past three weeks. He mentally traced his steps through his confrontation with his target, Amahd al-Tikriti.

He fully believed that he terminated only those who had done little to earn a pass in this life. That qualification was the primary consideration in his decision to accept or decline an engagement. He did have the unique right to refuse an assignment. His engagements would always be with individuals or groups who preyed on defenseless people. Al-Tikriti had met the criteria to a T. Caleb knew that the father and family of the dead boy in Baghdad would learn of al-Tikriti's long-delayed death. It would appear in the Iraqi press. That was all they would ever know, and he wanted them to know. It was done—closure, if that was ever possible, for a greatly bereaved and abused family and justice for a child whose only mistake was being born into hell.

Events such as this one caused "mental saboteurs" to attack Caleb's mind—saboteurs invading in search of remorse, launching corrosive self-accusations and doubts. He shoved the event and its memories into the cage he reserved for saboteurs in his mind. Nighttime, in the early, sweat-dampened hours, was the battlefield upon which he fought them. Caleb was well aware that he was still learning to live with himself—to live with the killing. His first assassination assignment, when he was graduating from Summer Camp, was a guy who was selling cocaine to high-school children. He had chosen to inject the man with a slow-acting, brain-deteriorating drug. He had wanted to make the guy suffer, knowing that he was slowly, painfully, and surely dying. "Oh, nasty," his instructor had said when Caleb proposed his methodology for approval. Caleb felt that rotting the man out for the terrible destruction he had caused was, in fact, true justice.

The lights of Modesto, California, slid beneath the Boeing 737's left wing. His mind turned to his sister, Rebecca. Reb, as she was called, was never far from his thoughts. Four years younger than he, she had responded differently to the violent death—the horrendously vicious murder—of their parents. At the age of fourteen, Caleb swore to avenge his parents' murder by hunting down and killing their killers. This commitment had kept him focused, leading him to his current profession. The old man from Georgetown, William Thorndike, had helped to educate, train, and mold him as a teenager. Bereft of the strong family influence in which he and Reb had been raised, Caleb grasped the guidance the old man offered the two children of his former employees.

Rebecca, a sensitive ten-year-old, developed into a beauty. Close to six feet tall with honey-blonde hair, she was not only a beauty but an athlete and intelligent enough to get into Stanford University. The social environment she tended to inhabit after graduation and a move back east to New York City was a major cause of concern to Caleb. On several occasions, he had used his many resources to distance his sister from bad men, women, or situations. The people he deemed unworthy for her to associate with never had an idea as to why major disasters befell them—credit problems, shady business deals revealed, and, sometimes, jail sentences resulted from their misfortune. Nor did his sister understand how acquaintances suddenly disappeared from her social circle.

His efforts to stay in touch with her were fruitless. At first, Reb used social obligations to excuse herself from spending time with Caleb. She blamed travel, meetings, and weekend trips for not getting together. He understood, but those commitments did not seem to add up to an insurmountable blockage for them to overcome. She always assured him that they would see each other "later."

"Well, let's set a date, okay?" Caleb would offer.

"Oh, Caleb, I'm so busy at the moment. Listen, I'll give you a call next week. Can't wait to see you. Love you ..." she would say and then *click*.

"Flight Attendants, prepare for landing," the captain said over the aircraft's intercom, interrupting Caleb's thoughts. With difficulty, he shelved his ongoing fears for Reb's future and his pain at being pushed away from her and her life.

He always liked the soundless, gliding float up San Francisco Bay from the south, past the small towns linking San Jose to San Francisco. The lights of the towns along the Peninsula glimmered like jewels on black velvet and cascaded down the slopes of the ridge to the bay waters. The parallel strobe-lit piers, extending from the airport runways into the bay, flashed beneath the aircraft as it settled softly on the runway.

The pressurized door wheezed open to the jetway. The flight attendants at the door bestowed "bye, byes" on departing passengers. The captain, still in shirt sleeves, stood outside the cockpit door, acknowledging those passengers who caught his eye or commented on the flight.

It was good to be home.

Being home among friends, people he could trust, meant a great deal to Caleb Frost. His team, despite the nature of their association, was composed of people he respected. Caleb had no compunction over his occupation. The people he assassinated deserved his brand of justice as far as he was concerned. His team concurred with his convictions and worked with him wholeheartedly. He would be glad to be back in their company.

Prior to departing from Washington on his location-scouting trip,

Caleb had been introduced to his recently formed team of agents at an organizational meeting in the old man's Georgetown townhouse.

Two of the team, Jake Corbett and Frank DeLong, were ex-Navy SEALs.

The fourth member of the team was a Greek. Her name was Irini Constant. When they first met, her eyes had raked over him like fingernails. They absorbed his look and probably his scent, given the way she tilted her chin, her long nose seeming to probe the air for signs, signals, alerts. Her eyes were as black as any he'd ever seen. Her elegance stunned his senses. She was an electrical force more than a physical entity.

The old man had laid the facts out for the four of them, described what was expected, and assigned the immediate task of setting up the home base to Caleb. Money was no object and real estate purchase no problem; they used only the best of anything that was needed, including communications equipment and weaponry. Security was mandatory, secrecy imperative. They were to blend into the environment, create no waves, and finally, fulfill the killing assignments without leaving a trace—as if there ever was a truly clean assassination. Mayhem, Caleb knew, tended to be messy.

As the meeting broke and Caleb gathered his briefcase, Irini stepped to his side, her long, dark hair framing her oval face. Her fingertips touched his forearm. He caught a very faint hint of spicy perfume on her skin.

She spoke in a muted tone with a very slight accent, which only served to add more mystery. "I have an idea for my cover, if it works for us," she said, looking him in the eyes. "It will be a very elegant dress shop, if our location is suitable. Keep that in mind when you select our base, would you? Please?" She smiled a tiny smile. As she turned to sit with the old man, her hair twirled in the air and heightened his awareness of her dusky perfume. She hesitated. Looking back to him, she said, "Oh, one other item ..." She stepped closer to him, lightly touching his arm with her slender fingertips. "I need to have access to you at all times. We need a credible reason to be close to one another."

She sat down next to the old man and smiled into his face. Thorndike, warmed by the sun of her presence, smiled happily back at her.

While Frank and Jake left to drive south of Washington to visit friends at Quantico before heading back to Kansas City to pack up their business tools and equipment, Caleb Frost left Georgetown to fly to San Francisco to locate a new place of business.

6

Jake Corbett was parked just outside the United baggage claim doors. The black F-350 truck sparkled. If it were possible to spit-shine such a vehicle, Jake would have done so. He and Frank DeLong had set up business in one of the two street-level shop spaces in the building Caleb had purchased. The truck, with a one-ton capacity, was used for pickups and deliveries. Given the value of the furniture the men muscled in and out of the F-350's bed, the customers deserved to see and be comforted by the massive, shiny vehicle that transported their valuable property. It was also useful for carrying the two men's favorite toys: ATVs, Jet Skis, and off-road motorcycles.

"So?" Jake said as Caleb tossed his luggage into the backseat of the cab and hoisted himself onto the passenger seat. "Went okay? Good to have you back."

"Yeah, it did. And I'm glad to be back, too."

"Got dinged, huh?" Jake said, glancing at Caleb's forehead.

"A scratch," he said, angling the rearview mirror to check his stitches. "Piece of a damned bullet casing. That medic Vesuvius recommended did an excellent job. He was a good one."

"Good? Vesuvius hires only the best. Many of them are ex–Foreign Legion doctors from Algeria. Lots of practical experience with the Legionnaires—knife wounds, gunshots, broken bones, bites, crushed *cojones*." Jake took a beat. "And that was just in the barracks."

"Ta dum," Caleb murmured and grinned. He lowered the window and let the cool night air sweep over his face. There was something about San Francisco air that was different from anywhere else. Perhaps it was the combination of the scent of the pine trees and redwoods and the ice-chip-filled sea fog banking up on the west side of the ridge running up the center of the Peninsula. The fragrance defied description. As the fog bank built up, it overflowed the restraining heights and, with ghostly, clutching, tendril fingers, slithered downward, picking its way through the dark-green spikes of trees to the valley below.

"How did you guys do in my absence? Business okay? Frank okay?" Caleb asked as Jake skillfully maneuvered the truck into the never-ending flow of 101 traffic heading south from San Francisco past the airport.

"Sure. We've been busy doing the furniture stuff. A great job from an estate sale in Los Gatos came in. A huge armoire. Eighteenth century. Beautiful. Come by the shop. I'll show you what great carving looks like. And ..."

"And Frank?" Caleb prompted, bringing Jake back to earth. "What's he been up to?"

"Oh, yeah, he's fine. He did the logistics for you. What weapon did you get from our contact?"

"He had a SIG Sauer P226, so I took it. Thanks for arranging the supplier. That gun seems to be the best for me," he said. "It did the work."

Before he had agreed to have Jake Corbett and Frank DeLong on his team, Caleb had studied the dossiers Thorndike had prepared on the two men. They were to become his tactics and weapons advisers, as well as skilled field operatives. The two of them had met as members of the Navy SEALs. They fought together in Iraq, did a few quiet jobs elsewhere, and found out they had many mutual interests. Weaponry, explosives, hand-to-hand combat, and antique furniture repair were high on their list of fun things. Both men were also well over six feet tall.

Frank DeLong was an African-American raised in a white

neighborhood in Mobile, Alabama. His parents, for some reason or other, had decided to integrate the neighborhood. Apparently, the family had stood up to any number of threats, indirect and direct, and his father and mother had faced their antagonists down. Eventually, they had earned the support of the neighbors and townspeople, and the DeLong family was allowed to live in peace. Frank's psychological profile indicated that the memories of his youth and the physical battles he had fought at school and elsewhere could still cause him to become unreasonably furious. The dossier also reported that he generally won the battles unless the numerical odds were overwhelming. Frank's adoration of his mother and deep respect for his father were only exceeded by his continuing distrust of people in general and many whites in particular. Frank's brown face frequently showed his emotions like a billboard when he had to deal with strangers. Of course, in the business conducted with Caleb Frost, distrust was a useful attitude. At thirty-seven years of age, Frank kept his head clean shaved. Caleb suspected that he knew it made him look meaner.

Caleb's initial impression of Jake Corbett was that he looked like a professional football player with large hands suited to carrying the ball. His dossier described his Navy SEAL career, and Caleb knew he had indeed "carried the ball" many times for the team, being first man on the beach or through a doorway. His broken nose, angled slightly to the left, belied his calm exterior. The son of an Iowa corn farmer and schoolteacher mother, Jake Corbett had faced the world with wide-eyed innocence and boundless energy and enthusiasm. Pictures included in Jake's profile showed him kneeling in a street in some Iraqi town with neighborhood children hanging all over him. He had apparently been giving coloring books, boxes of crayons, and water to the children. A broad grin across a rugged face, topped by a closely cropped military haircut, gave him a clean-cut, All-American appearance. Caleb knew that, in Jake's case, looks were definitely deceiving. He was as much a hardened killer as anyone on his team.

In action in the field or in the furniture-refinishing shop, where their huge hands cradled wood with a softness normally reserved for handling infants, Jake Corbett and Frank DeLong were a well-oiled team. Before moving to Burlingame as part of Caleb's team, they were running an antique-furniture-repair business out of their home's garage in a solid, middle-class neighborhood in Kansas City, Kansas. During the interview process, they had acknowledged to Thorndike that they would die for a decent shop in an affluent location. A move to California suited them just fine. In San Francisco, they lived in a Victorian brownstone on Dolores Street. The three-story home was their pride and always seemed to be under construction.

As Jake leaned the truck into the Broadway exit, Caleb appreciated the first twinges of relaxation coursing through his body. On a job, he never allowed himself to think about what he might be doing rather than what he was doing. It was getting easier to keep his focus as he got older, although, he reminded himself, thirty-two was certainly not old. Being able to focus made it safer, as well. In his twenties, he had frequently been distracted by thoughts of whatever young woman was currently receptive to his company in bed. Now, he successfully compartmentalized his work from the rest of his life. Recently, that had been accomplished by simply not having a young lady to distract him. A serious moth hole in the fabric of his life, he decided.

Caleb Frost had arrived in the small city of Burlingame on the San Francisco Peninsula two years earlier, when William Thorndike decided to shift his base of operations out of New York. The requirements for a suitable location were few: a major airport, a large city nearby, and large bodies of water. Together, these requirements met his need for various forms of transportation, escape routes, and a place where he could dissolve into the chosen locale's atmosphere. Among the West Coast options, the San Francisco Bay Area provided the best opportunities. Plus, he believed that Rebecca was still in the Bay Area.

From San Francisco International, he had checked into a hotel close to the airport. He smelled the air and saw the water and, in the distance, the skyline of a great city.

During the ensuing days, he had driven north to the City of San Francisco and further north across the Golden Gate Bridge to Sonoma, Napa, and Marin Counties. He had crossed the Bay Bridge to the East Bay Hills behind Oakland and then gone south around the tip of San Francisco Bay through Milpitas. He had taken a jog south to San Jose and then wound his way through Los Gatos, Atherton, Menlo Park, and Palo Alto. He'd followed Highway 101 north, exiting at Burlingame.

One afternoon, Caleb had stopped at a coffee shop on Burlingame's Broadway. Il Piccolo Caffé was a local shop with unique charm. The rich smell of roasted coffee filled the air. Patrons focused on their plates of pastries. The chatter was fast and happy. After a few days, he had found that people were nodding greetings to him. He felt comfortable in the café's sidewalk patio, leaning back in a wrought-iron chair, reading local papers, watching the street's life pass by—and appreciating the women who came in for their morning jolt on their way to work.

Caleb engaged Il Piccolo's owner, Dave, in discussion about the town, the politics, the 49ers, and the Giants. Caleb's father had followed the Giants when they played at the Polo Grounds in New York through the mid-1950s. From a very early age, Caleb had been instructed to hold the team in the highest esteem.

Dave's success was his ability to create an environment that was inviting, friendly, and nonintrusive. And the slender, dark-haired proprietor seemed to know everyone's name ... as long as it was "Buddy." His talent for knowing each patron's drink preference, however, was legitimate and legendary.

Caleb had presented himself as a management consultant moving from Minneapolis to warmer climes. He had indicated that he was looking for a place to settle down and run his largely Internet-based, global business. No, he wasn't married. Yes, he indeed preferred women. Dave's determination of his new customer's preferences was handled skillfully through oblique questions. No, there was no personal baggage. Caleb's Minneapolis cover story had been built carefully by Georgetown should any inquiries be made there. Gradually, Dave had extracted as much information about Caleb as he wanted him to have.

Although he could manage his real business from any location over the Internet and by telephone, Caleb liked Burlingame. San Francisco International offered ready access to domestic and international flights to anywhere in the United States, Europe, South America, and the Pacific Rim. He explained that his business took him out of town for extended periods from time to time. Dave did not persist. Apparently, good café owners, like good bartenders, had a finely tuned sense of propriety. Nosing into their customers' business was handled delicately.

It was Dave who had brought Caleb's attention to the fact that the building across the street from Il Piccolo was going to be up for sale. It was a three-story building with two shop spaces to rent at street level. Caleb had bought it.

7

Caleb Frost's stitches itched. Despite a few hours of sleep after arriving from Paris, he was seriously jet-lagged. His cell phone rested on his shoulder. Irini Constant was on the other end, two floors below him in her store. He was stretched out on his living-room couch.

"One finger?" he asked.

"Yes," Irini confirmed.

"FedEx, eh?"

"Yes. FedEx."

"And then?"

"Three more fingers. In a baggy. UPS," Irini said, her softly accented voice sultry and seductive to Caleb, particularly in his drowsy condition. He could understand what made Irini mysterious to the men in her life. Instead of risking rejection with a humorous but intimate comment, he yanked his focus back to the issue of severed fingers, asking, "How do we know these fingers belonged to Mr. Partrain?"

"Pinkie ring, apparently. Mrs. Partrain gave it to him for their last anniversary. Still on the little finger. Fingerprints from their home and office confirmed it."

"Those are usually solid gold with a gem of some sort, aren't they?" Caleb asked. "So, we can count out robbery as a motive."

"You are tired, aren't you?" Irini responded sarcastically.

Almost worse than rejection, Caleb thought, tracing the tiny row of suture knots across the ridge of his eyebrow. His afternoon couch attire was a pair of baggy cargo shorts and an ancient orange-and-black Princeton T-shirt. The California sun, sliced by his front room's window blinds, lay like thin, warm slats across his bare legs The image of Mrs. Partrain sorting out her husband's digits momentarily amused the black portion of his soul. He often wondered about that dried, crusty, corrosive part of himself. Where had it come from?

"Why involve us, Irini?" he asked. "I don't see our interest here."

"It seems that there is a whiff of national security in this one."

"Feds interested, huh?" Caleb said, concerned about federal involvement in how he might choose to conduct an engagement. The FBI or the CIA had the habit of over-the-shoulder watching, particularly when they had special interests or agency objectives associated with an operation. This disturbing aspect of working with such agencies frequently compromised Caleb's management of an operation. He and his team much preferred to conduct their business in the dark and without meddlesome intrusions.

"I think so, Caleb. It was different with al-Tikriti. State Department wanted that slimy bastard eliminated to get control of the boy's father's pro-American vote in the young Iraqi government. Despite the rationale, Caleb, it was a justified kill," she hastened to add.

"Okay. You're right as usual, Irini," Caleb acknowledged, rearranging himself on the couch. "Who has the fingers?"

"Under lock and key in the Hillsborough PD's forensics freezer. They guaranteed Georgetown full cooperation."

"Damn, this is all happening in our backyard, Irini. I just don't like the proximity."

"I don't think a 'not-in-my-backyard' argument will work, Caleb," she said softly.

"I know, and it may not stay local. Hell, we're talking China. Just a starting point, perhaps. What do you think?"

"Well, 'Wild Willie' Thorndike wants a conference call to discuss the engagement. You can always decline. May we meet in an hour or so? I'll close the shop and come up early."

"Yeah. Good. Oh, before we talk with Thorndike, you set a fee for the engagement?"

"The usual one hundred and fifty grand flat fee for the job, twenty thousand a day on top, plus expenses. The base fee in advance, of course. Is that satisfactory, Caleb?"

"Yes. Thank you, Irini. See you after you lockup."

He thumbed the HTC scrambler cell phone off and stretched, feeling his muscles protest as they were loosened up. His stitches were driving him crazy. Fortunately, his grazed forearm was responding to the painkillers the French doctor had supplied in quantity.

A large blue-black crow, rapacious claws hanging down beneath its belly, flapped by Caleb's open window cawing raucously. The bird cast what Caleb felt was a malevolent eye toward him, as if inspecting him as potential for dinner. Caleb wished he knew when the fucking crows were going to fly by. He would have loved to pick them off one by one. They evoked bad memories for Caleb Frost. It seemed appropriate to him that a flock of crows was called a "murder" of crows. They certainly were.

8

William Horstfeld Thorndike, sitting in his customary place at his desk in his Georgetown DC townhouse, adjusted his writing tools with blue-veined hands whose bone-defined fingers set his age well into his eighties. Ever since his time in Europe during the Second World War, Thorndike had chosen to wear Savile Row suits. Even though his bedroom on the brownstone's second floor was just a few steps from his office, he dressed in a freshly-pressed suit each day. Starched, pure-white shirts were all he owned. He also chose neckwear that ran counter to the traditional look well-dressed Londoners affected. He favored bow ties, many of which were brightly colored and definitely jaunty for a man of his age. To those who knew Thorndike well, the frequency with which his fingertips adjusted his bow tie was a "tell," indicating the level of tension he was experiencing at a given moment. He straightened his bow tie with both hands and leaned back in his leather chair.

A carpet of documents covered his large mahogany desk. The pages lapped like ocean waves against a computer and two monitors built into the desk. The electronics glowed in the room's gloom, a darkness created by heavy, dark-green, ceiling-to-floor curtains hanging behind him. Thorndike used a desk lamp as his main source of illumination. The curtains were tied back to allow daylight to filter into the office, but restrictive enough to effectively limit observation from the outside. The tall windows' glass was also bulletproof.

The rest of Thorndike's office was very much like any other den to be found in the homes of the wealthy residents of Georgetown—except this den was thoroughly swept electronically on three randomly selected days per week by counterintelligence professionals who could detect any eavesdropping device known to the technical world. The den also housed a computer server disguised as an old Wurlitzer jukebox set in the far corner of the room, well away from Thorndike's desk. The Wurlitzer actually worked as a traditional jukebox, for a quarter a tune.

Thorndike explained the quarter-per-play he charged by saying that, "If I have to listen to your musical preferences, I deserve to be compensated for my time." Many of his visitors dropped coins into the slot simply, it seemed to Thorndike, to annoy him with their selections.

Once a month, Thorndike opened the coin box, took whatever coins there were, and purchased a supply of jelly beans for the Baccarat candy dish on his desk. It was a mystery to him how the sugary delights he kept for his visitors' pleasure disappeared despite the fact that he rarely had visitors.

Four high-backed leather club chairs surrounded a coffee table filling the center of Thorndike's room. The coffee table was topped by glass through which a century-old Persian carpet of dark-blue and red design could be admired, but, most important, nothing could be hidden beneath the tabletop.

"Evening, Caleb," William Thorndike said over the conference call speaker on Caleb's multipurpose dining room and conference table.

"Evening, sir," he answered.

Thorndike's voice was parchment dry with a faint New England accent. It sounded of autumn leaves blown tumbling across bricks by a stiff wind. Irini and Caleb were bent toward the speakerphone to better hear the old man.

"Ms. Constant with us, Caleb?" Thorndike asked.

"Here, sir," Irini said.

"Good evening, Irini. How are you?"

"Very well, sir. Thank you. And you?"

"As well as can be expected. Another damn birthday coming up. How's the shop doing?"

"Also very well, sir. Thank you," Irini said. Thorndike thought he could hear her smile.

"Irini's Finery is it, the name of your shop?"

"Yes, sir."

"Well, don't sell those women so much that you don't need us to support you."

"You could always invest, sir. Then we could both retire."

"I thought we had already invested in you, Irini. But then, if you do decide that you need to take on partners over and above the common interest we already have, I might be persuaded to part with a piece of my hard-earned pension, eh?"

"I'll let you know at an appropriate moment, sir," she said.

Irini and the two SEALs had been recruited by "Wild Willie" Thorndike, long after he had decided to build a team around his protégé Caleb Frost, whose focus had been on finding his parents' killer by getting into the "assassination game" himself. Intensive testing, subsequent to Thorndike's assumption of Caleb's and Rebecca's guardianship, had profiled Caleb as an excellent recruit to the business. Caleb was entering his senior year at Princeton when Thorndike laid out his plans. Naturally, they included the opportunity to find out who killed his parents. Caleb accepted the offer.

Irini Constant, four years older than Caleb, had just completed a master of business administration degree in finance at New York University. She was also engaged in social activities that provided her an exorbitant amount of cash and were of professional interest to William Thorndike. She consorted with domestic and international movers and shakers—political, diplomatic, military, business, and underworld. Her social contacts were Thorndike's gold.

After agreeing to Thorndike's proposals, Caleb and Irini had entered into rigorous training in the art of assassination at Summer

Camp, the clandestine training organization. While Caleb Frost was learning how to kill and working with international and domestic law enforcement agencies, Irini learned the finer details of assassination. She had come to the program fairly adept in many of the cruder street methods. She continued to work at expanding her "customer base," as Thorndike called it. Irini preferred to call the carefully guarded list of coded names, numbers, history, and sexual preferences her "Good Friends Roster."

Jake Corbett and Frank DeLong were brought on board later in the team's development. Thorndike had scoured the histories of Special Forces, SEALs, and Delta Force to find the right men to join Caleb's team. They came with skills and required no extra training in the arts of assassination.

With the exception of Irini Constant, whose annual income at the time of her recruitment far exceeded all of their salaries combined, Thorndike's proposal offered each of them substantial money, an opportunity to right a few wrongs in the world, and plenty of excitement. It also promised total anonymity.

"To business, then," Thorndike said, pulling a few sheets of paper from the stack next to his elbow to the center of his desk. "I have before me a copy of a forensics report prepared by Byron Fleming of the FBI's office in San Francisco. It describes the condition of poor Mr. Partrain's fingers. As you already know, fingerprint analysis has proven the postal fingers to be part of Mr. Partrain's God-given original complement." He paused. "Comments? Questions on procedure, et cetera?"

Sitting three thousand miles away, Thorndike could not see Caleb and Irini's glance at each other. "No sir," they intoned together. Nor could Thorndike catch Frost's wink at Irini. She nodded and grinned back like a conspiratorial high-school girl.

"So, has anyone been able to find the rest of Mr. Partrain, sir?" Frost asked, pulling his laptop toward him. He also had a yellow legal pad covered with indecipherable chicken scratches, which he defended as his writing. Caleb rarely was able to read his notes five minutes after writing them. Irini had been taking notes on her laptop.

"Ahhh, let's begin at the beginning. In short, however, no, we do not have the remaining sections of Mr. Partrain, much to his wife's disappointment. Fortunately, we will never have to deal with the soon-to-be-officially widowed Mrs. Partrain.

"There is a strong Chinese component to what I will say. Let's use a Chinese menu analogy to tell the story. We'll start with 'Column A' for the Partrain story and 'Column B' for the Chinese story, as we understand it at this time from our sometimes friends in Beijing.

"Column A: The Partrains run a Chinese antiques, furniture, and object d'arts import business. The business, Eastern Partners, is headquartered in San Francisco, but its customers happen to be mainly in New Orleans. They have been in business for twenty years and, according to what we understand from Customs and Border Protection, their compliance on both sides of the Pacific has been perfect. Customs cannot check every container arriving in a US port, so the Eastern Partners' shipments, which have originated from the same distributor's warehouse in Shanghai for the past twenty years, frequently get a pass. Ninety-five percent of the time, in fact. This, by the way, is not unusual for many companies who are well known to the authorities. US Customs and Border Protection has been promoting and trying to gain traction for programs designed to increase container security by pushing back the borders and clearing containers for shipping into the US at the port of departure. The global economy is beginning to require much greater collaboration in matters of security than ever before. September 11, 2001, started that ball rolling. The idea is to get security-measure compliance started in the plants of the off-shore vendors—a bit tough when doing business with a jungle factory in Malaysia, of course. Maybe electricity, probably no Internet or computers."

"Sir," Caleb interjected, "how does Eastern Partners import their product?"

"Eastern Partners and their distributor in Shanghai, Asian

Artifacts, have always been among the first to cooperate fully with antiterrorist and antismuggling measures." Thorndike paused for a sip of Gerolsteiner sparkling spring water from a crystal goblet on a side table.

"As you know, sir, I am acquainted with several drug cartel members," Irini said. "Their comments indicate that it is a fairly easy matter to get goods into this country."

Thorndike's sigh whispered through the tiny holes in the speakerphone. "True then, and still true," the old man acknowledged. "Over the past five years or so, radio frequency identification, RFID, tag technology, is suddenly finding applications in transportation. Global positioning systems, or GPS, can track the containers off-loaded onto trailers at the ports and driven to US destinations. None of these systems is perfect."

"How did Mr. Partrain come to lose his fingers?" Caleb pushed the old man. Irini brought some fresh coffee from the kitchen.

"Well," Thorndike said, "it seems that Mr. Partrain found a time gap in the drop shipment schedule records the GPS system was transmitting to the office in San Francisco. According to the Hillsborough police interviews with Mrs. Partrain, she recalls that her husband brought it to the attention of Long Distance Freight, Inc., which is Eastern Partners' carrier and distribution service in the US. LDF reported that they had checked their records and found that all deliveries were made on time. They claim to have only their best and most trustworthy drivers at the wheel on Eastern Partners' deliveries."

"Yeah, right. There's a real healthy work ethic out there on the road. The drivers works long, long hours; are never home; and if they do long hauls, don't earn enough to make the hardships worth it. Industry seems to be unwilling to deal with those facts and wonders why there is a driver shortage," Caleb said sitting back in his chair. He sounded tired.

"An interesting summary, Caleb," Thorndike said. "But cutting off fingers doesn't describe most businessmen's response to a service inquiry from one of their customers, now does it?"

"No, sir."

"The Partrains have political clout, I believe. They called around and even had the chutzpah to contact the governor's offices in Sacramento. As they say, inquiries were made. Nothing much came of them. The focus was on LDF, Inc., the hauling company the Partrains used. The owner is a fellow named Curtis Rathmann, about whom we have very sketchy intel."

"This guy Curtis Rathmann's an interesting fellow," Thorndike continued. "Virtually raised in the gutters of Oakland, he turned out to be a genius with an IQ around one hundred and seventy or some ungodly number like that. So, a do-gooder philanthropist arranged for him to receive a full-boat scholarship to Harvard, including a living expenses allowance of better than five thousand dollars a month for room, books, food, lodging, travel, and whatever. Magna cum laude and Phi Beta Kappa. Then on to the Harvard Business School. And then poof, a puff of smoke, and Mr. Rathmann disappears, until his name comes up as the owner of Long Distance Freight. Again, he fades into the background and cannot be found.

"A woman named Cleo Solchow, who serves as the LDF office manager, order taker, and dispatcher, tells the local law that Mr. Rathmann travels abroad for extended periods of time. She hears from him by email as a rule. The police have spoken to the drivers as well. Nothing there. According to the reports, the drivers are the roughest crew the detectives have ever run into outside of a biker bar. They suspect they may be members of the Angels or possibly a new MC in Alameda called the Visigoths. The guys weren't wearing colors on the job, of course, but the investigators used the old 'If it looks like a duck and walks like a duck, it must be a duck' analogy." Thorndike's papery chuckle crinkled across the miles of airborne transmissions and fiberglass wires.

"And how does Column B come into the picture, sir?" Irini asked.

"Well, Column B, then," Thorndike said. "Did you know that a large number of the people who live in western China are Muslims? Ardent Muslims, like Chechnya Muslims?"

"Nope."

"Neither did I," the old man said, sounding surprised at not knowing something. "It seems that the Chinese government has identified a Chinese citizen ..." He paused to pull a sheet of paper out of the stack. "Name of Zhou Jing, who is just wealthy enough, politically well-connected enough, and criminally oriented enough to set himself up in an armed fortress in the western mountains. He is also more than slightly strange in that he lives and dresses like a fifteenth-century Chinese warlord. A warlord-wannabe, you might say. Although he is an ethnic Han Chinese, he has effectively bought the loyalty of the toughest, most anti-Chinese fighters from among the local Muslims.

"The Uighur Muslim population of the far western Xinjiang Uighur autonomous region are descended from Turkic peoples who ruled for more than a thousand years. The Uighurs hate the Chinese for their oppression, genocide, and cultural repression. For precisely this hatred, Zhou Jing chose to associate himself with them. He taught them to fight, armed them with the most modern weaponry available, and they swore allegiance to him alone.

"They are on his payroll," Thorndike explained, "and are treated exceptionally well. All of his one hundred and fifty some odd soldiers and their families live in his mountain compound. He has built a mosque, a school, and a small hospital on his property. Uighur farmers raise the community's food requirements and, of course, the opium crop, which is processed in an underground factory on Zhou's property.

"The Chinese government cannot mount a major offensive without drawing international scrutiny, and the Uighurs have proven to be tough fighters. The practice of Islam has been repressed, which has provided a cause for rebellion."

"I can see why the Chinese government is concerned," Caleb said. "We know from recent events the fervor such treatment can create in a desperate populace. But why are we supposed to be concerned?"

"Zhou is suspected of exporting drugs—excellent heroin, we are told—through his interest in the Shanghai-based business, Asian

Artifacts, which in turn supplies antiques and artifacts for sale in the United States to the Partrains' company, Eastern Partners. If for no other reason than the Chinese authorities find it an interesting coincidence, they have informed Uncle Sam that they speculate that the point of entry into the United States is the Port of Oakland."

Thorndike paused to take a sip of sparkling water. Holding the goblet up to a shaft of afternoon sunlight coming through a crack between the curtains, he spent a moment appreciating the light dancing through the cut-crystal surface of the goblet before continuing.

"We've been asked by the Chinese government to see if there is a knot of some kind between these strings and then determine what and who is involved—and eliminate the problems. Your option, as usual, Caleb, is to agree to the job or not. But that is why you were invited along for the ride."

The old man's leather desk chair creaked as he leaned back.

Silence.

Caleb wondered if Thorndike had gone to sleep or maybe expired sitting there, having made his last assignment. If the old man kicked off, who would care or know? The entire operation, based in Thorndike's Georgetown townhouse, was an "off-the-books" venture—a black and, frequently, wet ops instrument of the government. No one but Thorndike knew how the funding transfers were structured from cover entities directly into his people's banks.

"Sir?" Caleb asked.

"Just thinking, Caleb, just thinking," Thorndike said softly. "Too much yabber, yabber these days. We always used to believe that we needed more communications. What we really need is some decent thinking. Not enough thinking these days, you know?" Thorndike paused, perhaps to make the point. Caleb couldn't know that the old man actually did close his eyes momentarily. "Give me a call tomorrow with an action plan of some sort, if you'd be so kind. We'll toss it around and get you started. That is, if you accept the engagement. Okay, folks?"

"Yes, sir," Caleb and Irini chorused.

"Oh …" Thorndike's voice whispered across the continent. "One last thing, Caleb. I saw your suggested quote for this job. The statement of work Irini sent was a good analysis. Earlier, you asked why you should care or we should get involved. Caleb, all the parties involved in this deal have proven to be killers. This will not be a stroll in the park, and your team should know that they should indeed shoot first and ask questions later. This time, my boy, you may have underestimated the cost. Reconsider the fee, if you wish."

Silence … Thorndike stabbed the button leaving the team listening to the drone of the dial tone.

Caleb bent forward and pushed the "Off" button on the speakerphone. He watched Irini collect the coffee cups and take them to the kitchen. Coming at him or walking away from him, Irini always received an appreciative glance.

For no particular reason, Caleb pulled off the Band-Aid on his eyebrow wound. He touched the tiny sutures, counting six of them. He felt an odd sense of release for having discarded the bandage. It was time to have the stitches out. Except for the lingering memory of the girl with the little white puff of a dog, Paris and al-Tikriti were forgotten.

Caleb's cell phone signaled that a text message had been received. The text read: "need help see u 2day? Rebecca." He suddenly felt a familiar weight in his chest. These days, it seemed that she really only contacted him when she felt unable to deal with whatever twist she'd gotten herself into at the moment. He messaged back: "okay, later, Caleb."

9

Slate-gray, February-chilled water stretched like a concrete slab to the shores of Oakland ten miles across San Francisco Bay. Caleb Frost sped up US 101 toward the city. The Porsche's raw power surged through his fingertips and into his body. He wanted to mash the pedal to the floor and let the car fly—perhaps fly away from the problems he would have to deal with when he arrived at Reb's door.

Sutro Tower, a fierce sentinel guarding the heights from attack, poked its way through the ocean fog. The enemies the tower guarded against were already in the city. San Francisco was no different from most major American cities when it came to crime, drugs, and corruption. It carried a promise of excitement, of pent-up energy ready to explode upon provocation—a promise of hidden pleasures and the suggestion that outrageous events were occurring just out of sight, delicious skullduggery behind closed doors in the street-lamp-lit and fog-distorted lanes. The mystique of San Francisco was always in the air.

The Seventh Street exit angled downward to city streets. Caleb swung the car northward, crossing San Francisco's throbbing main vein, Market Street. He found a parking garage for his car three blocks from his destination, San Francisco's Tenderloin. There was no mystique about the Tenderloin. There, the dregs of humanity clustered together in common misery. In contrast, students and young businessmen and women took advantage of the low rents and the cheap living and overlooked the slovenly environment, seeing it all as an advantage. They knew they could leave. The down-and-outers were welded in place. Everything was for sale in the Tenderloin—flesh of either sex and in any fashion, substances to help one forget hunger, pain, lives of struggle, and fear of the future.

In her personal despair, Reb had taken a room by the week in a small hotel on Larkin. It was a dump by any standard. The pages of the "Sporting Green" section of the *San Francisco Chronicle* left on a lower step of the hotel's entrance had assumed a life of their own, flapping and turning in the street breeze. Caleb stepped over a Colt 44 can lying in a shallow gully worn into a marble step. His shoes squashed cigarette butts, and he felt the grit on the unswept steps under his feet.

The hotel reception area was small and overheated by a single space heater. The reception desk countertop was chest high. An elderly man with a shiny bald head resting on crossed arms slept behind it. The clerk's knobby shoulders rose and fell gently, stretching worn, red suspenders as he breathed. The man's slumber was that of someone who held two or three jobs to try to make ends meet—and they never did quite touch. A bell sat expectantly next to the thick, yellowing register on the worn countertop. Open-ended letter boxes lined the wall behind the desk, and a rack with hooks for keys hung beside it. The room numbers had, over decades, practically faded to illegibility. Only two keys remained. Full house. *This looks like something out of a Western film,* Caleb thought as he approached. He dinged the bell.

"Yessir, yessir," the clerk, jerking up in response to the bell, croaked groggily even before his head was fully upright. "At ya' service, sir. Wha' kin I do for ya?"

Even though Caleb was wearing faded jeans, a well-worn sweatshirt, and old Converse sneakers, he did not look like a Tenderloin resident. Tough-looking in a lean, muscled sort of way and with a bit of a menacing stare in faded gray eyes, he was definitely not from around the neighborhood—not dingy enough in body and clothing for one thing. Soul? Well, Caleb did not present any indicators of his soul, and if he did, it probably was a dingy soul at best. Even dingy souls deserved attention though, and Caleb wasn't about to pander to the man's need to know.

"Looking for a girl named Reb. Tall. Blonde. Gimme her room number," Caleb demanded.

"Can't do that, sir. That's 'gainst the law, ya know?" the clerk said, taking no chances on Caleb's possible occupation.

Pointing at an old phone by the clerk's elbow, Caleb said, "Call." He watched as the clerk checked a piece of paper under the counter and with an arthritic forefinger dialed three, zero, four. Caleb didn't wait for an answer. He turned to the stairway leading to the upper floors.

"Hol' on there, fella!" the clerk called, rising from his chair, his scrawny arm extending a French-fry-thin finger. Anyone having business with an occupant of the establishment was a drug dealer, a junkie, or someone looking to get laid. The clerk didn't owe him any particular respect.

"Sit down, and go back to sleep," Caleb snapped, shooting a laser glance at the man behind the counter, his legs disappearing from the clerk's sight up the creaking, narrow stairs.

Grocery bags, grease stained and torn, sat spilling their contents on the floor in front of doors along the dark hallway. The odors of wood rot, garbage, and compressed humanity assailed his nostrils. Sounds seeped from rooms—sex in progress, he guessed, by the sound of ecstasy, feigned or real, produced by a woman on a bed with springs badly in need of a rest. As he climbed to the third floor, the stairs groaned. A puddle rippled on a stair halfway up. At least it wasn't vomit. The air was pungent with the acrid odors of crack and grass and the urine being absorbed by the stair below him. Now, the silence was visceral and threatening. Shadowed recesses along the corridor held prospects of sudden violence. Low voices slid out from under doors as Caleb crept by them. At the end of the hall, a figure lay propped up in a corner; light from a dirty window softly illuminated the person—sex unknowable with long, greasy tangles of hair covering the face and an emaciated body denying any indications of gender.

The number "304" was painted on a brownish door in what he thought might have been an attempt at a gold color but was just mustard-looking now. There were no hall lights, and a sense of foreboding overcame him. He paused, preparing himself for this encounter with his sister. For a moment, a recollection of the fresh-faced, blonde-haired little girl she had been floated in his memory, tickling remembrances of a time when safety lay in the family unit. He thought of his mom and dad and Reb and himself canoeing on a lake. He couldn't place the lake or the occasion. The sense of a long-gone security faded rapidly as his knuckle rapped on the cracked paint.

A soft moan. He pushed lightly on the door. It swung open. The yellow, mottle-stained window shade, drawn down to the sill, served as a rectangular light for the room. The outlines of a bureau, a table with a telephone, and a stool appeared as his eyes adjusted to the dim light. Along the back wall of the one room was a narrow bed upon which he could see a low mound. Rebecca.

"Reb?" he said softly, more out of sorrow than expectation of a response.

"Caleb?" came the wavering reply.

"It's me, Reb. I'm here." She burst into soul-wrenching sobs.

There was nothing else to say to the slender woman curled on the bed facing the wall. He sat on the edge and laid his hand on her side. He felt the jutting ribs and protruding blade of hip through the damp sheet. Reb's sobbing breaths filled his ears. She smelled of sweat, urine, and the faintly medicinal odor of drugs. As he sat with his sister, the time passed like a viscous fluid; the light of day faded, turning from pale yellow to gray. A faint breeze lifted a corner of the shade causing a fragment of cheery red paper to dance merrily across the floor.

"I hurt," she said, speaking softly. The intensity of her pain injected wonderment into her voice. A sliver of life issued through cracked lips. "Need something, Caleb."

"I know; I'm calling Barney to come help you."

"Ohhhh, noooo!" It was a wail so desperate, so deep from her shrunken gut that Caleb wanted to hold her, do some magic, make it all better with a soft kiss. He had done that when she was a child cupping a scraped a knee. Now his sister lay in squalor, strands of sweat-darkened hair stuck to her face, fetid bed clothing encasing her limbs. Helplessness inundated Caleb as his eyes filled with tears. He speed-dialed a number and spoke softly, urgently into the phone.

He knew that Dr. Barney Flannery would probe Reb until he had found and dissolved the last bit of her willpower and then, like an ember in a dying campfire, breathe on it until she had enough strength to burn on her own. Barney and his staff would challenge her to take command of her life, give her lifelines to clutch, and wrench closeted truths to be faced and dealt with out of her mind like festering organs. Months of withdrawal agony, of confrontations with her own deeply embedded devils, lay ahead for Reb. Again.

Barney Flannery arrived with a female staffer, Margie Silas, carrying a doctor's black bag and a couple of blankets under her arm. Barney was a huge man, a bear of a guy, in his midsixties; he wore his long, silver hair tied in a ponytail. A drooping Fu Manchu mustache graced his upper lip under twinkling blue eyes. He wore corduroy pants, a denim work shirt, and hiking boots. His degree in psychiatry came from Johns Hopkins. His life experience came from the streets of San Francisco, Oakland, and Berkeley. He dealt with the city's human wreckage.

Barney had been blessed with a personality that opened doors and pocketbooks. So the funding for his private rehabilitation center came from a few corporations with a social conscience, private citizens, and numerous rock musicians and entertainment celebrities who had been patients. Set up in a row of three Victorian houses in San Francisco's Haight-Ashbury, near free clinics and other outreach services, the Flannery Center had an international reputation for good results. Rebecca Frost was a challenge, though. She had already been through one stay of seven months at the center and had fallen or been pushed off the wagon within three weeks of leaving. It had been a tough two years for Reb.

Margie Silas was a stocky woman, dressed in comfortable, loose-fitting clothing. She wore her hair in a severe bun. There was no evidence of makeup on her round, pleasant face. What did standout about Margie were her soulful brown eyes. When she smiled, the room lit up. She had rosy cheeks and perfect skin to complete the farm-girl look she had brought to San Francisco from Idaho. It was rumored—and Caleb knew it was true—that she was Barney's woman. At the Center, she was able to calm the most disturbed patients. Staffers turned to her during tough stretches of patient treatment. She went straight to Reb and began soothing her, reassuring her, and immediately preparing her for the trip to the Center.

Barney and Caleb moved to the window. Caleb raised the shade, letting the fading sun in. The sallow, afternoon light brought the squalor of the filthy floor and the stained walls into sharp focus. The men looked out through the dirty glass at the crowd passing below.

"How long has she been this way?" Barney asked.

"Don't know," Caleb said. "I've been away. Sent me a text message, about two hours ago. She said she needed my help. So, here I am. She's my sister for God's sake."

Barney reached out his hand and laid it gently on his shoulder. "We'll see her through this, Caleb. I feel that we've failed, too, you know. We thought we had her in the right place when we released her last year." Barney's hand came up to grasp Caleb's chin and turned his face to the dim light. "Neat sewing job there," he said, inspecting the stitches in his eyebrow.

"Did it myself," Caleb said with a trace of smile. Barney knew that was the end of the explanation.

Barney and Caleb watched the neon lights flashing on the people on the street below—people who were just a short step away from being like Reb. Drugs were available in any doorway, on any street corner. Someone out there had tampered with his sister, and Caleb intended to find out who that bastard was.

Margie Silas joined them at the window. "I've sedated her and wrapped her in a couple of blankets. We'll wash her up at the Center. None of her clothes here are worth salvaging. I'll get some for her at St. Vincent's. We'll get her down for a good long sleep tonight.

Here's her cell. She's not allowed to have it," she said handing Reb's cell phone to Caleb. "You might find it interesting to know this. Reb muttered something about wanting more 'red.' The fixings on the floor say heroin, but among the many description I've heard for 'horse,' none had anything to do with the color red. Anyway, guys, we're all set to go. Soon as possible, please."

Barney carried Reb down the stairs like he was carrying a child. Doors creaked open, and eyes surveyed them as they passed. An occasional snicker accompanied them. Someone sang Queen's rock tune refrain, "… and another one bites the dust," from behind the door to room 201. A knowing and warning glance from Barney kept Caleb walking. He filed the room number away for a future visit, perhaps. He probably wouldn't do anything, but the thought gave his craving for action against any person even remotely associated with his sister's plight something to chew on.

The clerk glanced up from his newspaper as they arrived at the bottom of the stairs. Then he went back to his reading. What he didn't know, he would not have to answer for.

They settled Reb on a gurney in the back of the Flannery van. She was still wrapped in blankets; her eyes fluttered open and found Caleb's. Tears welled up and trembled down her cheeks. He looked directly into her eyes and gave her a slow nod. A message of love and commitment passed unspoken between brother and sister. He took her hand, held it a few moments, and then gave it a squeeze. He backed out of the van to the sidewalk.

Margie, seated beside Reb's head, regarded him. "Caleb," she said, getting out of the van and leading him aside. "This isn't your fault," she said softly. "Don't let it be your burden. We'll be in touch with you the day after tomorrow. We'll review the program and the visiting schedule for the future. You take care of yourself, Caleb. We'll take care of Reb."

The van's door slid shut. Barney moved out into the evening traffic, and Caleb was alone. He ran his finger down the thin line of knots on his eyebrow. He turned and looked at the building, wondering if he should go back into the hotel to visit room 201 for a chat about the guy's taste in music.

10

Irini leaned against the edge of Caleb's kitchen sink, peering out the window to the west toward San Bruno Mountain and San Francisco. She was thinking about Caleb and Rebecca and the hell Rebecca would be facing as she rehabbed from her drug addiction. She would offer whatever assistance she could to Caleb during this period of extreme stress.

Caleb's kitchen was well equipped, and she enjoyed cooking there occasionally. Of course, having three large, always hungry men around to enjoy what she prepared gave her pleasure, not that she ever thought of herself as a housewife or anything less than absolutely equal to each of the male team members. She would never stoop to picking up behind them.

Caleb had called to say that he was on his way home on 101 and would be "in the office," as he called his apartment, shortly. He said that he had found Rebecca and Dr. Barney Flannery had taken her to the Flannery Center. He sounded somber, sad over the phone. Irini's heart went out to him and Reb.

Irini and Rebecca complemented each other physically and emotionally. Reb, a lean, graceful blonde, and Irini with flowing, raven-black hair and a svelte figure, both approached six feet in height. Irini enjoyed dressing Rebecca's model-perfect figure from her store's merchandise, including the latest fashions from Paris, Rome, and, recently, from Moscow. When Rebecca was well and Caleb took them both out in San Francisco, they were truly a sensation wherever they went.

Irini's concern for Rebecca's health was genuine. The two women had become close over the past two years and each filled a gap in the other's life. Rebecca provided Irini a trusted confidante and friend, while Reb needed the older woman as a friend and, just perhaps, a bit of a mother. The two had shared secrets, which each of them held inviolate for the other.

With the exception of William Thorndike, who knew everything there was to know about her, no one on Caleb's team really knew Irini's story. They were aware that she was Greek by birth, but not where she was born or the circumstances of her life. They had met her as an elegant woman and still saw her in that light. Her skills as an assassin aside, she continued to be a highly respected individual and a viable and valuable member of the team. She took comfort in the feeling that she was accepted unconditionally.

She was born Irini Constantinopolou, in the seaport of Piraeus, Greece. She had always felt that her life had been defined by an incident when she was ten. Her mother's lover had raped her. In an odd convolution, she discovered a native curiosity and intelligence while becoming sexually skilled by thirteen. With a combination of fondness and repulsion, she remembered the handicapped war veteran who owned the corner newsstand. He taught her to read as she sat on his lap. She became older, and he became more instructive as she continued to sit on his lap. Her family left Greece for New York after her father killed the man who had raped her and made a cuckold of him. She had learned to defend herself. She had no brothers to stand up for her, and her father was up to his elbows in soapy water sixteen hours a day washing pots, pans, and dishes in the back of his brother's Eighth Avenue Greek restaurant. Irini's recollections of life in Hell's Kitchen were filled with confrontations. She hadn't found it easy to be a beautiful young girl in that environment. In her neighborhood, she eventually earned a reputation as a dangerous person. The young men understood her hands-off policy. She had Americanized her name to Irini Constant and set out to deal with the world on her own terms.

With luck, talent, and the financial help of an adoring uncle, Irini was well educated by the age of twenty. She had earned her MBA in finance at twenty-two and had become an exceptionally successful escort. She had spent her days at New York University earning her degree and her evenings, nights, and weekends—who knew where?

As it turned out, William Thorndike knew not only where, but with whom.

Irini's clients were men—and women—from the international diplomatic corps at the United Nations and the foreign embassies, business executives from around the globe, and the military brass of many countries. She was also a favorite among the members of South America's drug cartels.

Her fee for a weekend of companionship, which frequently did not require sex and generally did include travel on private aircraft to luxurious accommodations, ranged from forty to fifty thousand dollars. One evening was fifteen thousand dollars. There usually were expensive gifts along with the fees from appreciative clients. And she garnered tips on investment opportunities, given intentionally by clients for her benefit or unintentionally by those who misjudged her intelligence and conducted confidential business in her presence.

She would attend state events on the arms of ambassadors, meeting leaders of countries and power brokers engaged in a variety of activities. She listened and collected information, while booze and egos flowed … and, of course, there was pillow talk.

Irini was well aware that William Thorndike only saw her as an asset, a tool to be applied. But then, as usual, Irini Constant had arranged to be very well paid.

11

The sound of the building's elevator brought Irini back to the present.

Frank and Jake would be along soon for lunch and the meeting Caleb had called. Irini had spent the morning gathering information. She would be doing the briefing.

The men were going to be having a late lunch or an early dinner of pizza and beer. Irini was having a yogurt, an apple, and a glass of chilled chardonnay. She smiled to herself. She could already hear Frank saying, "Christ, I'd die on a diet like that."

Frank's firm, muscular body put the lie to the evils of consuming large quantities of pizza, spaghetti, grits, biscuits 'n' gravy, and the fast-food delicacies he loved to eat. "Jes' like Mama made at home in 'Bama," he would say pulling out all of the stops on the Southern accent. The crushing exercise regimen he and Jake followed allowed no fat to collect on their bodies despite the huge caloric intake.

The elevator hummed to a stop. Caleb and Frank entered the spacious kitchen.

"Garlic?" Caleb asked sniffing the air around the two Amici's pizza boxes Frank carried.

Frank grinned and nodded. "Just like Mama never, ever made for us down home in 'Bama."

The oak table had been set for dinner. Frank placed the pizza boxes in the center of the table. With the exception of the place setting at the end of the table, each place had a pint beer glass. The setting at the end of the table included a crystal wineglass. A carafe of white wine sat next to it.

"Can you believe it? Glasses?" Frank said surveying the table and lifting one of the pint beer glasses up to the light as if to inspect it for lipstick or finger smears.

"Yes, glasses," Irini Constant said, emerging from the kitchen with a fistful of cloth napkins. "Drinking out of a can is crude. And, young men, let's be gentlemen tonight and please use the napkins."

"Yes, ma'am," Frank said as contritely as possible without bursting into laughter.

"Hey, ease up on Frank," Jake Corbett said, following Irini in with three plates in one large hand and a six-pack of Budweiser beer in the other. His laptop was wedged under an arm. After setting the plates down, he put two beers at each of three places on the table. "By the way, Frank's a great cook, as you'll see when you come up to the city for dinner, as soon as we get the new kitchen installed, that is." The two men fist-bumped across the table.

Sitting at the opposite end of the table from Irini, Caleb leaned forward to take two pieces of pizza, which he slid onto his plate with practiced dexterity.

Irini sliced her apple into quarters. Wielding her knife expertly, she cut out core and seeds. "I could have been having dinner with the former ambassador of Lithuania tonight at the Baker Street Bistro," she commented. "He's an old friend." She sighed as she watched Jake manipulate a slice of combination pizza to his mouth using two hands to corral the sagging tip and dripping toppings. "Instead, I'm here, in suburbia, in an attic, with three men, two of whom are carpenters, and one of whom has no apparent means of support. I'm spending my time watching them eat pizza laced with garlic and guzzle American beer."

She picked up a jar of cinnamon and sprinkled a spoonful of the spice on top of her yogurt. She gave the mix a couple of swirls with her spoon. "Aha!" she exclaimed, pointing down the table at Caleb. "And there you go pouring more cheese on your pizza. Wouldn't your mother object, Caleb?"

Silence fell. "Oh, I'm so sorry, Caleb. Please forgive me," Irini said leaning forward toward Caleb, truly sorry for her unthinking comment, as he deliberately dug into the ceramic bowl of shredded parmesan and spooned more of the cheese on his slices.

"That's all right," Caleb said quietly. "Yes, as a matter of fact, she did object, Irini, but it seems that horrible habits persist."

"Carpenters?" Jake said jumping into the conversation and changing the subject as quickly as possible. They all knew a little about Caleb's background and avoided any reference to his parents. "We're artisans, masters of woodworking," he claimed proudly.

Frank nodded his agreement. "And our high fees prove it!" He laughed, stuffing half a slice of pizza with extra freshly ground garlic and a heavy sprinkling of red pepper flakes into his mouth.

Irini reached down to the floor beside her and brought up her laptop. "I have an agenda for us. It's rather long, so let's get started while we eat. You'll find it under 'current business.'" Caleb reached behind him to a small breakfront and grabbed his laptop from it. The other two men keyed into the group site.

There were three agenda items on their screens: 1) Partrain Update; 2) Chinese Connection; and 3) Drug Distribution. Several subtopics were bulleted under each main item.

"First item, please," Irini said, tapping her forefinger's highly lacquered, peach-colored nail on the table. She moved her yogurt bowl and apple plate to one side, adjusting the computer in front of her. The sweep of her eyes, surveying the pizza boxes, the crusts, the crumpled and stained napkins, and the beer can wreckage in front of the three men, earned them each a piercing shaft of disdain from her suddenly dead-black eyes.

She smiled tightly and continued, "Among the materials sent by Georgetown is a report from the Hillsborough police, in cooperation with the San Francisco FBI office. All of this is in the file. There is no doubt that Mr. Partrain's fingers were delivered by FedEx and UPS to the family home. The fingers were severed with garden shears. Snip, snip, snip. Clean cuts," she said nonchalantly, arching an eyebrow as she raised her right hand, making scissoring snips in the air with her long fingers. "If not professional, at least efficient. We believe he was still alive when the fingers were acquired."

A glance flew between Jake and Frank, eyes dark and filled with understanding. A slim smile curled the corners of Irini's lips as she tucked away the insight she had gained from the exchange between the two SEALs.

"The home deliveries," she continued, "indicate some knowledge of the family beyond a simple business connection, since the Partrains are not listed in the telephone directory. My guess is that the perpetrators knew them fairly well, although any professional could have located their residence easily.

"You have several documents in the files going more deeply on the Partrains and their backgrounds. You can read these later, please," she said. "Eastern Partners, LLC, was owned equally by Albert and Cheryl Partrain. Eastern Partners' business was the acquisition, importation, and marketing of Chinese antiques and artifacts. Like many businesses today, Eastern Partners outsourced the main services, such as shipping and transportation. Their primary participation was in striking the deals to acquire product in China, which they did through an independent antiques expert, Chen Wei Ming, whose company, Asian Artifacts, also served as the Partrains' shipping agent. Cheryl and Albert worked with their dealer customers here in the States. Their major customers are in New Orleans. They have a few favored accounts, who would get first crack at particularly valuable and desirable pieces."

"Why are they selling so far away from the point of entry?" Frank asked.

"Simple. Marketing," Irini said. "They pretty much own the New Orleans market by virtue of long-term relationships. Any other questions?"

Jake raised his hand to pose a question. "Do we have any import and distribution details? Past records? Copies of customs declarations and inspection reports? Any information about projected new shipment arrivals, delivery schedules based on purchases? Backgrounds on the outsourcing companies they deal with?"

"None of the Eastern Partners' customers' backgrounds flagged any attention from the FBI," she said. The container ship, the *Orient Star Maru*, is arriving in the next couple of days with the most recent order from Shanghai. We'll know when and where the ship will unload a half day beforehand."

Caleb interjected, "Jake, I would like you to babysit the container at the dock and get some photos of the drivers who pick up the Asian Artifacts box for Frank to ID."

"Frank, you access the Oakland Port Authority computer," Irini continued. "Find out the pickup time slot assigned to the freight company." She paused to skim a few handwritten notes.

"The routine will probably remain the same. New Orleans is the first and probably only destination," Irini said. "We know the route the truck should follow: I-5 down to I-10 and East to New Orleans. It takes about two and a half days to make the trip with professional drivers."

"And the delivery locations?" Jake Corbett broke in.

"We know from orders in the Partrain office when the dealers are expecting deliveries."

"So, I'm to handle logistics?" Frank DeLong asked.

"And weapons," Caleb said. "We'll decide on the artillery I'll need in New Orleans and what Jake might need on the drive. Get what you need ready as soon as you can, Jake, okay? After the pickup, the container will be on its way right from the dock. Let's see where they lead us, and then we'll conduct our business."

Jake nodded and gave Caleb a grin as he typed notes into his computer. "Gotcha."

"So, to reiterate," Irini said studying her notes on the screen and indicating Frank and Jake with a sweep of her finger, "please cover the arrival and off-loading of the container and then track it to New Orleans. Jake, let's get a GPS tracking device attached to the container, ASAP, okay?" Jake nodded, making a note.

Her finger swung back to Frank. "Caleb said it, Frank. You will be monitoring and responding to all of the Internet traffic, telecommunications, and the GPS tracking signals. Call Georgetown and ask to be tied into the RFID SmartTag signal from the container."

Caleb, who had been sitting back listening to Irini organize the project, knew that his assignment was to ride on top of the groundwork Irini was laying with the team.

"Item two," Irini announced. "The Chinese connection." She bowed her head and held up her hands, palms outward, to squelch any immediate comments from the three men. "I know, I know, I know. You guys have strong feelings on the subject."

During their careers prior to joining the Georgetown organization, all three of the men in the cell had been engaged in covert warfare operations involving, for good or bad, Chinese agents and agendas. Whatever the operation, if it involved the Chinese, it always reeked of specific, but undeclared, objectives.

"Mr. Thorndike says that, as usual, the messages from China are difficult to interpret. The bare bone of it is that the Chinese think that ... *perhaps* ..." She paused to emphasize the word. "... there is a drug-smuggling operation in place from western China running through Shanghai and possibly on to the US through the Port of Oakland." She raised her eyebrows, rolling her eyes and feigning wonderment.

"Oh, no, say it isn't so," Jake murmured, shaking his crew-cut head of hair in mock despair.

Jake's own pretense of incredulity seemed to call the end to dinner as they all finished the last crust of pizza, set aside their plates, and repositioned their laptops.

"So, now we're buddies with the Chinese?" Jake said, his face slightly flushed. Irini knew his background with China's activities included several highly sensitive missions into the country to meet disaffected Chinese who wanted to pass documents but would not or could not gain access to safe electronic communications, so human assets had to go in. One evening after a few beers, he had told her about how he spent two days in a snow cave avoiding an intense search by the Red Army. He lost a toe as a result of frostbite. He told Irini that even now, on some nights, the toe still ached, bringing it all back, reminding him and hurting him once again. She had hugged him long and hard, an experience Jake had seldom engaged in with a woman.

"Well, it seems that the concept of 'the enemy of my enemy is my friend' applies," Caleb said. "It is a bit strong to call them 'Buddies,' I think."

Irini said, "We don't have irrefutable evidence establishing the connection between the antiques the Partrains import from China and the possibility of a drug-smuggling operation. Proving it and tacking down those proofs is our job ... and cleaning up the mess if we find the necessary evidence. Speculation runs rampant, of course."

Scrolling down on his laptop, Caleb urged the meeting along, saying, "And that brings us to item three, drug distribution. This is the crux of our involvement, as Irini said. If we cannot discover a connection between drugs and antiques quickly, we are to leave the Partrain murder investigation to the local police and focus on discovering, independently, whether or not there is in fact a drug-distribution operation. When we find the people engaged in drug smuggling, we terminate them. There is something unique in this situation though. That being that most heroin is reputed to come through Europe to the East Coast. If, in fact, horse is coming through Oakland, we are looking for someone with smarts, initiative, and big balls." Caleb stopped and turned to Irini, who checked her notes.

She continued, "So, while Frank cranks up communications and Jake concentrates on preparing to track the container, tonight I'm going make contact with a person who knows about drug sources and distribution from the inside."

Irini collected Caleb's smug smile from the opposite end of the table. His soft "Ahhhh" was accompanied with a knowing nod of his head. She smiled back, sweetly, with stiletto eyes.

"Frank, you and Jake can take off if you wish. I think that Irini has some reading materials she wants to lay on me," Caleb said to the two SEALs. "I'm leaving for New Orleans tomorrow to take a look around and scout out the antique shops on Eastern Partners' customer list. We'll meet up on the road to New Orleans, Jake. Have a good trip."

Chairs scrapped across the varnished oak floor as they all pushed back from the table. Irini smiled, murmuring, "Love military training," as she watched the two SEALs collect the plates, pizza boxes, and beer cans and carry it all into the kitchen for disposal.

Jake returned to grab his and Frank's laptops. The two excused themselves. Meeting over.

12

"What have you got for me?" Caleb asked Irini after Jake and Frank had left for their home in San Francisco.

"For you," Irini said, "I have intelligence on our friend Mr. Curtis Rathmann. Background, business, and known associates. You'll find it all under Rathmann, double N. Sit down here," she said, motioning for him to sit beside her on the couch. Her laptop perched on her knees. "We can work off one screen."

Caleb sat down next to her, and she shifted her screen so the two of them could both see it. She scrolled through the document. His brow furrowed as page after page slid by. Her thigh was warm against his. He furrowed his brow even more deeply to show how intently he was focused on the screen material.

"God, this must be a hundred pages long, Irini," he complained. "You know I'm really more into getting started on the action part of our projects than I am reading up on background information on a guy." He caught the pursed lips, sour-lemon, evil-eye look for which Irini was famous. Even expressing her displeasure, she was still one of the most beautiful women Caleb had ever known.

"I know, I know," he said holding up his hand to ward off her standard comment on his penchant for action versus preparation. "I'll read it. Tonight! Okay?" She nodded, patting his hand. Her hand rested on his, while she studied the screen for pertinent data.

"The pieces of the patchwork seem to be coming together. Mr. Rathmann's college buddy and Harvard B School study group partner, Collier Berwick, lives in New Orleans and has a restaurant,

Le Couteau Bleu. I have no idea what the blue knife represents." She flicked her hand in a dismissive gesture.

"I've printed out the list of customer drops and street locations," she said, passing him a couple of pieces of paper. "You should take the time to scout these stores out before the container truck arrives.

"And, finally, the Drug Enforcement folks suspect a heroin pipeline up the Mississippi from New Orleans to Chicago," she said as she scrolled through documents on her laptop. "If you discover something to indicate a broader distribution of the suspected heroin beyond New Orleans, we can offer some assistance to the Feds."

"So, I head out to New Orleans, scope out Le Couteau Bleu and Rathmann's buddy, and check out the stores expecting antiques deliveries," Caleb said.

"And meet up with Jake," Irini added.

"If there is a direct connection between the Partrains and the Chinese drug dealer," he said, "it's certainly going to come together in New Orleans."

"That's the distribution issue I mentioned in my agenda," Irini said.

"Has Frank arranged for my travel and ID?"

"I have a ticket for you here, nonstop to New Orleans leaving at 11:00 a.m. tomorrow. When the truck's released by customs, it will leave Oakland and take approximately two and a half days to get to New Orleans."

She passed him a manila envelope. He spilled the contents onto the table in front of him. In the name of George Garland, President, Peerless Barbed Wire, Inc., Enid, Oklahoma, he found a driver's license, some credit and bank cards, and a stack of business cards. The Delta coach airline ticket had its own little envelope. "I'm a barbed-wire manufacturer?" Caleb asked with wonder in his voice. "Really? Is this the best Frank could come up with? Barbed wire?"

"There's a farm equipment convention starting today in New Orleans according to Frank," Irini explained, laughing. "You will fit right in, I'm sure." She smiled brightly at him. "I have a room for you at the Royal Sonesta … George."

Forgoing the opportunity to bitch and moan, he scrolled through the material on his screen a second time. "Well, now, if we all have enough to work on …" Caleb suggested with heavy sarcasm, "I'd like to get to my reading. I'll set up our contact schedule. Do we have fresh satellite phones for everyone?"

Irini nodded. "And finally," she said, "the state cops are scrupulous in their attention to out-of-state visitors and their vehicles. Even though the alterations the guys have made to the Malibu should conceal what we want Jake to carry with him, we can't afford to have him hauling serious firepower in his trunk on this route. Jake and Frank have a source in New Orleans who will deliver the weapons to you, okay?"

"Jake mentioned him to me. The guy was in the Navy SEALs during 'Nam," Caleb said. "He deals in illegal weaponry and is totally freelance, no affiliations. According to Frank, he's the guy you want on your side in a fight. Georgetown approved him as an outside source, so that must mean there is a level of confidence in him on Mr. Thorndike's part."

"You'll be contacted at the airport with a car. We'll receive the rendezvous location instructions tonight," Irini assured Caleb.

He nodded.

Irini glanced at Caleb, trying to read his mood. Unable to do so, she wished him a good night of reading. Her heels clicked on the wood floor. She left the apartment to go to her home and change for the evening. She wished she had stayed.

A single lamp illuminated his space on the couch; his laptop balanced on his knees. The cars passing below on Broadway lent the only texture to the silence of the minutes he sat in lonely reflection. He imagined that he could feel the energy and tension contained in the documents beneath his fingertips on the keyboard. He clicked to the top of the file.

The beginning of any engagement was a mixture of emotions, the Devil's own mixture.

He started to read.

13

The limousine pulled up in front of the Cheshire Hotel. The hotel doorman helped Irini Constant out of the limo. Jose Maria Jimenez de Cordova greeted her with a warm kiss to both cheeks and, taking her hand, led her through the lavish lobby. Conversations stopped as they passed. Heads turned, and admiring whispers were exchanged. Irini looked particularly elegant in a blood-red Donna Karan sheath. De Cordova thought that she looked as fresh and beautiful as she had long ago at the soiree at New York's Modern Museum of Art, where they had first met. Her velvet tentacles had captured him in a way that to this day still eluded him. That was six years ago, and since then, de Cordova had found himself offering her huge amounts of money for spending time with him. He presented her with lavish gifts worth small fortunes to maintain her restive attentions.

The doors of the private elevator closed silently, and, with the very slightest sensation of lift, the elevator soared to the restaurant, The Marquis Room. Looking at her, de Cordova ached to stroke her smooth skin and touch her in those intimate places that never failed to drive him wild. The elevator doors slid open soundlessly. An attentive maître d' led them to a table by a window overlooking the waterfront.

De Cordova was slight of build and dark complexioned with piercing black eyes under a high, clear brow. Taller than most Colombians, whose roots were entwined with the Indio people of South America, de Cordova had used his size, native intelligence, and a willingness to do whatever was necessary to achieve his goals. He had forged a successful, if precarious, career among the Colombian drug cartels. Never a landowner or a member of the ruling families, he had made himself useful on the business side. And, in the contentious world of drugs, inevitably, his guile assured that in any battle, he was the last man standing.

Most of the reputed drug lords were peasants who had just enough intelligence to rise to the top of the turgid heap of thugs who had gravitated to the allure of the easy money. Life was short at the top. These people existed long enough to become targets for elimination by other drug families. De Cordova had maneuvered the dangerous terrain with skill. His global distribution network connections were invaluable to whomever was building an organization. He had never been caught betraying his employers, and that alone made him unique in a society in which relatives killed each other with apparent abandon for real or imagined slights, betrayals, or self-advancement.

When the dirty work began in the jungles and the cities of Colombia and other South American drug centers, the machete of vengeance sliced mercilessly and mindlessly. The violence, in the name of conducting business, was moving northward into Mexico and already seeping across the US border. If the United States, the mightiest nation of them all, couldn't stop the flow across its borders of illegal aliens looking for an honest job, how could they hope to stop the ruthless drug traffickers? Dozens of people were being slaughtered by gun, grenade, machete, shiv, or garrote as the battle to gain the upper hand in the drug world grew more intense and vicious. Nobody was safe.

De Cordova's sensitivity to the internal political currents of the drug business and the potential for mayhem led him to take frequent business trips out of town. He usually headed for New York, where he could spend his money, rub elbows with United Nations contacts, and enjoy the unique pleasures such a city made available. Over the years, Irini Constant's companionship was one of those special pleasures. Her position by his side during the social seasons' events had made her a subject of discussion and rumor among the social elite of New York. It also grew her client list.

De Cordova was sure that she was his intellectual equal, maybe even more intelligent, but Irini never challenged his macho-driven self-esteem. She understood and exploited the male ego.

In bed, she was also the most accomplished woman he had ever known. After being thoroughly drained by her enthusiasm for what he was sure was proof of his sexual prowess, he found it relaxing to rummage through his thoughts with Irini snuggled at his side. He would sort his issues into convenient boxes, describing the patterns he saw in the tea leaves of his life. Irini was an excellent listener, rarely interrupting his monologues, except for the occasional carefully worded question. These skillfully molded questions opened new doors for de Cordova's consideration and resolution. The two talked far into the nights they spent in his suites.

A table next to a window provided a panoramic view of San Francisco's Embarcadero and the many piers lining the Bay. Irini's classic Greek profile never ceased to enchant him. The city lights from below caressed her face and long, gracefully curved neck. De Cordova was once again captivated by her sensuality as she gazed out over the waterfront. He wondered if he could ever bring himself to ask her to join him in South America. At moments like this, he felt inferior to her—a unique position for a man in his business.

She turned to face him. "What brings you to San Francisco, *mi Jose Maria*?" she asked. "Business, as usual?" The use of "Jose Maria" was an intimacy that had grown out of their relationship. At moments of sublime passion, she found that calling him "Maria" stimulated him to achieve the heights of ecstasy. This bisexual implication during sex intrigued Irini, and she used it to her advantage. It was never discussed. Machismo was still to be respected with Latino men, and Irini knew the rules.

He reached across the table to take her hand in his. "I would like you to believe that I came here to see you, *cara mia*, but that would not be true. And you would know that."

"Shall I pout?" she asked smiling. She made a cushion of her lips followed by a small kissing sound. "I know that your business motivates your every waking moment. I'm just pleased to have some of your attention."

"I do have some business to tend to here in the city, but tonight is for us. That is, if you will share it with me?"

"Only on the condition that you do not feel compelled to send me gifts, Jose Maria. I know you like to do that. You also know it is not necessary. We have much too much history of the soul to allow material things to intrude. Let's just be together and enjoy each other while we can. You have much to tell me about how terrible your job is, no?"

"Ah, Irini ..." He sighed, swirling his Chateau Neuf du Pape in lazy circles, his body noticeably relaxing. "You make me feel at ease. I'm so very glad to be here with you."

His eyes devoured her as she lifted her wineglass and held it to him. Their glasses barely touched. The intimate softness of the gesture, its sensual delicacy, sent electricity thrilling through them both.

Irini gazed deeply into de Cordova's coal-black eyes, her mind calculating the value of her "friendship" with him. He was in on most of the major drug deals involving international trafficking and had a finger on the pulse of the far-flung business of drug distribution. The man in Georgetown supported her relationship with de Cordova and, indeed, had always encouraged her activities as a means to an end. As for the opportunity to bed de Cordova, she was not averse to some pleasures for herself.

After she had become William Thorndike's associate, she had found it advantageous to admit to de Cordova that she occasionally provided small quantities of drugs to her clients. Nothing large, she had explained, but some of the powerful men and women with whom she socialized as clients or acquaintances needed safe sources to feed their habits. They could hardly pull their Mercedes up to a Spanish Harlem street corner to deal with some macho thug leaning in the window with his pants hanging off his ass and a gun stuck in his waistband.

De Cordova arranged to meet her meager needs through his contacts with the Jamaican Posse in the Borough of Brooklyn. Her drugs were delivered to her apartment on Manhattan's Upper Eastside by a young, coffee-colored Jamaican carrying a long flower box. Irini would engage him in conversation as she sorted the powders, pills, and rocks at her kitchen table. The lilting accent entertained her, while she arranged the flowers from the box. He would talk about how powerful his posse was and how he was rising in the leadership ranks. She'd tip the delivery boy with a small rock of cocaine.

As far as de Cordova knew, she was just one of the thousands of Americans he had hooked on drugs. He had no idea that the eventual bust of the Jamaican Posse was a direct result of the deliveries he had arranged.

As they were sipping Remy Martin cognac after dinner, she broached the issues at the top of her mind. "I used to think that Chinese product came to us through France. I hear that some is now available through West Coast ports. True?" De Cordova nodded in acknowledgement.

"Would it cost me less buying product, horse, locally, so to speak?"

He sighed. "The global market is causing all sorts of problems. New competitors and sources arriving on a daily basis. New fads, as well. The chemists have been busy. And, here on the West Coast, we've had problems with Mexicans, Russians, and local motorcycle gang distribution systems and their methamphetamine labs. Why, *cara mia*? Are you looking for a source—other than me?" he said, peering at her, searching her eyes. "You know that I will have my people arrange for anything you need."

"That's not what I want your opinion about. You know that I don't want to bother you, Maria." She lifted his hand and kissed his fingertips. A tongue flick drew a smile to his lips. "You have told me that China has always been in the market with heroin," she said, bringing him back to her main question.

"*Si*, Irini, China White. But now I hear there is a maverick producer out in the mountains of western China. The quality of his product is very good, I am told. He has decided not to follow the traditional distribution routes through Europe and has arranged to import through the West Coast. Why are you interested, my love?"

She took his hand and turned it over in hers. She slowly and gently traced a line from his wrist, across his palm to a fingertip with the elegantly polished nail of her forefinger. She looked up into his eyes and, holding his gaze, leaned forward, raised his hand, and kissed his fingertips, very briefly holding one between her lips. She raised her head, and, as if thinking about something and coming to a decision, she gave her head a tiny shake causing her hair to slide across one eye before falling back in place.

"Only want to make a bit more money to invest in both my businesses," she said. "I want to get a good price so that I can make a decent profit from my ladies who enjoy the release they get from the products. I think they are sharing with friends and lovers, you know? Demand is up. Anything new you come across would find a ready market with me." She sat back, repositioning her napkin across her lap. The idea of expanding her personal business outside the guidelines for her activities set by Thorndike had always been at the back of her mind. It was encroaching on her attention in recent days, and de Cordova was a safe source for drugs right under Thorndike's and Caleb's noses. "I don't think that these women have enough to do. In addition, the extra cash would help expand my shop's business. So, that's why I'm interested. Are you … interested?"

"Of course I'm interested. But not in business at the moment. *Mañana, cara mia, mañana.* Enough of business for tonight. It will give me lines on my face," he joked. "May I suggest that we have a night cap in my suite?"

"Mmmm. Yes, if that will help my business. That's the only reason I have for visiting your suite." She lowered her eyes demurely.

He grinned. "Shall we go, señorita?" Not waiting for her answer, he signaled their waiter to bring the check, which he initialed, adding a substantial tip. He remembered the jobs of his youth, when the gratuities added up to rent or food for the family.

After retrieving her coat from the checkroom, the two of them entered the elevator, he thinking of the hours ahead and she thinking of how to return to the subject of heroin from China without setting off any bells leading to his scrutiny of her motives.

Standing close in front of him, Irini could feel the direction de Cordova's thoughts were taking him. Her hand slid back between them, and she grasped his erection firmly, squeezing it rhythmically. Moving with her stroke, he pressed against her and kissed her ear. The evening ahead was promising for both of them.

14

Irini Constant set the red, plastic hands on the paper clock on the "Closed" sign on the store's front door for a ten o'clock return and locked the door. There was a spring in her step as she climbed the stairs to Caleb's apartment. De Cordova had always been a satisfactory lover, as well as being a fountain of information during pillow-talk time. All in all, it had been an evening well spent. It also reconfirmed her appeal to men, her primary survival resource.

Frank met her at the kitchen table and spread out his information about the weapons source in New Orleans. As she scanned the material, Caleb came from his bedroom stretching and muttering about meetings being held in his kitchen. He was wearing pajamas low on his waist, his torso bare. Irini appraised him with a professional eye. She could imagine how it would feel to have his body inside her arms. It was becoming increasingly difficult for her to avoid highly erotic thoughts about Caleb. She was unused to having to restrain her imagination.

Caleb looked at the collection of papers on the table and suggested that they telephone Thorndike to fill him in. Irini suggested that he first take a shower while she and Frank sorted out the materials and sent them to Wild Willie before having the meeting.

He showered and, after wiping steam from his bathroom mirror, as he shaved, checked the pinkish line left behind as a reminder of where the stitches, recently removed, had been. A thin, bare space cut diagonally through his left eyebrow. The doctor in Paris had assured him that it would be barely noticeable and that it should disappear in his eyebrow's hair.

When Caleb reappeared, dressed in sweater and jeans and with bare feet, he apologized for taking so long. He suggested that his shower would have been faster had Irini done his back. "No, it wouldn't have," she murmured, giving him a seductive smile. Irini dialed Georgetown, and Thorndike answered on the second ring.

"Good morning, California," his thin voice said. "I assume you want to discuss the recently transmitted materials regarding our friends?"

"Yes, sir," Caleb said. "Frank and Jake have been busy the last couple of days."

"Someday, Frank, you'll have to tell me how you access this material so efficiently," Thorndike said. "I'm sure I could arrange for you to have legitimate access. Not as much fun though, eh?"

"Yessir," Frank said, leaving well enough alone.

"When do you leave for … what do they call that place … the Big Easy?"

"Yes, sir," Caleb confirmed. "The Big Easy. I'm flying out this morning. I have a couple of tasks to take care of before Jake and the container arrive."

"We wanted to update you on matters as they stand," Irini said, leaning toward the speakerphone. You have the up-to-the-minute information in the packet we sent you a few moments ago."

"Go on," Thorndike said. They could hear him settling down in his chair. Papers rustled as he squared the stack of printouts Irini had sent him. The tall, grandfather clock in Thorndike's office struck the hour. It was ten in the morning in Washington DC.

"Yes, sir," Irini began. "The *Orient Star Maru* is due into the Port of Oakland at eight tonight according to the ship's master's communications regarding his ETA. She will begin unloading at three o'clock tomorrow morning and should be ready to off-load our subject container between nine and nine thirty tomorrow morning. The container is listed as the property of Eastern Partners. A flatbed from Long Distance Freight is listed as the recipient of the container.

Jake will take shots of the drivers of record who are authorized to make the pickup. We ran their names through the FBI system to ID them and get their records. You have that in the packet we sent."

Frank took over the briefing. "The two men are members in good standing of the Visigoths MC, Alameda Chapter. They are Francis Patrick O'Riley, a.k.a. 'Pork Chop,' and Robert Fredrickson, apparently known very colorlessly, for these people at least, as just plain old, basic Bob. Aside from arrest records, which provide a list of crimes for each man ranging from petty theft to grand theft auto and up the scale to attempted murder and some murder charges to add spice, these boys have spotless employment records. On time to work. No traffic violations or run-ins. No accidents. Nada."

Irini said, "They are soldiers within the Visigoths organization. They do as they're told and the information we have indicates that their performance of duty to the Goths is as admirable as their performance on their day jobs. Point them and fire," she concluded.

"Well, well, well. An outlaw motorcycle club—gang, I mean. Let's call it what it is, a gang. Have you more information on the Visigoths?" Thorndike asked. A pen scratched on a pad in Georgetown. They all knew that Thorndike used an old fountain pen rather than any newfangled gel pen or electronic devices. He had a computer and was expert at it, but when he was in meetings, the scratch of the nib's point could always be heard. And they all recognized his crabbed handwriting too. Not a birthday or a major holiday passed without a card and handwritten note from "William Thorndike" acknowledging the event.

"Frank has been in discussion with the San Francisco PD's computer and has some info on them. Frank?" Caleb said, turning to Frank, who opened a file on his computer screen.

"Lots of suspicions here, sir. Not much proof. The Visigoths MC was founded in December of 1998 in Alameda. That was the first chapter, and the president was and still is a guy named Wrath. That's it … Wrath … one name and obviously not the one his mama gave him." He spelled it and heard pen scratches through the speakerphone. "They added chapters at a rate of one or two a month for the next year. Some of the chapters were seeded with as few as three or four members to start. They now have twenty-four chapters, and most of them have twenty to twenty-five members. The chapters' locations fall on a line from San Francisco through the Southwest to Texas and then to Slidell, Louisiana, and north ending up in Joliet, Illinois. Nothing out of country. Not even a personal trip by Wrath to Canada. They have Angels and Diablos up there. Lots of opportunities for the nasties there in the frozen north, but Wrath is not interested apparently. A real home boy."

"The suspicions I mentioned have to do with some altercations among their fellow MCs around the Bay Area and a bit further afield up and down the coast. Rumors of murders and theft in amphetamine country. Rumors of drug deals and hijacking of trucks carrying everything from cigarettes to imported food, like caviar. Not a very clear picture of someone who seems to be an evil genius. At the moment, every law enforcement agency has an inquiry for input on them."

"A few days ago, some cops out in Albuquerque busted up the Visigoths' chapter house," Caleb added. "The cops smashed bikes, which, excuse me, sir, even I think is going a bit too far. In any event, three days later, the rank in front of the house was filled with brand-new Harleys paid for by the national headquarters in Alameda. Every member, a full complement of twenty-four members, is mounted again."

"Back to Wrath," Frank said and paused to scroll through his notes. "No dope on him. He carries cash or has one of his guys pay. He does not meet with anyone and leaves no paper trails. Gets no mail. Wrath has the size and demeanor to scare the shit … excuse me, sir, outta everyone, if he wanted. He doesn't, and that's what makes him interesting. He has this fairly powerful organization and seems to be hiding in the shadows. Avoiding the light. I'd love to tap their house and find out about these guys, if this outfit proves to be of interest to us." Frank stopped and sat back looking at Caleb. He nodded.

"Frost? Your analysis, please," Thorndike asked.

"The obvious, sir. The chapter house locations track the route the

Eastern Partners' trucks take. They have drivers working for LDF. But what's the connection with China other than the transport of Chinese antiques? Is their interest in New Orleans just coincidental and part of the delivery job? This is a raw mixture, sir. Explosive, I think."

"Well, it's a wait-and-see situation, isn't it? As you say, there's lots of speculation, but we are lacking actionable proof for our clients," Thorndike interjected.

"I'll check in from New Orleans."

"Good-bye, Frost," Thorndike said. "Please give me a daily update, Irini. Good job, Frank. Same to Jake. Have a good day, everyone." The speakerphone went dead.

Frank asked if Caleb was ready for his input about New Orleans.

"Yeah, Frank. Let's have it," he said.

"Brought you the info on the meet with the supplier Zipperman in New Orleans tonight," Frank said. "There's an alley just to the left of the Acme Oyster House on Iberville. At 1645, a guy with a red bandana on his head and cockatoos on his Hawaiian shirt will enter the alley carrying a New Orleans Saints sports bag. The bag will contain some goodies for you. Ask him if the Saints found a kicker yet. They haven't. If he says they have, strangle the bastard. He's not ours."

"What have you got for me this time?"

"Well, at the moment, we think you'll only need a handgun, so we got a Smith and Wesson forty-five. It tends to stop whoever gets in the slug's way. Twenty-five rounds in the sports bag. You can buy more in the stores down there. That's my kinda town; New Orleans is my—"

"Thanks, Frank." Caleb cut him off. "Stay close to the phone. Huh?"

Frank gave him a small salute followed by a thumbs-up and left through the kitchen, calling, " Stay out of the honky-tonks," over his shoulder. "Oh, by the way," he added, leaning back into the room, "Be careful, Caleb." He disappeared behind the kitchen doorframe. Caleb heard his footsteps descending the stairs.

His cell phone rang. Barney Flannery's name showed on the phone's screen.

"Yeah, Barney, what's the word on Reb?" He listened to the Flannery Center's director describe Rebecca's condition. He nodded a couple of times. He had had this discussion with Barney before during Reb's past attempt at rehabilitation. "Well, I'm out of town for a week or so. Please leave me messages on my phone each day, buddy. I'll pick them up and get back to you if necessary. You remember Irini? You met her that time at the Stanford-USC game? She's my tenant in the shop downstairs. She said that she'd be around this week and would help out. She's a good person, and she knows Rebecca. I trust her." He gave Barney Irini's number.

"If something has to happen locally, give her a shout, okay? And, Barney, you get any information about Reb's pusher, I want to know immediately. None of the patient's privileged information shit here, okay? None of that, right, Barney?"

After a short silence on the phone, Caleb heard Barney's murmured agreement. They had determined that Rebecca had been mainlining a very high grade of heroin. Bending rules was sometimes necessary to clean up the pusher scum, and that activity was very much a priority for the Flannery Center.

"Okay, see you soon, Barney, and, Barney ..." Caleb paused, "thanks for your help." He ended the call and laid the cell phone on the table.

With a sigh, he stood and gathered his papers. Given enough advance time, Caleb was in the habit of packing his bag the day before his departure. Packing for an engagement trip was close to a meditative activity for him. This was a jeans trip, but he also included a good sports jacket, dark slacks, a dark-blue shirt, and a yellow tie for checking out the Le Couteau Bleu restaurant Rathmann's buddy owned. New Orleans was not much for formal wear, but sharp did count for something.

The backgrounders Georgetown had supplied on Curtis Rathmann, trucking firm owner, and Collin Berwick, restaurateur, were making for interesting reading. He'd go over them one more time on the plane. He would read the dossiers, which were copied on dissolvable lightweight paper, and then, immediately after landing at New Orleans, he would visit a men's room and flush them to oblivion. Thorndike's note on the biographies indicated that he felt that the "Harvard Boys," as he called Rathmann and Berwick, deserved some "fine-tooth combing," code for intense investigation and extreme treatment if necessary.

At nine thirty, Caleb zipped his battered leather suitcase shut and hoisted it off the bed. He crossed Broadway to Il Piccolo to grab a morning coffee and wait for his taxi to take him to his eleven o'clock flight at San Francisco International. Caleb's disdain for TSA's rule of being two hours early for a flight was well known by his team and friends. He hadn't missed a flight yet, arriving at airports a half hour ahead of schedule. His taxi was scheduled to pick him up at ten fifteen.

Caleb caught sight of Irini standing in her store window watching him when he climbed into the taxi. As much as they both tried to be cool and dispassionate about his departures on engagements, concern for his safe return was always a part of the emotional mix. It seemed to him that he could still feel her eyes on the back of his head as he drove off. *Not a bad feeling,* he thought.

15

Caleb's bag swung loosely from its shoulder strap as he walked through the Louis Armstrong New Orleans International Airport terminal's long corridors. Traveling light, avoiding involvement with baggage service, carrying as little metal as possible, and sticking to TSA's rules once he was in their grasp kept him out of the limelight when he traveled.

He punched speed dial. He had received an urgent text message during the flight to call as soon as possible.

"For safety, I changed your hotel reservations, if you don't mind."

"Frank, you're in charge of logistics. Tell me … what changes can I expect? What else has changed?"

"The Royal Sonesta Hotel was a bit too high profile, if someone is on the lookout for a strange face in the crowd," Frank said. "So I decided to make you as unavailable as possible. Do what you have to do at the restaurant but then vanish."

"Okay by me."

"I contacted the guy supplying you with your gear. Told him to find a safe house and to add a shotgun to your bag, plus some explosives to go with it. Also got you some appropriate clothes. Make you fit into the Bourbon Street scene and the alleys of New Orleans. Sit in a jazz club and nobody notices you. The guy's got everything ready for you. Same alley, same time."

"And, exactly where am I holing up?" Caleb asked with a note of suspicion in his voice. A long silence followed.

"Ahhh, well, Caleb, ya know …" Frank paused, clearing his throat. "It occurred to me that your residence should be, ahhh, obscure. Agree?" Caleb imagined Frank flicking nonexistent particles of dust off the equipment in the communications room while he waited for his response. Caleb then pictured Frank smiling a touch maliciously, knowing full well where he was housing his leader. Several of Frank's relatives had the misfortune of having to live in the Ninth Ward at one time.

"Yeah?" Caleb said slowly drawing out the question. Frank was making him sweat this. He knew it wasn't going to be even as upscale as the Motel 6 chain.

"Well," Frank said, "we've found a really nice, inexpensive, and out-of-the-way house to rent for the week."

"Where, Frank?"

"In the lower Ninth Ward district. Garden spot, Caleb, really or so my local source said. A small house, just for sleeping, of course. Pretty isolated. You'll need a car. I've arranged for a junker … nothing flashy. The guy's outside the front door of baggage claim now. It's a slightly used car."

"Couldn't find something ostentatious, Frank?" he asked.

"Where you are going in the Ninth Ward, this is the car to have. I exaggerated when I said slightly used, Caleb—exaggerated both words, *slightly* and *used*, but under the hood, there is a brand-new powerhouse. Nobody is going to envy you your ride, until you whip them on a straightaway."

"And how do I find this luxury pad?"

"Map in the sports bag your contact has for you. The bag you'll get in the alley."

"Hope nobody hijacks him with the bag," Caleb said.

"Oh, Caleb …" Frank chuckled. "They really wouldn't want to try to do that."

"You know this guy?"

"Only by reputation. Verified by guys I do know. In Vietnam, he was known as the Zipperman. Knife and wire specialist."

"So, I don't want to try to get physical with him if he doesn't recall the answer to our password test?"

"Nossir. If you can, stay better than arm's length away from this dude. Do it."

"Can I count on him for support, if I need something else?"

"You can set that up with him, Caleb. You can rely on him. Anything you need, he can get."

"Well," Caleb said, "better pick up my new ride. I'll check in from my digs later, Frank. That's if my cell works out in the garden neighborhood you've selected for me. I'm sure there's no phone or TV, right?" Silence. "Towels and soap?" More silence. "Yeah, well, thanks for your good work. You can get a job with Priceline when you need a new job, which may be soon, Frank."

"Okay, Caleb. I'll work on my résumé today, if I can find time."

Caleb laughed. "That's okay; we'll keep you on until the end of the month. Listen, Thorndike mentioned the Visigoths in his briefing. Can you amplify data on that little group and have it for me ASAP?"

"Sure thing, Caleb. And Jake will get the GPS tracker on the truck as soon as possible, so I'll chart its route and give you a heads-up on their ETA and their approach route into New Orleans. You and Jake will want to pick them up well out in the suburbs before they reach New Orleans."

"That's right. If they unload before the city, we want to be there. Stay in touch. Talk to you later, Frank. Bye." Caleb ended the call and stuffed the phone into his shirt pocket.

Adjusting the bag on his shoulder, he headed for the baggage claim area's exit doors.

16

Caleb mixed with the crowd exiting the airline terminal to the bustling sidewalk. Sitting across the street in the "No Parking" zone was a faded queen, a rusting relic, a rambling wreck from the looks of her. He decided that the pink Cadillac Seville was a "her," like a ship. She had mismatched tires—a white wall on the front right and a grungy black tire on the rear and dented fenders. The front and rear doors didn't match color-wise. He circled the car, noting a bullet hole in the front left quarter panel over the tire. The roof of the car was painted orange.

One of the skinniest men Caleb had ever seen was slouched in the front seat. He wore a wife-beater undershirt under a shirt featuring pineapples and the color fuchsia. A dirty panama hat was pulled down over his eyes, the brim, grimy with finger tugs.

"You him?" the skeletal man asked, a toothpick switching sides in his cracked-lip mouth.

Taking a couple of moments to study the man further, Caleb responded, "Do I look like him?"

"Name of the coffee shop cross the street from where ya all live?" the bony man said, craning his scrawny neck upward to see Caleb better. His squinting eyes were glittering slits beneath the brim of the Panama. They searched his face through the open driver's side window.

"Il Piccolo," Caleb answered.

"Now you lookin' just like him. Welcome to N'awlins, suh. Your keys are in the ignition. Enjoy your stay in our fair city."

"I hope you won't be missing this beauty for the few days I'll be using it," Caleb said and smiled.

Moving so slowly Caleb thought he must be in pain, the man unfolded himself from the Caddy's driver's seat. Then, giving Caleb a slow up-and-down appraisal, he tugged at the brim of the hat, patted the car's roof, switched the toothpick to the other side of his mouth, and sauntered down the street. Caleb's nostrils searched for fresh air as the man passed him in a cloud of rank body odor and cheap bay rum.

The engine turned over on the first flick of the ignition key.

As he drove the surprisingly responsive Caddy into New Orleans, Caleb considered his next moves—first, the alley and Zipperman and then Le Couteau Bleu restaurant. He felt he should get a feel for the restaurant and Collier Berwick before his transformation into a New Orleans native tomorrow morning. He parked the Caddy in the Hotel Monteleone parking garage and walked up Royal Street to Iberville and Felix's Restaurant and Oyster Bar. Felix's had been Caleb's father's favorite oyster bar in New Orleans. He had introduced him to the fine art of swallowing oysters at Felix's during a family trip. In the same block on the other side of the street was the equally famous Acme Oyster House. And tonight, Felix's large front window afforded Caleb a view of the Acme Oyster House's side of the street and an alley nearby. This was the location of Caleb's meeting with Zipperman.

A couple dozen raw oysters, with his own special blend of horseradish, tomato sauce, salt, and pepper and several dashes of Tabasco mixed at the oyster bar, plus a cold beer to wash down the fresh oysters, would be a good prelude to dinner at Le Couteau Bleu. Standing at the marble bar, he gestured to the oyster shucker on the other side to start shucking.

The spirit of Mardi Gras hung, suspended in the air for anyone to breathe. It was too early in February, but the festival vibes in the Big Easy were definitively beginning to hum like tight wires in the wind.

Nature's potential for delivering furious and successful assaults on New Orleans was well documented. Yet the great city's jazz played on, the politicians pandered to special interests, and the city was served by indifferent state and federal governments.

The other variety of liquid hurricanes, those carried on the streets of the French Quarter and served from hole-in-the-wall bars along the sidewalks, continued to flow down the throats of tourists whose pockets were expertly vacuumed by the sleazy shops on Bourbon Street and the side-street rip-off joints. Of course, the ten-fingered street thief found excellent pickings in the pockets of the tourists too.

Caleb knew that the music, the restaurants, and the shops in many sections of town made New Orleans a world-class city, "a delightful city of mystique," his father had always called it in his rare poetic moments. When his father and mother visited from Connecticut for Mardi Gras, they stayed with friends whose home balconies fronted on Bourbon Street. His mom and dad would bring back strings of colorful beads and boxes of pralines for Reb and him.

Caleb sighed with the memories of better times. The task ahead crept back into his consciousness when he caught sight of a figure shuffling along the sidewalk. He watched as the slouching man approached the crosswalk and stepped onto the street as the traffic signal turned green. Despite the coolness of the early evening, Zipperman wore a short-sleeve Hawaiian shirt with what Caleb assumed were the cockatoos Frank had alluded to. A red bandana was wrapped around his head. His khaki pants drooped to the point of exposing his butt crack. Red Converse sneakers added panache to his outfit. His gait across the street made him appear old and feeble. A large New Orleans Saints sports bag hung from his shoulder. The football Saints logo was worn and almost indistinct. Passersby probably saw him as a homeless person changing locations for the night ahead. Zipperman sidestepped into the alley just past the Acme Oyster House and disappeared into the evening darkness.

It was four thirty on Caleb's watch. Fifteen minutes early. That boded well in Caleb's opinion, showed the man was cautious. He watched for ten minutes before he called for his tab. The oyster shucker toted up the number of oyster shells on the counter in front of Caleb, added in the two beers he had consumed, and slid a small piece of paper with the scribbled charges on it across the marble bar top. Caleb paid the amount, shoving cash, including a healthy tip, back. The tip earned him the first eye contact and acknowledgment he had received from the oysterman. A curt nod of thanks and the shucking began again for another patron.

Caleb crossed Iberville Street with a crowd of tourists and walked leisurely past the front of the Acme Oyster Bar. A step or two from the alley, Caleb paused and checked the streets, acting like a tourist looking for a new source of entertainment in a city that offered diversions through every doorway. Stepping up the street and angling into the alley, he paused for a few seconds to let his eyes adjust. A shadow moved, and Zipperman emerged, hands hanging at his sides, head cocked, taking a careful reading of Caleb, who stood stock-still. Zipperman stood straighter and taller than his street posture had presented. His hands clenched and unclenched. Caleb had seen this particular twitch in many Green Berets with whom he had worked in the past ten years.

The men eyed each other, and then Caleb asked if the Saints had gotten a new kicker yet.

"This is silly, isn't it?" Zipperman said. "Of course they ain't got a new kicker. And when they do, they still won't have a kicker. Damn Saints! They really suck sometimes."

"So I understand, but enough chitchat, you got something for me?" Caleb asked.

"Well, aren't we in a hurry? Christ, this ain't just a pass-along, dude. I got stuff to tell you."

"Okay, let's get started then," Caleb said.

"Ya know, I don't know where y'all got this attitude, man, but lemme tell you that I don' like attitude."

"Hey, I'm cool. This has not been a super day, and I thought we might just get at it. That's all," Caleb said. "I know we got stuff to discuss." He looked around for the bag.

"Okay. I figured something was fucked up when we got the order 'bout increase'n your baggage," Zipperman said, motioning Caleb to follow him into the deeper shadows down the alley. The Saints sports bag lay against the brick wall. Zipperman shifted the bag out a couple of feet and then leaned back into the wall keeping the bag between his feet. Caleb could now read the black message on the T-shirt. "Shuck Me, Suck Me, Eat Me Raw" were the words. The artwork was of some oysters.

"First of all, there's no key to your safe house, but there's a map to git you to the Ninth Ward there in the bag," Zipperman said and nodded toward the gym bag between his feet. "And now let's talk about your bag of tools." He bent down and zipped open the bag. He reached in and touched objects as he reviewed the inventory. "Kimber forty-five an' five mags of eight apiece. A KA-BAR and sheath in case some close work is required, ya dig?" His voice had caressed the word KA-BAR like a favorite cat. "A coupla grenades and a flash bang for some variety and fun." He looked up and smiled a snaggle-toothed grin. "And a recent addition to your collection, a fine Mossberg 500 twelve-gauge shotgun and thirty shells. It's a FLEX model, and y'all can configure it for many uses, but you ain't goin' on a turkey shoot, are ya? So we set it up for the bear you might hafta hunt. Put on the pistol grip fer ya. Y'ever shoot a pump action?"

"Yeah, I have, but isn't this one a beauty?" Caleb said admiring the black-matte-finished weapon. "How many shells does it hold?"

"Fully loaded it holds six shells. Both the Kimber and the Mossberg weapons're clean and never been fired. You don' use 'em, call me and I'll collect them an' credit yer account. Memorize my number, buddy," he said, handing Caleb a small slip of paper. He waited for Caleb to read the number and indicate that he had committed it to memory. Zipperman reached out, took the paper, stuffed it into his mouth, and swallowed. Caleb blinked. "Remember, you don' use 'em, I want 'em back," Zipperman said giving a final gulp to the bit of paper. "That's our deal. But you use 'em, you go to your local, friendly bayou, wipe 'em clean of yore prints, an' chuck these puppies as far as you can inta an alligator nest. Gators will probably eat 'em."

"I have heard a bit about you," Caleb said with a short laugh. "And

I know that you're known as the Zipperman. Your skills are useful. Do you hire them out?" There was silence in the alley.

"Rather you didn't bring back some old memories," the voice said from the darkness. "Fuck, those were not the 'good ol' days,' and I was definitely one bad actor. Jungle heat perhaps. Bad ganja, more likely. Trying to reform by staying out of direct action. I'm part of the sooo-ply chain now. Although, ya know, if something comes a long … ah do like to test my luck, jes' ta stay in shape, y'unnerstan?"

Caleb heard hands scrabbling in the bag. "Got ya some local clothes ta go with yore car, yore home away from home, and the streets where you'll wanna walk. Help you blend in a bit, eh? Also added a coupl'a thermal blankets. The nights can get cool here. Where you stayin', there ain't no maid to leave you blankets. Nobody to turn on the heat neither. Actually, no heater anyway."

"I'll bet. So, let me have the bag," Caleb said. "You've done a good job for us. I've got your number and may have to call, if I'm in a jam. You up for that?"

"Yeah, okay, I guess so. Anythin' for a buck, buddy," Zipperman said.

"One last thing. What's this Ninth Ward like? Katrina sort of targeted on them, right?"

"Well, the word devastatin' applies to what Katrina done to 'em there. We were able to find a house well away from any other shacks. An' I do mean shacks. You'll be alone there. Shed in the back's good ta pull the Caddy inta. Cain't see it from the street."

"Well, I'd better get going. I have a dinner reservation."

"Okay. *Laissez les bons temps rouler* as we say in Creole and *bonne chance, mon vieux*," Zipperman said.

"Appreciate the wish for good luck," Caleb said, "but as far as the good times rolling, I'm not so sure we're going to have fun for the next few days."

He felt the sports bag land across his feet. The presence in the deep shadows melted silently into the darkness. Caleb soon sensed he was alone. He hoisted the bag's strap over his shoulder and left the alley to join the noisy sidewalk crowd streaming down Bourbon

Street in the multicolored night. He ran Zipperman's telephone number through his mind again. Even with Jake, Zipperman could be a valuable addition to this engagement.

17

In the Cadillac, Caleb pulled out the map once he had settled himself in the concave driver's seat. Since the Caddy's interior lights didn't work and the light of day was fading, he relied on the glare of a streetlight to read the instructions he found in the sports bag. The note contained explicit directions to his safe house. He hoped the house would actually prove to be safe, because he knew that bad people would ultimately be looking for him for nonsocial reasons.

He glided into traffic heading toward the airport and the Ninth Ward. A half hour later, he had found the house. Zipperman was right. It was a shack, but the shed at the back looked large enough to hide the Cadillac. He sat for twenty minutes in what had been a driveway entrance one hundred yards away watching the house, watching for a light and a movement inside or outside indicating an occupant waiting for him. It was not that he didn't trust Zipperman. He did, because he trusted Frank DeLong. That being said, he didn't trust Zipperman to honor his agreement with Frank.

The house was a clapboard shack. Caleb had heard small houses like this one described generically as "shotgun shacks" because you could fire a shotgun from the front of the shack straight through the house and out the back door. It had four windows—one window in the front, one in the back, and one on either side of the structure. The Cadillac fit beautifully into the remnants of the garage. With the Mossberg shotgun in hand, Caleb entered the building through the door leading into the kitchen at the rear of the house. A narrow hallway ran from the kitchen down the middle of the house to the living room at the front. Bedroom and bathroom doors faced each other halfway down the hallway. Caleb let his eyes get accustomed to the dark and, listening intently, cleared each of the four rooms— "cutting the pie" as the sweeping routine was called in some circles, making sure no bad guys lurked in the corners of rooms.

A bed, a bureau, and a rickety chair with one broken spindle leg furnished the small bedroom.

The cold water in the bathroom worked, and Caleb hoped that the toilet flushed. He tested it, after checking it for snakes—or was it rats? He then mentally slapped himself for doing his over-the-top precautions. *Old wives' tale,* he thought. It flushed—sluggishly. There was no chance in hell that the tub along the bathroom's exterior wall would be useful.

There was one wooden chair in the front room. Through the cracked front room window, he had a view of the potholed street, along which he could make out two nonfunctional streetlights. The poles appeared as tilted stakes in the ground, stark against New Orleans's city glow. No houses faced his, and the closest shacks on his side of the street were at least two hundred yards or better away on either side. Yawning foundations gave evidence of dwellings having been there at one time. In the dark, he couldn't determine the causes of their demises. *Katrina most likely,* he thought, *or fire, perhaps.*

He sat on the single chair in the living room and tried his cell phone. It worked. Frank answered. "Frost here," Caleb said. "What's the news?"

"The truck's been picked up and is underway. Jake hasn't been able to plant the GPS yet, but he expects to do so at the first truck stop. So we'll be in business soon."

"Okay, thanks, Frank. Listen, I'm all checked in to the suite you arranged for me. I want to thank you very much. I hate to leave the luxury of the accommodations, but I'm going to town now to visit the restaurant. Oh, by the way, your man's a good one. He delivered."

"Zipperman's okay," Frank said. "Anything else?"

"No. I'll check for messages. When you speak to Jake, tell him that I'll give him a call tomorrow. I'm driving a pink Cadillac. As soon as the truck goes by me, I'll pull into the parade. He should then lag behind me, and I'll track the truck to wherever it goes to unload. He'll be my backup. When you tell me that the container is, let's say, fifteen miles away, I'll call him on his cell phone."

"Oh, hold on, Caleb," Frank said. "You got a call from Barney Flannery. He said to say that everything is as expected, no better, no worse, and that you are not to be concerned. Progress is assured. Call when you get back. End of message."

"Thanks, Frank. I'll give him a call. Talk to you later. Bye." Caleb didn't wait for Frank to sign off.

He dialed Barney Flannery at his clinic. "Barney," he said when the clinic director came on the line. "It's Caleb. How's it going with Rebecca?"

"Caleb. Nice to hear from you." His tone included "finally" in his comment. "I take it you're still out of town. I won't ask where, because you always lie to me anyhow. Well," he said, drawing the word out, "as for Rebecca ..." Another pause, a throat-clearing rumbled across the line. "There is never much good news to report the first few days or sometimes weeks, for that matter. However, we are prepared to be optimistic and suggest that there is some good news. Apparently, she had just shot up when she called you and had not been on a run as we feared. We do find her to be surprisingly communicative and somewhat interested in cooperating with us. Not sure whether that's to lull us or whether she really has had enough and wants to get better. Margie tends to feel that she is on the right track. But, as you know, Margie is a pure optimist. Frankly, Caleb, Reb still looks a mess from all the shit she's poked into her veins, if you'll excuse such a politically incorrect and totally unprofessional evaluation. Margie is right in her feeling that we can work with Reb and make some rapid progress in her physical state. We might even take a short walk in the fresh air. The mental profile is something else, buddy."

"Hey," Caleb said, "I know that you and Margie are doing the best you can. I just don't know how many times she can come back and look fresh again. You know the look they get from leading the life? Like grit has been ground into their skin. It just makes me sick when

I think about us before my folks were killed. Damn. You just can't recapture some things, can you? Tell me, Barney, has Rebecca talked about her dealer at all?"

"Yes. He's a biker from the Visigoths over in Alameda. He met her down on the Embarcadero by the Villancourt Fountains and gave her a taste some months ago. Sometimes, he doesn't answer his cell phone when she wants to score some shit. It seems that he travels or, for a dealer, is independent as hell. When they did have a meet, he actually rode his hog. The Harley 'vroom' is probably how he announces his arrival. In any event, Rebecca says the shit's really potent. Hardly stepped on apparently."

"Any physical description?" Caleb asked.

"He has a swastika bleached into his beard. He's white, of course; outlaw clubs tend to be racist. She doesn't know … or offer up a name, Caleb. She did say that she thought that he wore Visigoths' colors."

"Doesn't look like the guy is overly concerned about his cover while conducting illegal transactions, does it?" Caleb said.

"Yeah, well these pushers get a bit of a god complex and believe that they are above the law. You remember the old Tom Lehrer song, 'The Old Dope Peddler' and the line about … 'spreading powdered happiness'? They cannot conceive of one of their 'clientele' dropping a dime on them. Ratting out your dealer is not a smart thing to do either. You'll have to move her out of the area as soon as she leaves our door, you know?"

"Yeah, I do know," he said. "Probably back to New England, someplace up in Vermont. St. Johnsbury or Burlington. Good towns. I know a lawyer up there in Vermont. Could help her go to ground."

"Well, there's not too much more to tell at this point, Caleb. We're in the deconstruction stage right now. We'll rebuild in a few weeks. She should be ready to leave us in June or July perhaps, if all goes well."

"Thanks, Barney. Give my best to your lady. I appreciate the care."

"One last thought about this dealer. The Visigoths are not noted for dealing, like some of the other outlaw clubs. This could be a freelance deal for this dude. That makes him a dangerous guy to fuck with. He himself is vulnerable to the club by the same token. They operate with very strict command from the top. If this guy is freelancing and stealing from the club's business, he could be in trouble. Like I said, the Goths aren't known for dealing. Talk to you soon then, Caleb. Bye."

Caleb sat, looking at the phone in his hand. Humpty Dumpty sat on a wall. But Rebecca was going to be put back together again.

Feeling along the baseboard in the bedroom, he found an electric outlet. He plugged his electric razor in to test for current. *Damn,* he thought. No red "on" light appeared on the razor in his hand. *All the comforts of home. Yeah, right!*

Pulling his Ranger-rolled clothing from his suitcase, Caleb dressed in the dark for his scouting trip at Le Couteau Bleu. He took his suitcase and the Saints bag to the shed for safety's sake, hiding them with the Mossberg and the shells high up on a board shelf in the rafters. He slipped the Kimber into his belt in the small of his back and took his belt up a notch to secure the weapon in place. The bulk of the gun gave him a sense of security and preparedness for whatever the night ahead held.

18

It was nine thirty in the evening when Caleb presented himself to the maître'd of Le Couteau Bleu to be seated for dinner. He had reserved his table under his George Garland alias. The crowd in the restaurant on Rue Delancey was primarily tourist. Caleb pointed to a small table in a rear corner and the maître d' nodded, anticipating a gratuity for this accommodation of the guest's wishes. Caleb followed the man to his table. As he was seated, he asked if Collier Berwick, the owner, was in. The maître d' said that he hadn't seen Mr. Berwick that evening.

"If he does come in, I'd like to say hello to him," George Garland said. "If the opportunity comes up, of course." He slipped the maître d' a couple of twenty-dollar bills to ensure he remembered the request.

Upon returning to his post at the front door, the maître d' punched a button on the wall phone. A voice answered, and the maître d' reported that "The customer at table 22 asked to meet Mr. Berwick." The voice thanked him. A small camera mounted in a darkly tinted plastic dome above the front window of the restaurant turned silently toward table 22. In a room above the restaurant, a finger pressed zoom. George Garland's image was captured and rapidly processed.

Despite the dozen oysters Caleb had eaten at Félix, he felt obliged to opt for an appetizer. He chose cold vichyssoise and ordered a lamb dish, salad frissé, and crème brulée for dessert. Coffee and a snifter of Remy Martin VSOP completed his order. He signaled to his waiter and asked for directions to the restroom. He had seen the camera above the front window as soon as he had been seated. He knew that cameras were tracking his movements.

When Caleb returned to his table, a large, round man was seated in the chair facing his place. The man's hand cradled a snifter, warming the amber liquid with languid swirls. He didn't raise his head at Caleb's approach.

"And what can I do for you, Mr. … ahhh …what's your name again?" the man asked.

"Mr. Berwick, I assume?" Caleb said.

"You have me at a disadvantage. You are here in my restaurant asking for me, and as of yet, I have no idea who you are or why you want to speak with me."

"George Garland, Enid, Oklahoma," Caleb said offering his hand across the table. Berwick ignored it, giving a final swirl to his drink and lifting the snifter to his lips for a sip. Caleb slid into his chair, taking a closer look at the restaurateur. He was midthirties with broad shoulders and a small round head. He looked fitter than Caleb's initial impression—perhaps not so round after all. His wavy blond hair looked streaked and not by natural sunlight. His fingers clutching the snifter showed nails that were professionally manicured. His eyes were a bright blue. And unfriendly. He wore a soft and pampered appearance like a cape, concealing a much more rugged and dangerous interior, Caleb thought.

"And you want to speak to me, why?" His voice was softly accented with the tones of the South.

"Well, a fellow from San Francisco suggested I should try Le Couteau Bleu and say hello to you if I ever was in New Orleans. Here I am."

"And who was kind enough to recommend my restaurant?" Berwick said leaning forward, eyes intense and probing.

"I'm in the barbed-wire business and ship tons of wire around the country. Every now and then, I try to find a better price from my carriers. Transportation costs are really skyrocketing with this crap in the Middle East and so forth, you know?"

Berwick nodded.

"Anyway, I'm looking for a better price and I find a listing for Long Distance Freight, and that's how I came to meet Curtis Rathmann."

"Nice fellow, isn't he?" Berwick said. "Short guy, if I recall. Suspect he wears lifts in his shoes. Comes here once or twice a year for the conventions. You're here for a show out at the Morial Convention Center?"

"Yeah, farm convention this time, and I've got some customers up north of New Orleans. Like to drop in and press the flesh, good for business, you know?" Garland paused, running his hand through his hair. "It seems to me, Mr. Berwick, at least my recollection of Mr. Rathmann is that he was quite tall. Are there two of them in the company, like father and son? The Rathmann I met was young, maybe late twenties, early thirties, ya know? Mebbe there are two, you think?" Berwick made no response. He just kept staring at Garland.

"So," Garland continued, "I look for good restaurants when I come to town and thought I'd take Rathmann's suggestion. Try to avoid the rip-off joints, know what I mean?"

"So, what can I do for my friend Rathmann's friend, Garfield, is it?"

"No, no, no," Garland said raising his hands and waving, as if he were flicking lint from a suit. "It's Garland. George Garland. Lots of people make that mistake though. That damn cartoon cat's more memorable than I am, and that's for sure." Caleb made George Garland chuckle at his lame joke.

"So, Mr. George Garland, what can I do for you?" Berwick repeated without changing his expression. He twirled a dinner knife through his fingers with amazing dexterity.

The background noise filled a long silence at the table. Garland studied his plate as if trying to come up with something to ask Berwick to do for him.

Finally, he raised his head and, lowering his voice, leaned forward to get closer to Berwick. "Well, Curtis suggested that you might be able to direct me to a source for some specific fun of the nonhuman variety. The human entertainment I can take care of myself," he said with a wink.

"Assuming you don't mean animals, when you say nonhuman, I'm taking your meaning to be that you're talking illegal substances. Do you think I sell drugs out of my restaurant, Mr. Garland? Is that what Rathmann told you? Or are you simply guessing that in New Orleans, we are all engaged in the drug business?" Berwick's voice hissed across the table; his words soaked in controlled anger. He swallowed the last of his drink and stood. His chair tilted back. A passing waiter caught it before it hit the floor.

"You, sir, have come to the wrong place. Please accept my sincere thanks for visiting us," Berwick said, his gentle Southern accent oozing like honey. "Remember this meal, because it's your last at Le Couteau Bleu. Enjoy New Orleans … elsewhere. Good evening, sir." And Collier Berwick strode away through the swinging kitchen doors without a backward glance.

Caleb sat for a few moments before beckoning the waiter over and ordering another cognac. "George Garland" might have been intimidated into leaving in haste, but not Caleb Frost. When he finished his cognac, he called for the check and paid with Garland's Black AMEX card.

He scanned the country French décor on his way to the front door of the restaurant—the colorful serving plates displayed on shelves, the wine racks in armoires positioned among the tables, and the surveillance cameras in strategic locations. On his trip to the men's room, he had checked out the kitchen and taken a headcount of the employees he could see throughout the restaurant. When he reached the front door, the maître d' was less than cordial as he bade him *"Bon soir, monsieur."*

Strolling down the sidewalk toward Bourbon Street, the usual caution alarm was set off in Caleb's subconscious alerting him to be wary of his surroundings. With so many people on the street, he couldn't determine whether or not he had a tail. But he sensed it in his gut.

When he reached his parking place, he kept on walking past the Cadillac for a couple of blocks. New Orleans was a city of strollers, and even at eleven o'clock at night, he found it difficult to pick out the tail in the crowd. After doing a figure eight around two blocks, he winnowed the people behind him down to one character: a young man with huge shoulders and a challenging gait who looked like the busboy who had cleared his plates and filled his water glass during dinner.

Caleb picked up the pace as he neared the street where his car was parked. He had seen an alleyway, and when he reached it, he stepped into the deep shadows. Not three seconds later, the busboy rounded the corner. His head cracked the brick wall with a resounding *thwock*; Caleb had used the guy's wrist and elbow as a fulcrum to leverage him face-first into the alley wall. It wasn't until the bricks were scraping the enamel off his front teeth that the young man thought to scream. With that, Caleb pulled him back and reintroduced him to the wall with enough force to rattle his brains for a few minutes and give him a headache for the next three days. A combination of gravity and rubber knees took the boy to the brick alley. He collapsed with a soft exhalation of his breath—or perhaps a sigh of relief—hoping that the beating was concluded.

It was.

Caleb stepped over the prone body lying in the open drain running down the center of the alley. The young man's clothes were soaking up whatever gunk was leaking into the drain from the businesses backing up to the alley.

Caleb walked casually to his Cadillac heap, cranked the engine, and drove back to the Ninth Ward. It had been an evening well spent, although he doubted that, despite the excellent food, he would ever recommend Le Couteau Bleu. The day's objectives had been met.

19

Dawn came to New Orleans like an infusion of milk into dark tea. Barely observable and then blooming in a burst of light.

Caleb had not slept well. He had startled awake in the morning experiencing one of his "flock of crows" nightmares. In it, he was attacked by huge crows, whose long, black beaks were lined with razor sharp teeth. Increasingly, the crows gained the upper hand in the battle. His mother always appeared just as he was about to be overwhelmed and eaten alive. "Mom, no!" he would cry out as the crows' talons raked her arms stripping flesh and causing large rivulets of blood.

Just as a particularly large crow was fixing its talons on his mother's shoulders, Caleb would jerk awake, drenched in sweat and with tears on his cheeks. "Mom, Mommy," he would be saying out loud in a terrified voice—at least he thought he heard himself say those words. His revulsion of crows was deeply seated in his psyche. He knew the origin of his nightmares. It was all related to his parents' death and the discovery of their mutilated bodies in the forest.

In his teen years, the surrogate parents Thorndike had arranged to assist in raising Rebecca and him had him visit a psychologist, a woman, whose sympathy and professional ministrations had guided him toward an understanding, if not an eradication, of the nightmare events.

Each time he had a nightmare about the crows, it reinforced his determination to find his parents' killers.

As he tumbled out of his restless sleep, the translucence of the flyspecked shade covering the one window on the side of the tiny house alerted him to the fact that the day was well underway. He checked his watch and found that it was nine fifteen.

He kicked aside the blankets Zipperman had provided and rolled off the sagging mattress. Peering through the peephole in the front door, he looked to see what was doing in the neighborhood. Nothing. Not a soul, car, or, for all he knew, a mule. He had jammed the back of the one chair the front room boasted under the doorknob, and it was still securely in place. A quick check of the chair-locked back door showed no signs of attempted entry either. Safe as a bug in a rug. He was sure that if this place had had a rug there definitely would be a bug in it.

He understood Zipperman's choice for his safe house. It's strength was its invisibility. As cover, it was ideal. Far away from the places people might expect to find him and a totally indigenous location, one an outsider would have had trouble finding. There was nothing about the house to keep people out. The doors and walls would fall to a swift kick, and aside from the studs in the walls, there was nothing to stop a bullet from penetrating and possibly exiting through the opposite side, width or length-wise. As Frank had said, even the car, a devastated hunk of corroding metal, fit the place and was also invisible.

He dialed Frank.

"Hello, Caleb," Frank answered on the first ring. "We've been waiting for you to call. How goes it?"

Caleb double-checked his watch and saw that it was only seven twenty in San Francisco.

"Well, good morning to you, too. The reason I slept in was because the silk sheets on this feather bed lulled me into a sound sleep." Caleb laughed. He heard others laughing with him. "Who else is on the line at this ungodly hour?"

"Good morning, Caleb," he heard Irini's voice.

"And I'm here too," William Thorndike said.

"Ditto," Jake called from the corner of the room where Caleb figured he was sprawled on the couch.

"Well, a gang which conferences together, et cetera, et cetera, et cetera," Caleb quipped. "How are you, Mr. Thorndike?"

"I'm great. It's snowing like hell. Can't get out of my garage. And the forecast is for two feet by this afternoon. Aside from that, it's a typical Georgetown sort of day. Thanks for asking."

"Sorry to have reminded you, sir," Caleb said. "Shall we get to the updates?"

"Absolutely. Carry on, Caleb," Thorndike said. Caleb imagined him lazily turning the silver teaspoon in the Lennox china cup holding the second of the two cups of black coffee he drank each morning. At his age, his "skyrocketing age" as he put it to his few friends who were still alive, he found that caffeine seemed to have him visiting the bathroom more frequently than in years gone by. Few of his really good friends, former associates, had died of natural causes. The business did not promote longevity. After a contented sip or two, he would be ready for the meeting.

"I'm curious about the information Irini has gathered from her friend in low places," Thorndike said, piquing Caleb's interest as well.

"Well, it was a quite profitable information-gathering evening, sir," Irini began, ignoring Thorndike's dig at de Cordova.

The cartel man's limo had dropped her off at 2:30 a.m. at her home in San Mateo Park. To Jake, she looked as alert and as stylishly dressed as always. Irini had done some Pilates stretches, taken a hot shower, and was in her shop by 7:00 a.m. with an Il Piccolo Alto, triple-shot latté, heavily dusted with chocolate, in hand.

She picked up a piece of paper with handwritten notes on it. "My contact is an interesting phenomenon in the drug trade. He is a major drug entrepreneur in the employ of several of the Colombian cartel families. He represents their interests abroad and is socially engaged with senior diplomats and business types and miscellaneous movers and shakers in just about every one of the one hundred major industrial countries in the world. He also has inside information on the drug importers and distributors operating in the United States. His knowledge is encyclopedic.

"I learned that there is a *muy loco* guy playing at being a seventeenth-century warlord and modern-day drug producer in the Xinjiang Uighur autonomous region of western China. He may be the pain in the side that led the Chinese to confide in us about their problem. My contact does not give him long to survive, but, to date, his fortress and his Muslim soldiers have held off every attack the Chinese have made. Apparently, he has moles deep in the government who alert him when a show is on. The pack of mercenaries he has formed is under the command of a notorious Muslim bandit who is not prisoner-friendly. He enjoys beheading people."

Thorndike said, "There's something about those renegade people that makes them want to chop people's heads off. Damned if I can see the benefit. And I do know that it's not part of Islam."

"I'm not sure what 'Tit' and 'Tat' actually are," Jake said, "but in Iraq, when we caught some of these sword nuts, a few of our guys gave them 'Tit for Tat.' Of course, there were people who thought of it as unusual torture. 'Spose we should've given them hot chocolate and cookies to make them talk."

"Well," Irini continued, "my informant said that they have a thoroughly modern heroin-processing operation sequestered away deep in the mountains. Even if the Chinese could find it, they probably couldn't get to it by land or air."

"How does he export the drugs, Irini?" Frank asked.

"All my contact knew was they were importing into the United States' West Coast ports. In the past, these drugs came in through the East Coast ports."

"Everybody else still seems to do so," Caleb added.

"It's a progressive move by the industry," Frank rumbled. "I have more to add to that story as well."

"Hold that for a moment. Let's finish up with Irini's intel first, okay?"

"Anything else, Irini?" Caleb's mind's eye saw Thorndike comfortably ensconced in the depths of his leather chair in the Georgetown townhouse, snow swirling furiously outside his curtained windows, a space heater warming his feet under his desk.

Caleb noticed a small furrow develop in her forehead as she spoke. "I have not been able to tie this fruitcake in the mountains to the Eastern Partners' antique company deal in San Francisco specifically, but the pieces of the Chinese puzzle are beginning to become a bit clearer," she said.

"Thanks. As those pieces do come together, please keep us all informed," Caleb said. "Okay, Frank, what have you got?"

"We know that the antiques buyer and exporting company Asian Artifacts, working in Shanghai with the Partrains, is owned by Chen Wei Ming. Like all of these characters, he's an interesting specimen. This man Chen's background, allegiances, associations, and debts are a large ball of Chinese noodles. No beginning and no end. He is known to travel to the Xinjiang Uighurs autonomous region frequently, disappearing for a day or two during each trip. Despite the fact that he is one of only a few dozen truly significant Chinese businessmen with international ties and influence, he is on the Chinese government's watch list—more so than the average capitalistic Chinese businessman. I'm presenting information I've picked up from friends at Customs and Border Security."

"We'll try to have a better fix on Chen later today," Irini said. "Caleb, I do have some intel on our warlord's end product."

"Let's hear it," Caleb said, his voice tightening.

"Well, my source said that the Chinese producer wraps his product in bright-red plastic. On the street, it has become customary to ask if the shit they're buying is 'China Red,' excuse the vernacular, Mr. Thorndike."

"I know they call it 'shit,' Irini," Thorndike said with a smile in his tone. "I may be old, but I'm not fragile and I've been there and back." With a chuckle in his voice, he said, "Please don't patronize this old man, young lady."

"Sorry, sir. I won't ever again watch my language, sir," Irini replied with false contrition. Thorndike's delighted laugh bubbled across the expanse.

"The thing I wonder," Caleb said, avoiding a derailment of the discussion, "is if the distribution drops are into the New Orleans and possibly the upriver markets like Chicago, what might China Red be doing in the Bay Area?"

"Could it be that, if the bikers are indeed involved, that one of them is skimming from the loads and bringing a kilo or two back to freelance and make a few more bucks?" Frank suggested.

"I like that," Caleb said. "Dr. Barney Flannery had the same scenario. You said you were going to try to dig up some more about this gang over in Alameda, Frank. Let's hear what you've got."

"Irini is not the only member of this team who has sleazy associates," Frank said, grinning broadly.

Irini gave him a haughty look and then studied her flawless nails, looking for flaws.

"I contacted a couple of guys that Jake and I have gone on motorcycle club rides with," Frank continued. "They were probationers with the Angels at one time. They are always a bit blurry about any specifics. And, me being an African-American, they are always cautious about speaking with me about biker information. They never divulge anything they may have learned during their association with the Angels or whoever, regardless how casual, brief, or trivial. But, they did admit to hanging out in bars with the Visigoths and doing some rides. It seems that the Goths are as picky as the Angels about who gets taken into the brotherhood. Our acquaintances didn't make the cut. Therefore, they do take opportunities to bitch and blame."

"Put all of the stuff you've got on the Visigoths online will you? Colors, names," Caleb interjected.

"Will do this morning. Gimme a couple of hours, and you can login. I'll post the list of the Visigoths' chapter locations. All told, they have twenty-four active chapters and three in development," Frank said.

"These are not nice guys," he continued. "The run-of-the-mill MC gang member has a day job on an assembly line or a job even more boring. But when the colors come out of the lockers at quitting time, these fellows transform into their rotten selves. Recently, a guy, a Visigoth, offered my pals some China Red. Probably been stepped on like the Bataan Death March. Talcum powder might be better. But they dug it. He then hit them up for future business."

"You get a name?" Caleb asked. He shifted the phone from his right ear to his left.

"Yup. One of your standard colorful names. Catch this one. Bangalore. That's his street moniker."

"Sounds Indian," Irini said.

"Not in an outlaw motorcycle club!" Frank exclaimed. "They are, despite the layers of grime, pure white. They are not specifically racist, but they sure as hell wouldn't invite me into their organization. They are definitely segregationists. A trust thing, honor among white thieves," Frank said.

"So, Bangalore has been spreading heroin around locally, huh?"

"Yeah, Caleb. And he's not too smart. If my buds are able to find out about it, then he'll foul up sooner than later."

"Frank," Caleb said, "do your computer magic and access some information from the local law's data files about ol' Bangalore. Don't want to pop him just yet. Let's get to know him better and how he fits into the larger Visigoth scheme of things."

"I'll see what I can get," Frank said.

"My sister's doctor says that she described her dealer as having a black beard with a swastika bleached into it."

"Okay, sounds like you're moving along on the gang issues. Tell us about your adventures in N'awlins, Caleb," Thorndike said.

"Yes, sir," Caleb said. "I drew some attention last night from Mr. Collier Berwick, proprietor of Le Couteau Bleu. Good food, inquisitive human service, and a lot of electronic surveillance. I met Mr. Berwick and exchanged pleasantries. I mentioned that I knew Mr. Curtis Rathmann and things went south from that point on. I had company when I left, and I had to engage the tail roughly … so to speak."

"Is he still walking and talking, Caleb?" Thorndike's dry voice came down the line.

Caleb assured him that no cleanup crew was required. "This guy is not likely to protest to the NOPD."

"So the point is that they know you are in town," Irini said, "and suspect that you're not who you are purporting to be, right, 'George'?"

"And they are certainly looking for you. Did Zipperman give you some undercover clothes?" Frank asked.

Caleb looked down at his frayed chino pants, worn plaid shirt, and leather car coat. He wore a stingy-brim gray straw hat missing the hatband. The unshaved planes of his face made him appear unwashed as well. Actually, he was unwashed. *A smelly devil,* he thought to himself. True enough, there was no hot water in the shack and he was having doubts about the quality of the cold water. He had not brushed his teeth and felt the beginnings of slime. "Yeah," he said. "He gave me a fine wardrobe. And a beauty of a forty-five to accessorize my outfit."

"Send snaps," Irini suggested.

"Let's summarize," Caleb said. "Irini, great job with your contact. Work the Chinese angle now. Spend some time checking the Partrains' business, and find out more about this guy Chen Wei Ming if possible. Frank, please coordinate the information Mr. Thorndike's contacts come up with regarding Bangalore."

"And what mischief are you going to be up to today, Caleb?" Thorndike asked.

"I'm going to familiarize myself with the city. Get to know the streets and the quick ways to get around town. Drive out and check the routes into the city that they are most likely to use."

"I sense that the engagement is picking up intensity," Thorndike said. "I'm going to be talking to some government types tomorrow. I'll also see what additional information about this Chen individual we can roust out of the Chinese client. Talk to you all tomorrow?"

"Sure. Okay, folks, good work!" Caleb said and signed off the call.

20

The *Orient Star Maru* shouldered her way toward San Francisco Bay through the dense bank of sea fog hunkering outside the Golden Gate Bridge. To Wrath, astride his 1958 Panhead Harley high on a bluff overlooking San Francisco Bay, the *Orient Star* reminded him of a sumo wrestler preparing for combat. Sitting low, squatting in the water, she dominated whatever sea she sailed. Emerging through the gathering dusk, the ship appeared ghostlike as she made way soundlessly in the distance. Swirling ropes of sea fog grappled with her hull in a vain effort to prevent her from passing beneath the bridge into San Francisco Bay. The launch that had delivered the port pilot to steer the *Orient Star* home to Alameda was a tiny speck in the murky light alongside the towering sides of the world's largest "hicube" container ship.

Wrath trained his binoculars on the containers stacked high on the ship. He inhaled deeply, sucking in the odors from the brackish waters below. The *Orient Star* slipped under the iconic Golden Gate Bridge into the broad Bay waters, her heading set past the storied Alcatraz Island prison, past the green hulk of Angel Island, and under the Bay Bridge and onward toward the Oakland Estuary and the Port of Oakland docks. He mentally checked off phase two: the safe voyage to port. The ship was virtually at its berth.

The fun had just begun, he thought. Phase three was getting the container cleared through Customs and Border Protection at dockside. Next to loading the container in China, this was the riskiest part of the venture. One discovery by US Customs and Border

Protection would blow the deal out of the water. But Chen Wei Ming, the owner of Asian Artifacts in Shanghai, had developed such a level of confidence among the US customs people in China and Alameda that he had even been able to insert several of his own relatives into both the Chinese and the US customs services in Shanghai. Family ties meant that he knew when a random inspection was going to take place.

Chen Wei Ming's years of successful smuggling made him one of the "good guys" as far as the government agencies were concerned. Few containers from well-known companies were actually searched as they came into US ports. There was no regulation or revision to codes that was not scrupulously obeyed by Chen Wei Ming's company. In fact, Asian Artifacts' technology staff often made technical and procedural suggestions to the Chinese and American customs authorities. Many of these improvements had been implemented with good results by the United States.

The Port of Oakland would call the trucking company, Long Distance Freight, and assign a time slot for the pickup of the container designated for them. The call would be taken by the Visigoths. The Visigoth chapters along the route to New Orleans would be given a timetable for the container's trip. Each chapter would assign members to shepherd the truck safely through their territory, passing it off to the next chapter's bikers along the route.

Wrath was becoming concerned that the routine had in fact become too routine. Anything that operated as smoothly as his operation was sure to run into a snag sooner or later. Anticipating the possible snags occupied a great deal of his time.

As he watched the progress of the ship, arms resting on his machine's ape hanger handle bars, his thoughts turned to the Partrain people, the owners of Eastern Partners, LLC. Their snooping had caused him problems, problems that he took as warnings of trouble ahead for his operation. He had Creek deal with those problems as only he could. Wrath wasn't sure he really meant to have Mr. Partrain taken out permanently. Creek assured him that Mr. Partrain's body would be fish food well outside the Golden Gate, courtesy of the strong current below the surface. Creek's response to the question regarding his unilateral decision to kill Partrain was, "So, what's the problem?" Pulling at the rat's leg bone woven into his beard, he growled, "The guy was a pimple on our ass. I just pinched the pus outta him. You're welcome, dude. Jest doing my fuckin' job," he had said before stalking away in a huff.

Wrath wondered if Partrain's corpse might not be reeling in the wake of the *Orient Star* at that very moment. He fired up the Harley for the run back to Alameda and, gripping the ape hanger handle bars, roared off toward San Francisco and the Bay Bridge. The scheduled container pickup time would be coming through from the port operations people later that night.

21

Jake Corbett hurriedly prepared for his surveillance on the Port of Oakland docks. The word had come that dock space had opened up and the *Orient Star Maru* would be docking that evening and unloading tomorrow. He chose his observation point by referencing satellite pictures of the area. Frank had lifted the photographs from an internal NASA website. The satellite pictures helped him locate a jumble of discarded containers stacked like cast-off railroad toys. The images were so clear and the enlargements so close-up that Jake could see which containers had open doors facing the docks located one hundred yards away.

In preparation for his trip chasing the container the following day, Jake packed an M4 rifle plus a box of ammunition and cleaning supplies in a compartment he and Frank had constructed under the backseat of the Malibu. The M4 was smaller and less cumbersome than previous versions in the rifle series. There was room enough in the compartment to stash the state-of-the-art camera Frank had arranged to get from a resource in the Defense Advanced Research Projects Agency, DARPA. It was one of the weapons development agency's recent creations for the military. Among the troops, the agency was known as DARPA-Vader.

The KA-BAR knife and the Glock Frank had given him fit into a compartment inside the driver-side door panel within a couple of inches' reach. The cover to the compartment slipped down in response to thumb pressure against a small button built into the Malibu's steering wheel and concealed under the wheel's leather cover.

Jake packed his personal gear for the extended engagement: underwear for seven days, an equal number of white T-shirts, an assortment of shirts and sweatshirts, three pairs of jeans, shaving gear, and toothbrush and paste. These, he placed in a sports bag, which he threw into the trunk of the gray Malibu.

For the stakeout, he wrapped the "camera" in two thin but very warm blankets and stowed the bundle in a seaman's duffel bag. He added the KA-BAR, a wool sweater, and some water. A large bag of food Frank had prepared for him completed the provisions for the night. He slipped a pair of heavy-duty wire cutters into his pea jacket pocket.

After dark, dressed as a crewman in dark clothing, he drove to a public parking lot close to the port. Duffle on his shoulder, he walked along the perimeter fence against which the old containers were stacked. In the darkness, he was virtually invisible. With his snips, he cut a three-sided doorway for himself in the chain-link fence—the more convenient to exit in the morning.

Climbing up to the highest vantage point he could find, he settled on a container whose open rear doors gave him a beautiful view of the dock area. Lying in a prone firing position inside the container and out of sight in the dark recess, he would be able to watch and record the unloading operations. According to the intel report from Georgetown, the Asian Antiques container would be unloaded sometime between 0700 and 1000 the following morning. Shipyards were not noted for meeting the tight schedules they set for everyone else. It would be a waiting game for him and the truck drivers who had been assigned to haul the container to New Orleans.

He pulled the camera out of the duffle bag and sighted a target on the well-lit dock through the high-powered electronic scope. The camera, if it could be called that since it looked nothing like a traditional digital camera, comprised a long tube mounted on top of what appeared to be an M4 rifle stock. The tube was a transmissions device through which images were sent to a satellite miles above in the sky. The telescope was the lens of the camera and was integrated

China Red | 123

into the transmission device when it was attached to the stock with metal thumb screws making the connection inside the stock.

Acne scars on the man's face were visible through the scope. Jake Corbett gently squeezed the trigger. A soft "ziiiip" sounded in his ear. The young man caught in the crosshairs of the lens never knew. He continued penciling data onto a form on his clipboard. A close-up shot of the *Orient Star Maru's* name on the bow of the huge container ship followed.

Jake's cheek was warm against the stock. He sighted more targets. With a gentle pull on the camera's rifle-like trigger, the image in the scope's lens was transmitted to a communications satellite stationed miles above. A split second later, a click in the rifle's stock announced that the image had been received back on earth.

"You get those shots?" Jake asked into the headset microphone he wore, the boom next to the corner of his mouth.

"Got it. Hey, nice, sharp focus. No shaking. You give up drinking?" Frank said from in front of the team's communications and security controls set up in a corner of Caleb's living room. Jake knew that several monitors would be stacked in front of him.

"Frank, cut the crap. I'm lying outdoors, in a metal corrugated box, in February, and you're making jokes."

"Hey, baby," Frank said. "You all snug there? I guess a campfire would be out of the question, wouldn't it?"

"Actually, not a bad idea. This crate is all metal. If I could cover the end of the container facing the docks, I could safely have a fire."

"Yeah, but you can't. Well, I miss you here. We could share one of the cots Caleb provides his guests."

Jake chuckled happily. He was missed, and he was doing a job he loved. "Miss you," he said. "I'll call as soon as the action starts here. Night, Frankie, sleep tight."

He arranged the blankets on the corrugated steel floor of the container and fell asleep quickly. The vibrator alarm on his wristwatch would have him awake by 0630 in the morning.

22

Zhou Jing could feel her tiny toes digging into his back as she stepped carefully to the pressure points intended to relax and restore his spirit, as well as his muscles. He felt tension seep out of him. Sweat, like blood from knife thrusts, trickled from his naked body, coming to rest in puddles on the sheets. A long, gray braid curled like a boa constrictor around the wrinkled skin of his neck. The hole in the massage table upon which he lay circled his face, which had sharp features, unlike most of the Chinese in his family and among his retainers in the fortress. Elegant eyes slanting upward at the corners held the penetrating stare of a hawk. His mouth, slightly open with the pleasure of the moment, was usually compressed and severe. A bitter line.

The girl stepped off his back and with soft, warm hands gently urged him to roll over. As he did, she pressed opened his legs and knelt between his knees. Slowly, she excited his thighs with her tongue, softly circling her palms on his flat stomach, tracing tingling paths across his skin. Zhou Jing resisted the urge to pull her head up higher and labored to allow the excitement of his senses to course through his entire body. Her flicking tongue moved further up his thighs, and every fiber in him anticipated the moment when she would consume him. Her circling hands inched up his sides, pinched his nipples until they were erect, and then slid downward. One hand rested on his belly while the other moved down to take him in her small hand. She stroked him until he was as hard as steel, and then, tossing her head to throw back her long, silky hair, she took him into her warm, wet mouth. He exhaled and shuddered in absolute pleasure, undulating his hips to encourage the movement of her head.

The moment came when he reached down and grasped her shoulders to pull her on top of him. With a practiced move, she took him inside and, knowing him well, moved quickly, urgently, back and forth, riding his hips, hands on his knees behind her, while he squeezed her small breasts and rose beneath her, penetrating deeply. She moaned with unfeigned pleasure at his thrusts. He exalted at how wet she was and how her vaginal muscles grasped him so rhythmically. His mind wandered to Mei Mei, his mistress of so many years. Now at the age of fifty, she had responsibility for training the girls who serviced him. Every now and then, at difficult times, he would ask her to join him, for her kind of affection still pleased him. He called her, Ma Ma. Mommy. She cuddled him as he sucked at her breast. Sometimes, he sobbed.

The day's meeting with Chen Wei Ming from Shanghai flitted across his mind, but a change in the urgency of the girl's motion brought him back to the present—his awareness of his total penetration and his feeling of his motion inside her brought a groan from his gaping mouth.

His passionate explosion came abruptly, his face contorted in the pleasurable pain of release. Her arrival at her personal pleasure with him at the same moment pleased him, proof of his sexual prowess. She too was pleased with her performance; giving him such a strong release, she thought, *Mei Mei will be proud of me when I tell her the details.*

The girl lay across his chest, head snuggled against his neck. He felt the slick of sweat on her skin and believed that she, too, had achieved total fulfillment. After a few minutes, she slipped off him, her hand caressing and squeezing his withering erection as if to indicate her pleasure and desire for more intimacy. She brought warm, damp, lilac-scented cloths to wash him. As she dried him with soft toweling, his mental focus shifted to the issues he had to face that day.

He grew impatient to dress and return to his desk. He arose from the massage table, towering over the petite thirteen-year-old girl. He caressed both her breasts with the palms of his hands, squeezing them before he stepped away from her. Turning his back, he held out his arms so that she could rub him with oil to keep his skin soft and youthful. She stood on a stool to wind his hair in an oiled topknot. She then assisted him to dress in several layers of robes. He stepped into jewel-encrusted slippers. The girl helped him position the heavy, ornamental jewelry he would wear that day. He preened in the mirror on the wall, combing his drooping mustache and long goatee. In the purposely darkened glass, the wrinkles in his face were invisible to his searching eyes. He only saw a powerful warrior.

The girl, still naked, stood before him with eyes cast down. "Tomorrow, my lord?" she asked.

"Of course, little one, and ask Mei Mei to teach you another game we can play, will you?"

"Yes, my lord. Thank you, my lord. Have a blissful day, my lord," she said, her small hand reaching out tentatively to touch his. Then she backed away, head still bowed. She turned and skipped out of the room, bending to gather up a bright-red gown lying on the floor near the doorway. Zhou watched her go, his lips twitching in a wolfish smile. He felt himself respond to his memories of the past hour.

Striding after the girl's bare, pattering feet, he left his personal rooms, passing pairs of guards stationed at each doorway. Each guard wore armor made of lacquered black metal squares sewn onto a wool tunic and a fearsome, horned helmet. In the seventeenth century, they would have carried swords and spears; today, each wore an RPT machine gun slung over a shoulder ready to use to protect his warlord. Zhou Jing had designed the uniforms himself from pictures he had found in old books. The guards were not ethnic Chinese, but people from the Muslim Uighur population of the Xinjiang Uighur autonomous region in westernmost China, well beyond the protective reach of the Great Wall of China. These men were peasant Uighurs, descended from the Turkic peoples who had ruled this land for more than a thousand years. The Uighurs hated the Chinese for their oppression, genocide, and cruelty.

They were Muslims, persecuted in the past and the present by a succession of ethnic Chinese governments. Religious repression led to the closure of mosques, and, in some cases, they were burned to the ground. While elsewhere in China, there were many mosques, the Uighurs presented social problems and virulent secessionist rhetoric leading to much stricter controls by the government regarding the practice of Islam in the region.

Zhou had chosen them and taught them to fight, and they, in return, had sworn allegiance to him alone.

23

Zhou Jing entered the great hall of the fortress. The hall was draped with tapestries, war banners, and flags, and armaments were on display along the walls. In the center of the marble-floored hall, a large, intricately carved, teak desk sat on an oriental carpet. Zhou Jing's blood-red, silk robes bearing gold-embroidered images of fire-breathing dragons curling around his body rustled as he walked to his throne-like chair behind the ornate desk. His presence had a powerful, threatening effect.

A guard pulled out the throne chair for Zhou and assisted him to be seated. A tall woman in a brown-silk robe and black scarf wrapped around her head, obscuring her face except for her bright black eyes shining from the shadow of the scarf, served him tea in a delicate bone china cup. Imported Oreo cookies lined the rim of the saucer. Zhou's eyes bored into the eyes of each of the three men seated in front of him as the tips of his fingers twisted open the chocolate halves of the Oreo. A Sony laptop sat on a corner of the ancient desk. He tapped a key, and the meeting's agenda appeared on a large monitor positioned on the desk so that the four men could see it. Sitting erect on the edge of his seat, Zhou cleared his throat.

"Allow me to quickly reintroduce these honorable gentlemen to you, Chen Wei Ming," Zhou said to the man in the business suit seated before him. "I say 'honorable' in the sense that my presumption is that your loyalty …" He made an inclusive sweep of his hand. "… to our organization—to me—is as solid as the walls of this fortress." His eyes slid to the left to look directly at Mou Shilan. Mou bowed his head in response and then, raising his head high, looked Zhou straight in the eye and said, "Yes, my lord."

"Mou Shilan is my chief of security," Zhou said to Chen Wei Ming. Mou wore a traditional seventeenth-century Chinese army general's uniform. At his side was a curved scimitar, which was said to have sliced the heads off dozens of men and women in defense of his lord, Zhou. His Arab heritage showed in his narrow brown face and piercing black eyes. He wore the characteristic thick mustache across his upper lip. Mou loved his work and would not let anyone else share the pleasure he felt at cleaving meat and bone with his scimitar.

A Uighur from the surrounding area, Mou Shilan had proven his loyalty in the number of Chinese soldiers and freelance pirates he and his men had captured and summarily executed without benefit of discussion. Prisoners' elbows were bound behind them, and they were marched high into the surrounding mountains to a place where bloodstained rocks edged a sheer cliff. At the bottom of the cliff was a yawning crevice. The punishment meted out in this place was beheading. The severed heads of prisoners bounced and tumbled down the abrasive sides of the chasm and were funneled into a deep, subterranean cave awash in seeping water and liquefying remains. The heads were quickly followed by the detached bodies dripping blood. The stench was pervasive for miles around, and myth kept the local populace from approaching the area.

Next to Mou, in a pin-striped blue suit, blinding white shirt, British rep tie, and gleaming black business shoes, sat Chen Wei Ming. An alligator briefcase lay flat on his thighs. He had flown from Shanghai to visit Zhou. He bowed over the briefcase. "Yes, my lord." He managed the exporting business, Asian Artifacts. He was responsible for strategizing and implementing the smuggling of heroin to drug addicts in the United States. In this far western aerie, high in the craggy peaks of the Xinjiang Uighur autonomous region, he was totally out of place. The men on either side of him were among the least desirable people he could imagine associating with under any circumstances. The general was a homicidal nutcase, in his opinion, and the bumpkins whom Zhou referred to as his colleagues were, well, they were mud people. Both were Muslim slime. His upper-class Han Chinese sensibilities were rubbed raw when he came to this land. He suspected Zhou enjoyed his discomfort from having to be in the same room with the Muslim rabble he gathered around him.

The third man, Ma Ching Hong, sitting to Chen's left, had the swarthy skin of a desert nomad. Chen was right to see the lower class in him.

Ma had actually come from a mud hut to take his place in the palace fortress. He was determined that he was never going to return to the impoverished town in which he had been raised. Nor were his children—his sons. His hair was cut close to his square head. The full mustache under his hooked nose was trimmed precisely each morning by his wife. His work clothes were clean and pressed. He was responsible for raising and processing the poppies from which he produced superior heroin. He was convinced that he made the finest heroin in the world. Zhou had sent him to Afghanistan to learn the secrets of poppy farming. Despite the Chinese government's effort to destroy the poppy fields in the mountains, he was always able to gather sufficient quality and quantities of the precious "milk" for his hidden processing plants. He pressed the palms of his hands together and bowed to Zhou. "As Allah commands, my lord," he said.

A wolfish smile broke over Zhou's narrow face with these reassurances. "Welcome, my friends," he said beaming at the three. "We have much to discuss, and I don't wish to keep you from your tasks. Let's start with your report, Chen Wei Ming. How is our work progressing from your side of the operation?"

"My lord," Chen said, "I am pleased to inform you that the vessel, *Orient Star*, is approaching the American port of Oakland as we speak. It carries a container of Chinese antiquities plus five hundred kilos of my esteemed colleague, Ma Ching Hong's, finest product." Chen gave a small bow in the direction of Ma, whose face tried unsuccessfully to appear modest in the presence of this recognition.

"And the delivery system still eludes the American customs people?" Zhou asked.

"Yes, my lord. Ma Ching Hong, again, continues to amaze us with his ingenuity."

"What do you hear of the government's proposed attacks on our brothers of the Islamic faith?" Zhou asked. He indicated the two Uighurs with a wave of his hand, which gesture left his hand hovering over the teacup saucer. He selected another Oreo and split it in half, careful to avoid breaking the cookies with his long fingernails. He inspected the creamy center. With his lower teeth, he scraped and savored the cookie's cream, eyes watching Chen over the edge of the cookie. Zhou smacked his thin lips.

"There is no mention of Muslims or the Uighurs, per se, in the press, my lord. There is, however, considerable government vitriol about the insurgencies in western China. The government cannot identify the insurgents as Muslim, because China has profitable relations with many of the Middle Eastern Islamic states. According to the press, the insurgents are thought to be located in Xinjiang and in other smaller provinces along China's borders. The eight contiguous countries create other political issues for the government. There are calls for a major offensive against known strongholds. As preparations for campaigns are made, you may be assured of the fact that you will be the first to know."

"Finally," Chen continued, "I have some bad news to report. Our antiques customer, Albert Partrain of Eastern Partners, has met with an unfortunate accident and is believed to be dead. This terrible incident was preceded by Mr. Partrain's recent interest in the delivery procedures of his transportation company, Long Distance Freight. His disappearance and certain unpleasant testimony to the fact that he is probably dead have led to unfortunate inquiries by a number of law enforcement agencies. We have dealt with these local investigations in the past. This time, there is something different about some recent probes. My local people do not know where they are coming from. I am concerned, my lord."

"For the benefit of our colleagues here this morning, will you please review how our delivery system works?" Zhou asked.

"We pack the antiques in my warehouse in Shanghai. When your vegetable trucks arrive, we remove the product from beneath the truck's floorboards. All inspections of the container's contents take place before the RFID seals are put on the container doors by the US customs people in our plant."

Chen nodded. "We leave the antiques unwrapped for inspection, since both governments want to be sure that we are shipping ordinary antiques and not state-regulated antiques. We intentionally add some very fine antiques, which invite additional work for everybody. All of which distracts attention from our main objective. When all of the antiques have been cleared by our own government and the American government, we wrap them to protect the shipment and load the container." Chen leaned back comfortably in his chair before saying, "All of this right in front of them." He beamed, expecting a respectful response.

The Muslim dogs sat with their hands in their laps and blank expressions.

Chen caught an amused smirk on Zhou's face. "RFID stands for radio frequency identification," he continued, "and these RFID SmartTags communicate the contents of the container, breaches of the container, and its general security, and in cases where temperature or humidity is of concern, the tags will report environmental changes. The data is reported electronically to what are called 'readers.' Everything that needs to be known about the condition of the container and its contents is reported to the readers and therefore brought to our attention by radio on predetermined frequencies. As a rule, once we pass inspection in Shanghai, the container is never opened again until we do so to unload the contents. You understand so far?" he asked the two Muslims. He had passed their level of comprehension with his description of "RFID."

"Get to the delivery of our goods, please. How does that work?" Ma asked.

"Well, before the container arrives at its New Orleans destination, our drivers circumvent the electrical circuitry on the SmartTags and enter the container to remove the product. There is no report of the entry, and the delay is less than one hour. The truck then drives to the warehouse to unload the antiques. The product is transferred to small vans and delivered to our safe house for distribution to our customers … and our partners make sure that we get the money."

Zhou, fully aware of the procedures used to deliver his product to market, smiled. The business was simple: produce the purest heroin possible and sell to the highest bidder. The people who bought his heroin knew that it would kill a user if it were not "stepped on" several times to reduce its potency. "Stepping on" the product means adding ingredients that double, triple, or quadruple the initial volume. And since volume determined price, profits skyrocketed. The initial group of dealers would sell their processed product to other buyers who might—probably would—step on it again. An initial kilo of heroin would hit the market as several kilos.

The man from Harvard had proposed the business relationship to Zhou. The fellow had stressed that selling pure heroin was safer than selling the cut product. The business was dangerous enough without working at the street level. Better to deal with a few large distributors for a premium price for the raw product than get involved with the smalltime distributors who, more likely than not, were hopped-up drug users as well. Ambushes, betrayals, and the killings that resulted were acknowledged and were ever-present possibilities in any drug transaction. The man in America had pretty much solved that problem with a unique solution. Zhou admired the patience, attention to detail, and the conservative approach to business his American colleague applied to their mutual interests.

"I would also like to make one more comment, my lord," Chen said, bowing to Zhou. "Your idea to package the product in the beautiful red color you have chosen has led to our product being known as 'China Red.' On the street, the customers want to know if they are buying red heroin from China. A brilliant marketing decision, my lord!"

Zhou opened a desk drawer and lifted out a colorful silk fan, which he spread with a flick of his wrist. He fanned himself slowly, before answering, "You flatter me, Chen Wei Ming, but I thank you. I am pleased that our small idea has contributed to your success on our behalf. Red is the color of happiness, and I'm very happy in this business. My customers are happy," his long, gray goatee drooped across his collar when his mouth opened wide as he cackled his glee. "Everyone is happy, my friends. A good report, Chen."

Folding the fan and pointing it at Chen's chest, he said, "The news of the death of Mr. Partrain does distress us, however. He was an unwitting dupe, but a vital player in our business. His death was not necessary, in my opinion. Please go to the Golden Mountain, express your condolences to Mrs. Albert Partrain, and verify that our Asian Artifacts business relationship will continue with her. Offer assistance, if need be. Then speak with the man at the trucking company, Mr. Rathmann, and verify that his business with us will continue as well. You may tell him that we are very sorry to learn of Mr. Partrain's death and that we would like to learn the details. You should also investigate the nature of the probes into our business you mentioned. If you can identify the source and terminate it, please do so. That will be a favor to me personally, Chen."

"Yes, my lord," Chen said, bowing his head.

"And now, Mou, my brave general, what do you have in store should the Red Army be foolish enough to come to invade us. How sharp is your scimitar? Does your cave need food? Tell me in detail what you have in mind for our uninvited visitors." Zhou rubbed his hands in anticipation. Cheng felt decidedly ill. Ma's eyes blinked uncontrollably in his stoic, Uighur face.

24

At 9:15 a.m., a flatbed pulled alongside the *Orient Star Maru*. The huge arm of the dock crane stretched out high above the ship and reached down to the stack of containers and the specific container awaiting its grasp. Crewmen hustled to attach the container's rings to the crane's steel cables. Slowly, the crane's brute force overcame inertia, lifting the container from the deck.

From his position in the rusting heap of containers, Jake shot pictures of the truck, its license plates, and the container markings as it soared high in the morning sunlight. The crane's operator swung it with hardly any sway to settle perfectly on the waiting truck's chassis bed. Dock workers ran forward to detach the crane's grip.

Most of Jake's photographs were of the driver and his helper. The driver had a full beard and a baseball cap worn backward on his head, giving a full frontal view of his craggy face. He was a muscular guy, but he seemed diminutive next to the tractor and the container hovering over his head. His co-driver sported a drooping mustache and wore tan work clothes over a roly-poly body. A crunched-up cowboy hat obscured his face. Jake followed him through the lens of the camera waiting for sunlight to get under the brim of the hat and give him a decent shot.

Within seconds of uploading the photos Jake took of the drivers, Frank's screen lit up with FBI pictures and information. The identifications of the two men Jake's scope had photographed were completed and rap sheets attached. He forwarded the intel on to William Thorndike in Georgetown and called Irini to come up to look at the material.

Jake's cell phone vibrated in his shirt pocket. Frank told him that the pictures were coming in perfectly and that he was running them through a patch he had created on the FBI's files—unauthorized of course. Jake knew that his partner's illegal hacking activities were simply all in a day's work.

Jake Corbett set his twenty-ounce paper cup of coffee in the Chevy Malibu's cup holder. Two blueberry scones were in a paper bag on the passenger seat close at hand. The sun was warm on his knuckles as he gunned the gray Chevy into the flow of the late-morning traffic heading south from Alameda on 880. The sky was a clear blue. *This is what California's all about,* he thought tromping on the accelerator. February and the sun was warming. Zigzagging through traffic, he made good time getting to 580 heading east. He checked in with Frank.

"Hey, big fella," Frank's big, warm voice resonated over the Blue Ant attached to the Malibu's visor. "Haven't spoken to you in ages. At least twenty or thirty minutes. Homesick already, baby?"

"Nah, just trying to make you think that I'm not having any fun and miss your home cookin'."

"So, you liked the little camera I got you?" Frank asked. "Your shots were almost professional. Some were even in focus."

"My ass, they are professional quality and should be award winners. But, listen, if Santa Claus was as good as you were, last night would have been my Kodak Christmas. Yeah, I liked the camera just fine. It's under the car's backseat in the locker with the pea shooter. I can see the possible need for the M4, but I hope I don't need the Glock or the KA-BAR."

"Want my man well protected," Frank said, shuffling through the photos on his screen. "Don't get tangled up with the law down there, if you can avoid it. They find these weapons they're going to make a pot full of trouble for us. They'll put you away for safekeeping."

"C'mon, Mommy!" Jake laughed, passing a couple of cars going the speed limit. "I've tidied up everything, and the interior is clean as a whistle. I'm secure from a better-than-casual search."

"Well, I'm not kidding about wanting you safe. I'm not there covering your butt. You recall the party in Somalia?"

"Yeah, I remember Somalia," Jake said, settling his shades on his nose. "How often do I have to thank you for that one, Frank?"

"Just remember who's got your back. Like always, Jake."

"Memorable firefights we have known, huh?"

"Back to business," Frank said, pushing aside the memories of the ambush in Somalia and the casualties they suffered. "How long before you catch up to the truck?"

"I figure I'm just a few miles, maybe ten minutes, behind them. I stopped to pick up some coffee. When I get onto I-5 in a half hour, I'll ratchet it up a notch and should have them in my sights in no time," Jake said, extricating a scone from the bag.

"We've checked them out through the DMV," Frank said. "Irini learned that they both have clean driving records, which tells me that they actually do follow the law. They won't be going too much over the speed limit. Everything taken into consideration, a professional driver will average about fifty-five miles per hour, including some mandatory stops for weigh stations and stops for food and sleeping. They do have two drivers, so it may be a long haul for you driving solo. That bothers me. Maybe they'll take a sleep break. I have the feeling that they follow the law perfectly, even to the extent that they may take longer than other truckers just to be safe."

"I wish we could have gotten the GPS tracker stuck on the truck back in Alameda. I could really hang back a distance."

"Yeah, well, we didn't. Shoulda, coulda, woulda, eh? So what's your plan?"

"I'm thinking that I'll get ahead of them and make it to the first big truck stop and wait to see if they stop. I'll stick the GPS on there. If they don't stop, I'll leapfrog them to the next."

"Gimme a call when you get it on, okay?"

"Yessir, Mr. Boss," Jake said signing off the call. He settled his rear more comfortably in the driver's seat and slipped a ZZ Top CD into the player for some "Cheap Sunglasses" Texas rock.

Jake loved the I-5 Interstate highway. Cars of all types hooked up in mini-convoys. At first, the lowly Malibu was suspect to the other drivers. The super-charged mill under the hood soon showed them that it was a player in this pickup game of speed and collaboration. They blasted along in and out of traffic at eighty to ninety miles per hour. Rarely would the convoy positions in the line change, as if the order were preordained. The rhythm, the sway of the line around the slower cars on the highway, the apparent teamwork was satisfying to the drivers. They swept by two guys on motorcycles who glowered as they were buffeted by the wake the speeding cars left behind. The bike riders exchanged glances but stayed steady in their speed.

The convoy had come upon the riders so quickly that Jake had not caught the colors on their clothing. In a few miles, the convoy passed a brightly painted red container truck. The golden dragon on the side was entwined with a company name, "Asian Artifacts."

Jake dropped out of the convoy at Exit 58 to the Buttonwillow Travel Center truck stop. As he had hoped, a few minutes later, the golden dragon on the red container truck pulled in and parked among the other semis lined up near the Country Pride diner. Jake waited in his parking slot among the vacationers' and business travelers' vehicles, while the two trucks' drivers climbed down from the cab and strolled to the restaurant's entrance. When he saw the drivers seat themselves at a table, Jake walked through the canyons of trucks until he was beside the Asian Artifacts container. He quickly squatted and stuck the magnetic GPS tracking device on the inside of the chassis' side rail and up close to the floor of the container.

Jake was entering the restaurant when two motorcyclists wheeled into the parking area. He couldn't tell if they were the two he and the other cars had passed a few minutes before. They rolled by him surveying the lot. Jake was able to make out the colors on the back of their vests. The Visigoths' name and death's head were easily visible.

The bottom rockers showed them to be members of the Fremont chapter. They braked in front of the Asian Artifacts truck, checking it out, and then circled around the parking lot to take up a position close to the truck-stop entrance. They were the outriders protecting the truck, just in case it needed any protection. And now they were on sentinel duty, while the drivers refreshed themselves.

Jake passed the two truckers as they were ordering their food. The waitress seemed to be auditioning for a ride out of town the way she giggled at their banter and shook her head making her hair swirl. Jake used the restroom and then ordered a double cheeseburger, coleslaw, and a root beer at the counter. He ate quickly and left to take up his own sentinel duties waiting in the Malibu for the drivers to take the road.

"It's on the rig. We are at the Buttonwillow Travel Center in Buttonwillow just off I-5," Jake reported to Frank.

"Okay. Good job. I'm picking up the locator signal. I see it. I see it," Frank muttered into his headset boom.

"Oh, yeah? What is 'it' doing?"

"Don't tempt me to tell you, baby. Don't start something you are definitely not in a position to finish."

"Yeah, you're right," Jake said. "I'm in the parking lot watching these bozos stuff their faces. One of them has a laptop out and is tapping away to someone."

"Probably just reporting in like you."

"Yup. Two guards have been following. Passed them a number of miles back. They maintained their distance and are now sitting at the entrance watching for hijackers, I suppose. They're from the Fremont chapter according to their colors. Their bikes are a Flathead and a Fat Boy. They must have changed guard shifts because the first two guys were on Shovelheads and wore Alameda colors. Good-looking machines these guys have got. I'm envious. Maybe I'll join up. Whaddya think?"

"May we talk business and reality here? Pictures? Got any?" Frank said, ignoring Jake's banter. He knew that Jake was getting tense over his situation. In the SEALs, it was Jake who would introduce humor into serious combat situations to ease his tension.

"Want 'em? Well, okay then. Give me a minute to get the lighting set up," Jake said.

"Yeah, you and God get the lights set up. If you have nothing better to do, partner, take a few shots. I'm at your service to ID the buggers."

"Hold on while I get the seat open," Jake said as he turned and fumbled to get a finger on the release latch to open the locker under the rear seat. With a soft "click" the latch released and he was able to get his fingers into the space and lift the seat.

Jake took a number of shots of the bikers and sent them to Frank. "Got 'em," Frank said. "I'll let you know who your traveling companions are. Call you later. Ciao."

Twenty minutes later, the Asian Antiques truck pulled out from the lot onto the highway. Jake let the two outriders enter the freeway ahead of him before he joined the parade moving south toward the junction with I-10 East.

25

Mrs. Cheryl Partrain was the poster girl for the adage that women can never be too thin or too rich. In the San Francisco, Los Angeles, and Washington society columns, cameras added just enough weight to make her look fit and especially attractive among the many women who lacked either the genes or the desire to maintain their physical beauty. Her blonde, pageboy cut became Cheryl Partrain's trademark. She was readily identifiable by her hairstyle in the midst of the crowds at the galas she and her husband, Albert, had attended and in the photographs in the following day's press reports of the events.

Today, however, as Chen Wei Ming, who had known the Partrains for twenty years, sat in the Partrain home in Hillsborough, he found her wan and seemingly ill. The skin around her eyes and jaw was loose and without sufficient tightness to keep her appearance youthful. He tried to hide his surprise, but Mrs. Partrain's intuition picked up on his reaction to her appearance.

She smiled ruefully and said, "I know I look poorly, Mr. Chen, but it has been a trying time since, since Albert …" She paused staring at her thin, veined hands, fingers interlaced and clutching each other in her lap. "… disappeared," she finished in a whisper. Looking up, she said, "We appreciate your coming. Yes, *we* …" She paused. "Albert and I, we appreciate your coming this distance to offer me support. It's the sort of regard and concern we have come to expect from you. Your generosity is welcome during these very distressing days."

"It was all I could do," Chen said. "I would not be a friend to do otherwise." His hand strayed across hers, and he gently patted her slender wrist.

"Well," she said, sitting up straight in her chair, adjusting herself and her mind to deal with the business discussion at hand, "we must move forward and maintain our perspective." Reaching for her teacup, she gave Chen a small smile. He sat in front of her, knees together, erect, saucer holding his teacup perfectly motionless, his leather briefcase by his side—the perfect Chinese businessman.

The walls of the day room at the back of the Partrains' mansion in which they sat were painted a bold yellow. The room's furnishings were Chinese, acquired by Albert and Cheryl Partrain during their antique-buying trips to China. French doors gave access to a flagstone patio alongside of which was a fifty-yard-long Olympic-length lap pool. Beyond the pool, closely trimmed lawns led down a slight decline into woods fifty yards beyond the house. Chen knew that thirty-five yards further into the woods, an eight-foot-tall stone wall stood guard. There was electrified wire, and coils of razor wire festooned the top. A complete sensor system, lying inside and outside along the wall, fed into the Hillsborough police security computer server. Security in Hillsborough was exceptionally high, so much so that by nightfall, the residents were essentially in prisons of their own design.

"We have much to discuss, Mrs. Partrain," Chen offered softly. "When you feel up to it, of course."

Cheryl Partrain's head jerked up. "What?" Her mind had been far away. She had, in fact, been thinking business rather than about her loss. Since the police had advised her that it looked unlikely that Albert would be returned alive, if at all, given the amount of time that had passed, she had pretty much assigned her husband of forty-eight years to the past. There would be a memorial service at St. Thomas's Episcopal Church in Burlingame. She would wear the mourning widow role for the expected period of time. She had also called in the company accountants and lawyers and advised them to assume the worst regarding her husband's prospects for returning to her. She had instructed them to prepare for her sole ownership and management of Eastern Partners. Albert had left his share of the company to her, so only the formalities remained.

"Do you have any idea about the circumstances of your husband's disappearance?" he asked and paused for a moment. Then he said, "Something you have not told the police, perhaps?"

Chen watched her nervous gesture, as she smoothed the fabric of her skirt, a delaying tactic she employed when she was searching for an appropriate response. "No," she said, clasping her hands in her lap. "The police have a credible witness who recognized Albert. This witness said that he saw Albert entering a white van with a large bearded man wearing a vest of some sort. It was dusk, and the witness's eyesight is not the best. He thought there was some sort of design on the back of the vest, but he could not make it out. It seemed odd to the witness that Albert, who was in a business suit, crawled into the van on his hands and knees through the side door rather than sitting in the front passenger seat. The big man climbed in after him and slid the door closed. The van drove off. End of story, I'm afraid."

She sighed, her gaze focused on her hands folded in her lap. Chen had noted the liver spots. A sign of aging and, he feared, an indication of weakness.

"No further identification of the vehicle?" Chen asked.

She shook her head. "He had been at the office, you know … working as usual. On his way home," she said, "it gets dark here around four thirty in the afternoon these days and the light was not good."

"Why do your police feel that Albert has come to harm?" Chen paused, struck by the callousness of his own words. "I mean," he said trying to soften the question, "why do they think that, despite the obvious misfortune poor Albert has suffered, he may not be coming back at all?"

Cheryl Partrain bowed her head as if in deep thought; her hair fell to shelter her face from view. Chen could see a thin gray root line along the part. "They feel that there actually was a message sent," she said from behind the curtain of hair. "They feel that since there was no follow-up after the ahhh, you know, the … ahhh … delivery of his … his fingers," she faltered and drew a deep breath, wiggling her own fingers a bit as she struggled to say the words. "The police think that we will hear no more. No ransom demand, no demand … no communications at all. And, no, before you ask, I haven't offered them much insight into our business. It seems that this all amounts to an assumption on the murderer's part …" She paused again, apparently thinking about her new burdens and shaping her words. "That assumption being … that I should somehow know what to do without being told."

Chen spoke slowly, confidentially, almost in a whisper, "And do you, my dear Mrs. Partrain? Do you know what they want and what you should do?"

"Yes. Yes, I think I do know. They want to be left alone. They were telling us to stop looking around. Poor Albert's fingers were the message to stop poking."

"Who wants to be left alone?" Chen pressed, eager to learn what she knew or thought she knew.

"I told the police that we suspected that someone was tampering with our shipments, but that we could not determine who, where, or how, since the containers are sealed in China under the noses of both US and Chinese customs authorities and the shipment contents were arriving without signs of tampering. None of our goods are missing from the containers. No damages and the insurance companies have no interest until something goes missing or is damaged in transit."

"I cannot believe that the containers have been compromised," Chen said with firm assurance, "since you have the GPS system tracking your containers in your office, do you not?"

"Of course, we do. You know how it works. You devised most of it," she said a bit snappishly. "And you mounted the RFID monitors collecting the data generated by the truck."

"So, Albert was suspicious," Chen said. "What did he do, and whom did he suspect?"

"He's always been a do-it-yourself man. From plumbing to keeping our books …" She smiled inwardly, remembering battles over pipes and leaks. "He decided that there was something about the carrier— you know, Mr. Rathmann's operation, Long Distance Freight. They have the container in their possession from dockside in Alameda through to New Orleans. So …" She paused for another long breath and a sip of lukewarm tea. "Albert made some inquiries, background checks with Better Business, local police departments, some of our acquaintances in the political arena. He also contacted other carriers to ask for bids, just in case a problem with LDF arose."

"Mrs. Partrain, I recommended Long Distance Freight. If they have been less than adequate and, worst of all, dishonest, I am responsible and I shall insist on speaking directly to Mr. Rathmann on the subject," Chen said.

"Mr. Chen? May I speak frankly, in confidence?"

"Of course, dear lady. Please tell me how I may be of assistance."

"I have no intention of changing Eastern Partners. We shall continue to be a good customer and partner to you. I also rely on your judgment. While I want Albert's killer caught and dealt with—perhaps you can help in that regard—I have no intention of dismantling a business that has served us all well for twenty years."

"Your strength is impressive, madam," Chen said bowing slightly at the waist. "I have no doubt that you can manage Eastern Partners, and we stand ready to help in any way possible." He relaxed a bit and sat back in his chair regarding Mrs. Partrain through half-closed eyes. "And your thoughts on continuing to investigate Long Distance Freight?" he asked.

"I think we rely too much on technology, don't you, Mr. Chen? It was only a blip in time that my husband noticed. And now he's gone," Cheryl Partrain said, reaching for the teapot.

26

"The trip to New Orleans is unavoidable," Curtis Rathmann said as Chen settled in his seat. "Sorry it came up during your visit, Mr. Chen."

"Of course. Business always comes first," Chen Wei Ming said, bowing slightly in the direction of the younger man. Chen had left Mrs. Partrain an hour earlier, intent on finding out what damage had been done to his export business from the man who was at the center of the distribution and collection operations. Despite the fact that Curtis Rathmann had devised the overall plan, neither Zhou Jing nor Chen felt any respect for this young foreigner. Perhaps they did not understand the ways of this Western country, but they knew a brash, uncultured criminal when they saw one. Chen's forced smile was broad.

"You are right, Mr. Chen, and the trip does involve our business."

"Problems?"

Chen followed Rathmann's gaze around his office. It had all the trappings of a legitimate freight carrier's office—scarred desk and wall shelves filled with bills of lading, drivers' reports, route maps. There were three mismatched wooden chairs for guests and a side-split leather swivel chair behind the desk, which Rathmann used as his desk chair. The only seemingly new piece of furniture in the room was a large couch with several big pillows. It sat under the window overlooking the street, four stories below. The fractured street surface was lined by warehouses—blank facades, small name plates or none, painted-out windows, and recessed doors with no handles.

Outside Rathmann's office, there was a decently appointed reception area and his right-hand girl, Cleo Solchow, who, Chen knew, aside from her intimate tasks for Curtis Rathmann, served as receptionist and a delightful first introduction to visitors. The report Chen had commissioned from a Boston detective service prior to entering into business with the young man said that Rathmann had met Cleo in Boston while he was at Harvard. She was attending Boston College majoring in biochemistry. They became roommates, sharing an apartment on Charles Street at the bottom of the Beacon Hill slope.

Cleo was apparently a high-maintenance companion, to say the least, but Rathmann's full scholarship and the revenue generated by his various side interests allowed him to afford their lifestyle easily enough. It wasn't only money that kept her on the straight and narrow in their relationship. Her addictions to Nordstrom, Bébé, and the lingerie outlets selling thongs, uplift bras, camisoles, and shoes from Italy and Argentina were secondary to her reliance on prescription drugs. Rathmann was a good provider in that regard as well.

When Rathmann graduated from the Harvard B School, he moved his operations to San Francisco. He brought her along as an employee and an on-the-spur-of-the-moment lover. They had evolved past sex as the prime mover as in their former steamy relationship. Drugs were Cleo's focus. The demands of Rathmann's business had his full attention. He paid her six figures a year to maintain her habits and her cooperation. As long as the money and the drugs were hers—she was his. It was a trade-off they both understood.

"Let's just say that in recent days, we are drawing some attention." Rathmann swiveled his chair back and forth, elbows on the arms, fingers steepled at his lips.

Chen noticed that Rathmann's fingernails seemed to have half-moons of dirt embedded under the nails. The whorls of his fingertips were dark and seemed to be grimy. Aside from being offensive to the Chinese gentleman, the dirt also seemed incongruous with the man's attire. He had on a gold-buttoned, dark-blue blazer; cream-colored, button-down business shirt; gray slacks; and highly polished loafers. Rathmann's long, well-washed and brushed hair was worn in a ponytail hanging down his back, well below his shoulders. It was held in place by a band, which Chen's experienced eye could see was solid gold.

"I don't like uninvited attention, Mr. Chen," Rathmann continued.

"The apparent murder of Mr. Partrain?" Mr. Chen ventured. "Do you think that his unfortunate circumstances led to these inquiries? And if so, how do you intend to deal with them?"

"You say the old lady is going to continue doing business without pressing for a resolution, for any closure?" Rathmann asked.

"Yes, we are most fortunate to be working with a woman who understands how the world makes its way," Chen said. "I would be most upset if anything were to happen to her, you understand? Zhou Jing would be very upset. He fancies her in his own unique way. He finds her charming. Never met her, of course, but he … well, he fancies her."

"Any blonde in a storm, huh?"

"I don't understand. An Americanism?"

Rathmann snapped, his mood changing abruptly. "Our wannabe warlord has a taste for blonde women is what it means, Chen. He wants to fuck Cheryl is what it means."

"My apologies for not understanding," Chen soothed, absorbing the verbal assault with increasing distaste for the thug across from him. Despite Rathmann's elegant appearance, the uncouth beast under the thin crust of civility was apparent. "Yes, I think your observation is correct. He finds Mrs. Partrain of interest."

"Interest, my foot. All he wants is to get her in the sack. He is one fucking badass. Crazy, you know what I mean? She's a fucking seventy-year-old, wrinkled-up broad. He's gaga over press photos. Absolutely fuckin' crazy and you …" Rathmann pointed a grimy finger at Chen. "You put up with that shit."

"Mr. Rathmann, Zhou Jing is a well-respected businessman with many connections in Beijing. His family is one of the oldest families in China. You should not speak that way of him," Chen challenged, defending a man whom he knew to be tottering on the brink of total madness. He thought to himself that he was surrounded by Muslim killers on the one hand and American criminals on the other. Business was presenting such problems of diplomacy at a rapidly increasing rate as the global economy expanded.

"Hold on, buddy," Rathmann said, leaning forward and again pointing a finger at Chen's face, his own countenance achieving an alarming reddening. "Let's get this straight. I brought this deal to you in Shanghai. I found your nutcase, Zhou Jing, hiding on his mountaintop, and I have all the risk in picking up and delivering the shit. Above all, I collect the money that goes back to you and Jing-a-ling. Don't you ever forget that," he said pounding the desk with his fist. "Without me and my organization, you'd still be smuggling cheap jade."

Chen sat pinned to his chair by the ferocity of Rathmann's words. He felt demeaned. The words stung like hornets. He wished for a blade with which to slit this impudent young man's throat, cut out his arrogant tongue, and ship it in homage to Zhou Jing. Instead, he bowed his head, offering subservience in response. It galled him.

"Now, to answer your question about problems," Rathmann said, instantly dropping the consuming fury and presenting a calm, reasonable demeanor. "We have had a couple of incidents, which may be unconnected, but which occurred almost simultaneously on this shipment. On the road to New Orleans, in Arizona actually, we feel that the truck is being followed. Some of our boys are checking that out. If it turns out that there is something hinky about the guy in the car, I've instructed my men to deal with it. Secondly, in New Orleans, my name was used in my partner's establishment."

"I was under the impression that your connection with this establishment was a well-guarded secret," Chen said.

"Right. I never mention it to anyone, nor does my partner. One of our boys followed the man in question and had the shit kicked outta him. There seems to be an inordinate amount of incapacitating going on," Rathmann mused, smiling with a twitch of his lips at his play with the word *incapacitating*. The smile left his face as quickly as it had come. "And then, the guy who we're trying to get a line on, the guy who clobbered our man and knows my name, disappears."

Emboldened by being included in some of the details, Chen asked, "Is that all that has happened?"

"No," Rathmann said. "A couple of nights ago, a major player in the Colombian drug market, Jose Maria Jimenez de Cordova, had dinner with a beautiful woman at The Marquis Room in the Cheshire Hotel here in San Francisco. We know who he is, but the woman is someone we don't know. The conversation, as best the waiter, an associate of ours, could overhear it, was not so much personal as it was about business. The drug business. The woman mentioned one of the local motorcycle clubs at some point, and our waiter called me."

"And this woman," Chen said. "She is important, do you think?"

"Don't know yet. She spent some time in this guy de Cordova's suite. Early this morning, his limo took her home to San Mateo down the Peninsula. No names on the mailboxes. My idiots didn't bother to stay and tail her this morning, so we have no idea what make car she drives, where she goes. Nada, baby. And it bothers me that this dude from Colombia is even in town. His being here, the woman's curiosity about the motorcycle club, the incident on the road, and the business in New Orleans add up to a major irritation for me and our operation."

"So, anything I can do to help, Mr. Rathmann?"

Rathmann stared at Chen pondering the benefits and risks involved in including the Chinese businessman in their local activities. "Perhaps you could be useful. Find out more about this woman." He pulled open a desk drawer, withdrew a manila envelope, and slid it across the desk to Chen. "Here's what we were able to get. The waiter took a few shots of her with his phone. And here's the address from the guy who followed her. A hell of a piece of ass, as you'll see. Pick her up tomorrow morning and follow her to wherever she goes. Call my cell as soon as you know anything."

"Yes, I can do that," Chen said. "I already have a rental car, and I do know the area fairly well. Yes, I will be glad to assist you."

"I should be back from New Orleans by the day after tomorrow, for sure," Rathmann said. "We'll meet here to discuss the current situation and what you've learned about the woman. Some of my boys'll keep an eye on the Colombian. We'll also discuss the next shipment. I think we should max our capacity. The market can absorb whatever we can bring in. 'Horse' is getting big again. Shootin' and smokin'. How much product can Zhou provide by next month?"

"No doubt we can double the kilos we ship. I'll contact Zhou tonight."

"Please give my favorite warlord my regards and very best wishes for his good health," Rathmann said in his most sincere voice. "I'll also have a coupla cases of Oreos dropped off at your hotel for you to take back as a gift."

"I shall mention your good wishes, sir," Chen promised. "The cookies will make an excellent surprise. He will be most appreciative."

Rathmann stood up. Chen rose, feeling dwarfed in front of this towering white man with freezer-cold eyes. Without offering his hand, Rathmann led the Chinese businessman to the office door. Cleo took the handoff and led him to the front door of the office. He willingly followed her enticingly swaying bottom. Her Anne Taylor gray suit's skirt was stretched skintight across her well-defined rear. As he passed through her trail of perfume and entered the wood-floored hallway, he heard the hard click of a deadbolt being thrown, followed by the clatter of the thin slat blinds on the window next to the office door being closed.

"A funny little man," Cleo said, turning from the closed venetian blind and stepping close to Rathmann.

"A dangerous, funny little man," Rathmann agreed. His hands pulled her roughly against him for a kiss. His flaring anger with Chen had left him aroused. Cleo's hand fondled him, feeling his immediate response.

––––––––––––

An hour after he left Rathmann's office, Chen was back in his hotel room near Chinatown in downtown San Francisco. Sitting on his bed, photos spread out, he contemplated the images of one of the most beautiful women he had ever seen. Elegance defined her as he tried to put words to his impressions. Her dark hair coiffed high on her head to fully reveal her oval face, large black eyes stared at him from beneath arched eyebrows. Her lips, smiling at the man she was with, the cartel man, de Cordova, made him want to crush them with his own lips.

In one shot, she and de Cordova were standing, and he could see she was an inch or two taller than he. Her figure looked perfect. One long, well-shaped leg was exposed by the slit in her evening gown as she turned away from the table. Her figure was breathtaking. In the photograph's background, he could see the faces of men turned toward her in what he imagined was wonder, awe, and lust in that order. Her face and body were burned into his memory as he stacked the pictures and slid them back into the envelope. His computer search provided Chen with directions to her home.

It was a shame, but he might have to kill her. Something to sleep on, he decided. The decision could wait until the morning. It might earn him some respect from that animal, Rathmann.

Chen called China to report. Then he walked up Grant Avenue into Chinatown looking for some home cooking.

27

"They're in for the night," Jake said over the cell phone. He was stretched out on a bed in the Desert Rose motel a short distance from Love's Travel Stop in Benson, Arizona, on Route 90, just past Tucson.

Frank could hear the weariness in his voice. He himself had been dozing fitfully at the console. "I've got IDs for you on those two riders."

"Too late, they're gone, man. Replaced when we went through Tucson. Tucson Chapter guys. I'm driving along, and all of a sudden, two guys tore by me. I'm going eighty, you know, and they left me like I'm driving in reverse. Five minutes later, the two guys I've been following come tear-assing the other direction. They're gone in a flash, so I speed up and catch sight of the two who just flew by. They're slowed down and chatting back and forth as if there's nothing doing in their lives at the moment. Replacements. Changing of the guard, literally."

"You haven't gotten into position to shoot them yet?"

"Nah, maybe in the morning. The drivers checked into this motel. I slipped the night guy some bucks to let me know if they checked out early. Set my alarm for when the night shift ends, so I can be out waiting for them to hit the road. The two guys from Tucson are sleeping in the truck's cab."

"Sounds good, babe. Long day, huh? Wish I was there to give you a neck rub down. Sounds like you could use it, huh?"

"It's been a bitch. They've done close to nine hundred miles in just under twelve hours, average around, what, seventy-five miles per hour? Better than average that's for sure. Well above the speed limit at times."

"Yeah, they didn't stop to eat between Buttonwillow and here. They took a piss break at the Arizona border and then at the New Mexico border. Marking their way like dogs across the country. Just pulled over, let it rip, and got rolling again. Forty-five-second stop."

"Have you got any idea of your ETA in New Orleans? Caleb's already down there. He's got a couple of things to do before you arrive, but I'd like to let him know when you think you'll be pulling in."

"At the rate they are going ..." Jake took a moment to quickly calculate. "I'd guess another day and a half, say midday, day after tomorrow."

"Sounds good, baby. Get some sleep, and send me pictures of the new guys tomorrow. We're making a scrapbook."

"Will do. G'bye. Love you, Frankie." Jake rolled over and fell fast asleep. His ability to go to sleep immediately upon closing his eyes drove Frank crazy.

28

Frank DeLong's cell phone hummed softly, intruding on the last moments of sleep he had hoped to enjoy before his alarm buzzed at 0700. He rolled over and answered the phone. His clock read 0538.

"Frank! It's Irini!" She was breathless. "I was just attacked a moment ago. Left quite a mess behind me. Can you track the police calls? Should start coming in soon. Somebody is going to find him in the San Mateo County Fairgrounds parking lot."

"Hold on, Irini. You okay?"

"Shaken and bruised by the damn airbag. I'll have bruises in unflattering places, but aside from that, I'm fine. You should see him!"

"What the hell do you mean 'attacked'? And 'him' who?"

"An Asian-looking guy. He followed me this morning. Waiting outside, down the block from my place. I noticed him pull a U-turn as I drove out. Nothing unusual about U-ies in my neighborhood, but it was only five fifteen. Nobody around here, absolutely nobody, is up at that hour. I was, because I have a report to write for Caleb."

"Go on," Frank urged.

"He followed me. I led him down El Camino toward the Hillsdale Mall. Wanted to be sure he was following me. If so, I wanted him out in the open. Vulnerable."

"Yeah. What happened?"

"Frank, the son of a bitch tried to kill me. You don't sound concerned. He tried to shoot me!"

"Irini, please calm down. You handled the situation and are pretty much out of it, at least as soon as we take care of a few things. Go on, tell me how it went down with this guy."

"Okay. I led him into the big parking lot on the north side of the county fairgrounds' exhibition halls. You know, those maintenance and service buildings close to the side entrance?" Frank murmured that he understood. He had seen the buildings and knew that the maintenance facilities were intersected by two roads crossing at the center of the small complex.

"I hear sirens, Frank. They're heading in that direction!"

"Where are you?"

"On 101. Almost to Peninsula."

"Don't drive like you're in downtown Athens. And I want you to go directly to Tony's Auto Repair. I'll alert him that you're coming and that we need immediate service. He'll drive you here," Frank said. "Now, Irini, gimme the facts. Tell me more."

"Well, I led him toward those parking lot buildings. I went through the center road. Came around the building. When he came through the intersection, I T-boned him right in the passenger door!"

Frank could imagine Irini's Mercedes G550 SUV racing its 382 horsepower V-8 engine and smashing the guy's car with the shiny chromed push bar she had installed on the front. The Mercedes, a box of a vehicle, became known by the team as "the Beast."

"Go on, Irini."

"The bastard had a gun in his hand. Looked me straight in the eye a split second before I hit him. He knew what was coming, Frank! Tried to bring his gun to bear on me. He was scared stiff. Could see it in his eyes. You know, when they know what's coming? That insight, that moment of pure knowledge and understanding of the future? I … I love that moment, Frank."

"Yeah, Irini …" He paused, "I know. I know what you mean." The air tingled with blood emotion. He heard her breathing heavily, felt her blood pounding and her physical tension crackling through the air to him.

"My airbag deployed on contact, and all I know is that the impact apparently drove the front of his car into the building on his left,"

Irini's breathless voice continued. "Right through the building's exterior wall and into a goddamned office. His car spun around. Crashed through the office furniture and hit the rear cinder-block wall backward. Blocks were knocked out of the wall."

"Hold on a moment," Frank said. "The police chatter's starting." He set his earbuds more firmly in his ears, turned to his laptop, and listened to the transmissions. "Police calling for an ambulance, Irini. Sounds like your guy's health is not looking so good," Frank reported.

"Good news, in my opinion. Where they taking him?"

"Peninsula Hospital. I want you to come in right away. We need to get you and the Beast checked out and both of you repaired immediately. I'm sure that a lot of that chrome flaked off the push bar and some smart detective will be looking for the source."

"The damage is minimal. You may be sure that I've checked both front ends ... mine and Beast's." As if it had just occurred to her, she said with wonder in her voice, "I could have been killed, Frank."

"I know that, Irini. Let's get on top of this quickly. What else can you tell me?" Frank tapped out an email to Tony Bologna, who owned the auto repair operation. His special services repair shop was in a large garage behind his home. Tony handled many automotive favors for various clients—on either side of the law.

She described how she had used her KA-BAR knife to cut the airbag free of its container, pushing it into the passenger side of the Mercedes. With the knife and her Beretta 92 FS in hand, she had approached the tangled car, peering into the front seat. Nobody there! A moan from the back.

"The guy was in the corner, directly behind the passenger seat. The driver's seat was flattened backward. The impact with the cinder-block wall must have driven him from the front to the back. Right out of his seat belt, Frank," Irini said, her voice indicating the wonder she felt as she described the violent destruction she had caused.

"What was his condition?"

"It looked like he'd bashed his head. Blood was pouring down his face. Lacerations all over. Blood running down his shirt from what looked like a chest wound actually glittered in the sunlight. That was weird, believe me … like bright, red, sparkling worms. The door was buckled, so I climbed in through the side window. Had to slice my way through the damn airbag with my knife. Cut the hell out of my knees on the broken glass all over the backseat. I've got bits of bloody safety glass embedded in me. I sure as hell hope he doesn't have AIDS, 'cause if he does, it's in my system now. His right shoulder was bent backward. Broken very badly, I suspect.

"You know how they describe blood smelling coppery? Never really noticed that until now. It does smell that way, but it smells thick in the air. He kept moaning and wheezing like it was hard for him to breathe. Lung damage perhaps? I was able to reach his inside suit pocket and grab his wallet and papers. Went to the glove box up front and took the rental papers too. Found his gun and his briefcase on the floor. Took them, and then I got out of there fast."

"That was very risky, sticking around like that, but good work getting the ID documentation."

"Have to know who this guy is, don't we?" Irini asked.

Frank was in his car and heading south on Highway 101 to Burlingame. He was about four miles away from the Broadway exit.

"Yeah, we did. I'm just interested in getting you home safely," Frank said. "How close are you to Tony's? Problems driving?"

"I'm about a block away. The only problem I have is that I've got my skirt up around my hips, trying to keep it out of the blood on my knees. That's a good reason to drive slowly. Be tough to explain to a police officer. Blood, glass … and thighs!" She giggled with the tension of the moment.

"How's the car driving?" Frank asked.

"The engine and steering seem to be unaffected by the collision. Let's hope that Tony can get the push bar replaced today and fix whatever else he thinks needs repair. The Beast is mine, and everyone knows it. So, in case anyone's looking, it will be as usual, all spic and span, no?"

"Irini, it will all be handled. Just get yourself to the office as soon as possible."

"We'll get a lot of answers to our questions about this guy from the stuff I grabbed. Can't wait to crack the briefcase. The police are right. He's not in good shape. A great hit, Frank! Damn! Got that bastard right in the middle of his car."

"Get back here, pronto." Frank paused a beat or two. "I'm glad you're okay, Irini. Let's get started on cleaning your traces from the incident ASAP. Tony's waiting for you."

"Almost to Tony's. Two or three minutes and I'll be there. We should get the word to Caleb, Frank. And Georgetown, I suppose." She clicked off. The KA-BAR was on the seat jabbing her naked thigh. Danger everywhere. She slid the knife into the sheath under the dashboard and her Beretta into the clip holster next to the knife.

She drove the Beast through a large door into the garage at the end of Tony's driveway. The garage door closed behind her. Bright lights illuminated the workshop. Tony, a burly man wearing a Giants baseball cap and sporting a well-clipped, white brush mustache bent over to peer at the front end of the Mercedes. Irini turned off the ignition and sat breathing deeply for a few moments.

Tony opened her door. "The Beast's no problem," he said offering her his hand to help her step down. When he saw the damage to her knees, he ohhed in sympathy. "Let's get you to Frank. I gotta call in the order for the push bar, and then I'll drive you to your shop. Frank called to see if you'd arrived. He said that he's about there and will expect me to deliver you in the next fifteen minutes. Let's go."

Her wristwatch showed that it was now 6:15 a.m.

29

Caleb's day started with Frank's call at eight thirty, two hours ahead of the Pacific Standard Time Zone. The call had roused him from a deep but uncomfortable sleep. His muscles still ached from the after-dinner exertions following his meal at Le Couteau Bleu. New Orleans's damp February weather didn't help, invading the house's rotting structure and taking possession of its contents. The ratio of moisture to bedding material seemed to be achieving a fifty-fifty balance. Caleb was sure he could squeeze water out of the mattress.

Apologizing to Frank, he put him on hold while he padded across the hallway to the bathroom and attended to some early morning business. Back in the bedroom, he stretched as many key muscles and joints as he could before settling himself on the bed and giving Frank the go-ahead for his report.

"We've had some excitement early this morning, Caleb. Irini picked up a tail on her way in." Frank relayed the details of what happened in Irini's encounter with the would-be assassin. "His prognosis for recovery is not good, according to the EMT transmissions to the Peninsula Hospital emergency room doctors. There's a good possibility we will not be able to talk to the guy soon, if ever."

"What's most important is how is Irini?" Caleb said with great concern.

"Shaken, a few dings and bruises, but otherwise fine. Aside from her knees, there aren't any visible wounds. I patched her knees and tried to send her home to get some rest, but you know Irini ..." Frank said with a touch of pride and admiration in his voice. "She's in her shop and is coming up later to see where we stand. I guess there will be a few aches for a day or two. The Beast's at Tony's for repairs. I think Irini's in the clear."

"So we've established that Chen from Asian Artifacts is here at the same time as the arrival of a shipment," Caleb said. "Any idea how Irini drew his attention?"

"I'm stumped. She had dinner with her cartel contact a couple of nights ago," Frank said. "Whoever they are may be trying to place her in the picture. How a Chinese guy we know is involved in one of our cases and also happens to be involved in this tailing business, I just can't figure out.

"Irini grabbed the guy's briefcase and wallet from the wreck. The papers show correspondence with Curtis Rathmann at Long Distance Freight about shipments. Veiled references to the business. He also had correspondence with Mrs. Partrain and had a meeting with her yesterday. The players are all in town, Caleb."

"Keep an eye on Chen. Bring Thorndike up to speed as well. Now, how're Jake and the truck doing?"

"The monitor tracking the GPS signal shows the target on the road. I calculate that it should be in the vicinity of Lafayette, Louisiana, around 1400 hours tomorrow," Frank reported. "The GPS signal from the tracking device is strong. Jake called in that the drivers laid up in a motel just east of Tucson last night."

He reminded Caleb to expect an escort of at least two outrider bikers about a mile back trailing the truck. "Wait for them to pass, before you chase the truck. Jake will fall in behind you."

There was nothing more for Frank to say to Caleb except to wish him good luck. They clicked off with Frank saying that he'd call back to keep him informed on the truck's progress toward New Orleans.

30

The idea that morning sneaked in softly was not a concept Jake Corbett particularly espoused. Morning was always a shock to his system. His wrist alarm woke him at 0630 with a jolt. He was showered, shaved, and in the Malibu with the heater on by 0700.

The first chore of the day had been to check to see that the Asian Artifacts truck was still parked at Love's truck stop. It was.

He walked around the truck to the place where he had attached the GPS. The truck was parked so that Jake could not be seen from the motel's front windows. He dropped to one knee as if to retie his boot laces and felt underneath the chassis to make sure the small, electronic device was still there. It was.

The smells of breakfast cooking wafted across the parking lot and drew him into the motel. Most motels didn't check to see who was and who wasn't a paying guest in their courtesy breakfast rooms. He helped himself to paper napkins, a couple sweet rolls, two yogurts, a plastic spoon, and a large paper cup of coffee with cream and sugar. On his way out, he practically tripped over the two truck drivers seated at a small table in the center of the room. Fortunately, the men were too engrossed in eating huge omelets, strips of bacon, and sourdough toast and jelly and slurping at hot coffee to pay any attention to him.

The second chore of the day was to get into a well-hidden position at the next truck stop down the road to wait for the parade to form up and pass by. Jake found a vantage point at a truck stop fifteen miles down the road. When the truck passed, he waited for the outriders to come by, and then he fell into line.

At noon, he sped up and passed the two Visigoth security team riders and the Asian Artifacts container. He calculated that the truck would pull off the road at the next truck stop for lunch, and he wanted to be there to observe and photograph from a concealed spot among the vehicles in the parking lot.

The drivers did choose to stop, and Jake took some shots of them as they emerged from the cab and stood in front of it stretching their cramped limbs. They strolled into the restaurant just as two bikers in Visigoths colors pulled up and parked near the truck. Through his telescopic camera lens, Jake could see that the newcomers were from the Tucson chapter. Taking turns, the bikers went into the restaurant to get some carryout food, which they ate slouched against the front bumper of the truck.

The bikers stood more erect and showed deference to the two drivers from Alameda when they returned to the truck. The four of them consulted a map and nodded agreement, and the drivers climbed into the cab. The Visigoths mounted their hogs. The roar of the engines shattered the noontime peace. As if in chorus with the rackety timbre of the bikes' engines, trucks up and down the line added their mellow throb to the growing thunder as they fell into place and took to the highway.

Jake Corbett gave them a few minutes to get organized on the road and then pulled to catch up behind the truck and its outriders.

Highway signs directing passersby to Las Cruces, New Mexico, and the New Mexico State University appeared and flashed away along I-10. A pair of bikers passed Jake's car, peering into the car as they pulled by slowly. Then they accelerated, disappearing into the flat horizon. He had an overwhelming sense of having been inspected, of having been under suspicion. He had done nothing that he could think of that would draw their attention to him.   They   wore Visigoth colors. The bottom rocker said, "Las Cruces." A stirring of apprehension alerted Jake's senses. Across the divided highway and too far away to see clearly, two other bikers raced westward past him.

The desolation of the roadway was another discomforting factor as Jake drove on. Suddenly, a motorcycle appeared in his side-view mirror. He hadn't heard it approaching. A second rider slid across past his rearview mirror slotting himself just behind the first.

The lead rider pulled forward, matching the Malibu's speed and stomped his foot against the car's fender. Jake's head turned toward the rider. At that split second, Jake saw the twin bores of a shotgun in the window. He jammed on the brake, and the barrels swerved toward him. Instinctively, he ducked. The blast spattered him with shards of glass and blew the door post in half.

Jake was aware of the physical impact to his face and shoulder but felt nothing other than wonder as his tires slipped into the roadside ditch. The world turned circles as he stared through the gaping space that had been his windshield.

31

Caleb had spent the day visiting Eastern Partners' client stores. The array of ceramics; cloisonné vases and platters; beautifully carved tables, chairs, and chests; and jewelry varied from store to store. After visiting the last of the five stores on his list, Caleb began to feel overwhelmed. He had no idea that Chinese antiques were so highly valued as to draw the stratospheric amounts the price tags requested. He saw a set of ceramic rings used by archers in China to assure a smooth release of the bowstring priced in multiples of thousands. It was interesting to him to see the varying atmospheres the shop owners created for displaying their goods. Some stores were dusty, dark caves packed with product. A couple were well laid out and organized efficiently. And there was one highly modern showroom offering a small number of priceless items exhibited in pools of spotlighting on pedestals placed around a huge showroom.

By the time he had visited all of the stores, his feet were killing him and his wallet required refilling at a convenience store ATM. He had used taxis to traverse the city and enter neighborhoods far removed from the sleazy patina Bourbon Street had gathered, perhaps unintentionally, over the years.

In each store, he had engaged managers in conversation. Wearing his sports jacket, open shirt collar, and Levis combination, his appearance implied that he was a moneyed tourist and therefore a promising prospect to the shopkeepers. He roamed each store, caressing the very expensive items as though he just might buy them.

None of the stores and the vibes emanating from their environments suggested that they were anything other than a store selling Chinese antiquities at scandalously high prices. If there was anything illegal going on, the pricing was it.

In search of a place to sit down to rest his feet, Caleb wandered down a side street to a narrow, dingy sandwich shop advertising, "Like Yo Momma's Best Po'boys," the famous New Orleans shrimp sandwiches. Despite the food-stand nature of the shop, it was typical of the tiny joints his parents had frequented when they visited New Orleans. Certainly nothing fancy and plenty of locals to look at as they enjoyed their inexpensive lunches. It was his memories that brought back the unique, delicious taste of po'boys—fresh shrimp in a roll with mystery sauce.

He placed his order for two of the sandwiches and a draft of locally brewed NOLA brown ale. An old woman, with a dark-brown face wrinkled by the years, shuffled to his table with his order. Well-worn, paisley-print slippers comforted her feet. Her face glowed with pride as she set his plate and glass of beer on his table. "Y'all enjoy your meal, suh. Glad you with us this fine day. Y'all need somethin', wave to me. I'll be here'n a jiffy." She turned and shuffled back to the counter leaving warmth behind her along with great food. Caleb took a huge bite of his po'boy. His phone chirped.

"Yeah, Frank, what's up?" he asked, shifting his mouthful of shrimp po'boy to his cheek for clearer speaking.

"Change of plans, Caleb." Frank DeLong's voice was hollow in his ear. He could hear the tension. There was a thundering silence on the line.

"Jake's been shot," Frank said after a couple of beats. It was said without emotion, but Caleb heard the forced control.

"What the hell happened?" Words tumbled out of Caleb's mouth as his mind spun trying to arrange everything in a comprehensible fashion. He left his food and stepped into the street to converse in private. The old lady at the counter looked confused and followed him to the door. He waved her back, giving her a thumbs-up and pointing to the phone at his ear.

"They ambushed him between Roscoe and Sweetwater, Texas, on I-10. They got him with a shotgun. Fucking bastards got him with a shotgun." His voice broke. "Goddamn it, Caleb."

"Frank, give me the details."

Frank told him what he knew. "Lucky that kid was hunting rabbits and saw what happened," Caleb said. "So he heard motorcycles and pops up in the tall grass to see what's goin' on. How'd he know they were bikers?"

"Kid saw the vests; they wore colors, but he couldn't make out whose they were. Riding Harleys, he said. He knew by the sound but was too far away to see anything useful. 'Weren't no ricers; they was Harleys' were his exact words. His daddy had taught him the different engine sounds apparently. As the motorcycles passed, the last rider brought up a stick. That's what it looked like to the kid."

"But it was a shotgun, right, Frank?"

"Fired into the driver's side. Jake lost control of the car, and it flipped into the ditch. The bikers just kept on riding. The kid had a cell phone and called nine-one-one."

"Good kid to have around. And Jake? What's his status, Frank?"

"They say Jake's going to live, all right. They're picking pellets and glass out of him right now, and then, according to the hospital, they have some pretty good surgeons to work on his shoulder and face," his voice shimmered over the last few words. "He's so good-looking, you know."

"I know that, Frank. I know. This is a tough one to handle, but you can't do anything to help Jake at this point. Your thoughts, all of our thoughts, are going to have to suffice right now. Let's focus on getting the sons of bitches, okay?"

"Yeah, sure. We'll get them. All through Desert Storm, Desert Shield, the fuckin' Yemen incursion, Somalia, and God knows how many other deals Jake and I've been through, he never got hit. He joked that it was 'cause he was such a good-looking guy. Shit, I'd tell him, 'If looks were the criteria for survival, you woulda been dead a long time ago.' Not so funny now, huh?"

"You're right, Frank," Caleb agreed. "Listen, have you advised Georgetown about Jake? Thorndike will want to know."

"Yeah, we did that. Irini called as soon as we heard. Thorndike said he'd take care of getting Jake home without any hassle from the cops. Told us not to worry."

"And I won't. You shouldn't either, man. Jake's going to be okay," Caleb said reassuringly. He fingered his eyebrow scar. It still itched. "What else?"

"Well, this indicates that somebody suspects that there's a probe," Frank said. "They don't care who it is. They just don't want snooping for any reason. They've shown that they're killers."

"Let's revisit Jake's situation for a moment," Caleb suggested. "I'll buy your idea that somebody suspects something. But for all they knew, Jake could have been an innocent business guy making his next sales call."

"Caleb, you know these guys don't give a rat's ass who they hurt or kill. Something stands in their way, they shoot. They smelled something."

"Yeah and they're protecting something precious and don't want any interference, no matter how innocent."

"Well, done is done. My main concern is getting him home so I can take care of him, you know?"

"You said he's going to be fine, huh? The car took most of the pellets. Damned lucky."

"Yeah, they're releasing him in a day or two. He'll be in a sling for a couple of days and then do some light rehab work. Thorndike's arranged for everything, including a private jet to bring him back to San Francisco."

"Okay then. He'll be in your custody in a day. Anything else of importance, Frank?" Caleb asked, trying to move Frank on and away from the subject of Jake's injuries.

"Well, should I fly out to take Jake's role in this engagement? Irini can manage the tracking. The truck should be arriving to you tomorrow afternoon. I could be there."

"Frank, I want you at the controls. I can handle the truck. Our main objective is to see what happens when it arrives in New Orleans and then makes its drop at the store. I've visited them all, and I can't get a whiff of anything other than the antique business as usual."

"Okay, Caleb. Be very careful with those bikers. They are not as stupid as we'd like to think they are. We saw that today."

Caleb returned to his table, receiving big smiles from the old lady at the counter. At least all was right with her world, now that her customer was eating her food.

There was nothing to do until the truck arrived, so he looked forward to a night of jazz at the clubs along Bourbon Street—maybe preceded by a meal at Galatoire's or Arnaud's since he doubted he would be welcome at Le Couteau Bleu.

He would try to control his rage at the people who had shot Jake.

32

Caleb Frost awakened on his fourth morning in New Orleans sure that he would have pneumonia by the time he returned to California. However, he comforted himself that this would be his last day in the Crescent City, if the truck was on time and it revealed its secrets. He worked on the assumption that he would be leaving the Ninth Ward that morning.

Frank answered his cell phone call on the first ring. Irini and William Thorndike were on the call.

"Let's start by getting an update on Corbett's condition," Caleb suggested.

"They let me speak to him last night. We hope that he'll take off for San Francisco tomorrow," Frank said. "He sounded quite good considering everything he's been through. It appears we've been pretty lucky."

"How is his shoulder?" Irini interjected. Just the sound of her voice was downright exciting, Caleb thought. He wished he were home rather than getting moisture-bite in New Orleans.

"His shoulder was the main injury of concern. The docs found that it was not as serious as originally thought, and they say that he should be well along to total recovery in a few days. He'll be back in the weapons-toting business in a week, possibly sooner. That's according to the doctors. According to Jake, we're looking at a day or two."

"Until that shoulder's really in good shape," Thorndike said, "keep him busy downstairs in the shop or upstairs in communications doing some light work. I called in a debt with somebody in the Interior secretary's office, and they muddied the waters and called the cops off."

"Yessir," Frank said. Caleb could hear the skepticism in Frank's voice. Keeping Jake tied down was virtually impossible, and everyone knew it.

"Frank, give Jake my best. Thoughts with him and so forth. Let me know what I can do to assist you. Whatever you need," Thorndike said.

"Now, what about the Asian Artifacts truck?" Caleb asked, feeling confident that Jake was going to be back in the game soon and believing they had commiserated enough for one meeting.

"The truck's located some one hundred and seventy-five miles from New Orleans at the moment," Frank said. "If you leave the city and drive out on Route 72, you'll pick it up at Coomagaleaux or there about. There are a lot of smaller towns along the road for you to hole up in."

"Have they visited the truck stops along the way with any regularity?" Thorndike asked.

"I know what you're thinking, sir. They may be doing whatever it is they do, other than delivering Chinese antiquities, on these stops for all we know. That's the intel we lost when they put Jake out of commission," Frank said. "However, the stops we do record seem to be natural stops for meals or spending nights."

"Regardless of what they may have done along the way, can we agree that New Orleans is where they will do the majority of their side business, whatever it is?" Caleb asked. He heard general agreement. "Okay. I'm on the road to pick up the truck and follow it. Anything further specific to me catching the truck?" There were no other issues. "All right, Frank, we'll stay in touch."

Thorndike and the others wished him well.

After dressing in the street clothes Zipperman had provided for the second odorous day, Caleb spent the next half hour cleaning the house of all traces of his presence. He knew that he might have to use the house for at least one more night, but if he could finish his engagement that day, perhaps he would catch a late flight back to San Francisco. When he was sure that the house was wiped clean, he carried his suitcase, the Saints bag, and his moist bedding to the Caddy in the shadows of the shed behind the house. The gym bag contained the extra ammunition and the grenades, which he did not think would be necessary but would have available in the trunk, if he needed some more firepower. He took two additional mags for the Kimber and six extra twelve-gauge shells for the Mossberg out of the bag, which he then stowed in the trunk of the Caddy along with his leather suitcase.

Using one of the two blankets Zipperman had provided, Caleb wrapped the Mossberg 500 and the extra shells into a long bundle and placed it behind the front seat on the floor. The forty-five, the extra mags, and the KA-BAR went onto the front seat under the second blanket. He ran Zipperman's telephone number through his mind to make sure he had it available.

The Cadillac's engine turned over immediately, and Caleb thought good things about the skinny man, Clarence, and his skills at automotive maintenance. Winding his way out to the highway, he saw a few children playing on flat, hard, dirt front yards. Puddles provided some extra fun. Cold weather and the rain were probably keeping many of the kids indoors, although he didn't think there was much appeal in that either. *Bleak* was the word that best described these people's lives—today, tomorrow, and forever.

As he pulled away from the Ninth Ward, he felt as though he was being released from an all-encompassing malignant cloud of pure misery and despair.

33

Caleb Frost drove to New Orleans's Jackson Square and parked across the street from Le Café du Monde, world-renowned for its beignets and chicory coffee. He bought half a dozen still-warm, heavily sugar-powdered beignets and three large, black chicory coffees to go. Savoring one of the beignets, he rolled westward toward Lafayette and the planned pickup point for the red Asian Partners container. He carefully tilted the plastic lid off one of the paper coffee cups, and the pungent odor of chicory filled the car. While certainly not all that comfortable on the car's decrepit bench seat, he felt warm and contented as he munched and drank his way out of New Orleans, west on I-10.

About twenty-four miles west of Lafayette, just west of Rayne, Louisiana, on I-10, an abandoned gas station, overlooking the interstate, provided a well-concealed vantage point from which to wait for the truck. Caleb backed the Cadillac into the shadows beside the paint-flaked clapboard side of the building. He had an excellent view of the highway looking west. A quarter mile off was an access ramp. The trees framing the rotting gas station were cloaked in Spanish moss that dripped from the branches. Even in broad daylight, the silver-gray moss looked sinister and ghostly, like desiccated fingers reaching for anyone who passed by. Thousands of trucks, cars, and buses did whiz by this spot daily. Few, if any, of the passers-by paid attention to the collapsing gas station building. Only the most desperate people would give any thought to the decrepit car nestled against the scabrous wall.

Slouching low in the sagging front seat of the Cadillac, Caleb let his eyes follow the stream of traffic on the highway in front of him. It was noon or "twelve hundred hours" in Frank DeLong's military parlance.

He shivered. The morning's dampness slithered over his body. The threadbare New Orleans Saints jacket Zipperman had provided hardly fought off the chill. Louisiana seemed to be struggling to stay ahead of the constant attacks by nature's moister elements. The city and the surrounding parishes were the victims of water and dampness. Hurricane Katrina's ravages were still in evidence. Bayous and creeks, home to alligators and snakes, typified the countryside.

Caleb speed-dialed Frank. "Yes, Caleb?"

"Frank, there is something you could do today. Get a fix on that guy, Bangalore, the Visigoth selling drugs. We were talking about him yesterday. The guy with the black beard and swastika bleached in it. Okay?"

"Will do. Can I use a freelance for this? I have a couple discreet guys I could hire."

"Okay, but just to peg the bastard down. No action. I'll deal with this guy myself." He hung up and settled back in the seat. He closed his eyes. Images of five-year-old Rebecca crept across the back of his lids. He remembered his feelings for her—his protectiveness, how she was the apple of all their eyes. His mom and dad adored them both, of course. His parents had made it clear, in their way, that he and Rebecca were equally loved. But Reb was a centerpiece for them all.

Rebecca's style, even as a child, was such that all of her classmates wanted to be included in her circle of friends. At moments, she was a tomboy, arms swinging left and right with tiny clenched fists as she battled for the soccer ball, and then she became a coy little girl who could persuade her older brother to buy the forbidden Cokes and cookies from the local soda shop. Caleb smiled as he thought about how Rebecca could charm their father into getting her whatever she wanted.

A silver Porsche swished by, disrupting his memories. His thoughts returned to Rebecca, the teenager. The boys began coming around.

They insisted they came to visit him. He knew otherwise, of course. He was the gatekeeper, vetting these fellows with whom he played sports and snapped towels in the locker room. At a point, he came to understand that the physical, emotional, and social changes in him and his friends were very significant. He recognized the visceral responses he experienced around some of the girls at school. He knew he wanted to touch them and, in a very vague way, knew what to do should the opportunity arise. At that teenage stage, *Playboy* magazine gave a lot of pointers, as did some other more explicit and titillating magazines he and his pals exchanged. Understanding all of this about himself made him downright fierce with the boys who were bold enough to ask Reb out for a soda or a movie.

A grin crossed Caleb's face now as he chuckled remembering how many intimidated boys had returned Rebecca to her doorstep on time, unkissed and untouched. She probably was confused by the lack of forwardness from these young boys to whom she was frequently attracted. She wanted to experience the intimacy the girls discussed and giggled about at slumber parties.

During her last years of high school, she made up for all of his interference and then some. Caleb was in college and unable to approve of and intimidate the young men who dated Reb. His absence allowed her to greatly expand her social activities and her experimentations. How she had arrived at her current condition wasn't much of a mystery to Caleb.

Reb was already into drugs when he brought her out to San Francisco from New York. He arranged for a job in advertising. She succeeded brilliantly and was promoted to a position of greatly increased corporate responsibility. A fast track lay ahead of her, and then, a year ago, she disappeared for a month. When she reappeared, now without a job, money, or an apartment, she suffered from debilitating mental distress, irrational fears, and the use of chemical and physical outlets to combat the recurring terrors.

A red truck speeding by on the highway brought Caleb upright, but it was not the Asian Antiques red container with a golden dragon on its side. He sat back checking his wristwatch. His cell phone vibrated just as he took a final gulp of cold coffee to wash down the last chewy bite of sugary beignet. Quickly wiping his fingers, he answered the call from Frank DeLong. "Yeah, Frank, are they breaking the speed limit?"

"Nah, the truck's on time, but we have some info from our freelancer based on your description. The target's an active member of the Visigoths and a tight buddy of the Goths' president, 'Wrath' … Wrath, as in pissed off. No momma's given name on either of them. We know where he lives: the Visigoths' mother chapter house in Alameda. I Googled it. The picture actually shows guards positioned around the lawns, like they're expecting some action. Satellite caught 'em."

"Good job, Frank. Have your man gather some more specifics. Perhaps about the house and the security schedules and so forth. No direct contact though, okay?"

"Sure, Caleb," Frank said. Caleb could hear key strokes on the computer. "Hold it, Caleb. The truck is now located approximately fifteen miles from you. As you thought, it is running fast. Get ready to jump in behind him when he goes by, but wait for the outriders. Stick with them, and you'll find the truck."

"All set, Frank. I'm next to the entrance. When I see the outriders go by, I'm on the ramp in twenty seconds. I'll check in as soon as I have anything. Did you call Georgetown?"

"Yeah. Mr. Thorndike called back. When you get a moment in your busy day—his words, not mine—he'd like you to give him a call. The Chinese want to make a move on the producer in Xinjiang. They need confirmation from us that we've got the goods and can trace them back to their guy in the mountains."

"A small request from our good friends the Chinese, huh?" Caleb said, emphasizing "small request" as he said it.

"Well, they are trying to cut off the head of this dragon. That's it for the moment. Watch for the truck, Caleb. It's coming at you."

"Got it, Frank. Thanks."

34

After sliding across the bench and behind the wheel, Caleb turned the old Caddy on. The engine sounded healthy and ready to roar. He peered through the Spanish moss down the ribbon of highway searching for a flash of red signaling the truck's arrival. Finally, he saw a red dot. It grew into a box. He inched the car out through the moss approaching the side-street curb. *Yes,* he said to himself. *That's it, golden dragon and all,* as the truck sped past him on the highway. Where were the backup riders? They should have been closer to the truck. Caleb waited, keeping the truck in sight as it sped east. He kept quickly glancing up the highway to the west for the security muscle. The truck disappeared. He couldn't wait. He jammed his foot to the floor.

The Cadillac leaped forward, screeching toward the ramp. Barreling onto the highway and careening across the first lane into the second, he managed to barely miss a Lexus. A good-looking young woman promptly hoisted her middle finger into his rearview mirror mouthing some choice words in his direction. *Southern Belle,* he thought as he accelerated to catch the truck.

The Golden Dragon crossed an overpass some distance ahead of him. Following the flash of red, he found himself among rows of pine trees. Arrayed like soldiers on parade, the trees stood uniform and perfectly in line. Following a plume of dust, Caleb turned down a side road. A worn sign announced "Scragg's Forest Product Woodlands." A smaller sign advised that trespassers would be shot. Caleb had no doubt on that score.

The dust from decaying pine needles mixed with ancient soil filled his nostrils as he glided the Caddy down the red-clay road. Civilization and mechanical monsters hurtling down the strip of highway behind him soon disappeared as the silence and menace of the woodlands fell over him. Tall, loblolly pines seemed to bow over the narrow dirt road. The sky was obscured by the treetops. The faint sound of the large truck stopped. Caleb came to a clearing with logging equipment parked hither and yon like forgotten Tonka toys. He hid the Cadillac alongside a huge log truck and cut the engine. He left the car and walked several yards into the woods where he stood still listening. He could hear muffled sounds in the distance. Picking his way cautiously across the blanket of needles, he moved in a crouch from tree to tree in the direction of the occasional clang of metal echoing through the woods.

Tree-farm trees were planted in straight rows with enough space between the rows to drive harvesting equipment through. The trees were about nineteen inches in diameter. Hiding—on his part or that of any pursuer—would be difficult. He felt exposed.

At the top of a small hill, he overlooked the red truck fifty yards below him in the center of a large clearing. Lying prone on the ground, he crept forward. A dozen or so men surrounded the truck. A delivery van, its back doors wide open, was parked next to it. A number of wine casks were stacked next to the van's doors. Large tarpaulins covered the ground between the rear of the truck and the van. Protective-moving-blanket-wrapped bundles lay on the tarps. The men had unloaded the entire cargo of antiques. The container was empty.

As Caleb watched, each bundle was unwrapped. Men brought stacks of blankets from the van and carefully rewrapped the carvings, vases, and pieces of furniture. Each bundle was then set back into the container. Off to the side, three men took the padded blankets, which had made the voyage from Shanghai and with careful, deft strokes of small knives shredded them. Others shook the slashed blanket strips. Crimson packets fell like droplets of fresh blood from open wounds.

Several of the men, their Visigoth colors visible, gathered the packets from the tarps and placed them in the barrels.

The genius of the operation became clear. China Red! Packets of heroin were sewn into the packing blankets. The blankets were wrapped around the Chinese antiquities as the customs representatives from the United States of America and the People's Republic of China watched, confident they were performing their duty by carefully inspecting and approving each and every antique. As the antiques passed their scrutiny, their attention turned to the next one. The inspected and "approved for export" items were carried away to be wrapped in protective blankets and loaded into the container without further supervision.

A twig snapped. Caleb started to spin around, but barely had his head begun to turn when a crushing blow to the back of his skull smashed his face deep into the carpet of needles beneath him. His last microsecond of consciousness recorded the smell of pine and dust.

35

The scent of pine needles mixed with the sour fragrance of spilled wine filled Caleb Frost's left nostril. The right nostril seemed to be clogged. The back of his head throbbed. A dull, persistent ache echoed throughout his skull, ricocheting like a twenty-two-caliber bullet without the power to exit.

There was enough dim light for him to make out the irregular surface of a slate floor. A few pine needles clung to his eyebrows like stalactites from a cavern's ceiling. He blew to clear them way. The screaming pain from a split lip soared an octave or two, joining the chorus of other pains reporting from his extremities.

Like a journalist organizing a first paragraph, his mind tried to sequence the who, what, when, where, why, and how leading up to the present. The answers to his questions floated just beyond his grasp. A tentative movement of his head sent a shaft of lightning through his eyeballs. *No fast head motions,* he told himself. He closed his eyes to rest them. The last images etched onto the back of his eyeballs were of bottles and racks and casks. He slipped into a state somewhat approaching sleep.

His memory slowly gathered enough hints to put him back on the ground of the piney woods. He recalled the blow to the back of his skull, his face being embedded into the pine needles, and the scent of earth and pine. And now he found himself still smelling the ground, but lying on slate.

His shoulder signaled shrilly from beneath his body. He rolled from his side to his stomach, arching on his forehead and knees to ease his position on the hard floor. The pressure on his forehead opened the Paris doctor's fine stitching in his eyebrow. Blood seeped out of the open wound, joining the droplet pattern on the slate floor started by other facial contusions. His feet were bound, and his hands were tied behind his back. The ropes were tightly tied. He felt nothing in his hands. They were numb—hunks of useless appendage. His fingers might as well have been on vacation. They did not respond to his call to action.

A flash of light seared his eyes as a door was flung open. The beat of boots on the floor reverberated in his head. He shut his eyes and pretended he was still out. Large hands grabbed his elbows and hauled him up. Relaxing his body as loosely as possible, Caleb opened his eyes a very narrow crack. In the dim light, he could make out denim-covered knees. Then a leather vest came into view. A "1%" patch scrolled down past his slitted eyelids as he was hoisted semierect. A huge hand grabbed his whole face and bent his head backward with a violent twisting motion. He found himself staring into a pair of black marbles. They were surrounded by wrinkled, bluish, red-veined skin. The wind-burned face of the biker was wreathed in short, black hair and a beard. The nose appeared to have been broken in two different directions multiple times. Black hairs bristled from nostrils.

"Wake up, asshole," the biker's rasping voice commanded. Bad breath accompanied the command. And the bad breath was followed by a backhand thrash across the left side of his face. He shook his head to fight off the pain bounding around inside his head like a jack rabbit trying to outrun a coyote. *Christ,* he thought, *if I ever get out of here, I'm coming right back to deliver some righteous damage to this guy.*

At the moment, all he could offer in the way of conversation was a murmured, "Uh-huh?" He was flung onto a chair. Then hands lifted his arms high behind him and over the back of the chair. By then, his eyes had cleared enough to pan the room through a squint. There were rows of racks filled with bottles of wine. The rows ended at a whitewashed wall. A stairway led up to what must have been a ground-level delivery door. He was seated in a chair in the middle of a wine cellar in a space that had been cleared of a wooden table, which was now lying on its side against a wall.

"Now, fuckhead, let's find out what you were doing spying on us." This statement of the meeting's objectives was followed by another wake-up-and-pay-attention slap across Caleb's face. "Talk or we'll avoid this whole mess by stuffing you into one of the casks and let you age for a year or so. Clear? Answer me, asshole! What were you doing and why?"

"Yeah, it's clear," he murmured, frantically searching for some diversionary conversational gambit to stop this guy from hitting him again. He knew he had to create a believable story to buy some time. "And who are you?" he asked. Obviously not the most diversionary question possible, but it might gain him five or ten seconds during which to come up with a plausible story or a long joke. *Did you hear the one about ...?* he thought. He struggled with the rope around his wrists. *If only I can get one hand free, I can damage this son of a bitch.*

"Wow, this guy has balls," Leather Vest said to a second person in the room.

"He came to the restaurant last night. Nosing around. Asking for me. We've got him on the security tape. Said his name was George Garland."

Caleb recognized Collier Berwick's voice. Add him to the list of appointments for a return visit.

Leather Vest said, "Can't prove that. His pockets are empty. Nothin' in the car. Anybody that clean ain't at all whatever he says he is."

"Tell you this," Berwick offered. "We sent one of our college football player interns out to track him. Find out where he went, you know? This fucker ambushed him. Kicked the shit outta our guy. Now I got a huge hospital bill for the intern and a nasty head coach at the university who'll be plenty pissed if the guy can't play next year."

"Yeah, we all got problems," the biker said dismissively. "None like the business this guy and us have got to discuss though."

Forcing his eyes open, Caleb looked Berwick in the eye. "The kid's a pansy."

Berwick's fist buried itself deep in his gut. Leather Vest stepped in and caught Berwick's second attempt in his huge fist.

"Hold it. I want this guy to talk, and I mean in the next minute," he said, pushing Berwick back and away from Caleb's chair.

The biker pulled a revolver from under his vest and poked him in the solar plexus. When he could breathe again, he looked up at the biker. "Untie me, why don't you, and we'll see who has the real balls around here. You Goths do well hitting people tied to chairs, but in a real fight, I'd guess that you'd run."

The biker laughed, blackened teeth lining his red gums. "Did you really think this was goin' to be a fair fight? Really, man? How stupid are you? Jes' fill me in a bit, like for starters, who do you work for?" He pressed the Glock under Caleb's chin so the muzzle dug deeply into the softness of his throat.

"Get that out of my throat, and we'll talk," he croaked around the finger of steel pressing against his windpipe.

"Okay," Leather Vest said, sticking the pistol back into his waistband. "Now let's hear it. Who do you work for, huh?"

"Listen," Caleb said, "are you the guy I should be talking to about my operation and the proposition I can offer you guys? I have something you need for your business. Can you make the decisions here? I can tell you all about it, but I don't want to go through it twice, you know what I mean? It can't be the creampuff over there who's in charge, is it?" he said nodding at Berwick. "Get me the first team, and we'll talk."

With a roar, the biker leaned down to within an inch of Caleb's face, spittle splashing, "Don't waste my fuckin' time. Who the fuck are you, and what are you doin' tracking us?" He pulled back his fist to smash Caleb's face. As he swung his raised fist, a black hole suddenly appeared in the center of his forehead. The row of bottles behind him exploded, mixing red wine with the blood spurting from the neat hole in the back of the biker's head. A black, metal tube thunked into the wall behind the biker whose body swayed before tilting forward, bowing from the waist, legs still holding him erect.

"Holy shit!" Berwick shouted, spinning around, waving his arms in terror, trying to understand what was happening. He caught a Bowie knife in the middle of his chest. His eyes showed white with surprise as he looked down at the magenta spray pumping his lifeblood onto the slate. Almost simultaneously, both Leather Vest and Berwick collapsed in a communal heap. A rapidly growing pool of blood inched toward Caleb's feet.

Stunned, he scanned the room, coming to a stop at the top of the staircase against the back wall. Zipperman stood just inside the door. Crossbow resting on his shoulder. "Anybody else at home?" he asked softly.

Caleb shook his head. "No, we're home alone. Don't know how you found me, but I'm very glad you're here."

Zipperman descended the stairs slowly, a nasty forty-five extended ahead of him, the muzzle sweeping left and right, like a deadly nose sniffing for more lurkers. When he reached the pile of bodies, he grasped the Bowie knife's handle protruding from Berwick's chest.

It seemed to Caleb that there was no question about exactly how dead Berwick was, but Zipperman wrenched the knife back and forth a few times, certainly cutting the vital internal organs just a touch more. "Jes' makin' sure, ya know?" Zipperman said catching Caleb's questioning glance. He wiped the blade clean on Berwick's silk suit jacket. Then he delicately sliced through the ropes tying Caleb's hands behind the back of the chair and around his ankles. The knife disappeared into a sheath on Zipperman's belt.

Caleb felt the welcome pain of his blood returning to his extremities. He winced as the delicious burning sensation brought feeling and the promise of function to his hands and feet. Rubbing his hands and forearms vigorously, he stood. Not feeling particularly confident in his ability to manage in an upright position, he held onto the back of the chair and stepped gingerly to one side to avoid the approaching spread of blood from the bodies on the floor. With difficulty, he bent over to rescue the biker's Glock from the approaching slick. The gun provided a small amount of reassurance. He popped the magazine and found that it was full.

"Well, how'd you find me?" he asked.

"One of the guys saw the Caddy drive down Bourbon Street without you at the wheel. He followed it here. My boy jumped the driver, and he's sound asleep in a dumpster. He called me to report and tell me where the car was. We know this place. Bad place. Drugs, girls. And ah do mean girls. Not women. Girls. Hell, donkeys, if ya want, fer god's sake. Only seen worse in Vietnam. Panama mebbe. The upper two floors are dedicated to such activities. Gives the neighborhood a bad rep, know what I mean?

"This guy ..." he said toeing Berwick's body over, "... is ... *was*, ah'm pleased to say ... a truly evil man. We knew you was here and should be extricated ASAP. So, we decided to kill two birds with one stone. That how they say it?"

"Yeah, it's exactly how they say it. Plus, you saved me two nasty follow-up chores, Zipperman," Caleb said, nodding his head toward the corpses on the floor. "We can scratch two. What next?"

"Well, Le Couteau Bleu is noted fer it's flamin' desserts, and dinner's jes' about over, baby."

As he spoke, the outer door at the top of the stairs swung open. A burly young man, six foot six or seven in Caleb's judgment with bulging muscles, sporting a totally bald head and wearing army cammie fatigue pants and a khaki T-shirt came down the stairs carrying several bottles in his arms.

"My nephew, Ezekiel," Zipperman said by way of introduction. "He's visitin' from Fort Polk to see his ol' uncle a bit, ain't ya, boy?"

"Yes, sir, Uncle Zip."

"Call him, Zeke. Anyhow, he'll be useful. Some special skills he learnt in Afghanistan."

"Welcome to the party, Zeke," Caleb said extending his hand.

"He's a mixologist of the first order," Zipperman continued. "Petroleum and accelerator—a cheery blend. This wine cellar runs halfway under the dining room and all the way under the kitchen," he explained. "We'll be kissin' this hellhole good-bye t'night."

Zeke started unscrewing bottle caps and placing the bottles around the wine cellar. Caleb picked one up and read that it contained the accelerant for Zeke's cocktail mix. Zeke climbed the stairs and returned with four red five-gallon gasoline cans with flexible nozzles.

"You walk okay?" Zipperman asked, looking Caleb over. "Whereas it's time for dessert at Le Couteau Bleu ... it's cocktail time fer us downstairs. You should be gone, dude."

Caleb nodded, moving toward the stairway. "I'm fine now, but I do need some sleep."

"Wow," Zeke said in a startled voice. He had been moving a few wine casks creating pathways through the cellar. One had caught his attention. He saw that the bunghole was empty. Zeke stuck his finger in and pulled off the round end of the barrel. He was looking down into a cask full of red, shrink-wrapped packages.

"Holy shit," Caleb said. "You've found the ... the shit. What about the other barrels?" Caleb asked. "Damn, I saw them loading these up out in the woods before they sapped me. Let's check all of these other casks."

Zipperman ran his hands deep into the cask Zeke had opened and hoisted a flowing stream of bright-red packages into the air. The three men started pulling the ends off the casks without spigots in their bungholes. In a couple of minutes, the floor was littered with fifteen barrels' worth of red packets. Caleb scooped up two and stuffed them in his pocket. "For our client," he explained. "Pour gas and accelerant over those packets. Burn 'em all. This is what this whole operation has been about, Zip."

"Tell you what, amigo," Zipperman said, tossing the Cadillac keys to Caleb. "You take these keys, an' ya drive back to your place in the house. Should be okay, huh?" Caleb nodded. "My bartender nephew and I have to spread some liquid happiness 'round the room here and then git the hell out of the way. Heavy equipment comin' through the Quarter tonight! Big, red equipment. Can you dig it, man?" Zipperman said, grinning broadly. Caleb headed for the stairs leading to the alley.

Keys rattled in the wine cellar door as he mounted the stairs. He turned, crouching, and raised the Glock. The maître d' from the night before walked through the door. He took in the scene in a split second and started to turn away. Caleb shot him in the chest and head in quick succession. The maître d' fell forward, adding his dead weight to the hump of bodies on the floor. A waiter who had accompanied the maître d' screeched and took off down the hallway. They could hear his feet pounding up the back stairs leading to the kitchen. Terrified voices and hurried footsteps echoed through the floor as the kitchen emptied. More shouting could be heard as the kitchen staff pounded into the dining room. Chairs were overturned, and more than one woman screamed as panic embraced the dinner patrons of Le Couteau Bleu.

"Well, I guess there's no need to alert the diners that somethin's up," Zipperman noted continuing to unscrew bottle caps and pass them to Zeke, who poured the gasoline throughout the room. "I wonder if they paid their dinner checks on the way out. Whaddya think, Zeke?"

"Thanks, Zip," Caleb said climbing the last few steps to the doorway. He exited on the back alley. "I'm outta here. By the way, don't forget your bolt there in the wall. It's reusable."

Zipperman nodded but kept his head down, intent on his task. He poured accelerant on Colin Berwick. "Guy deserved what he got, eh?" he muttered. Yanking his crossbow bolt out of the wall, he turned to Zeke and said, "Let's light 'er up and git the fuck outta here, boy!"

36

Caleb found the Caddy halfway down the alley. It was raining hard. Water poured from the rooftops in sheets. The rain felt good as it soaked his clothes. Four blocks and two corners later, he pulled to the side of the street. He got out of the car and sat on the front fender, cupping his hands to catch some water to splash on his face. He stretched. Pain reported in from several locations, but there were no broken bones despite the thrashing he had received.

The rain had driven the tourists into the bars. He made his way out of the main district to the highway rapidly, tires humming. Fire engine sirens sounded in the distance. A red glare danced in his rearview mirror. An occasional, spiked red flame reflected off the rain-shimmered slate roofs of the French Quarter. The Couteau Bleu, the blue knife, was red hot.

At one point, he felt an intuitive itch. He looked for a tail, but, in the rain and with few cars on the road, he could not find anything to tip a tail's presence. Shrugging off the feeling as being a product of the day's harsh activities, he drove toward the shack. He turned on the car radio and caught the news that the famous Le Couteau Bleu was fully involved in a fire that the fire chief was calling suspicious.

Pulling into the shack's ramshackle garage, he suddenly felt safe—not home safe, but generally in control of his environment safe. He popped the Caddy's trunk and pulled out the blanket-wrapped shotgun and shells. The rest he left locked up in the car. *Basic security,* he thought as he trudged into the kitchen at the back of the little house with the shotgun under his arm. He climbed into bed fully clothed, the shotgun snuggled next to his leg. He pulled the damp blankets up to his chin. He was fast asleep within minutes.

An hour later, he came to the edge of consciousness. A smell alerted his senses, the smell of wet wool. Not a noise so much as a feeling of a presence, a filling of space, aroused and jangled his survival instincts. He freed the shotgun from the blankets and rested it on his knees as he inched up to a sitting position against the wall behind him. The room was pitch-black, but the frame of the doorway was slightly visible in the dark.

Rain, staccato on the roof, interfered with his ability to hear anything else. There was a creek. It sounded like leather. Caleb's finger tightened on the trigger, eyes straining to pierce the dense darkness. Focusing on the doorway directly in front of the barrels of the shotgun, he felt hot sweat oozing out of his scalp.

Sensing, more than actually seeing, a shape in the doorway, he squeezed the trigger. The flash of the Mossberg's barrel painted the intruder dead. The impact of the shot, tearing out his chest and stomach, hurled him backward across the hallway. The sound of a weapon clattering on the floor was the only sound beyond the echoing of the blast in Caleb's ears. He lay with the shotgun's barrel against his knees, straining to hear any noise from inside or outside. Nothing. He waited a few minutes, listening, and then climbed out of bed.

He took his flashlight and the Kimber forty-five from beneath his damp pillow and crept across the hallway to the bathroom. A pair of greasy Levi-clad legs hung motionless over the side of the bathtub. The cone of flashlight illumination exposed the remains of a former member of the Visigoths MC. Caleb guessed that he had been one of the outriders following the truck. A shotgun lay on the hall floor. He added it to his collection of weapons for the local alligators to chew on.

He dressed in the George Garland clothes he had worn to Le Couteau Bleu. His street clothes, shotguns and handgun, and the ID he had taken from the biker's pocket went into the Saints gym bag. He then wiped down whatever surfaces he might have touched throughout the house. He loaded the Cadillac and drove without lights for three miles through the deserted townscape. At a spot out of sight from any habitation, he stopped and burned the contents of the biker's wallet. He broke the melted plastic cards under his heel and between his fingers. He crumbled the paper ashes into dust and spread them along the road. The bits of plastic he threw out the window randomly as he drove. He wondered behind which shack the biker had hidden his bike and what the property owner would do when he discovered it. Sell or ride? Probably the former. The Goths would find it eventually and take it back. Finding the body sprawled in the bathtub would happen much sooner. Somebody had sent the biker to kill him and would follow up when the guy didn't return with his scalp in hand.

Finding a bayou, or 'gator nest, as Zipperman had instructed, was a more daunting challenge. Caleb decided to drive until he found a waterway that looked deep and assume an alligator lived there. He'd chuck the shotguns into the alligator's front room and head for the airport. He'd leave the unfired Kimber and all the ammo among the disreputable contents of the Saints gym bag for Zipperman. When he called Zipperman to meet him at the airport for the return of the Caddy, Zipperman said he'd send Zeke at that hour of the morning. They wished each other well.

Caleb texted Frank. "Hi, honey. Arrive pm. Let U know flt. #. Love Charlie.☺." DeLong would understand. He'd share with Corbett. So much for spy-craft.

37

William Thorndike watched the blue snake of a vein slither across the back of his left hand. His fingers, clawlike, grasped the solid-gold lion's head handle of his black stag-horn cane. Recently, he had grown more dependent on the cane for support. Stenosis, the Bethesda doctors had said, pointing to MRI images showing an hourglass-pinched spinal cord. They had pointed to CT scans of Thorndike's spine, nodding their heads knowingly. Treatable by exercise, epidural injection, or surgical repair, they had said. The thickness of the blue snake under his transparent parchment skin reassured him. Blood still coursed aggressively through his veins. His life force was strong, matching his will to continue with his work. He felt oppressed, not depressed, by the information the Bethesda doctors presented to him. He rarely allowed himself to feel depressed. He had determined a long time ago that depression impeded performance. Thorndike's business, his entire career, was essentially depressing enough.

He used to think of the work as a game. Back in the early days of the OSS, they had a flair for the business of espionage. Like the pilots' white scarves, the trench coat had become a symbol of their dangerous occupation. There were rules of etiquette for spies and assassins back then. Or so it seemed. Unlike today, kills in the early days did not occur with so much devastation to others than the intended target. A gunshot here. A knife thrust there. A few drops of powerful poison in two fingers of excellent whiskey or on the sharpened tip of an umbrella. No RPGs were shot through windows then. Over the past couple of years, Thorndike had occasionally experienced a strange feeling. His careful examination of his feelings seemed to point to a sense of remorse—very strange and atypical of his usual mind-set.

Thorndike fingered the array of colorful medications prescribed for his lower back pain and other ailments. The collection of pharmaceutical delights was the devil's own rainbow in his jampacked medicine cabinet. The alternatives to medicating himself were daunting and unacceptable, so, as instructed, he obediently, even ritualistically, swallowed the pills. His baseline assessment of his current condition was that growing old was a pain in the ass.

The Chinese wanted an update on the progress his team had made. They were eager to confirm their suspicions about Zhou Jing and his drug trade. They wanted to attack Zhou's stronghold again. Confirmation by the Americans that drugs were being exported by Zhou would justify the Red Army's huge military assault planned against the Muslims defending Zhou and his operation. They would describe the attack as being conducted on behalf of their good friend, the United States of America, in support of their fight against rampant drug addiction among their citizenry. The genocide angle would be rebuffed by professing hurt feelings.

A muted jangle from his telephone interrupted his train of thought. The screen on the phone told him that it was the San Francisco cell. Caleb Frost's operation.

He pushed the speaker button. "Hello, California, what can we effete Easterners do for you today?"

"Good morning, sir. This is Frank DeLong speaking, sir. Jake is with me. Sorry to interrupt your morning. Caleb is on his way back from New Orleans. We expect him in an hour or so. But something has come up you should know about. We'd appreciate your advice, sir." Thorndike pictured the two young, muscular men hunched over the table in Burlingame, intense and waiting for his leadership.

"Is Caleb aware of this call?"

"No, sir. He's in the air at the moment on his way back from New Orleans. This seemed important enough for us to call you. We'll bring him up to speed as soon as he lands. The matter is extremely personal to him, sir." Jake and DeLong exchanged glances, reaffirming their decision to break protocol by contacting Georgetown without Caleb's approval.

Damn, "Wild Willie" Thorndike thought, tapping his cane on the toe of his well-polished shoe, *that's no fewer than five "sirs" in less than a minute.* These military types never ceased to amaze him with their politeness. Sincerity? Ah, that was another thing. In Thorndike's opinion, they were all just mercenaries, bought and paid for.

"Well, Frank, what is it?" he asked.

"We just received a call or, I should say, a call came for Caleb. It was a secretary from Flannery Center, the rehab center in San Francisco. She was distraught and in tears most of the time. She said that the director of the facility, Barney Flannery, had been shot and that Caleb's sister, Rebecca, had been kidnapped."

Thorndike, stunned by the enormity of Frank's message, sat up straight in his red leather desk chair. "Are you sure of your facts?"

"Yes, sir. Triple checked the information. Flannery is dead of one shot to the forehead at close range. It happened late yesterday afternoon in a secluded area of Golden Gate Park. I asked to speak to the director's assistant, Margie Silas. Margie also happens to be Barney's wife, sorta. They're not married but have lived together since the sixties. The girl said that Margie had to go to the morgue to identify Flannery. The police are all over this. Barney was well known and well regarded, sir."

"Yes, yes, I know," Thorndike muttered, his mind already searching for threats, implications, and consequences. *What does this have to do with us?* he wondered.

"Aside from delivering this terrible news," Thorndike continued, "why are you calling me? Don't mean to be cold about Rebecca and all, son, but how do these people impact our operations?"

"Sir, we have an unconfirmed report that a guy with a girl on the back of a motorcycle was seen leaving the area at high speed around that time of the day. Flannery's body was not found until about 1730 Pacific time yesterday. Now, we have an unconfirmed sighting and a very shaky witness to be sure, but we tend to discount coincidence and make the assumption that the lead is of value. Combined with our current operation and dealings with the Visigoths, we suspect some involvement on their part."

"Makes you wonder how they put two and two together in this case, though," Thorndike pondered aloud. "How would they know about Rebecca, and, secondly, how would they locate her? Why kill the doctor? Well, he would have been witness to the kidnapping and all that, I suppose. We are indeed dealing with subhumans, are we not?"

"Sir?" Jake's voice filled the room in Georgetown.

"Yes, is that you, Jake?"

"Yes, sir; how are you, sir?"

"I'm fine," Thorndike said with a wry thought to the battery of chemicals making his system tick. "The question is how are you? Fit as a fiddle already? Ah, youth."

"The medics did a great job on me. They kicked me as soon as they could. I appreciate the ride you set up for me, sir. And I'm eager to get back on the case. Can't run and jump much at the moment, sir, but I'm up for light lifting."

"Good man," Thorndike said. "I think that we are going to need everyone on board for this one. How do you read the situation, and where's Irini by the way?"

"She followed up on all the intel we could gather about Barney's murder," Frank interjected, taking over the discussion. He placed a placating hand on Jake's arm and squeezed gently, apologizing for taking over. "And then she went to look at the scene herself. Get a sense of the place. We know that it's one of the side areas in the park with playground stuff for kids. She wanted to see where the guy arrived and left the scene, as well as talk to anyone who may have seen something. Maybe find a witness."

"Good, and what of the Chinese gentleman she sent to the hospital?"

"I accessed his hospital records an hour ago. He's in a very bad way, sir," Jake offered. "The crunching Irini gave him did damage to his internals, and the outcome is bleak, to say the least."

"Bleak, indeed. I imagine the Chinese would like to speak with him, but would not be overly inconvenienced should he pass on to a better place with his ancestors, eh?" Thorndike said.

"Yes, sir," Frank said. "We have created a scenario based on our involvement with the Visigoths. Something like this. If, and we have to verify this, a member of the Visigoths kidnapped Rebecca Frost, we then must ask, is this because of the Chinese connection or coincidence and related to something else? It could be a total coincidence, but we tend not to believe in them. However, our focus is going to be on the Visigoths, their membership, and their house in Alameda. We are not against taking a few more of these lowlifes off the streets as part of the Chinese contract."

"You will recall, sir," Jake said, "we hired a freelance operator to learn more about Bangalore, the assumed dealer, and to observe the Visigoths. He is still undercover in the Goths' neighborhood. We've described Rebecca to him and instructed him to look for any unusual activity involving young women other than known Visigoths ol' ladies and mamas."

"Our gut says," Frank continued, "and Irini agrees, that Rebecca has been taken to their house and is locked up there. We are concerned for her well-being, as you can imagine, and therefore want permission to proactively proceed with locating her and extracting her as rapidly as possible."

"Let's hold on a moment," Thorndike said. "Caleb is responsible for the activities of this unit and will be held accountable for the outcome of any of its projects … as will I, ultimately. I want Caleb briefed as soon as he lands. I want his concurrence on the action plan, and I expect him to lead it. And finally, I don't want any local authorities involved. If you identify areas in which assistance would be of value, you contact me. Got that, gentlemen?"

"Yes, sir," chorused DeLong and Corbett.

"Make sure that Caleb and Irini receive that message as well. When does Caleb land?"

"ETA 1320 at SFO, sir," Frank DeLong answered immediately, his delivery sounding as if he were at attention. "Irini is going to meet him. We felt that she could brief him better than we could."

"You have some serious work ahead, gentlemen. A bit sensitive, since it may fall well outside our government charter, but let's find out how it all fits together. Generally speaking, our policy is that nobody touches our people without retribution. In this case, I sense that Rebecca is one of our people. Right? So let's bend the policy to our satisfaction, gentlemen."

"Yes, sir!"

"Good. Get at it. No local authorities. Get it done fast. Keep me in the loop. Oh, by the way, well done on the Chinese account. The destruction in New Orleans seems to have wiped out their inventory and distribution hub. We may have terminated the folks who shot you, Jake. Let us hope so. Now, perhaps we can cut the head off the snake. Let's get this guy Wrath one way or another."

The phone clicked dead.

38

Irini picked Caleb up in front of Delta's departures doors on the upper level of San Francisco International. Caleb climbed into her vehicle, the repaired Beast, looking tired. The cuts and bruises on his face told her all she needed to know about what had happened on the trip to New Orleans. There he was though, battered but alive and therefore well.

Instead of taking him to the house on Broadway, she drove to a park alongside San Francisco Bay. They walked to the far end of the area and sat close to one another on a bench along the water's edge.

As Irini briefed him on Dr. Barney Flannery's murder and his sister Rebecca's kidnapping, Caleb Frost could feel the familiar shroud settle across his shoulders, wrapping around him, transporting him to a state of icy-cold detachment. It was as if gravity had lost its restraint and he could float, intensely aware, absorbing information, data, and facts, while soaring above everything around him. Time slowed. His questions were brief and concise, gathering specifics, ignoring unnecessary information. His emotions were rigid inside him.

Irini laid her hand on his as she spoke. Leaning close to his ear, she told him the incident details the team had gathered. To passersby along the park walkway, they might have been lovers planning their next weekend get-away. Her urge was to hold him and stroke his face to calm him; the tic she had noticed at the corner of his right eye was the only proof of internal turmoil.

Irini Constant had seen that tic before. Several months earlier, she and Caleb, acting on a tip from an informant, had approached a dilapidated, three-story tenement in Brooklyn's waterfront district. They had been informed that a man living there had information regarding the deaths of Caleb's parents. They had burst into the two-room apartment. The man, Steve Curley, according to the pencil-scrawled name on the mailbox in the entrance foyer, tried to escape through the kitchen window. She had dropped him with a very swift kick to one of his knees. As he tried to regain his footing, she further damaged his flight instinct by crushing his gonads with a spearing toe-kick. He lay clutching his balls with both hands and vomiting into the cracks of the kitchen's decayed linoleum. Avoiding drips of spew, she and Caleb hoisted the man off the floor and tied him in a kitchen chair.

Curley made the mistake of thinking that being macho might in some manner reduce his peril. He acknowledged that he had been a driver that night. He hadn't even transported the victims. He had gang guys in his car, so, therefore, he reasoned, he was innocent of the activity that followed. Boldly, he detailed the events leading up to the murders that dark night—how the woman had fought like a tiger. He described how one gang member had produced an ornate samurai sword and had sliced the woman's breasts with the tip of the blade before turning her over to the other men to rape in front of her husband. Then the swordsman dispatched the two captives. And everyone drove home.

Steven Curley did not know that Caleb Frost was that woman's son, nor did Steve Curley know that he was sweating his last drops of water through his slimy, wet pores. Not until he himself was skewered through his neck and just before the serrated bread knife found on the kitchen counter sawed open his jugular vein, spilling his evil life fluid across the floor, did he know who Caleb was. In that instant, before he died, the man—and Irini—saw the tic in Caleb's eye and the hot tears that washed his cheeks.

Killing was not a pleasure for Caleb Frost; when he killed, a shroud fell around him before the act. He had come to define the terrifying feeling that engaged his soul as a shroud, a vast calmness that encompassed his being. He felt power and a sense of ultimate justice sweep through him, filling his veins, muscles, and eyes with perfect clarity. He validated the action he was about to take by reminding himself that killing was his job description and his primary responsibility.

After each termination, he would analyze the sensation, the shroud. He could not tell if it occurred because of fear, hate, and isolation or a subconscious *knowing* that the inevitable result would be violence and mayhem. A bloodlust seemed to fill his soul, bubbling past his eyes, filling his brain, and driving his actions. He felt himself physically harden. He felt an internal force, and his actions were taken with great clarity and coldness. The recuperation was equally painful and slow.

When Irini had finished her briefing about the kidnapping, she laid her head on his shoulder. Her hand softly pulled his head to rest on hers. They stayed that way for several minutes, staring at the gentle waves of the incoming tide. Irini shifted and put her arm around his shoulder pulling her face close to his neck. He felt her soft lips on his skin and the light kisses she gave him. She pulled back, and they sat for a few moments more, wrapped in the union of the moment. Then Caleb stood.

"Thanks for telling me all of this, Irini. I think I'll go to the park now and see if I can't find another eyewitness. Verify all of this before we make a move. Let's go home. I want to get my car and, no …" He held up his hand anticipating her offer. "I don't want you to come along. Thanks for the thought, though," he said with a small smile. "Frank told me about your adventures. Go home, and get some rest. We are going to get Reb back and finish the business with the Goths. We have a lot to pay them back for: Jake, you—and now Reb." As they stood, Caleb wrapped her in a hug, squeezing her until she thought she was going to lose her breath.

Releasing her reluctantly, he walked down the path to her car, beckoning her to follow. There was no arguing.

39

At first, the park seemed deserted. Afternoon sun created pools of light and dark. Out of the corner of his eye, Caleb sensed a form sitting on a bench in the deep shade of an oak tree. The figure clutched a heavy walking stick. Bent forward, his head rested against the stick's shaft; the brimmed, soft hat he wore covered his face. He was indeed brown from hat to toe. Caleb approached him.

"I hear you walking," a soft voice said from beneath the brim of the crumpled hat. "You walk like you wanna stop."

"I didn't know that I could walk tentatively. May I join you?" Caleb asked, matching the softness with which the brown man spoke.

"Free country … park … and bench, too. Of course, I'm free to move on, if …" His voice trailed off.

Caleb sat on the worn bench slats. He left a respectful distance between them. No encroaching on the other man's space. No triggering a flight response. Rebecca's life could well depend on the information this man might provide. He peered sideways to see the man beneath the hat—a scruffy beard; cheeks flat, lined, and dirty. He smelled. Caleb caught the odor emanating from the man, indicating someone who lived out of doors and slept in alleys, under bushes, in doorways, perhaps. Maybe he drank too much, ate too little, and took long vacations from bath to bath, change of clothing to change of clothing. It was a dirty, steely smell. The hands gripping the cane were surprisingly delicate—long fingers on diminutive hands. The hands seemed as though they might come from someone else and had another purpose besides holding a walking staff.

"Nice place to watch the world," Caleb suggested.

"Yeah."

"World's not so nice these days. You think?"

The staff became an extension of the man's right arm. He toyed with the dead leaves along the path, poking them into place before him.

"You're not sitting here with me to discuss the state of the world, friend." The tone of the brown man's voice changed for the worse. "Whaddya want, buddy?"

"Okay. You're right. You here yesterday afternoon around three?" he asked.

"Uh-huh."

"You see a guy shot and a girl get grabbed?"

"Saw a guy shot. Yeah, I did. Sudden. No history there, ya know. Bang. No preamble that I could see." The use of the word *preamble* sent an enlightening slice of information to Caleb. He realized that the brown man was not at all the vulnerable homeless guy he wanted to seem to be. A street person by choice, Caleb decided.

"Saw a girl go away with the shooter. Seemed he had something she wanted, and the word *grabbed* doesn't seem to be the interpretation I'd lay on it."

"Okay. How'd she go with him then?" Caleb asked.

"She's sitting over there by the playground swings." The brown man paused. His hands tightened on the stick.

Perhaps he's revisiting the scene, Caleb thought, the abrupt snuffing of a human life.

"Dead guy lying on the path behind the swings." His head inclined a hair's breadth in the direction of the distant sidewalk. "She didn't seem upset by the guy gettin' off'd that way. She just swingin' and starin' out. Watchin' some kids in that sandbox way over there." He pointed his stick to a play area fifty yards away. "Nobody seemed to see what had happened. Man, life just continued. Children played on." He paused, his eyes closed. He seemed to be putting the right phrasing together. "Those kids just continued to grow up while all this tragedy was happenin' 'round 'em. Just continuin' to grow. Moms didn't know that someone, a living man, was now dead. Slaughtered within their sight. They were otherwise occupied with the happy children. Girl ... just swinging. Back 'n' forth. Back 'n' forth. So fuckin' depressing, man ... ya know? Those kids. Shit what a mess we mortals make, huh?" He sat up straighter, arranging his clothing with little pulls and tugs.

He seemed to shrink as he sighed; the sigh shivered along his lanky frame from his shoulders on down. His reverie broke with a nod of his head, as if dismissing the ghosts. When he spoke again, his voice conveyed a huge tiredness—one memory more to truck around in his satchel of life. He said, "Well, so this guy finishes pulling the dead guy into the bushes and goes to sit nexta her on the other swing. She don't pay no attention to him until he holds out his fist and opens his fingers. Bingo! She's interested in what he's sayin'. Can't hear nothin' over here though, 'cept the guy's fist is closed and she's tryin' ta pry his fingers open."

Caleb watched the man's face. The weathering was total—wrinkled forehead, eyes watery, and eyeballs yellowed. But the sad, weary voice and the words he used were those of a man whose brain was not scrambled.

"You see the guy arrive? How'd he come to this place?"

"Oh, yeah. I saw 'im arrive. Guy's a Visigoth. Hoody unner his colors. A gang guy. He rode a Harley. Ape hanger bars."

"They don't ride anything else. Harleys is all they use," Caleb said.

"Nah, they don't. Had one once, but I was no 1 percent-er. Rode with the Angels couple of times. Didn't get invited in. Didn't even make probationer for Christ sakes. Failed t' do the deed test or whatever."

"What do you know about the Visigoths?"

"New. Alameda. Guy named Wrath runs 'em. Mean son of a bitch. Hair-trigger temper, which is 'ow he got his street name I 'spose, Wrath, ya know?"

"Yeah, I got it. Wrath. What's his story?" Caleb, body tense, was intent on the brown man's words.

"Well, it seems that once he gets a heat on 'im, he can't maintain control. Flies off the handle. Does a lot of fuckin' damage. Psycho, you ask me."

"Ever see him around town?"

"Embarcadero. Riding 'round on his hog. Not here in the park though. Deals're done here. Wrath don't do deals. Actually, Goths don't deal much. Made me wonder 'bout that guy and the girl. It was drugs, for sure. Not a Goth's gig, ya know? The guy could be freelancing. That being the case, the girl could be in deep shit. He was lurin' her, for sure. Maybe he don't want anyone talking. Maybe he wanted the girl for himself."

Caleb stiffened at the brown man's suggestion of the intention behind it all. He knew all too well what was possible.

"Not sure how the Goths make the cash they spend on bikes," the man said, shifting on the bench. "And that hooch they hang out in. There's not a bad bike in the club, they say. Takes bucks, ya know?"

"Tell me about the guy who took the girl. ID the dude."

"Buddy," the brown man said from beneath his brim, "you seem like a guy needs some help. Help ain't cheap. Good help, leastwise." Silence. The cane reorganized some more leaves. A heavy sigh. Dappled light mottled the brown hat.

"Yeah, I do need help," Caleb said. "Why I'm here, you know?"

The brown man tilted his head. A yellowed eye appraised Caleb. He noticed the tic in his eye. "Well," he said, "don't need much … my lifestyle 'n' all. But a bit does make it some easier day to day." Silence. "Cops don't pay nothin' for good info."

"Cops didn't know you were here."

The hat tilted further. Now two yellowed eyes focused on him. "Ya know that? Fer sure? A fact?" New interest or possibly suspicion flittered behind the eyes. "P'raps I should be movin' on, buddy?" The slender hand moved down the shaft of the heavy stick. A leverage point gained in the hand's slender grip.

"No hurry, fella," Caleb murmured, not moving. He raised his hand slowly, palm out to calm the man. "No problem. Not a cop. I just know things. Shit's out there to be had, you know? I hear things is all. We're cool. Stay a while … just some talk."

"Let's see some commitment first, buddy. Then we'll chat some more."

"Hundred bucks," Caleb said.

The brown man threw a reappraising eye over Caleb. "Sounds like you lookin' to form a partnership wi' that kind of money. Who these people to you … if I c'n ask?"

"Girl's my sister. Guy got shot was my friend. Give."

The brown man's head dropped lower. His face disappeared under the brim. "Buddy, your sister's got a bad problem an' bad friends to boot. Ya know?"

"Yes, I do. Tell me about the guy." Caleb turned sideways on the park bench to face the brown man squarely. A cloud passed in front of the sun. A chill crept into the air. No more sun on the brown man. He began to fade into the shadow of the oak.

"*Tell me!*" Caleb repeated, pulling a wad of bills from his pants pocket and thumbing five twenties into a neat packet in his hand.

"Didn't lift my head too much. Didn't wan'im to see muh face. Maybe he would think I didn't see anything, ya know? Lookin' out under the brim. Ugly, big motherfucker, three hundred pounds … mebbe more. Mor'n six feet tall. Long hair … beard … some sorta symbol on the beard. Thin hair so the thing on his beard moved in the little wind that day, ya dig? When he talked or moved that thing in the beard shit moved too. Scary shit, man. Mean cocksucker from his look, and a'course, blowin' the guy away without a word. He qualifies as the cruelest dude in the valley, ya ask me. That's the coldest thing I ever seen, man."

"So they left. And the girl, how'd she go? Willingly or fighting?"

"Shit, man, she climbed on the hog with that guy, and they peeled outta here. Cloud of smoke. Adios, amigos. Gone. Her clutching 'im round the waist like they were bosom buddies. She like wallpaper glued to his back."

The brown man pulled the hiking stick upright between his knees. A brown hand reached out of a frayed cuff and grasped the bills from Caleb's fingers, vanishing the hundred into a pocket of the brown canvas coat. "Thanks, man. Good luck with your sister. Really, man, that's a tough one." He stood and shuffled away down the path, hiking stick beginning the rhythmic swing of someone used to walking distances.

"Wait!" Caleb called. "I may want to talk to you later. I'll keep our partnership going."

"Nah, we're done, buddy. Time to split. Don' need visitors like that Goth guy or the police in case you let slip about our conversation. Big world. Lots more to see. I'm off. The yellow brick road, Route 66, all that shit, man. You …" He stopped and peered intently over his shoulder at Caleb, eyes glowing from the darkness beneath the brim. "You, buddy, you take care." The walking stick came up, an extension of the brown sleeve. It jabbed gently in Caleb's direction, punctuating the advice. The brown man turned and shuffled down the path.

Caleb looked down at his clasped hands, appreciating the concern in the brown man's voice. When he looked up, the brown figure had disappeared.

Caleb left the park, his understanding of the situation and the necessary action crystallizing in his mind.

He headed toward Haight Street and the clinic. He wanted to see Margie to console her and offer his help in any manner possible. She was a tough lady in most ways, but this, this was not something you trained for. This was human anguish without the distortions of drugs or psychosis. This was life—or rather death—full force, in your face. She would need understanding and support. Her love for Barney Flannery was deep. They were as one. And half of them had just been ripped away without warning or expectation. He knew from experience how a simple presence at times like that helped to sustain the most fragile people through their personal hell.

He would provide that presence, if needed, but his mind would be within the shroud, focused on Rebecca and her recovery.

The tic at the corner of his eye continued to flicker.

40

"I'm not very good at this, Caleb. I apologize," William Thorndike said from his office in Georgetown. His voice was gruff and unsure. He realized that the circumstances called for an intense show of concern, not that he really felt any. He hadn't shown much empathy when he first heard about the abduction. The girl had never shown him much appreciation for all he had done for them as they grew up. As far as he could see, Rebecca's kidnapping was a sideshow to the main event.

"Your predicament is terrible," he said. "Rebecca is very dear to me, and I support whatever effort you make to rectify the situation. You know that, I trust?" A glass of 1945 calvados sat close to his hand. The equally old glass wine bottle in which the golden liquor had been packaged on a farm in Lower Normandy sat on a silver tray within easy reach. A wine cork stoppered the bottle. Packaging had not been an issue or much of a problem for the calvados distillers. *Fermier* or "farm-made" calvados had been one of Thorndike's many tastes acquired during World War II. Most of his other acquired tastes were not quite as civilized as calvados.

"I understand, sir," Caleb said. "And thank you for your support. I know that Reb will thank you in person very shortly." Thorndike wondered if his concern for Reb's well-being was really closely tied to Caleb's service. The burden of dealing with the two children equally had always been difficult, and he, truth be told, was more interested in Caleb's success.

Caleb took a long pull of his pint of Stone's Arrogant Bastard Ale.

The team was assembled around the office table. An Amici's extra-large New York pizza with fresh chopped garlic was in the center. Even Irini was dining Italian that evening and was sipping a glass of Merlot. DeLong and Corbett had dark-amber ales. The mood was somber. "We were just discussing our plan of attack when you called. Do you want to sit in on the discussion?" Caleb asked.

"Certainly," Thorndike said. "I'll be glad to contribute whatever I can." He finished his calvados and reached for the bottle to replenish his glass. Three healthy shots were all he allowed himself of the potent liquid. He held the glass to his nose and sniffed the apple liquor's fragrance. It stung his nostrils and burned his throat as he swallowed. He loved it.

"All the help we can get will be appreciated," Caleb responded. "I just asked Jake to go into public records to get all of the information we can scrape up about the building the Visigoths call their mother chapter house." He paused and drank some ale. "Irini is going to Alameda to recon the building and the environment around the house. She will also make contact with the freelancer who has settled into the neighborhood and believes that he saw Rebecca on the day she was kidnapped."

"Good evening, Mr. Thorndike," Irini said, leaning forward toward the speakerphone.

"Good evening, my dear."

"We have preliminary intel on the building, the neighborhood, the neighbors themselves, and police files and reports on the various activities that have drawn the attention of the police and local politicians to the Visigoths. Frank has done a great job of building our file."

Frank, addressing Thorndike over the speakerphone, said, "Sir, the building and property are actually guarded by armed bikers, as we have noted before. All they've done is set up shooting nests for their guys. In our opinion, cross-fire might do more damage to them than an armed intruder would. We have access to all of the standard armaments we need to take the place down, sir."

"May I assume you are contemplating a night operation?"

"Yes, sir."

"I could arrange for a surveillance drone with heat-seeking capability, if it would help. The technology allows us to penetrate a building and get a 3-D simulation identifying where warm bodies are located," Thorndike offered, swirling his calvados in the paper-thin, crystal snifter. "Vandenberg would be our resource, and they could inform law enforcement people and local airports that they were conducting a drone training flight. I could take care of that."

Caleb said that they would appreciate his assistance. Raised eyebrows and some rolling eyes defined the group's thoughts about the idea of dropping a Hellfire missile down the chimney in an American residential neighborhood. While a great deal of fun, the results would make for a very difficult public relations effort.

"As for personnel, four of us are sufficient manpower to achieve our goal of retrieving Rebecca," Caleb said brushing red pepper flakes off his fingertips. The thought of his sister in the hands of the Visigoths festered in his guts. The shroud, screaming to release his anger, enclosed him more tightly. "The faster and the sooner, the better. Before they can think very far ahead," he concluded.

"Our study of the layout of the building and some of the city documents indicates that there is a sizeable attic and storage space on the third floor," Irini said. "Frank has access to a tiny camera; we may be able to attach it to the upper window and take a look."

"We have a number of unanswered questions before we can make a move," Caleb said. "First of all, why kill Barney and abduct Rebecca? How do they know who she is? Do they know who I am and how I fit into the picture?"

"As for you, Caleb, that's fairly easy," Thorndike responded through the speaker on the table. "If they had surveillance cameras in the restaurant you sautéed in New Orleans, they might have pulled facial match-ups. Even without knowing specifically what you are up to, they would know your name, address, but not your occupation. Then again, it would not take much intelligence for them to put you together with the disaster that befell their drug enterprise, which I must say, gentlemen and lady, was exceptionally effective."

"If leaving a charred hole in the middle of a major city is an accomplishment, I guess we are very accomplished," Caleb said with a small attempt at gallows humor. Around the table, tight smiles creased faces for a moment. Video of the firestorm at Le Couteau Bleu made national and international TV news. Three bodies were discovered at the source of the fire in the restaurant's wine cellar, but no patrons or staff members were injured. The New Orleans coroner had surmised on local television that three different methods of killing the victims had been used. A mysterious hole was found in the head of one victim. A stab wound in the chest was found in another, and the third appeared to have been shot through the forehead. Tune in at eleven o'clock. More news later.

"But," Thorndike said, "it's entirely possible they have no idea about you and your team, and this whole mess revolves around some drug-related business on their part. Can't divine what the purpose of the killing and kidnapping might be though. It's a stretch to think that they were out for revenge so soon after the fricassee." He chuckled softly.

"Do you mean that they may have kidnapped Rebecca because of how she might have exposed them to Barney Flannery during her treatment, sir?" Jake asked. "She might identify the Visigoths as her supplier?"

"Hey, I can see that," Frank said slapping the table. "Let's assume that they don't even know about us, and, aside from a potential police investigation, they are in the clear. The police they can handle. We are a different story."

"It sounds like you are on top of the situation," Thorndike said. "It's late here, and you have much to plan for. Give me a call tomorrow with your shopping list. I have a few strings I can pull for you."

"Thank you for your help, sir," Caleb said. "I intend to implement our plan quickly."

"I'm sure you do," Thorndike answered. "We don't want Rebecca in their clutches a second longer than necessary. Good luck."

The line went dead.

Clutches. That was a good one. Great word, Thorndike thought, chuckling to himself as he drained the last drop of his second calvados of the evening and reached for the bottle, still chuckling. "Clutches." Hah!

41

"The fuck you mean?" Wrath said from behind the biker known as Bangalore, who was seated, bound, on a kitchen chair in the center of the Visigoths' mother chapter house's living room. The entire club was present to watch him sweat. The swastika on his beard was soaked with drool and beer. The piss might come later.

"Do you mean to tell me that you figured that you should kill some guy, grab a girl, throw her on your bike, bring her back here to our fuckin' goddamn chapter house, and hide her ass in our attic stoned out of her fuckin' mind? What you got, turds for brains, you motherfuckin' jerk-off?" The laughter died with a glance from Wrath's blazing eyes.

"I'm sorry, Wrath," Bangalore whimpered. "I know it was stupid, yeah, but I … I foun' out she'd gone to the clinic. He'd make her tell where she got the shit, and he'd tell the pigs for sure. He's no friend of ours, ya know. Said so yerself. Thought I was doin' a good thing."

"How come she got the shit from you, Bangalore? We are not in the drug-dealing business, are we, guys?" Wrath scanned the room for compliance and received the assurances he expected.

"Tell me, asshole, the fuck did you get the shit to sell this girl? You been stealing from our club, huh?" Wrath prodded the man hard behind his right ear with the muzzle of the Glock he'd pulled from his waistband. "Tell me before I just blow your stupid head off and your ol' lady's and your goddamn kids' heads as well, you fuckin' traitor."

"It was just one bag, honest. It fell out of a blanket I was cuttin'.

Jes' put it … jes' put it …" Bangalore's voice rose a couple octaves. "Jes' put it in my pocket without thinking. Rode back home, and there it was. We needed some stuff, so I went on the street. Shit, Wrath, was only one pack, fuck!"

"Yeah, I know. You need stuff! You got to get it, don't you? Even when you know the rules, huh, Bangalore?" Wrath paused and then grabbed the chair Bangalore was in and pulled it backward. He roared downward into the man's face, "Rule fuckin' number one! We do not deal in drugs!" He let the chair drop backward. It crashed to the floor, bashing Bangalore's head and leaving him lying on his back. Wrath's face was contorted with uncontrolled rage. Spittle from his curling lips dripped down into Bangalore's eye. He squirmed and blinked, trying to clear his already unfocused view.

"Won't happen again, please, Wrath," the man begged. His bound hands strained upward in supplication against the binding ropes holding his elbows to the chair. His jeans were now wet as well. His sweat-soaked hair, a mass of slimy earthworms, stuck to his face.

Wrath stood up straight and looked across the room at Creek. They stared at each other, a long look passing between the two as if a decision were being discussed by telepathy, a decision being studied from all angles. Then, a final decision was reached. Not a word was spoken.

With a deep sigh, Wrath hoisted Bangalore and his chair upright. Pulling a hunting knife from its sheath on his belt, Wrath sliced the ropes binding Bangalore and stood him on his feet. He patted the man's dripping shoulder.

"Creek, take our man here and clean him up. I'm sure that he is going to live up to our rules and regs in the future, aren't you, boy?"

"Yeah, I will. Thanks, Wrath. No more screwing up, okay … okay, Wrath? You'll see."

"Yeah, okay. I'll see," Wrath assured him. With a twitch of his head, he urged Creek to take the man. As Creek helped Bangalore walk on trembling legs, Wrath took his seat in front of the members. He arranged a couple papers on his desk, laid a few well-sharpened pencils side by side, and calmly surveyed the men in front of him. He didn't blink when a muffled shot sounded. Then a second.

"Item one on the agenda," Wrath said calmly, "what do we know about this girl and what are we going to do about her? Coyote, tell me the story as you know it. I want a plan before anyone leaves tonight." Creek returned and took a seat to Wrath's right. A glance passed between the two men. Electricity crackled in the air between them.

Wrath raised his fist and, in a flash of rage, crashed it down on the desk. The neatly arranged pencils flew into the air, points snapping as they hit the desk or hopped in all directions off their erasers. Wrath cleared the debris from the table in a wide, sweeping motion. His head drooped as if he was thoroughly tired out from the wildfire of emotion that had swept through his mind. He struggled to regain control, looking from beneath his black eyebrows at his assembled troops.

"And the executive committee will stay," he said, "until we figure out what to do with our business that turned to fuckin' toast in g'damn New Orleans last night. What the shit is goin' on around here, and who's after us? Everyone, heads up! I want you to touch our networks, ol' ladies, mamas, buddies outside the club … any contacts you have. Keep it close to your vest. Don't let on what's happenin', but find out if the Goths are bein' talked about. You hear somethin', you call Creek, pronto, got it?"

Nods, grunts, and a few "fuckin' A's" followed.

"Okay, everybody, get your asses on the street. Executive committee, sit tight."

42

Wrath glanced across the room to Creek who had sprawled on a couch. Again, the silent communication and Creek left the room. His thudding boots traced a path up the central stairway to the third floor and then down to a tour of the second floor. The lumbering giant returned to the living room. A twitch of his head told Wrath that the house was empty. Creek dragged a chair over to the doorway leading to the front hall and foyer and plunked down to keep watch.

"Let's get to business," Wrath said. "First, the bitch upstairs!"

Dog Shit raised his hand. Dog Shit got his street name because at a time when he was under grave duress in a street fight, he had extricated himself by grabbing a handful of some conveniently located dog poop and jamming it into the mouth of his adversary, who promptly forgot the death grip he had on Dog Shit's neck.

"Yeah, Dog?" Wrath said.

"I'm lookin' for a connection between the bitch upstairs and the guys who trashed us in New Orleans. Anything in that direction?"

"Good thinking, Dog," Wrath said hitching his chair closer to the desk. "'S why you're on the board, man. Keep it comin'. Coyote? Wanna jump in here?"

Coyote stood, pulling a crumpled piece of paper from his right hip pocket. Smoothing it out on his thigh, he said, "Here's what we have discovered through Charlie Z's woman, who works in records for the SFPD. This guy Flannery has a psycho shop in the Haight. Small, but successful operation. Deals with drugged-out assholes.

Been there since the seventies, eighties, thereabouts. Cops and him are tight. We got the broad's name, Rebecca Tilden. Ran her through and found that she has a guardian in Washington, but the name is in code and we haven't been able to make head or tail yet. A brother is listed. Ran him and hit a fuckin' stone wall."

Wrath assumed control of the conversation saying, "Girl exists; guardian and brother are phantoms of the opera. I hate opera, but this makes me curious."

Creek, grasping the top of the living room door frame, leaned into the room. "We got pictures of the dude who mebbe turned pyro on us," he said. "The guys at the restaurant saved the security disc. Why not have them push New Orleans PD to do a face match. At least we have a picture to pass around."

"Better yet, Creek," Wrath said, "have them email the picture to Charlie Z's ol' lady. Have her run it and gather dope on the goddamned fucker. Run prints for the guys to use to try to ID this guy on the street."

"'Nother thought, Wrath," Dog Shit said.

"Yeah, Dog. What you got?" Wrath turned his attention to the older man.

"Just on the side of caution and anticipation. What if this guy decides to extend his meddling to Alameda and attacks our house? Maybe he's the same guy the road crew caught in the woods watching us unload. He was taken to the restaurant. Apparently, the guy they caught wasn't one of the three dead ones. Bruno was going to interrogate him. Shit, knowin' Bruno, and what he could do in a short discussion, I'd be fuckin' pissed at everyone and would want revenge somehow. Maybe he's on his way here. Whaddya think?"

"I think you're on the right track. Back in my college years, we used the 'What if …?' process to anticipate the unexpected. That's the way business operates. Course we never expected last night, did we, huh?"

Up to this point, the fifth member of the Visigoths MC Executive Committee had not participated. He was known as "Pony" because he typically wore his long, salt-and-pepper hair in a flowing ponytail.

Today, his hair peaked from the center of his hairline and hung loosely across his shoulders, his head in deep shadow. A drooping walrus mustache, full mutton-chop sideburns, and the framing hair fairly well obscured any identifying facial characteristics. His arms, extending from the short sleeves of a red T-shirt beneath a black leather vest bearing the Visigoths identification were bare—except for the colorful mélange of ornate tattoos covering his skin with ink. The artwork stopped midway down his forearms. "You never want the judge to see your tats," Pony would say to explain the abrupt stoppage.

Since Wrath had handpicked the executive committee, there was general respect for Pony. He tended to be the last to speak, spending his time in meetings gathering opinions and ideas, and then he would offer an analytical summary and suggest a plan of action when the flow of new concepts dried up.

Wrath gave Pony a sidelong look and a nod. As with Creek, Wrath and Pony seemed to communicate wordlessly. Pony sat up, with some difficulty, in the beanbag seat he occupied. No one laughed.

"My suggestion to the executive committee is that we recognize a state of war. Prepare for an attack from an unidentified enemy. Our departed brother Bangalore was a total asshole, but, despite having perhaps put us into this mess, he may have unwittingly given us the out we need. A hostage or ..." Pony paused for emphasis. "... maybe a lure. Fact is, we don't know who we are up against or really why, since our shipment got crisped last night. All security and retaliatory measures must be implemented." Pony crunched back into the beanbag seat.

Wrath sat, head bowed. "Yeah. Well said, Pony. Thanks. Okay, I agree. We need the picture of this guy and some intelligence about him. We have to make the assumption that somebody, this guy or somebody else, is going to try to do something to us. Creek, I want to install a surprise package in the attic on the door to our visitor's door. Let's get Pringle in here and assign him to be on lookout up there. Tell him to stop anyone from going into that storage closet." Creek nodded and left.

"Coyote," Wrath continued, "put out a call for everyone to come in. Everyone, no excuses. Go over the defenses once again. Inside and out. Get everyone in position with their weapons."

Dog Shit stood and stretched. Pony's head lolled back against the beanbag. The silence of the house crept softly into the room. Wrath could hear the noises Coyote and Creek were making as they moved to their assignments. Ignoring the other two men in the room, Wrath let his thoughts turn to his escape route options.

Wrath knew there was a point at which you cut your losses. Chen dead, Mrs. Partrain sure to collapse with Chen's demise, a huge chunk of change owed to the Chinese guy in the mountains for the last shipment, and the Visigoths exposed to someone who might be strong enough to attack him and win—those were the negatives.

The positives were that huge profits had been socked away from the success of the business. A high percentage of the gross profit had been funneled to his personal account off shore. The men in the Visigoths had no idea how large the profit was nor how the earnings were distributed. The executive committee was part of management. The B school always emphasized that the management team shared big-time. Again, they had no real idea of how large the profits were. As for the membership, "Hell," Wrath had always said on the subject, "banquet 'em, booze 'em, bike 'em, and bed 'em and they're ours for as long as we want."

Any of the troops left after this war, which he was sure Pony had projected accurately, would hook up with another MC and just keep on riding.

The key, he said to himself, *is knowing when to split.* He sensed that time approaching.

43

The handwritten note on Irini's shop door read, "Gone to Paris SHOPPING! Back in a few." In fact, Irini was in Alameda, in a condo directly across the street from the Visigoths' mother chapter house. Caleb smiled as he read the sign on his way across the street to Il Piccolo for a much-needed espresso. A couple of hours of sleep were all he had managed since the drone had started to circle over the Visigoths' house the night before. It was a long day and night ahead.

The coffee shop was bustling with the morning crowd. Caleb acknowledged a few of the folks he had come to know. There was a large round table dubbed the "Algonquin Table" after Dorothy Parker's famous gathering spot in the Algonquin Hotel in New York City. There, the world's problems, failings, political disappointments, fiascos, and scandals were all dissected, debated, and solved before it was time for refills from the coffee urns. The solutions the group arrived at for the various discussion topics were frequently right on target. However, Caleb Frost knew too much about political realities and the commission of horrendous resolutions to the issues being debated at Il Piccolo to hold any hope for peaceful conclusions. These kind people would never have to know his world. Caleb returned to his living room, hot espresso and a bag with some bagels and cream cheese in hand.

Frank, at the drone control console, sat back in his chair, stretching his arms high over his head. He rubbed his eyes. Caleb passed him a plate of bagels and small containers of the cream cheeses he had picked up at the café. Frank helped himself to an everything bagel and spread generous amounts of the cheese on the two halves. "Needed that. Thanks," he said munching hungrily. "Man, this drone is my sort of magic." Frank had been huddled in front of the monitor for as long as the drone had been available and in position over the target.

Loaded with electronics, the drone provided a three-dimensional image of the interior of the target building from a mile high. It allowed the operator to track and tag heat signatures generated by objects—people—in the building. He had recorded everything the drone's equipment had captured and was in the process of analyzing and tagging the heat-generating objects with numbers or, as ID's became available through photo recognition, with individuals' names.

In Alameda, deep inside the living room of the condo, aiming through the open window, Irini was using a powerful sniper rifle with a camera attachment to shoot people as they appeared inside the house at windows or outside on what passed as the Visigoths' front yard. These photos were processed, and IDs, attached to rap sheets, were returned to Frank, who applied a name. Occupants were shown as glowing dots within the 3-D representation of the structure. As long as the drone was in orbit, the dots' movements could be tracked.

"Got some action up in the attic, Caleb. Come see how this is working," he said. "Number Seventeen is approaching the attic." Frank isolated the floor's image on the monitor. "He's going to the front of the house. See, see there. That's another person right at the edge, which is a window. Irini has him in her sights. She has already taken a photograph, and we are running an ID process on him. Anytime one of them shows himself or herself—as it turns out, there are several women in the house—we snap them and process the photos for IDs."

The one motionless dot on the third floor was tagged, "Rebecca." The other dots in the house and yard were tagged one through nineteen. As he surveyed the images on the monitors, Caleb could feel his soul turning as black as a moonstone in a closet.

Irini's voice broke in over the communications line. "Got another photo for you, Frank. Guy at the window joined by someone else. Sending it through. As soon as Jake takes his shot and gets the camera and voice-transmission devices attached, we'll be able to listen in."

"Irini? Caleb here. Any unusual activity other than the attic that you can see?"

"Well, out of twenty-five known members, we have sixteen in the house plus three women. That seems to be quite a lot for early evening, and they are scattered throughout the floors of the house," she said. "It does look like the people are located in strategic spots in the building. Could they be expecting us, do you think?"

"They can't be expecting the surprise party we have in store for them," Caleb answered, "and we know where they are."

"Jake," Frank said leaning toward the microphone, "how you coming?"

"Just about ready to launch," Jake muttered as he loaded the sleek projectile into the dart rifle.

"What're you putting in place, Jake?" Caleb asked.

"I've got an XR22-Dart 12 camera with extendible, remote-controlled video arm and a voice transmission cup device. I'm going to position it on the window frame above the third-floor front window. After this, I'll be moving to a school down the street and north of the target. From the school's roof, I'll be firing a listening device dart, which will penetrate the roof and should protrude an inch or so into the space where Rebecca is held. Give me fifteen."

"The images and sound will come through here," Frank said to Caleb, pointing to several monitors arrayed in front of him. "Jake, take your camera shot as soon as you want. Hold on the microphone implant until I give you the go-ahead. We want that guy, Number Seventeen, clear of Rebecca's space before we penetrate the roof. Don't want him hearing the strike."

"Roger that," Jake responded. "Ready for camera placement." Silence. "Okay, Frank, it's implanted and under your control."

A blurry picture appeared on the monitor. Frank turned knobs and made adjustments. Gradually an image became clearer, and Caleb and Frank could see a right ear and some greasy hair along the right side of the camera's frame. Beyond the head, partially obscuring the picture, they could see a long room with a pool table in the middle.

"Good job, Jake," Caleb murmured. "We've got it."

"Movement on Number Seventeen!" Frank exclaimed. Both men peered intently at the glowing dot in motion on the attic view. A figure appeared on the video screen. It was a tall, slender man with long hair. They had a full frontal view as Number Seventeen walked across the room toward the camera. The figure to the right on the screen turned his back, effectively blocking the camera lens. They heard a door open.

"Look, Number Seventeen is moving toward Rebecca. There seems to be a door. He's with her. The glows are close, but not close enough to overlap. He's away from her. Talking, I guess. Shit, I wish we had sound."

A few seconds later, a door shut. A voice, almost unintelligible, could be heard. "Fucking chick's still stoned. What the hell did Bangalore feed her? Hate those fuckin' drugs. If it didn't make us so much money, I'd dump this business in a heartbeat, you know what I mean, Coyote?"

"You got that right, Wrath. This mess plus the shit that went down in N'awlins makes me fuckin' nervous."

"Right now," the man called Wrath said, "let's just hunker down in our cozy bunker until things become clearer. Got to think this one through, man. Maybe it is time to fold the tents and split. Too bad. Listen. A coupla things. First, I want a crack at that girl as soon as she's straight enough to speak coherently. Secondly, get someone up here to take this spot and you check around the perimeter and the house to make sure our security is tighter than an ant's asshole. Get the communications gear passed out so that I can talk to everyone. Got it? Oh, and I want a meet in the living room in fifteen minutes to discuss strategy. Check to make sure they know what their assignments are before the meeting, and then get them together for the meet. Leave perimeter guys out there."

"Yeah," Coyote said. "I'll get Pringle up here. He's reliable." The camera showed two men disappearing down the stairway at the rear of the long room.

"That fucker's mine," Caleb said.

"What about I get a clear shot at him?" Irini asked over the speaker.

"He's mine. Get the tags set, Frank. Wrath is Number Seventeen, and the other guy is Coyote. Next up is Pringle. Run them, and get their bios."

"Got Coyote coming out the front door," Irini reported. "See his dot moving?"

"Got 'im," Frank acknowledged. The glowing dot now tagged "Coyote" stopped in the middle of the house's front yard. Four dots appeared from the perimeter and joined Coyote. After a couple of minutes, the group separated and one dot moved swiftly to the front door and through the house to the back. It ascended to the attic.

"Who's this?" Caleb asked. The dot, tagged Number Five, turned into a short, fat guy with a ponytail on the video screen. As he arrived in the attic, he walked full-face toward the camera.

"Welcome, Mr. Pringle," Irini said. "Smile. Your eight-by-ten glossy will be ready in no time at all. Frank, incoming mail."

"Thanks," Frank said, his fingers flying on the keyboard as he entered Pringle into the ID processing system. "Let's see what a charming life you've led, huh, baby cakes?"

Jake's voice came through the speaker. "I'm on the school's roof. Ready to shoot, Frank. On your command, buddy."

"Fire your probe, Jake," Frank DeLong said, his voice increasingly tight. Fewer words were being spoken. The tension was building.

Caleb checked his watch. Four o'clock in the afternoon. "I'm looking for an early morning conclusion to this mess. Launch at one, okay?"

"Roger," came Irini's response.

"Shot away," Jake said. "Good contact. And I'm ready when you guys are."

"Amping up for sound. You'll all hear whatever our probes pick up over the headsets," Frank said as he bent over his instruments. "Time to get personal."

A sobbing voice echoed through the team's earphones, piercing Caleb's soul. "Help me! I hurt so much … Gimme some. Gimme some! Oh, please, help me." The girl's voice, sobbing and moaning, scorched the listening ears and minds. "Oh, God, let me die … I wanna die! God … please, let me die … I don't want to …" The sound of wrenching vomiting could be heard. "Oh, God! Oh, God!" Wailing, Rebecca Frost's voice pleading for death assaulted them. "Please, somebody help me. I hurt so much … Please, help me. Just one fix, that's all … oh, God!" For once in his life, Caleb felt helpless, listening to the torture his sister was experiencing. With great effort, he controlled his urge to simply attack immediately.

Banging sounds from outside Rebecca's prison could be heard. The video monitor showed Pringle kicking a door. Then his voice, very clearly, said, "Shut the fuck up, you stupid bitch, or I'll come in there and beat the shit outta you!"

Rebecca's cries became tortured whimpers.

Caleb Frost's face hardened. The tic at the corner of his eye flickered rapidly.

44

Caleb and Frank had shifted the necessary gear from Burlingame to the condo across the street from the Visigoths' house in Alameda by nine o'clock in the evening. Jake had installed the surveillance gear and had control of the Vandenberg drone circling above the house, as well as the Hummingbird drone Thorndike had arranged for. The data received from the two drones' surveillance allowed the team to continue to monitor and track the positions of the occupants within the house. Caleb and Jake checked armaments.

Key among the weaponry were several ugly handguns capable of firing darts loaded with a high-powered sedative. The decision had been made to have as little blood-letting as possible. The use of traditional grenades had been abandoned in favor of the darts and silence. Glocks were also available as sidearms.

Lying lengthwise down the center of the condo's dining room table was a Dragunov SVD sniper rifle. An assortment of attachments were laid out next to it. Irini assembled the weapon carefully. It had not been range-tested, so all care had to be taken to make sure that the attachments and threaded parts were seated perfectly.

Wrath appeared on the video screen focused on the interior of the attic. Jake had aimed the tiny lens on the door leading to the room in which Reb was kept. Caleb and the others gathered around the monitor to see what was going to happen.

Wrath had a paper bag in his hand. On the green baize of the pool table, he laid out some wire, a plastic pill bottle; a half a brick-sized rectangle of white, clay-looking material; a small battery device with wires attached to a detonator; and a marble-size steel ball bearing. He also produced a pair of pliers, a roll of silver duct tape, and an awl with which he punched two holes in the cap of the pill bottle. Wrath inserted a wire into each hole.

He dropped the ball bearing into the pill bottle and shook it to make sure that the round object would move freely inside the container. He went to the door of Rebecca's prison and opened it. As Caleb's team watched their monitor's screen, Wrath affixed the pill bottle using the duct tape to the interior doorknob in an upright position, cap at the top. His body obscured their view for a few minutes.

When the biker stepped back, a white block was now attached by tape to the center of the door. Wires ran from the cap of the pill bottle to the battery and from it to the detonator embedded in the block.

Frank gave a low "Ohhhhhhhh, wow. Neat! C'mere, Jake, and look at this. Man, gives me goose bumps. It looks like C-4 or Semtex. Half a brick of the stuff. What do you think? That will open the door for sure."

Jake, hand on Frank's shoulder, leaned over for a closer look. "Not only the door, buddy, not only the door. That house will be missing an attic real fast. Remember Ar Ramadi, Frank? Remember that bunker the Marines found for us? Damn, that was a beaut. Uhrah for the Marines. Our Semtex surprise left a hole so deep—"

"How deep was it?" Frank chimed in.

"It was so deep," Jake responded, picking up a vaudeville cadence in his voice, "that, if it had snowed, the Iraqis could have skied down the hole."

"Da daah!" they both concluded giving it a performance flourish and then laughed at their own humor.

Irini stared at them coldly, as if they were infantile at best, crazy for sure. Her stare was delivered over the top of the PSO-1 optical sight scope she was mounting on the Dragonuv sniper rifle. Frank nodded pleasantly to her, a broad grin stuck across his face. Irini finally cracked a small smile and went back to installing the scope.

"Now that's dirty," she said to nobody in particular referring to the bomb the scumbag had just affixed to the doorknob of Rebecca's prison room.

"I guess we won't be rescuing Reb through the front door," Caleb said as he watched Wrath gently close the door without turning the knob.

"Well," Frank said, "another little opportunity to show our unique B-and-E skills. That wallboard should be easy enough to cut through, eh, Jake?"

"Yup. Piece of delicate cake. No sweat. Don't wanna hang around though. There'll be plenty of shaking going on, and just a touch of that steel ball to those wires, and it's 'how high can you jump' time?"

The microphone on the window picked up the sound of footsteps ascending the stairs to the attic. Coyote appeared on the monitor. "You got it done?" he asked Wrath.

"Yeah," Wrath said.

"What about the bitch?"

"She's out … worn out, passed out, or dead. Doesn't make any difference. If someone comes for her and goes through that door, they'll be pink dust in a split second. Pringle, you understand what I just said?"

"Gotcha. Don't fuck with the door," Pringle answered, his fingers tracing quote marks in the air as he repeated the warning.

"Well, either you keep whoever gets this far into the house out of the attic, or if they make it to the door, you'd be wise to be dead first. You'll be dead one way or another when they turn the knob."

"Yeah, pink dust. I heard you, Wrath." Pringle turned back to continue his watch over the front yard below. A hummingbird flew by the window. *A pretty thing,* he thought to himself. The bird made another pass, its breast facing Pringle.

Pictures flickered on a monitor seventy-five yards away in the condo.

Jake deftly twirled a knob controlling the speed of the tiny hummingbird drone's flight. With a joystick, he made the bird swerve and dive. He flew up and down the street, pinpointing the locations of the sentries Coyote had posted to watch the approaches to the

Visigoths' house. He circled the house, snapping shots at each window and then went down the alley in the back of the house to locate the sentries guarding the rear entrance.

Just then, a tromping of boots could be heard coming up the attic stairway. Five bikers appeared, moving toward the door in the wall. Pringle shouted, "Stop right there. Don't move a fuckin' muscle. Where you guys going?"

"Coyote told us to get guns."

"Well, it's not through that door," Pringle said. "Stay well away from it. We have that broad in there. Wrath don't want no one to disturb her sleep, dig?"

"Okay, so where's the guns," a skinny guy with a Mohawk asked, rubbing his palms together in anticipation. "I want a Glock and a shotgun."

"You guys can help yourselves. See that panel there? Give it a gentle push. It's spring-loaded."

One of the men the team was watching said, "Fuck me," in awe as the panel swung open revealing a shallow room with weapons clipped to the underside of the slanting roof. Boxes of ammunition for the arms lay beneath each weapon.

The team watched the bikers arm themselves. Jake gave Frank's shoulder a punch. "What d'ya think? That's some neat collection of firepower. Shit, they've even got a machete over there." Frank, who understood his partner's interests in weapons, nodded. "Let's stick to business, babe. We can talk machetes later, okay?"

"Yeah, well, there's your entrance, Caleb," Jake said. "That room with the weapons is adjacent to the room with the door bomb. Your KA-BAR will cut through the wallboard with no trouble. Will that work for you?"

"That works for me," Caleb said. His eyes were fixed on the monitor screen, his mind with Reb on the other side of the door … waiting for him.

45

Caleb looked up from diagrams spread across the dining-room table. The team had been preparing for their assault, and all of the details had been covered. "This sounds like a line from a B movie it's so corny, but let's synchronize our watches," he said with a thin smile. "On my mark, I have zero-zero-forty-five ... on the dot ... now." He raised his hand.

"Aren't we tuned to the same satellite?" Jake asked, checking his watch with a sideways glance at Frank, who, head bowed, smirked.

"Okay, all synced up, Captain America!" Frank made a show of looking at his watch, tapping the glass.

"Who's this Captain America?" Irini inquired as she loaded 7.62x54mmR steel-jacketed cartridges into the rifle's curved, ten-round magazine. A second fully loaded magazine lay next to a box of extra ammunition.

She was dressed in skin-tight black motorcycle leathers. Caleb admired the look. Frank and Jake appreciated the look but were more interested in the quality of the leather.

"Obviously not a well-read foreign visitor to our shores," Frank said under his breath to Jake.

"It probably was all Greek to her," Jake agreed chuckling.

"And," Irini said, "I don't think you want me to point this weapon in your direction, do you, Frank?" She swung the rifle's slotted, flash-suppressor-tipped barrel in his direction.

"I surrender, I surrender!" Frank said, his face contorted into mock fear and trembling, eyes wide and popping, hands raised and waggling.

Smiling, she lay the weapon down on the table.

"Probably the first time the Greeks have ever had anybody surrender to them," Jake said.

Irini's eyes flashed fury. In one fluid motion, she drew her KA-BAR knife from its sheath on her hip and buried the blade between Jake's arms, firmly nailing a diagram he had been studying to the mahogany dining-room table. All eyes went to the knife quivering in the table and then to Irini.

"Well. There goes the condo's security deposit," Frank said softly.

Irini laughed, her temper dissipating as rapidly as it had appeared. Reaching across the table, she reclaimed her knife. She looked up at the two men from under her eyebrows. "I don't have to tell you boys about Greeks, now do I?" Acidic innuendo dripped from her lips.

The three of them burst into laughter.

"If I may have your attention for a split second, please," Caleb said clinking his coffee cup with a pen. "I want to attack at zero-one-hundred, if that's okay with this fun group. We should not be engaged for more than ten minutes, only four or five of them during which there may be resistance. In and out. Fast and furious. Knock them back onto their heels."

"How much blood do you want to leave behind, Caleb?" Irini asked fondling the hilt of her KA-BAR. "If it was up to me and they had my little sister, I'd leave some of their delicate parts nailed to the front door."

"Appreciate the thought, Irini, but Thorndike doesn't want an inquiry. Heaps of bodies are not in the bargain with his client agencies. That's why we have these dart guns and …" He reached for a handful of darts. "… plenty of drugs in the darts to use on those people. The drug is fast working, one or two seconds in most cases, and the recipient is down and out for six hours. These came from a federal testing lab. They work, but you have to be within six or seven feet to have accuracy."

"Then what's this beauty for?" Irini wanted to know, stroking the rifle's metal stock frame.

"Ah, the one exception. As we discussed, you'll be returning to the condo window as soon as you, Jake, and Frank have finished off the guys along the street and on the front lawn. As I said, the dart delivery is suspect at distance. Unreliable. As soon as you finish your assignment, Irini, I expect you back up here in the window with the rifle. We're counting on you to cover our butts as required."

"I know what you're saying, Caleb, but Jake's the firearms expert," Frank said.

"That's okay." Jake placed his hand on Frank's forearm. "She's a dead shot."

Irini dipped her head in acknowledgement.

"The Dragunov comes with a flame suppressor," Caleb continued. "The lights will be out here, of course, and she'll still be in black clothes. Her position will be as invisible as possible. Irini will take out anyone she can target inside the house through the windows. Questions, anyone?"

There were none.

"Let's go," Caleb said. "Check your night-vision goggles and Bluetooth communications earpieces. We will be able to talk to anyone at any time, so no idle gossip, okay? Since all of us will be on the move, it is important that necessary information flows smoothly. Let's be brief, concise, and serious," Caleb concluded eyeing Jake and Frank, who nodded, having received the message.

Irini smiled and held the sniper rifle up to her shoulder, sighting down the barrel's length, getting a feel for its weight.

"Any last-minute issues?" Caleb asked. "No, then let's do it."

From his position in the shadows of the condo building across from the Visigoths' house, Caleb watched Frank DeLong and Jake Corbett creep around opposite ends of the building. The street was not well lit at any nighttime hour, and at this hour, it was black. Night-vision goggles made it like daylight. Moving silently and invisibly, the two men reached opposite ends of the block in a matter of seconds. Caleb could see the sentry at Frank's end of the street. He was sitting under an oak tree in the front yard of a home two doors down from the entrance to the Visigoth house. A close-up shot into the guard's neck with a dart guaranteed a surprise for the home owner the next morning. "One down," Frank whispered into the Bluetooth.

"Good work, Frank," Caleb said softly.

"In position Jake?" Caleb asked.

"Guy's in a clump of bushes," Jake responded. "Thinks he's invisible. I don't believe it. He's smoking."

Caleb heard a soft grunt. "What's happening, big guy?"

"Just crawling, trying to get a decent shot," Jake said. "Think these darts will work on a skull?"

"Sure," Caleb said over Jake's earpiece. "But if it doesn't, he'll be out and doing a rabbit run for the house. If he runs, Frank, you take him."

"Yessir," Frank said.

"Irini, all set?" Caleb asked.

"Ready." The soft rumble of a motorcycle filled the early morning air.

"Two down," Jake reported softly to the team's earbuds. "His head wasn't all that hard after all."

Tires screeched, an engine roared, and a black Harley rose up on its rear wheel, leaping forward down the street. As the front tire touched down, Caleb could make out Irini's sleek, black-leather-clad figure on top of the huge bike. She was hunched forward, her helmeted head low over the handlebars. She raced past the entrance to the Visigoths' house and screeched a U-turn at the far end of the street. It occurred to Caleb that if the dead were sleeping, they would be up and howling now.

Thundering back up the street, Irini ripped a right turn. Halfway up the driveway, she jammed on the brakes and slid the back wheel around so that the bike was facing the street. Three men raced from the bushes, guns drawn, but not in firing position. Irini's entrance had startled them but had not alerted them to danger. In rapid succession, Irini shot each of the men in the middle of his chest. They fell on the run. One skidded across the grass to lie in the center of the driveway. Irini ran him over as she powered the bike forward and down the driveway.

"I thought there were four guards. Look for the fourth," she said quietly into her headset as she reached the end of the driveway. "I only got three of them." A slash of fire across her right arm caused her to lose control of her bike for a split second. "Now these guys are cheating, using real bullets!" she yelled over the intercom as much surprised as pained. Gaining control of the bike, she careened onto the street. "The bastard nicked me. Somebody get him!"

The sound of a pistol shot echoed through the night air.

"Got the motherfucker, Irini. Sorry I didn't see him coming sooner. Want me to finish the sonofabitch off?" Frank asked calmly over the intercom.

Caleb's voice broke in. "You okay, Irini? How bad is it?" He knew the dangers. She knew the risks and took them without question or reluctance. But his acceptance of the possibility of the worst occurring did not extend to Irini.

"Just a scratch. No need to off the bastard, Frank. Just put him to sleep with the rest of his buddies. No worries."

"Guys, back door, pronto," Caleb commanded as he charged across the street and raced along the side of the house to the backyard. "That shot will have the natives up and restless. Move it! Cut the power to the building as soon as you get to the back."

Caleb dispatched the two guards in the easement behind the house. It passed through his mind as he sank darts into the necks of both the sentry bikers that the lack of discipline was going to make this operation easier. Apparently, the two had become bored with guard duty and came together to share a joint. They were no more than three feet apart when he came up behind them.

Caleb joined Frank and Jake, pressed against the back of the house. The doorway was in the center of the building. Caleb gave a forward signal, and Jake wheeled around and kicked the door open, shattering the knob and lock. "I'm home, honey!" he called softly, crouching low and entering the kitchen with his dart gun held in two hands ahead of him. Looking left and right, he surveyed the kitchen through his night-vision goggles. He took a position with his back against the kitchen wall. He had a clear view of the swinging door leading to the front of the house. Anyone entering through that door was his meat.

"Clear," he said.

On Frank's "Clear," Caleb Frost entered the kitchen swiftly, followed by Jake. Caleb went to his right to a doorway. Behind the door a long stairway led up the back of the house to the third floor.

"This is it, guys," he called softly. "Frank, control the kitchen. Irini," he said into his Bluetooth, "I count eight down and possibly eleven left in the house, right?"

"Roger," Irini responded. "I do count eleven still moving about. Only Pringle and Reb on the third floor at the moment."

"Guys," Caleb said, glancing at Jake and Frank, "you see Wrath, shoot him with a dart."

"How about me?" Irini asked.

"Know you'd love to do him, but I want him alive. Track Wrath on the monitor," he said. "You can plink away at anyone who shows up in an attic window."

"Jake," he said, "take control of the second floor. Use your handgun if necessary; otherwise, stick to the darts."

"Frank, the kitchen is yours. It's our only way out of here, so hold it," Caleb said.

"Okay," Jake said. "I hear company coming down the stairs."

The three men waited for the arrival and entrance of whoever was coming down the stairs. The door flew open, and a woman appeared, shotgun held in one hand and a knife in the other. The woman had a pink, flowered bandana tied around her head. She was dressed in a tube top, denim vest, and cammie pants.

Caleb shot her with a dart in her exposed rounded tummy. The sting of the dart caused her to stop and look down at her wound. The drug's paralyzing effect froze her limbs, and she tottered forward. Caleb stepped to her falling body, grabbing the shotgun from her hand before she hit the floor. He tossed it to Frank. "Only if necessary, Frank," he said gesturing with a tilt of his head to the weapon.

Frank saluted, touching the shotgun's barrel to his forehead. "Only on the white devils, boss." Sweat made his dark features glow.

"Yeah, something like that," Caleb said, going through the door to the stairway.

Jake stepped over the woman's body and charged through the open doorway and up the stairs to the second floor following closely behind Caleb, who was heading to the attic.

"Irini, have you got Pringle in your sights?" Caleb asked, pausing on the stairway.

"Yes," Irini answered adjusting her headset to better accommodate the stock of her rifle against her cheek.

"Take him out," Caleb's voice whispered in her ear. The moment was sexual, a visceral decision between a man and a woman. She exhaled slowly. Her finger tightened on the trigger, moving cautiously toward the death of a man whose left eye appeared in her scope's lens.

The sound of glass shattering, a grunt, and a thud on the floor confirmed Irini's accuracy.

"Attic clear," Irini said, voice gone husky and cold.

Caleb tore across the attic around the pool table. Everything was clearly visible through the night-vision goggles' lenses. He slammed the panel next to the door in the center of the wall. It popped open revealing the brackets for weapons. Ammunition boxes lay scattered on the floor. Caleb stepped across the growing pool of Pringle's blood gathering in front of the open panel door. He drew his KA-BAR and plunged it into the drywall. The wallboard sliced easily, and soon, he was able to pull away enough material to make a hole large enough for him to step through into Rebecca's prison room.

Make her okay, he prayed to an entity he rarely addressed himself.

I love her. She's my sister, and I'm here to make her safe. His eyes swept the space searching for Rebecca. The goggles turned the room green.

The rattle of gunfire came from the staircase.

"Sons of bitches are using machine guns!" Jake shouted.

The sound of the pistol shot punctuated the groupings of machine gunfire.

"Got 'em comin' in from the front of the house," Frank reported. "Christ, there's another woman with a shotgun. Bitch!" A shotgun blast echoed through the house followed by two rapid pistol shots. A machine gun rattled.

"Need me there?" Irini called. Her tone of voice pleaded for a "yes."

"No! Stay there. Cover us and tell us where people are in the building. Jake, go downstairs. Help Frank," Caleb said.

He located Reb's still body in the darkness. *God, let me see her breathe.* He felt her feeble pulse. *She's so weak,* he thought as he hoisted her skeletal body into his arms.

"Caleb, I'm in the kitchen with Frank. Someone's on his way up!" Jake shouted over the intercom.

"I have his ID, Caleb," Irini said her voice low and calm. "It's that guy, Creek. Bad guy to tussle with while you're trying to get Reb out. I'll try for a shot if I see him through the window."

As Caleb emerged with Reb, a huge man appeared at the top of the stairs. Small bones rattled in his beard as he swung a machine gun toward Caleb. He was running across the attic. In the darkness, Creek's hip crashed into the corner of the mahogany pool table. Grasping his SIG Sauer, Caleb threw off a quick shot, which caught the biker in his right shoulder causing him to drop his weapon. Creek's momentum kept his body coming, hitting Caleb and sending him crashing to the floor. Reb was thrown to the floor like a rag doll. Caleb found himself lying against the door, the one with the explosive knob. Rolling away from the door, he dragged Reb after him by her arm. He left her lying against the wall. Turning to face Creek, he caught a powerful forearm chop on his shoulder. Dropping to a squat,

Caleb lashed out at the bigger man with his leg, kicking his feet out from under him and bringing the giant down hard on the floor. Creek was on his feet in a split second, foot lashing out at Caleb's gun hand. The SIG Sauer skittered across the floor under a chair against the far wall. A follow-up blow to Caleb's head knocked the night-vision goggles into the darkness. Creek's little bones kept giving his position away as he moved around the room. Caleb tackled him, driving him into the pool table. A man with a lesser physique would have broken his back from the impact, but Creek simply roared and threw a flurry of wild punches into the darkness.

Caleb moved around the pool table and away from both the biker and Reb, who was beginning to moan and roll around on the far side of the attic. He found the wall rack and grabbed a pool cue. Brandishing the cue with both hands, he swung at where he thought Creek was in the darkness. Strong hands tore the cue from his grasp. He heard the cue bashed against the table and the splintering of the hard wood as Creek snapped it in half. He could hear the chuckle in the biker's throat as he moved closer with his pool-cue spear swishing back and forth searching for him.

Caleb's back was to the weapons cache. He whirled and dashed to the wall. His desperate search in the darkness proved that the guns had been taken earlier, but the machete remained. He gripped the machete's handle. Sensing Creek's rush, he swung the blade in a wide arc. He twisted his body around with all of the force he could summon. Caleb felt the blade strike and bite flesh and bone. Creek howled with pain clutching his slashed arm to his body and trying to maintain his balance.

The tiny bones in his hair and beard tinkled gaily in accompaniment to the agonized dance. The biker staggered and, in the darkness, tripped over Pringle's sprawled body, sending him staggering backward toward the dormer window. As Creek crashed through the window, he tried to save himself by reaching out to grasp the window frame. As he did so, he let go of the arm he had pinioned to his chest. The severed limb fell off his body, preceding the rest of him to the cracked cement two stories below.

"Sorry," Irini's controlled voice spoke in Caleb's ear. "Couldn't get a clean shot at Mr. Creek while you two were dancing. What's the situation? I saw him leave the party."

"We seem to be okay. Reb's in bad shape." Caleb kicked his goggles as he moved toward Rebecca in the dark attic. With the night-vision goggles in place again, he was able to see his sister's limp figure on the floor. He gathered her up in his arms and made his way to the stairway. "Check in, guys. Jake? Frank?" The tic no longer flickered at the corner of his eye.

"Kitchen has fresh meat all over the floor, but it ain't my meat, boss," Frank reported.

"Good job. What about you, Jake?"

"Check here. A couple of dings but nothing to ruin my looks much. Can we go home now?"

"Okay, coming down," Caleb said as he walked carefully down the servants' staircase. "Irini, any movement in the house other than us?"

"No. Nothing."

"Good. Did anybody see Wrath?"

No response.

"Hey, hold on," Irini interjected. "Movement in the back. Someone leaving the backyard. Going through the alley. I'll get the hummingbird drone launched."

"Frank. Grab a live one and take him or her back to Burlingame for some Q and A. We'll find out from the coroner and the police who was ID'd in the house," Caleb said. "I'm on my way to San Francisco with Reb. You guys clear out of here. The police will probably show up sooner than expected because of the gunfire."

"Shit, I can't get the damn bird to fly," Irini said. "And the figure seems to have left the area the drone covers. It might have been Number Seventeen, Wrath."

"We'll make a quick pass through all of the rooms we've been in," Jake said. "See what I can wipe clean, okay?"

"Okay," Caleb said, "check the third floor for the Glock I had. Lost it in my scuffle."

"Right. I'll get it," Jake said. "Frank, see you at the condo. Irini, make sure it's wiped clean, please. Let's move, everyone. See you at the condo."

"I've got you your live one, Caleb, here in the kitchen. It's that guy they call Coyote," Frank said. "I got him with a dart. Another couple hours of sleep, before he'll be ready to talk. We'll pack him up in the van. I'm looking forward to persuading him to discuss matters."

"Okay, let's get out of here!" Caleb passed through the kitchen and out the back door. Reb moaned and circled an arm around his neck.

Running down the alley, Caleb fumbled the car-key remote while carrying Rebecca over his shoulder. He had the doors unlocked when he reached the car's rear door. He laid Reb down on the backseat, tossed a heavy blanket on top of her, and sped away into the early morning.

"Hold it," Irini's voice jarred the team's ears. "There's someone moving on the second floor."

"Can't worry about them now, Irini," Caleb said. "Everyone, clear the area."

"Good idea," Irini said. "Whoever it is, is heading for the third floor. Oh, me, this looks bad, guys. Jake? Frank? Where are you?"

"In the van behind the condo. We dumped Sleeping Beauty in the back of the van. All trussed up and ready for cooking. Just about to go in and come up," Frank said.

"I'm assuming nobody defused the little popper, eh?" Jake asked.

"Nope. Didn't have time to. Actually didn't even think to do it," Caleb said as he sped toward the Bay Bridge. "And I'm now about one mile away, and I'm not coming back. Nor are any of you. We are done there. Pack and split, fast."

"It's Number Sixteen. The guy they call Pony. I've got him coming to the top of the stairs," Irini said using the rifle scope. "Should I shoot him, Caleb?"

"No. We've had enough gunfire for the night."

"He's heading to the door, Caleb," Irini said tension building in her voice. "Oh, God, he's going to open that damn door. Oh, no!"

A torrent of Greek came across the earbuds followed by a flash of light and the roar of an explosion. Frank and Jake rushed into the condo living room just in time to see the roof lift off the Visigoths' house and the wreckage rain down onto the roofs and yards of the neighboring houses. Irini, who had watched the blast through the high-powered scope, was partially blinded by the flash. She stood by the window rubbing her eyes. The torrent of Greek continued.

"Holy shit," Jake swore. "Poor old Sixteen definitely ain't no more. I wonder about the folks on the floors below."

"Not your worry," Caleb said over the Bluetooth. "There's going to be a lot of confusion. Continue with our plan, and get away immediately."

"Right," Frank said. "Five minutes and we are out of here. Let's move."

Sirens filled the early morning air. Neighborhood house windows lit up like Christmas trees as people scrambled to see what the matter was.

46

Caleb checked his watch. It was one fifteen in the morning. The action had taken only twelve minutes. He was thankful for the lack of traffic and stayed at the speed limit, driving in the right-hand lane, not wanting to attract attention. Every now and then, a moan would escape from Rebecca, who was lying on the backseat wrapped in a blanket. She was shaking from the cold or illness or withdrawal, Caleb didn't know which. He just wanted her back in the Flannery Center.

Caleb's cell rang. It was Thorndike.

"Good morning, Caleb. Heard from Vandenberg. Ungodly hours you work," he said chuckling dryly. "They reported that you had released them and that the results of their testing, quote unquote, were most satisfying."

"We've just finished the party. All objectives were achieved. Extraction completed. On the way to deliver the goods back to San Francisco."

"And her condition is acceptable?" Caleb could hear Thorndike turning pages of a document on his desk.

"Yes." Caleb looked back at Reb. "Tired, confused, basically still under the influence. Sort of aware. That's about it, sir."

"Well, take care. Nothing but the best for my girl, you know that, son?"

"Yes, sir, and thank you," Caleb said. He could imagine the old man readjusting a lap rug against the early morning Georgetown chill.

"Get some rest, and let's talk later today. Wrap up this Chinese business. The thugs in the motorcycle gang are another issue now. Shall we say three o'clock your time?"

"Sounds right to me, sir."

"Talk to you then," Thorndike said. The phone clicked off. The Bay Bridge toll plaza loomed ahead of him. Traffic was nonexistent at this hour. He would have Reb in the center's care in a few minutes.

47

Wrath's departure led him into the secret tunnel between the Visigoths' house and his secret residence at the far end of the underground passageway. Silence had descended on the Visigoths' stronghold. He knew it was time to split. There were no more shouts from his people, no heavy motorcycle boots tromping around, no explosion from the attic.

Rather than face whatever nemesis had taken his empire down in shambles, his preference was for flight. Closing the passageway door, he threw the large bolt lock he had installed months earlier. The simple, precautionary action of barring the door increased his confidence. His long strides took him down the length of the tunnel and into the basement of the home on Clifton Way.

The appearance of the basement was a typically middle-class family room. Anyone visiting the space would have admired the comfortable furniture and the playroom's mahogany bar with a full complement of the best booze around. A wine cabinet covered a major portion of one wall. Dartboard, air hockey table, treadmill, plasma TV—it was all there. A waist-high divider separated the playroom from the two-car garage.

A highly polished red Maserati sat on one side of the parking area. Wrath's Harley occupied the second space. Wrath, or more properly the owner of 2727 Clifton Way, Curtis Rathmann, unlocked a cabinet standing by the garage wall near the bike. Without hesitation, he lifted a saddlebag from a hook in the cabinet. The saddlebag compartments contained a passport, some bank papers, a hundred thousand dollars in bundled cash, a Glock, and several magazines of ammunition. A long coil of heavy link chain hung on a hook next to the cabinet. Wrath hung the coiled chain over his head and under his right arm. After slinging his getaway-kit saddlebags behind the seat over the rear of the bike, he pulled on the helmet resting on the seat and mounted the saddle. A pair of leather gloves with fringed cuffs hung over the high, ape hanger handlebar. He pulled them on and fired up the bike's engine. In the enclosed garage, the sound was exhilarating. His losses of the past two days faded from his mind and were replaced by the thrill and the challenge of a new adventure—an adventure of survival. He pulled a cord over his head; the garage door opened, and Wrath roared into the dawn. *This'll wake up these uptight assholes,* he thought as he wrestled the huge bike up the driveway and onto the road.

Wrath rode as quietly as possible on the big Harley so as not to disturb his neighborhood's uptight burghers who might call the police about the disturbance.

Wrath wound his way toward the Posey Tunnel, which emptied him onto the familiar streets of his hometown, Oakland. The feeling of freedom continued to energize him. His bike swept across the San Mateo Bridge westward to Half Moon Bay and US 1 South, weaving around big trucks delivering goods to San Francisco and San Jose, passing the small cars driven by the small people for whom his disdain was monumental.

Passing through Half Moon Bay, he was tempted to indulge himself in some comfort food. Forgoing that momentary luxury would result in arriving at his hideaway before most people were up and about. He would sleep, rest, and eat when he had arrived at his destination, his rustic shack way back from the road and up a ravine out of sight. The shack was in a remote, heavily forested area.

It was well protected. Wrath had been given a volatile, deadly solution to his security concern by a young woman who worked in one of the Lawrence Livermore government labs. She was looking for some excitement in the woods, she said, when they met in a local bar. "You've found it," Wrath said.

Deadly gases were her specialty. Oral sex was her pleasure. Wrath and she had enjoyed a two-way street for a weekend in his shack. She had told him about her project, an odorless gas that would weaken and incapacitate a person and stop one's lungs in a matter of two minutes. She was tasked by the government, she told him, giggling all the while as she played with his penis, to figure out how to make it faster acting.

As the weekend progressed from one sex position to the next, Wrath gradually drew more information out of her. They consumed each other. She gave Wrath the details, thinking that there was no way this biker could ever absorb the chemical formulations she was describing. How wrong she was.

It was a powder that in contact with plain water would produce a deadly gas. If a tablespoon of the powder was poured into a dish of water, whoever did the pouring would be dead in two minutes.

He knew the gas did work. Wrath had arrived in Big Sur one day and found a hippie-type kid sprawled in the middle of his shack. Obviously intent on theft, the kid had tipped over a test tube of powder into the dish of water when he forced open the door. Wrath was intrigued by the kid's bright-blue skin. He decided that the color suited the kid. That night, he dragged the rotting body down the ravine to the beach. Refuse for the crabs to munch on and then, probably, die from the poison in the young man's body.

Wrath, pissed off about having to sleep outside while the shack aired out, had cursed the motherfucking hippie dying like that and stinking up his place. He drifted off to dreamless sleep.

48

The team sat at the big table in Caleb's apartment, sharing hot coffee and toasted bagels, cream cheese, and lox from Il Piccolo. The midmorning sun streamed in the windows. Gone were the leathers and cammies, replaced by jeans, sweats, and sweaters. Irini, nursing the wound she had received, kicked her shoes into a corner and tucked her bare feet up beneath her. Frank and Jake looked fresh despite the few hours of sleep and the dings they had received.

"Okay," Caleb said, pulling his chair closer to the dining room table in front of his laptop. "Medical report first. Irini, flesh wound on her right arm. Jake, devilish good looks slightly marred by some flying glass. This job has definitely been tough on you, big guy."

"Poor, baby," Irini murmured stroking Jake's bandaged shoulder and patting him on his cheek.

"Frank," Caleb continued, "it appears that, aside from a shower of ceiling plaster, you didn't participate in this event. No dings, dents, slashes? What were you doing the entire time?"

"Hey, you guys were doing such a good job I decided to watch and learn. I'm particularly impressed by Irini's skills on the bike. That was some riding."

"The shooting was excellent too, Irini," Jake added. "Those dart guns are really finicky, even up close. Good job."

"I'm afraid my language lacked a bit of propriety when I took that hit. Sorry," Irini said.

"Hell, shoot me and you'll hear a lot worse language coming from me," Frank said. "You did fine." His dark face beaming expansively, he raised his coffee mug to Irini. "You had one hell of a night, lady. Shot one in the window, darted three on the ground, and ran over another. Wheew! Glad you're with us." Irini bowed graciously, giving him a wink at the end of her bow.

"You all did the job. Great work," Caleb said. "That's why this team succeeds." He held up a folder. "We have reports from the police department and the EMTs on the scene. The damned FBI was notified of the ruckus by some police desk jockey with not enough to do. Mr. Thorndike will have to get involved and intervene for us. Get those buggers off our tails."

"The police accounted for seventeen Goths. We know that they missed one in their count, since we saw Number Sixteen blown to smithereens by the door bomb in the attic. Eleven of the sixteen were inexplicably drugged and unable to stand. Six were inexplicably dead—well, not inexplicably, exactly. One guy fell out a window. One guy armed with a machine gun lay at peace in the second floor entrance to the stairway. Another guy with a machine gun and a woman with a shotgun died in the kitchen from what appear to be multiple nine-millimeter gunshot wounds. The kitchen looked like the main battlefield according to the report. There is massive evidence that both the machine guns and the shotgun had been fired. The ceiling and the wall area around the kitchen's back door were severely damaged.

"One gentleman, who they think was peering out the attic window, was shot straight through the forehead." He gestured toward Irini. "Courtesy of our own Annie Oakley. And one died later from complications resulting from being run over by a motorcycle, as well as being shot and drugged by a dart. Again, the artistic work of our *femme fatale*," Caleb said gesturing toward Irini. He looked up and smiled. "Confusion reigned at the scene. No answers yet about what went down.

"Then, of course, there was the instance wherein a major section of the roof and the third floor attic were destroyed by a makeshift explosive device," Caleb noted. "While they don't know what happened, the police supposition is that there was a bomb-making operation going on in the gang's house. That will suffice for their purposes. It allows the authorities to arrest whomever they wish as terrorists. We have just about fulfilled our contract regarding the Visigoths and their role in the drug deal."

"Except for one other small detail," Irini said. "We know that nobody matching Wrath's description was found dead or alive."

Caleb slapped the file folder on the table. "Yes. We know Wrath was in the house. We all saw him. And the drone showed an image we believe was him moving away from the house, but the scan area did not include neighboring areas, and Wrath was not caught, goddamn it!"

"Somebody must know where he'd run and hide," Jake offered. "Maybe we can get something out of this Coyote character in the basement, eh, Frank?" he said glancing over at his partner. A barely noticeable nod was his answer.

"Water boarding?" Irini asked, her eyes glittering. She touched her hair, pushing it back over her left ear.

"Wanna watch, sweetheart?" Jake did a questionable Bogart imitation.

"I'll pour," she answered, "just like at my tea parties for the ladies in my shop."

"Enough!" Caleb said, getting the team focus back on the point. "Irini, here's what I want you to do. We know now that Wrath is Curtis Rathmann, owner of the shipping company, Long Distance Freight, which transported the heroin, the China Red, from Alameda into the distribution point in New Orleans. The FBI has provided us with some information on one Ms. Cleo Solchow. She's personal secretary and a great deal more to Mr. Rathmann. We have the office address. I'd like you to go there and find out what she knows about where Wrath might hide—this morning, before she understands what has really happened and splits. Here's some dope on the young lady from the FBI." He slid a sheet of paper across the table to Irini.

"Use whatever persuasive talents you need to get the information, but preferably she should be talking of her own volition … if you can swing it. If not …" He shrugged.

"What about our visitor downstairs?" Jake asked.

"Don't want the neighbors alarmed," Caleb said, sipping his coffee. "After he's wrung dry, shoot him up again and drop him off in the woods off Seventeen, toward Santa Cruz."

"That it?" Irini asked, stepping into her shoes.

"Yeah. Let's all report back here by three o'clock for the conference call with Mr. Thorndike."

They all stood to leave for their assigned chores. Caleb turned to the two men. "Hold it, guys," Caleb said. "See what you can learn about Mr. Partrain's demise from Coyote. We should provide something to the Hillsborough PD, so they can close their case. Okay?"

The meeting was adjourned.

49

Irini Constant smelled the Long Distance Freight office before she identified the reception door—cheap perfume mixed with the unmistakable odor of grass. The reception area was neat in the sense it looked unused. Freight and transport magazines available in a magazine wall rack were two years old.

A young woman sat at an uncluttered desk. Her attention was on the Solitaire game she was playing on her computer. She finished a couple of moves before looking up.

"How may I help you?" she asked with a tone of irritation for having her game interrupted. Looking at her face, Irini wondered how Cleo Solchow, for that was who Irini expected was the only employee, could possibly see through the tiny pinholes in the center of her irises. Thoroughly stoned was Irini's snap evaluation.

"I'm looking for Mr. Curtis Rathmann," Irini said. "He suggested that I stop by to discuss some freight business we are going to be contracting."

Cleo Solchow was not too out of it to notice Irini's Paris original. The suit fit perfectly. The total package belied the content's potential for truly unladylike violence.

The discussion started cordially, if one sided. It became evident fairly soon that Cleo Solchow's denials about knowing anything about Rathmann's current whereabouts rang true. Irini dropped all pretenses.

"Listen closely," Irini said, challenging the woman's capabilities. Leaning forward into the cloud of cheap perfume, she continued,

"Your boyfriend has split. The drug business is finished, as is the motorcycle gang you are associated with. The police and FBI are involved and I should imagine that they will be coming through that door any minute. It's over. And since Rathmann hasn't bothered to collect your sweet ass and take it with him, you're over as well. Kiss your deal with him good-bye; you understand what I'm telling you, sweetie?"

Jumping to her feet with the desk letter opener clutched in her fist, Solchow swung a sweeping thrust at Irini's face. Irini stepped back just outside the arc of the blade. Back in the streets of Piraeus, Irini had learned early on that an immediate response to somebody throwing a punch at you—or a letter opener for that matter—negated the initiative gained by the instigator of the fight. Irini learned that once you attacked, you should keep on the attack until the opponent was defeated.

Irini's initial salvo of physical persuasion, which included a clobber to Cleo's right eye, only produced sketchy information regarding Rathmann's general location. "Big Sur or somewhere like that. He has a shack he goes to down there," Cleo mumbled, tears stinging her eyes. Liquid mascara streamed down her cheeks.

"I'm not using Google Maps here, woman," Irini said, working to drag specific information out of her reluctant informant. "Where is Wrath's hideout, this shack he's got? How do I get to his front door?" Irini launched a short, sharp jab to Cleo's left eye, knocking her and her chair to the floor. The chair rested on top of the sprawling woman. What little skirt there was to her ensemble was rolled up around her waist. Irini's blow to the eye guaranteed that Cleo would look like a raccoon for days to come.

To Irini's amusement, she watched Cleo Solchow pick herself up awkwardly from the office floor. Cleo's desk chair tripped her again as she tried to regain her balance on four-inch heels. As blurred as her mind was from her consumption of pills and powders and the occasional pummel to her face, Cleo was beginning to appreciate the fact that Wrath, her source for what made life good, was possibly not going to be available in the immediate future. That being the case, she knew of some stashes of money, drugs, and weaponry she could use or sell. Some of the assets were right there in the office. She had forged his signature on checks enough times in the past for both company and personal business that it occurred to her that she could write her own severance. Other treasure troves were in Rathmann's personal home in Alameda.

Perhaps the sooner Curtis Rathmann was otherwise occupied, the better. But ratting him out didn't appeal to her given her long history of abetting his crimes. Perhaps she could clean out the pots of gold, if she moved quickly, beating the police and FBI to them. Then she could head back to Boston.

The time Cleo Solchow took to absorb Irini's information, sort it out, and arrive at her own plan took longer than Irini's patience lasted.

Irini's *pièce de résistance* was a haymaker. The punch resulted in a sickening cracking sound like dry reeds being broken. Cleo went down, landing sitting upright in a corner between her credenza and the office printer. Bright-red blood dripped on her white silk blouse. This apparently did the trick for Cleo. She made like a faucet, providing information as quickly as she could.

"South of Lucia, down a steep hill, there's a white bridge crossing the bottom of a really deep ravine." She mopped up blood, tears, and makeup with a handful of tissues Irini handed her. Her voice was becoming difficult to understand. "Jes' before the white bridge der's a path. Goes down bottom of the ravine der. Go to the bottom an' go up the ravine." Cleo pressed another handful of tissues against the flood of blood from her nose. "Gotta hike inta his place. Up along the stream." She dabbed more blood from her chin. "There's a turn in the stream. Place ya come to … his cabin sorta hid in bushes. Can't see from anywhere 'cept right'n front." She looked up at Irini, both hands filled with soggy masses of blood-soaked tissues. "Tha's it. Now gedda fuck outta m' office."

"Yes, Ms. Solchow, I'm leaving," Irini said, smoothing her skirt and straightening her suit jacket. "I do like your outfit. Gucci, isn't it? The blood really distracts the eye though." She turned and walked to the reception office door. As if having an afterthought, she stopped, her hand resting on the doorknob, and turned back to face Solchow.

"By the way, dear," she said sweetly, "if this information is wrong, I'm coming back and I'll use your entire body for a workout with my fists." She opened and closed the door quietly behind her. A stream of truck-driver-worthy swearing echoed down the hall in her wake.

She called Caleb from the car and gave him directions to Wrath. Her wounded arm ached from all of the exercise.

———

The sun was slanting in from its western descent. A gradual afternoon chill invaded the apartment. Caleb and Irini were in Caleb's living room waiting for the guys to arrive. A somnolent state left them quiet, each engaged in his or her own privacy. The prior day's activity and the lack of sleep were catching up to both of them. Caleb stretched his long frame out on the couch.

Irini had raided her store for a warm cashmere sweater. Curled up in a club chair, she nursed bruised knuckles on both hands in a bowl of ice sitting on her lap. An ice pack was wrapped around her upper arm where she had been nicked. Despite the aches, she smiled.

Caleb was thinking about Rebecca, who was back in Margie's hands at the Flannery Center. He felt confident that the rehab program would bring Reb back to a wiser, stronger mental state.

"While we're waiting, tell me more about the meeting with Wrath's girlfriend," Caleb said, stretching his arms high and settling his long body more comfortably. "I want to leave tonight." He continued to lie on the couch but pulled himself up to rest his head on the padded arm so that he could look at her.

"Overall, I think I would describe it as a collection of emotional extremes," Irini said. "I would guess that she'd been shooting heroin and mixing in a joint or two before I arrived. Her pupils were like pinholes. Her cover-up perfume damned near asphyxiated me it was so strong."

"Did she seem to know what had gone down that morning?"

"No. That's what's so strange. This guy Wrath is no gentleman; that's for sure," Irini said with a sniff in her voice. "She could be the overlooked loose thread in his sweater. Of course, being stoned all of the time does tend to obliterate a lot of the details."

Feet pounding up the stairway sent vibrations through the house.

"The boys are here." Irini sighed. "Why is everything so loud with them?"

The door burst open, and Jake staggered into the room, roaring with laughter and slapping his thigh. He was followed by Frank laughing just as hard and shaking his huge fist.

"No, no, Jake, babe!" Frank was able to shout before he hit the floor, arms outstretched. "You cheated. Cutting through backyards is cheating. God damn it, we have rules!"

Jake collapsed in a chair, chest heaving, sweat pouring down his face, choking with laughter. "I won, sweet man. Give it up!" Jake crowed.

"Jake. Frank. What's going on?" Caleb demanded.

Irini sat with disapproval flaring in her coal-black eyes. *Twenty-nine-year-old children,* she thought. *How unprofessional they are.*

"We … we … ran from BART to here. Our truck's in the garage, so we took BART," Frank gasped. "He …" His finger wavered at Jake. "… cheated. He … he … he ran through somebody's backyard. That's cheating, Jake."

"Come on, boys; that's only a three-mile run. A piece of cake for you Navy SEALs, isn't it?" Irini chided them, smiling at the two men gasping for breath.

"All right, I declare it a tie," Caleb said slapping the coffee table. The telephone on the table rang at that exact moment. "Okay, that's Mr. Thorndike. Straighten up."

50

Thorndike spoke into his phone, "Good evening, Caleb. All present?"

"Good evening, sir. Yes, Irini, Jake, and Frank are here," Caleb said.

"You had a highly successful evening last night, and I am very pleased that you met your objective so well. You all know that I have a special concern for Rebecca Frost. Congratulations."

A chorus of "Thank you, sir," rolled across the airwaves to Georgetown and William Thorndike's appreciative ear. He smiled and sipped from his ice-cold dry martini, his first of the evening. He allowed himself two before dinner—sometimes three and then an early-to-bed evening.

"Now to business," Thorndike began. "In sealed diplomatic pouches, the Chinese government has thanked the US government for the assistance they received in disrupting the heroin business in their western province. You will never hear about this. Yesterday, the Chinese launched a major air and ground offensive attack on a heroin operation in the Xinjiang Uighur autonomous region. Should any recognition of the event become public, it will be reported as an action precipitated on behalf of the United States of America because of our drug problems. Dozens of Uighur field hands, women and children, were killed in the raid, along with many soldiers manning artillery pieces and in the barracks. It seems that Zhou Jing escaped with his household. A manhunt is on.

"The gentleman from Shanghai died of his injuries. A one-car accident is how the San Mateo police have recorded it. Family had the body shipped to China. Done. Case closed."

Irini's chin dropped to her chest. She wondered why this should bother her. But it did. She had been taught to set aside personal emotions and personal involvement when it came to killing. In this instance, the proximity to the action and the lack of planning or collaboration with Caleb and the team made it seem like freelancing. She did not like killing on a whim, which this seemed to be. He did track her, however, and she was sure that he was trying to kill her. It was, on the other hand, thrilling to relive the moment. The kill. The smashing into the enemy.

"What about the Alameda authorities? The Vandenberg people? Are they in the fold?" Caleb inquired.

"Yes. Altercation within the motorcycle gang is the Alameda police report. Possible charges of terrorism against those in custody, because of the bomb exploding and raining shingles, et cetera, all over the law-abiding neighbors. It's in tomorrow's *Oakland Tribune*. The use of drugged darts is a new one to the police. They are checking to see where darts have been used in the past. There are no incidents for them to discover, but it will keep them busy and at work for some time. Personally, I'm betting that the gangs will develop it as a weapon."

"Has Zipperman been paid?" Caleb asked.

"Ah, yes, Zipperman. An interesting sobriquet, no? Frank's friend, I believe," Thorndike said. "Quite innovative. Yes, he's been paid. Over and above the contracted price covering time and materials for the pyrotechnic extravaganza. I'd like you to evaluate him and his crew for future assignments, when you have a moment, please."

Caleb made a note.

"Speaking of finances," Thorndike continued, twirling the crystal-clear liquid in his glass and holding it up to the light for closer inspection. "The Chinese government added a bonus for the speed with which you resolved their issue. That gratuity plus our agreed-upon fee will be in your bank by tomorrow evening. Any medical expenses—send them to me."

Caleb gave a thumbs-up signal to the team. Grins all around. Frank threw his arm around Jake's shoulders and whispered in his ear. Caleb wondered if there was a home renovation plan working for the two men requiring some extra money.

"Then, sir," Caleb said, "we can close this account and wait for another assignment?"

"Yes. We are done. I'll be in touch when something suitable comes up. Things in Africa are beginning to boil, and there are some real nasties who are not playing nice in Somalia. Yemen. Even Egypt. Then, there's still Iran. Hmmmm. Yes, I suspect we'll be back in business soon."

"Well, thanks for the engagements, sir. We'll expect to hear from you. By the way, we have fairly strong evidence that Mr. Partrain is indeed dead, killed by a biker whose name is Creek. That's all we have by way of a name, Creek. He's the guy who dove out the third-floor window, so that case is closed as well."

"Yes, I'll let the Hillsborough police know that. By the way, Caleb, keep me informed about Rebecca's progress. Good-bye." The line went dead.

Silence filled the room.

After a moment, Jake stretched and said, "Well, that's that. It's a wrap."

"Caleb, Wrath did not come up in the conversation," Irini said, watching Caleb's face.

"Yeah, sort of an elephant in the room, and you ignored him," Frank said.

"Wrath's mine," Caleb said. "I go and collect him."

"Want some company, some backup?" Irini offered putting a hand on his forearm and squeezing it gently. He barely shook his head, but it was a "no!"

51

Caleb watched as Jake laid out the weapons he had chosen for him. "Looky, looky," Jake said as he held up a gray nine-millimeter pistol. "Found this up at Jackson Arms. You liked the SIG Sauer P226, so I got you an upgraded version. It's the Combat TB—great accuracy from a distance. Well, of course, the accuracy depends on the shooter, doesn't it?"

"Thanks," Caleb said. "I'll try to meet the weapon's expectations."

"Just meet mine and we'll be happy."

"Uh-rah," Frank added pumping his fist.

Irini sat watching the process, her thoughts concerned with the outcome of the venture. Seeing Caleb off on another solo mission brought back the niggling concerns she felt for his safe return. *Stop that,* she scolded herself.

Based on Irini's description of Wrath's hideout location and the shack, Caleb agreed with Jake's selection. He packed his saddlebag.

Caleb Frost removed his motorcycle helmet. The dense sea fog washed his face with swirling gray mist. The smell of seawater filled his nostrils. He felt as though he could drink the air, it held so much moisture. Visibility was nil. He had ridden the last fifteen miles to Big Sur on the centerline with his headlight out. The light's reflection bouncing back into his eyes was worse than riding without lights at all. Only one or two other drivers were stupid enough to be driving in the pea soup, and Caleb dodged them as they appeared. In his black helmet and leather jacket and pants, fog swirling around him like wisps of smoke, he was a wraith in the darkness to anyone who caught a glimpse of him as he roared by. Driving in the fog was mesmerizing and played games with one's mind.

The white bridge over the creek at the bottom of the steep ravine was exactly as Wrath's girlfriend had described it. A pathway led off to the left of the bridge. Caleb almost missed it in the fog. He rolled down the rocky path to creek side and turned off his bike. Visibility improved during his descent to the bottom of the ravine. The Pacific Ocean lay off to his right under the bridge's expanse. Cooking spots outlined with streambed rocks were evident along the creek's edge. The occasional beer can announced civilization's intrusion on nature.

Pulling the Combat TB from his jacket pocket, Caleb checked to be sure a round was nestled in the chamber.

The only sound he could hear as he prepared to ascend the creek bed was the faint rippling of the stream's water off to his right. He gathered the grenades and the gas container from his saddlebag and headed up the stream's bank. He stuffed the explosives into his jacket pockets.

He had no idea how far up the creek Wrath's shack might be. He wanted to be ready for whatever might come up, so he held the pistol in his hand as he walked, safety off. There was always a good possibility that he could walk right by the shack in the fog and darkness. *Or trip on the welcome mat,* he thought.

Fifty yards up the creek, a whisper of breeze sliced a clearing in the fog for a moment. He thought he saw the shack and moved in that direction as quietly as possible. He had the fleeting impression of a wooden doorway in the moment of visibility. He could just about make out what he thought was the outline of a building. No lights were in evidence. It was a cabin, backed up to the side of the ravine. The structure seemed quite large and square. Maybe twenty by twenty feet. The bushes were thick around it. *No access from the rear probably,* he thought.

The fog ebbed and flowed like an incoming tide. During a moment of clearing, Caleb moved closer, bending beneath the low branches on the path leading to the front door. He could just make out the unpainted board siding. He took a step closer to listen.

A whirring noise caused him to flinch and throw up a protective forearm. The bushes on his left shattered in an explosion of leaves and twigs as a large chain tore through them and slashed against his upraised arm. Stunned by the suddenness of the attack and the pain coursing down his arm and along his side, Caleb was only able to crab-crawl himself backward away from the shack.

"What do you want here, asshole?" a voice snarled. Caleb stood, backing away through the bushes. The sound of a chain being gathered up seemed to be close by. A second slicing blow from the chain lashed across his chest and thigh. He staggered away from the source of the attack. Scrambling through the undergrowth, he stepped into the fog hoping that Wrath, for that was who he was sure was attacking him, was as blinded by the blanket of fog as he was. Pistol in hand, he listened for a noise, heard a branch move, and fired three rapid shots in the direction of the sound.

"Motherfucker!" Wrath cursed. Caleb could hear the other man stumble through the bushes. Had he hit him? He couldn't know. "Enough games. Who the hell are you, and what do you want?" Wrath challenged.

"I came to personally put you out of business, Wrath. For what you did to my sister. For what you did to users of your drugs. I decided to put you down!" Caleb shouted into the fog. In response, a barrage of bullets spattered the area around Caleb. He lay still behind a large rock, listening, gripping his weapon, ready to fire, searching the fog for something to shoot at.

Wrath was no doubt in the vicinity of the shack, either in it or just outside, lying in wait for Caleb to make a move. "I finished you and your asshole buddy off in New Orleans. A nice toasty fire, wasn't it? Burn, baby, burn. Horse makes a great fire. How many millions do you suppose that would have been worth on the street? We took you down in that hovel you call home in Alameda. I cut off that freak Creek's arm before he fell out the window."

Let's see how you like this move, Caleb thought as he eased a grenade from his pocket.

"You can take your Harvard degree and stuff it, loser." He paused to stare into the fog, to listen for the slightest sound. "I don't hear you, Curtis Rathmann, you failure. Nothin' to say, little man? By the way, your girlfriend is long gone. Yeah, we had a conversation with her too. Spoke with Coyote under our personal waterfall. Oh, what a lowlife you are, Curtis Rathmann. This is the end of your road. Putting you back into the gutter you came from."

Pulling the pin, Caleb lobbed the M67 grenade into the fog toward the cabin's front door. The M7 shrapnel would open doors, windows … and walls. The grenade made a single echoing knock on the wooden door. *Knock, knock, who's there?* Caleb thought to himself. The answer was an explosion, which rocked the ground. Shrapnel and shredded leaves and twigs rained down on him. The large boulder rocked, barely providing protection from the debris pelting the area.

"Still with the program, asshole?" he called as he threw the second grenade. It bounced on a floor, not a wall, not a door. It was inside the cabin. Again, there was an earthshaking explosion.

"You're dead meat!" Wrath roared through the smoke and dust floating in the moist fog. More gunshots sprayed the area around Caleb. A kick like a horse hit his left shoulder. An involuntary "Owww!" brought a raucous laugh from Wrath. "Tag!" Wrath screamed. "You son of a bitch. Just the beginning. Stay where you are, you bastard. I'm coming for you."

Caleb heard what he believed were sounds of shuffling coming from the shack. Rearing back like a baseball pitcher and forgoing the recommended lobbing style, he flung the gas container in the direction of the cabin, sure that its front had been obliterated. The canister clanged around on the building's floor and then released its evil gas with an eerie hissing sound. Strike!

A motorcycle engine's roar and the bike's growling passage three feet above his head startled him and made him duck behind the security of the boulder. Caleb raced down the creek to his bike. It lay on its side. Wrath had kicked it over as he tore by. Caleb heard the hollow sound of a motorcycle crossing the bridge above his head. Heading South to LA? Santa Barbara? Mexico?

It took him a couple of minutes to wrestle the bike's three hundred and fifty pounds upright. Adrenalin helped to do its part in the effort, overcoming the increasing pain and weakness from the shoulder wound. He stuffed a handkerchief inside his jacket over the bullet's entry hole hoping that the tightness of the jacket would apply much-needed pressure on the site. His helmet had disappeared in the brook's current and was probably floating along the creek toward the sea. Mounting the bike, he raced up the hill to the roadway.

Wrath had made a skidding left turn at the top of the path, leaving a large rut in the wet soil, which Caleb's front wheel slipped into as he crested the slope. He took a moment to calculate the combat tactics Wrath might employ. The best option, aside from simply shooting Caleb, was to ambush him in the fog, using the heavy chain.

Caleb urged his bike through the gears, aiming for as much speed as possible given that he couldn't see where he was going through the impenetrable fog.

At the top of the hill, on the far side of the ravine, Caleb's bike slewed violently on a parking lot's sandy surface. The fog lifted enough for him to see that he was a yard away from the edge of a bluff as he regained control. Along this road, the cliffs were three to four hundred feet above the rocky, wave-battered coastline.

The roadway was narrow with many switchbacks as well as pull-off points for parking and picture taking. Good places for ambushes. *Got to make him commit himself. Get my hands on him up close,* Caleb thought.

He raced along the road, his front tire tracing the white centerline pathway. He leaned into the curves as they leaped at him out of the fog. A dip in the road sent him flying several yards across the depression. As he landed, Wrath's chain whipped out in front of him, wrapping itself around his chest. Pain radiated from his shoulder as the chain tightened around him.

Gunning the bike and clutching the handle bars in a death grip, he saw his front wheel almost above his line of sight. He hung on, straining forward as much as he could to pull the chain with him as he accelerated. His shoulder burned fiercely. Blood pooled in the tight leather jacket, warm against his skin.

The chain went slack and fell away from around his chest. Caleb forced the front wheel down. The sounds of a heavy crash and the screech of metal on asphalt sliced through the curtain of fog as Wrath and his bike hit the ground skidding. The chain clattered and clanged for a few seconds as if it were following Caleb, hoping to catch him again. Then, the only sound was the roar of his own engine.

In the dense fog, a leading position was better than a trailing one. Caleb slowed his speed. He thought he could hear Wrath's motorcycle coming fast behind him. *In a hurry. Trying to catch me. Come on, you son of a bitch.*

Caleb rode on, looking for what he thought was a straightaway. He loosed a few shots behind him. A volley of shots answered his, sparking in the road to his left. He flipped on his lights. Red taillights and headlight glowed, beckoning to Wrath through the dirty-gray, cotton-textured fog.

Caleb slanted into a curve just as another shot flew by his shoulder, pulling at the leather. Realizing how close behind him Wrath was, Caleb decided it was time to finish this tour of the coast. He turned off his machine's lights, giving the impression to Wrath that he had turned a corner and was well ahead of him.

Climbing a long, winding, uphill curve, bending low in the saddle and trying to see the road under the layer of fog, Caleb searched desperately for the telltale strip of dirt indicating a scenic viewing area turnoff. Slowing down even more, he listened intently for Wrath's Harley. It sounded very close. Caleb flipped on his lights again and went straight toward the strip of dirt he sensed more than saw up ahead. As he passed from asphalt to dirt—hoping this was indeed a viewing area, he turned off his lights. Jamming his brakes, he spun his bike to face the road. He hoped that Wrath would think that he had gone around a tight curve.

He sat in the darkness of the fog for a few seconds before he heard the high-pitched whine of Wrath's bike reaching the top of the hill. He was racing straight ahead and accelerating as he flew forward, trying to catch Caleb.

The vacuum of Wrath's passage by him, not a foot away in the fog, pulled at Caleb's body. He thrilled to the power of the man whose nemesis he had become. He could smell his leathers, the grease of his bike, and the total commitment to the chase. Wrath's bike shrieked in agony as he tore the engine to shreds trying to wring even more speed from the heart of the machine.

This was, in fact, the moment at which the transference of spirit occurred. In that split second, Caleb owned Wrath.

There was no sound of tires chewing the earth. There was no creak of saddle or rush of wind around a body clutching the back of a monster. There was no scream from the lips of Wrath.

There was only the banshee wail of a tortured engine ... accelerating ... fading ... and then ... nothing.

52

Rebecca Frost loved Caleb Frost in a more passionate manner than was common between brothers and sisters. She would never have allowed herself to have a physical relationship with him, although she readily acknowledged the taboo desire in her dreams and during moments of introspection. She had never mentioned her deeply felt, bordering on carnal, feelings for Caleb to the many psychiatrists and counselors who had been brought to her over the years since their parents' deaths—since the atrocity that was their murder.

She wondered if the feelings were reciprocated. Did Caleb have feelings for her beyond the brotherly affection he had always shown her? Perhaps the problems she had created—which he inevitably fixed for her—stood in the way of his view of who Rebecca really was.

She knew that the past nine months had not been easy for Caleb because of her. The rescue from the Visigoths motorcycle gang's house had been dangerous, fraught with the possibility of sudden death.

Her emotional deconstruction and rebuilding by the staff at the Flannery Center had been an agony, a grueling journey of despair and mental corrosion through valleys she had wished never to visit again. Yet, she girded herself to fight her way through the daily ordeal of looking at herself and learning who she was.

Reb was treading on an emotional high wire far above a rocky chasm. In her nightmares, she felt impending doom throbbing in the darkness just out of sight, just out of comprehension. She would scream, "Come get me, you bastard!" to the evil being in her tattered psyche. She challenged the specter to show itself, to get it over with.

Her screams would bring Flannery Center staff to her room. They would hold her, reassure her, while she sobbed uncontrollably.

Gradually, she, the jigsaw, was pieced back together again, although she still felt as if something might give way, that a rivet was going to pop in her mind's protective shell and that the slime of her past would squeeze through the cracks, attack her mind ... and devour it.

During rehab at the Flannery Center, the subject of emotional dependence transference came up in a group session. She had wondered if, after her parents' murder, she had, in her intense sorrow, transferred her love of her father to her older brother.

And now, years later, Caleb's career path, though they had never discussed it specifically, emulated their parents' lifestyle— disappearances for varying lengths of time for inexplicable reasons. She had never believed his marketing consultant cover story. He suffered strange injuries, frequently requiring extensive recuperation. And, sometimes, even when they were together in traditionally happy social circumstances, there were prolonged silences when he was totally lost in thought. And then there was the tic in his eye. She had mentioned it and suggested that he have it checked. He had brushed her suggestion off. And there was William Thorndike, who was a constant influence in Caleb's career.

She recalled that as a child, Thorndike's name had come up every now and then when her parents thought the children were not within earshot of their conversations. Thorndike's appearance in their lives immediately after their parents' murder had provided a major safety net for the children. On the rim of Reb's memory, he had always been present.

Her most prominent memory of William Thorndike was that he sent birthday gifts—books on history, autobiographies, little microscopes, a BB gun for Caleb, Barbie dolls for her. She had no idea about the substance of the business relationship between Thorndike and her parents and—now—her brother.

Thorndike had become a surrogate grandfather. He took control of their lives, seeing to their care in a house with loving "foster parents";

he sent them to small private schools and arranged for psychological testing for reasons Rebecca never fully understood or appreciated; and he saw to it that they were given unusual opportunities to develop unique skills. Rebecca was unaware that they were being raised differently from other children.

Caleb devoured the education Thorndike arranged for him. He spent weeks away at a place he called Summer Camp and became more and more secretive and vague about his camp experiences. He changed, becoming more serious, more introspective, and more judgmental.

Rebecca, on the other hand, embraced being a girl, wearing the styles of the day, and gaining popularity among classmates in her large social circle. She had a happy childhood with the occasional scary remembrance of the loss of her real parents.

Rebecca attracted boys like a golden flame attracts amorous moths. The boys were a problem Caleb was able to address, until he went away to college. Then Reb managed to embrace all of the wrong people, to engage in dangerous sexual practices and consume illegal and destructive substances.

The lure of drugs, the release from her fears and the plagues of the past drew her into a dependency, which she could not dismiss. She felt as if she were bouncing on the end of a diving board. In her new recurring dream, there was no water in the swimming pool over which she stood. No matter how hard she tried, she could not repress the constant urge to dive.

The long plunge into the gutters of San Francisco began many years later.

One afternoon, toward the end of her rehab at the Flannery Center, Reb was given permission to leave the Center for a few hours with her brother. They chose to go to a local playground. They sat on swings side by side. His shoulder was still stiff from the gunshot wound he had received several months earlier. He swung holding on with one hand.

"Show-off," Reb said. Caleb smiled contentedly.

She listened to Caleb ask her how she was, how she felt. Rebecca explained how she had been able to achieve an acceptance of events and had been able to weave them together into a relatively viable pattern.

"The trauma of that animal killing Barney will never really leave me, I know," she said, head bent as her mind thought back on recent events. "Barney was talking softly to me in that way of his, getting through my mental haze. All of a sudden, that man appeared out of nowhere. I remember looking up and seeing that he was pointing something at Barney. Barney was backlit by the sun, all blurry and golden. Then blood sprayed out of a hole in his forehead, turning his white shirt dark red. It was all confusion. I couldn't understand. The man with the beard showed me a packet of China Red. The next thing I knew, we were on his bike, and then I woke up in that dark space." Highlights flared in her long blonde hair as the sun sent shafts through the leaves in the park trees. Tears dampened her cheeks. Caleb said nothing but took her hand in his as they swung gently in the warmth of the autumn sun.

She spoke about the terrors she had felt when she was abducted, at least what shards of memory she could muster. In sessions at the Flannery Center, the retelling and the detailed analysis of the experience with the Visigoths triggered a switch in her perceptions of life; her world view was altered.

"It seems that pieces of my mind have changed gears," she said. "I've opened doors and addressed closeted issues I've avoided for years. My basic emotions related to Mom and Dad's murder and the hideous urges I have for revenge are issues I'm facing for the first time.

"I feel grounded. Like my feet are touching solid earth for the first time in years. Like before Mom and Dad left us." She squeezed his hand. "You've been so supportive, Caleb. To say I couldn't have survived without you may sound trite, but damn it, it's true. Since Mom and Dad, you've been there. Always. Through thick and thin."

"Ups and downs," Caleb said, his lips beginning to smile.

"Ins and outs," Reb added smiling broadly.

That's more like it, Caleb thought. Their swinging picked up a bit of speed. "I've had an epiphany, sort of."

"Tell me, Reb."

"You remember the training, the games, the—what did you call them—Summer Camps you went to? I didn't want to go and leave my friends and …" She paused. "Oh, all the boys, la-di-da." She waved her free hand, as if trying to erase the memories. Drawing a deep breath, she took her hand back from Caleb. With both hands on the swing's ropes, she swung hard and fast until her feet stretched up into the sky as if to fly away. Caleb waited.

"Well," she said when her momentum had died down, "about this epiphany thing. Man, have I done a one-eighty turnaround."

"This epiphany thing of yours—" Caleb started to say, but Reb kept talking.

"During all of the testing and game playing, our benefactor, Mr. Thorndike, arranged to educate us when we were kids," she said the with some sarcasm in her voice. "All of the tenets, philosophies, rationalizations dealing with good and evil, rotten guys and good guys, all that shit meant nothing to me at the time. Until now, Caleb. Suddenly, all of that has new meaning and relevance for me."

"How do you mean *relevance*?" Caleb asked leaning forward, intently studying his sister's face.

"Realizations slammed into my brain, clearing out spaces clogged up by my drug abuse. It was like a fresh broom swept away the crap of years of misinformation, false truths taught me by false prophets. Hell, Caleb, I had a trophy wall in my head—maybe my soul—hung with offers of redemption from well-meaning people who I essentially told to go fuck themselves."

Caleb listened intently as they swung side by side on the playground swings.

She started to sob. Her shoulders shook, and she clutched the swing ropes to her chest. Caleb stood, helped her up from the swing seat, and hugged her.

They moved to a park bench. She wanted to know specifically what he did. She told him what she suspected, and given the fact that his earlier assignments had been openly associated with international law enforcement, her guesses were close.

And was he going to avenge their parents? She suspected he could, and she wanted to be a part of it.

They bought two gelatos from a small Italian store on the corner of the park. With cones in one hand and the other's hand firmly clasped in the other, they ended the afternoon strolling across the park lawns. They spoke of their parents and better times. They spoke about acting on convictions versus talking about them. Action. Conclusive action. Making a substantial difference.

They spoke of revenge and how sweet it would be.

Wind-blown leaves, like brown ripples on a sea of green, flew across the expanse of lawn. The sky looked lead gray. The day grew colder.

53

Caleb called Thorndike that evening to discuss Rebecca Frost's future.

"You say that she's ready for training, Caleb?" Thorndike asked over the scrambled telephone on his desk in Georgetown. His silk-sock-clad feet were stuffed into comfy, Vermont-made sheep's wool slippers. He still wore the pin-striped suit he had worn during the day.

"Yes, she is," Caleb said. "Physically, she has a little way further to travel before she's totally fit."

"Does she understand the pleasure you take in your work?" Thorndike's fingers pushed a colorful array of pills into neat rows on his desk—tablets and capsules prescribed to keep him alive. *Barely keeping me alive some days,* he thought. *So much to do, to rectify ... and truly, so little time in which to do it.* The pills on his desk were his p.m. selection. The a.m. pills he took with grapefruit juice each morning. Sometimes V-8 juice with a dash of Tabasco. It used to be a Bloody Mary. He truly hated, resented aging and the pills bore testimony.

"No. Not yet. She will have to come to that on her own, don't you agree?"

"Yes," Thorndike murmured. "You, however, were raised to it, because I surmised that a combination of parentage, environment, and values taught and learned through your observation and our association formed your capabilities. You do not lack compassion, an unfortunate affliction in our business, which is why we allow you to accept or decline assignments." He sighed as his aged fingertips created medicinal groupings of pills by color. Red dominated the piles.

"I don't terminate because I enjoy it, Mr. Thorndike," Caleb said somewhat stung by his controller's assumption.

"Hmmm," Thorndike acknowledged. "Does Rebecca have the necessary—what shall we say—*instincts*, do you suppose?"

"Don't know. The instructors at Summer Camp will know."

"How's her rehab coming along? You think she'll make it this time, that she won't backslide? You believe that the treatment will take?"

"Margie Silas at the Flannery Center says that Rebecca has made remarkable progress since her return from the kidnapping. She and Margie had several sessions dealing with Barney's murder. Both had lost someone dear to them. Reb now recalls the cold-bloodedness of the killing. The suddenness. The man with the swastika dyed in his beard, and the gun. She and Margie have worked through it. A good process for both of them. They have come to acknowledge it. However, Reb does seek justice for Margie and her loss of Barney."

"Justice?" Thorndike made a random pile of pills. He couldn't find his glass of water.

"Our kind of justice, sir, my kind of justice," Caleb said and paused for a few seconds. "This is why I encouraged her to talk today, to outline her feelings, to tell me what she wanted to do in detail."

"And?" Thorndike asked, spinning his chair around to his credenza. The silver tray, which usually held a carafe of water and a Baccarat water goblet, was bare. "Damn it all!" he exclaimed under his breath. "Jorgen's getting too old for this job," he added, referencing his longtime aide and bodyguard. There was little Jorgen Pedersen didn't know about Thorndike—and, in his turn, there were events in their long association he would never discuss with anyone other than Thorndike.

"It was like listening to myself," Caleb continued, describing his conversation with his sister. "Her passion is cold, as it should be. Incidentally, I have not yet told her that we have evidence that

Barney's killer, Bangalore, was himself killed by the Goths. Ironically, his killing was in fact for having kidnapped Rebecca and bringing the heat on the gang, according to our talkative captive, Coyote. I'm not sure I will tell Reb that. It seems to be a motivating factor, as is the unsolved murder of our mom and dad."

"I see, yes, quite right," Thorndike agreed. "Keep her focused. I suppose it does us more good to be quiet about Barney's killer's demise than it would if Rebecca knew and lost the motivation she has now."

"I'd like you to get a slot for her at the Summer Camp up in Donner," Caleb said. He thought for a moment. "And I want a good first kill for her, sir, at the end of her training. See the aftermath of her first experience, you know? Testing and all."

"I'll arrange that," Thorndike said. "Get her to Donner as soon as she's released from the center. I'll take care of the details." There was a silence from William Thorndike's end of the conversation. Thorndike chuckled softly and said, "You know, Caleb, we've never had a brother-and-sister act in our business. It was unique enough having your parents."

Thorndike hung up, his hand scooping the pharmaceutical confetti on his desk into his other cupped hand. He stomped off in search of water. He was tempted to dispose of the pills, virtually stamping his feet in a childish manner as he rejected the doctors' instructions to swallow them. Dire consequences, the doctors had said, should he not take his medicine. *Someday,* he thought, *someday, I'm simply going to stop the pills. But not tonight. But someday I'll stop all of this.*

In California, Caleb stared at his cell phone for a long time. He wondered if he had a right to contort his sister's life by bringing her into his world of stark reality and death.

54

The wind wrapped itself around two black helmets. Darkly tinted visors obscured the faces of the riders on a powerful Harley-Davidson bike. Tight-fitting leather clothing rippled and shimmered in the bright September sunlight. The riders could feel the machine's muscle as the driver throttled and shifted along the rolling highway north of San Francisco.

Rebecca Frost clung to Caleb's back, aware of his strong body through her arms encircling his waist and her breasts and thighs where they made intimate contact.

At moments like this, sitting on the back of Caleb's bike, she felt superior to her terrors, seeing them in daylight rather than peeking at them through fingers clamped over her eyes in the middle of the night. No shaking body. No feelings of vulnerability.

The Harley's roar prohibited any conversation between brother and sister. Actually, there was little to be said between the two of them. Decisions had been made, and Reb was stepping into the challenge of leading her own life. For the first time, she felt in control and confident in her direction.

She had been released from the Flannery Center. "Rehabilitated, no longer addicted to heroin. At least at the moment," Margie Silas, recently appointed director of the Flannery Center, had explained in her parting interview. The two women had forged a close relationship during the rehab process. The murder of Barney Flannery had impacted the women's lives, and their mutual survival was reinforced by their open and frank discussions about the event.

"I won't be back," Reb had said. Margie had smiled and assured her that coming back to say "Hello" was encouraged. "I don't want you back as a patient, Rebecca," Margie had said holding Reb's hands in hers. Tears filled both women's eyes as Reb stepped into the street.

Reb had found Caleb waiting for her as she left the Flannery Center. Since then, they had spent time in his apartment in Burlingame. Irini and the guys, Jake and Frank, had been concerned for her. Irini felt that feeding her plates of Greek food would in some way help her reentry into the world. *As a chubby woman,* Reb had thought as she chewed home-baked baklava dripping with honey and chopped walnuts and almonds from Irini's kitchen.

Reb and Caleb had discussed her future for hours. Her enrollment in Summer Camp had been arranged. A date set. Caleb's words still rang clearly in her memory. "The path you choose is up to you. If you follow me, you will be tested to the extremes of your physical and mental endurance—and, possibly more critically, your moral strength. Your objectives are correct, but let's acknowledge that you've proven yourself to be as fragile as the next person. You have much to prove over the next few months."

"Wait a minute—" she had started to say, but Caleb held up his hand.

"No, you listen to me, Reb," Caleb had said softly. "You aren't anything yet. Not a whole person yet." He had stroked her slender shoulder gently. "There are some people waiting for you … expecting you to fail. People in your life who have pulled you down before and anticipate doing it again. They will not be surprised if you do fail. I wouldn't be surprised if you failed either. If you succeed, you damn well know I'll be among the most proud. I'm convinced you will succeed, but I can't help you once you enter Summer Camp."

"I understand," she had said, looking up at him. He had taken her in his arms and hugged her. She hugged him back, holding onto him tightly, absorbing his strength—his essence.

Now, two weeks later, she was traveling to the threshold of her second life. The bike and riders moved in concert, diving through the curves, gravity pressing them into the saddle, pulling them back as

Caleb accelerated the bike out of the curves and onto the flat, black strip of highway disappearing over the horizon.

The temperature dropped as they roared uphill through the forest. The closeness of the trees on either side created a feeling of being contained; it was a bit claustrophobic. Convoys of trucks passed in the other direction heading westward toward coastal cities, the huge semis' transmissions straining against the downhill run. The smell and smoke of burned diesel fuel and scorched metal stretched behind the trucks' giant exhaust pipes with a lingering stream of stench. Caleb pushed the bike to greater speed up the winding road.

As a Donner Pass sign flew by, Reb felt the bike decelerate. Caleb downshifted, leaning the bike into a sharp, right-hand turn. She saw a virtually invisible dirt road over Caleb's shoulder. The rear of the bike kicked up a cloud of dirt clods behind Rebecca. She pressed her body more tightly against her brother.

The forest grew closer to the road, and Caleb drove more slowly now. Boughs swept across their helmets, brushing shoulders, as if to pull the riders off the devil machine spewing smoke into the pristine mountain air. A grassy clearing appeared. There was no road to travel ahead. The trees, forming a circle, grew together too closely to allow the motorcycle to pass through them.

Turning the bike, Caleb stopped facing back in the direction they had come. The engine rumbled, as if irritated by the stoppage. Reb climbed down from the saddle. She stood next to her brother.

"Welcome to Summer Camp, Reb." Caleb flipped up his helmet visor. "Follow the trail past the sign over there." He pointed a gloved hand across the clearing. "Just keep walking and they will find you. I love you, Reb. Good luck." With a twist of the throttle, the beast in the motorcycle roared, and Caleb was gone.

Rebecca stood for a moment watching her brother's back disappear through the trees. As he vanished, so did the sound of his bike. Silence crashed around her ears. She pushed the helmet's visor up and smelled the pine-scented air. A gentle breeze caused fine threads of her golden hair to ripple across her face.

Boots crunching on the blanket of twigs and leaves, she walked to the sign Caleb had pointed out.

The rusty sign's barely legible letters, worn from years of exposure to the mountain's weathering elements, warned faintly against trespassing. The sign was pockmarked and punctured by shotgun pellets and rifle bullets.

Without looking back, Reb walked into the woods.

55

Caleb sped west on I-80 from Donner toward San Francisco. He set his own pace in the light traffic, weaving gracefully through the assorted vehicles. The sounds of the ride, the powerful engine's roar, the whistling wind, and the humming of the motorcycle's tires on the road, blended into a cocoon of comforting white noise. His mind filled with thoughts of Rebecca, her past, present, and future. The emotional and physical trials Reb would deal with at Summer Camp would either toughen her or result in the collapse he feared for her. She was, still and foremost, his little sister.

After parking the Harley in the basement garage in Burlingame, Caleb checked his cell phone for calls. There was one. No message, just a number he recognized as a secure phone. Riding the elevator to his apartment, he called Thorndike.

"Hello, Caleb," Thorndike's dry, impersonal voice came on the line. "It went well at Summer Camp? Rebecca's in place?"

"Yes. I dropped her off about two hours ago."

"We wish her good luck, of course. I'm sure she will excel. Since she'll be occupied for a while, what are your immediate plans?"

"I thought that I might take a few days in Las Vegas. Relax. Loosen up a bit."

"Las Vegas," Thorndike mused. Silence. "Hmmm. Are you on a secure line?"

"Yes, I am."

"An interesting opportunity came across my desk today. A request for an immediate solution to a problem. It's time sensitive. Can't divulge who the client is, but we've worked with them before." Silence.

"Okay," Caleb said. "I'm listening." He didn't know and didn't care if Thorndike could hear the sigh that accompanied the comment.

"Our subject is a Swiss citizen, a Sigmund Wohlenberger. He's an arms dealer, responsible for supplying weapons to terrorist groups around the globe. Wohlenberger, through his business, is responsible for the indiscriminate slaughter of hundreds of innocent, noncombatant people—men, women, and children." Caleb could hear Thorndike rifling through some papers. "They want the situation normalized within three weeks from this coming Friday. By the twelfth of next month."

"Why that date?" Caleb asked.

"A meeting is scheduled for the fourteenth between Wohlenberger and African buyers from Somalia. Our client wants to terminate him just prior to the meeting. Read the file in our drop box, and let me know if you'll accept."

Caleb downloaded the file after they hung up. Sigmund Wohlenberger: fifty-four years of age, five foot two inches tall, weighing three hundred and sixteen pounds. His out-of-focus picture showed a wispy-haired, balding guy with bad teeth. His teeth could be seen in the one picture in which Wohlenberger was smiling. "Resident: Zurich, Switzerland. Business: illegal arms and munitions dealer." As he read more, his understanding of the man evolved. This guy, Wohlenberger, was dedicated to creating chaos and havoc in the free world by making the tools of destruction available to demented men intent on pulling civilized structures down.

"I'll take the engagement," Caleb said into the mouthpiece on his return call to Thorndike.

"I thought you would," Thorndike said, swirling his second martini of the night. He smiled and took a long sip of the crystal-clear, iced liquid. "Your advance will be in the bank tomorrow morning. Our client will be pleased. Good luck. And, Caleb, don't worry; after the job is finished, Las Vegas will still be there."

Caleb disconnected.

ACKNOWLEDGEMENTS

It may take a village to raise a child, but it has taken an entire metropolis to shepherd me through the writing of this debut novel. I acknowledge the following people who have all supported, taught, and contributed to the writing of *China Red*.

My wife Susan's love, understanding, and support overcame the doubts that assailed me at three in the morning. My sons, Ethan, Wyeth, and Adam Towle, and their wives, Jenny, Gina, and Kim, respectively, probably could not have imagined that one day I would write an action thriller. They never asked, "What the hell are you doing, Dad?"

In *China Red*, I refer to an "Algonquin Table" in the Il Piccolo Caffé. The café and the people at the table exist, as does Dave Armanino, the owner of Il Piccolo. At the table, offering ideas and encouragement as the writing went on … and on … were these interesting and intelligent folks: Ellen Bond, "Basically," Bob Macalusa, Rich Montana, John Spreitz, Betty Wuestefeld, Patrick Stewart, Dave Abeyte, Lon Parker, Paolo Canton, Mary Sheedy, Rodger McBride, Elmer Benson, Bob Cameron, Juliana Fuerbringer, and Neil Murphy, my political advisor, Tony Stagnaro, and, of course, Jessica Ibarra and Gina Mallos, baristas without whom Il Piccolo Caffé would not be so attractive. These people's interest kept me going.

Among my friends who brought specific support to my endeavor is Ron Sosnick, life coach, guide, motivator, and friend extraordinaire. Gator Walter and Daryl Zellers shared their knowledge of Harley Davidson bikes and the folks who ride them. My Mid-Peninsula Clique Mastermind Group of Andrea White, Alec Keit, Lelana Crayne, Lena Griffin, Julie Malta, and Bill Dwyer tracked my progress on a weekly basis.

And then there are the pros who taught me so much, starting with Jill Ferguson, who introduced me to the wonderful world of imagination, the creative process, and to a passion I had always suspected was within me somewhere.

Ed Kaufman, bookseller and the owner of the greatest crime and mystery independent bookstore, M is for Mystery, was the president of my personal educational institution. Ed passed away before I could give him a copy of *China Red*. A great loss for me personally. The "professors" in Ed Kaufman's "M University" were the dozens of authors who came to read their new books and stayed to share the essence of their craft with people like me. I particularly want to thank Cara Black, George Pelecanos, and John Lescroart, who wrote me notes of encouragement as they signed their books. All of the M is for Mystery authors set the standards by which I try to write. I will always be grateful to Ed Kaufman for bringing the best mystery and crime writers in the world to his bookstore.

A word about writing groups. A good writing group critiques your work with a combination of honesty, creativity, experience, and compassion. My writing groups nurtured me all the way and will continue to do so as I move on to future efforts. Antoinette May and Lucy Sanna, both published authors, brought me into their writing groups, and I can never thank them enough for that introduction. Through them, I met and learned from Rob Swigert, Jim Spencer, Mercedes Cerna, Kevin Arnold, Brent Barker, and Sally Henry. At Gold Rush Writers Workshops, authors Pam Mondale, Bob Yeager, and Rick Glaze critiqued, advised, and contributed to *China Red*.

And, of course, my editors at iUniverse and Lucy Sanna—thank you for your hard work. Thank you to my manuscript readers, Georgeanne Marchese, Pam Mondale, my sons Ethan and Wyeth, my daughter-in-law Gina, and my sister Kathie Hession. They all offered observations, suggestions, corrections, and contributions to the writing.

So, my thanks to all of the super people above and to you, the reader, for having given me the opportunity to present you with a story.

Read on!